COURTING
TROUBLE

COURTING TROUBLE

LISA SCOTTOLINE

BOOKSPAN LARGE PRINT EDITION

HarperCollins*Publishers*

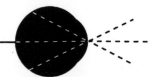

This Large Print Book carries the Seal of Approval of N.A.V.H.

May you always be courageous.
—Bob Dylan,
"Forever Young"

Lucy Ricardo and Ethel Mertz (singing): When other friendships have been forgot, ours will still be hot.
—*I Love Lucy,*
"Lucy and Ethel Buy the
Same Dress," Episode
No. 69, October 19, 1953,
singing Cole Porter's
"Friendship"

1

Anne Murphy barreled through the bustling lobby of the William Green Federal Courthouse, her long, auburn hair flying. She was about to do something crazy in court and couldn't wait to get upstairs. If she won, she'd be a hero. If she lost, she'd go to jail. Anne didn't think twice about the if-she-lost part. She was a redhead, which is a blonde with poor impulse control.

"Ms. Murphy, Ms. Murphy, just one question!" a reporter shouted, dogging her heels, but Anne charged ahead, trying to ditch him in the crowd.

Federal employees, lawyers, and jurors crisscrossed the lobby to the exits, hurrying home to start the Fourth of July weekend, but heads turned at the sight of the stunning young woman. Anne had wide-set eyes of willow-green, a straight nose dusted with freckles, and a largish mouth, glossy with an artful swipe of raisiny lipstick. Very female curves filled out a suit of cream-colored silk, and her long, lean legs tapered to fine ankles, ending in impractical Manolo Blahnik heels. Anne looked like a model, but given her past didn't even think of herself as pretty. None of us outgrows the kid in the bathroom mirror.

"Uh-oh, here comes trouble!" called one of the court security officers, as Anne approached the group of dark polyester blazers clustered around the metal detectors. Manning the machines were five older guards, all retired Philly cops, flashing appreciative grins. The guard calling to Anne was the most talkative, with a still-trim figure, improbably black hair, and a nameplate that read OFFICER SALVATORE BONANNO. "Gangway, fellas! It's Red, and she's loaded for bear!"

"Right again, Sal." Anne tossed her leather briefcase and a Kate Spade messenger bag onto the conveyor belt. "Wish me luck."

"What's cookin', good-lookin'?"

"The usual. Striking a blow for justice. Paying too much for shoes." Anne strode through the security portal as her bags glided through the X-ray machine. "You gentlemen got plans for the holiday weekend?"

"I'm takin' you dancin'," Officer Bonanno

answered with a dentured smile, and the other guards burst into guffaws made gravelly by cigarette breaks at the loading dock off of Seventh Street. Bonanno ignored them cheerfully. "I'm gonna teach you to jitterbug, ain't I, Red?"

"Ha!" Officer Sean Feeney broke in, grinning. "You and the lovely Miss Murphy, Sal? In your dreams!" Feeney was a ruddy-faced, heavyset sixty-five-year-old, with eyebrows as furry as caterpillars. "She's an Irish girl and she's savin' herself for me." He turned to Anne. "Your people from County Galway, right, Annie? You got pretty skin, like the girls in Galway."

"Galway, that near Glendale?" Anne asked, and they laughed. She never knew what to say when someone commented on her looks. The X-ray machine surrendered her belongings, and she reached for them as two reporters caught up with her, threw their bags onto the conveyor belt, and started firing questions.

"Ms. Murphy, any comment on the trial next week?" "Why won't your client settle this case?" "Isn't this ruining Chipster's chance to go public?" They kept interrupting each other. "Anne, what's this motion about today?" "Why do you want to keep this evidence from the jury?"

"No comment, please." Anne broke free, grabbed her bags, and bolted from the press, but it turned out she didn't have to. Officer Bonanno was confronting the reporters, hard-eyed behind his bifocals.

"Yo, people!" he bellowed, Philly-style. "You know the rules! None o' that in the courthouse! Why you gotta give the young lady a hard time?"

Officer Feeney frowned at the first reporter and motioned him over. "Come 'ere a minute, sir. I think you need a full-body scan." He reached under the security counter and emerged with a handheld metal detector. "Come on, in fact, both of youse." He waved the wand at the second reporter, and the other security guards lined up behind him like an aged phalanx.

"But I'm the press!" the reporter protested. "This is my beat! You see me every day. I'm Allen Collins, I have an ID." Behind him, his canvas briefcase stalled suddenly in the X-ray machine, and the guard watching the monitor was already confiscating it. The reporter turned back, puzzled. "Hey, wait a minute!"

Officer Bonanno dismissed Anne to the elevators with a newly authoritative air. "Go on up, Miss!"

"Thanks, Officer," Anne said, suppressing a smile as she grabbed the open elevator and hit the button for the ninth floor. She hadn't asked for the assist and felt vaguely guilty accepting it. But only vaguely.

Minutes later, Anne reached the ninth floor and entered the spacious, modern court-room, which was packed. The Chipster case, for sexual harassment against Gil Martin, Philadelphia's best-known Internet millionaire, had attracted press attention since the day it was filed, and reporters, sketch artists, and the public filled the sleek modern pews of dark wood. Their faces swiveled almost as one toward Anne as she strode down the carpeted center aisle.

Bailiffs in blue blazers stopped conferring over the docket sheets, law clerks straight-ened new ties, and a female court reporter shot daggers over her blue steno machine, on its spindly metal legs. Anne had grown accustomed to the reaction; men adored her, women hated her. She had nevertheless joined the all-woman law firm of Rosato & Associates, which had turned out to be a very redheaded career move. But that was another story.

She reached counsel table and set down her briefcase and purse, then looked back. A young man dressed in a lightweight trench coat was sitting, as planned, on the aisle in the front row behind her. Anne acknowledged him discreetly, then took her seat, opened her briefcase, and took out a copy of her motion papers. The motion and the young man on the aisle had been Anne's latest idea. Chipster.com was her first big client at Rosato, and Gil Martin had hired her because they'd known each other at law school. She had never tried a case of this magnitude, and in the beginning wondered if she had bitten off more than she could chew. Then she decided that she had, and stopped wondering.

"Happy Fourth!" whispered a voice at her ear, and she looked up.

Matt Booker was a year older than Anne's twenty-eight, and he stood over her, with dark, wavy hair, light-blue eyes, and eyelashes too thick to be wasted on a man. She would have been wildly attracted to him if he hadn't been opposing counsel, but that was an alternate reality. Matt represented the plaintiffs in this case, a female programmer named Beth Dietz and her husband Bill, who had filed a derivative claim against Chipster. Though Anne hadn't dated anyone for the year she'd been in Philly, Matt Booker was the first time she'd been tempted. Really tempted, but opposing counsel was about as forbidden as fruit gets.

"Go away," she said, but Matt leaned closer.

"I just want you to know that I'm not asking you out today." His whisper smelled like Crest. "You've turned me down 329 times, and I'm detecting a pattern. Stop me before I ask again."

Anne blushed. "Matt, has it occurred to you that you are sexually harassing me, in a sexual harassment lawsuit?"

"Come on, my advances are welcome, aren't they? Sort of?"

Anne didn't answer. She was deciding. It had been so long since she'd let herself trust anyone. But she had known Matt for almost a year, since the complaint in this case was filed, and he was an overconfident pain in the ass, which she liked in a man.

"A little? Slim to none?" Matt was asking,

bracing a hand on the polished counsel table, and she took a chance.

"Okay. After the trial is over, I will go out with you. But only after."

"*Really?*" Matt's voice cracked, which Anne found cute. He was always so cool, it was as if his veneer had cracked, too. He looked astounded, his jaw dropping unself-consciously. "Anne, are you on drugs?"

"No."

"Will you sign an affidavit to that effect?"

"Go away." Anne studied her brief. "I'm preparing to kick your ass."

"What if I win this case?"

"Not possible. You're in the wrong, and you're against me."

"I won the last evidentiary motion, re-member?"

"That was a battle, not the war." Anne eyed the bailiffs over her papers. "Now go away. Everyone knows you're flirting."

"You're flirting back."

"I don't flirt with opposing counsel."

"I'm not opposing, you are." Matt snorted, then stepped away and crossed to plaintiff's counsel table. Beyond it lay the jury box, a polished mahogany rail cordoning off four-teen empty chairs in various states of swivelhood. They made an interesting back-drop, and Anne wondered if Matt would still want to see her after the verdict came back. She thought of the young man sitting behind her and suppressed a guilty twinge. That made a total of two guilty twinges she'd had in her whole life, and Anne wasn't good at suppressing them, on account of such sporadic practice.

"All rise!" the bailiff cried, from beyond the bar of the court. The golden seal of the United States Courts rose like the sun on the paneled wall, behind a huge mahogany dais of contemporary design. Gilt-framed portraits of past judges hung on the walls, their thick oil paint glistening darkly in the recessed lights. The bailiff stood near one, his chest puffed out as if it bore medals. "All rise! Court is now in session! The Honorable Albert D. Hoffmeier, presiding."

"Good afternoon, everybody," Judge Hoffmeier called out, emerging from the paneled pocket door, carrying a thick accordion case-file. The gallery greeted the stocky little judge in return, and he bustled into the courtroom, the hem of his shiny black robes brushing the carpet as he chugged past the American flag and onto the large, wooden dais, then plopped the file onto the cluttered desktop, seated himself in his chair, and pushed up his tortoiseshell glasses.

"Good afternoon, Ms. Murphy." Judge Hoffmeier smiled down at her, his eyes bright. His wiry hair was flecked salt-and-pepper, and he wore a Stars-and-Stripes bow tie that evidenced a sense of humor legendary on the district court bench. "What is it you're troubling us with, young lady? My favorite holiday is almost upon us, and we should all be out buying hot dogs and sunblock." The gallery chuckled, as did the judge. "Yes, I like sunblock on my hot dogs."

The gallery laughed again, and Anne rose and took her brief to the lectern. "Sorry to keep you, Your Honor, but I do have this pesky evidentiary motion. As you know, I represent Chipster.com, the defendant company in this matter, and I am asking the Court to exclude the testimony of Susan Feldman, whom plaintiff intends to call as a witness at trial next week."

"You don't think the jury should meet Ms. Feldman, counsel?" If Judge Hoffmeier appreciated Anne's beauty he hid it well, and she didn't kid herself that he'd let it influence him. It took more than a pretty face to win in a federal forum. Usually.

"Not at all, Your Honor. I think Ms. Feldman and her testimony should be excluded under Federal Rule of Evidence 401, because it is irrelevant. Ms. Feldman alleges that one of Chipster's programmers, named Phillip Leaver, sexually harassed her, in a rather bizarre incident." The judge's already-twinkling eye told Anne that he knew the underlying facts. "Neither Ms. Feldman nor Mr. Leaver have anything to do with this case or either of the parties at issue. The incident concerning Ms. Feldman occurred in a different department, at a different time, between different people."

"I read your motion papers." Judge Hoffmeier patted the accordion file. "Am I correct that defendant company concedes that the incident involving Ms. Feldman is true?"

"Correct, Your Honor." Anne took a deep, preparatory breath. "We concede that this incident took place, but we do not concede that it constitutes sexual harassment. The incident was a prank, and even though Mr. Leaver's conduct wasn't actionable, Chipster found it inappropriate and terminated him that very day."

"Oh really? A prank?" Judge Hoffmeier peered in amusement over the top of his glasses. "Let's talk turkey, Ms. Murphy. Mr. Leaver came out of his cubicle at work—and he was naked as a jaybird!"

"True." Anne suppressed her smile, and the gallery reacted with muffled laughter. "But it was a joke, Your Honor. And, just for the record, Mr. Leaver was wearing ankle bands with little wings. They were made out of Reynolds Wrap."

"Ankle bands with wings, of course. A fan of Hermes, or Pan, perhaps, eh?" Judge Hoffmeier chuckled, and the gallery with him, since they'd been given judicial permission. "Why wings, counsel?"

"Why not, Your Honor? Though I doubt Mr. Leaver studies mythology. He's twenty-three years old and watches way too much *Jackass.*"

"Jackass?"

"It's a show on MTV. Young men skateboard naked or dressed like gorillas." Anne loved the show, but wasn't eager to reveal as much to a sixty-year-old judge with Article III powers. "In any event, Mr. Leaver came out of his cubicle and stood for a moment in front of Ms. Feldman, but said nothing inappropriate and made no lewd gesture. He merely flapped his arms and pretended to fly, which I admit is silly and tasteless, but is not yet a violation of federal law."

Judge Hoffmeier burst into laughter. "This is why NASDAQ's in the crapper! This is the Internet revolution we hear so much about! The nation's economy is run by children wearing kitchen supplies!"

Anne waited until the laughter in the gallery had subsided. The holiday mood had already started, and she hoped it would flow in her favor, five minutes hence. "It is funny, Your Honor, and in fact, Ms. Feldman clearly took Mr. Leaver's actions as a joke. When he started flapping, she laughed until she fell off her chair. Mr. Leaver was so embarrassed, he ran into the men's room and refused to come out until the close of business."

The gallery laughed louder, and Judge Hoffmeier let it spend itself, then turned serious. "Well. This is a unique fact situation, to be sure. Your client, Chipster.com, doesn't want Ms. Feldman to tell the story about the tinfoil wings at trial?"

"No. Her story, her evidence, is irrelevant. The upcoming trial, *Dietz v. Chipster,* is a quid pro quo case of sexual harassment. In it, plaintiff alleges that Gil Martin, the company's CEO, forced Beth Dietz, a female programmer, to have sex with him in his office on a number of occasions, in order to keep her job. What happened between Mr. Martin and Ms. Dietz is a credibility question for the jury, and we will prove that plaintiff's allegations are false. But whether Mr. Leaver streaked, flapped, or struck a pose for Ms. Feldman doesn't make it any more or less likely that Gil Martin harassed Beth Dietz."

"Standard relevance analysis, eh, Ms. Murphy?"

"Exactly, with one addition." Anne rechecked her brief. "While that evidence may be admissible in a 'hostile environment' theory, in which the number and pervasiveness of alleged other incidents are relevant, it is clearly inadmissible as irrelevant in this, a quid pro quo case."

"So, you rest on the difference between a hostile environment theory and a quid pro quo theory of sexual harassment." Judge Hoffmeier frowned in thought. "It's quite a technical argument."

"Think of it as precise, Your Honor." To Anne, precision mattered in the law, brain surgery, and lipliner. Otherwise it was no fun at all. "The distinction makes a difference because of the impact the evidence will have. Plaintiff's counsel will be using this incident involving Mr. Leaver to bootstrap his meager proofs regarding Mr. Martin."

Judge Hoffmeier rubbed his chin, clean-shaven even at this hour. "Any guidance from upstairs, Ms. Murphy? I've found no appellate cases on point."

"Frankly, no, Your Honor. I briefed *Becker v. ARCO*, which supports my position, but it's not precisely on point. It does emphasize the danger in admitting evidence of this kind, in that it enables the plaintiff to prove the defendant's liability only in the loosest and most illogical fashion, like guilt by association."

"Thank you. I have your argument, Ms. Murphy." Judge Hoffmeier nodded and turned to plaintiff's counsel table. "You want in, Mr. Booker?"

"Sure do, Your Honor." Matt went to the lectern as Anne stepped back. "Your Honor, I like a joke as much as the next guy, and I agree this incident may sound funny to us now. But contrary to defense counsel's assertion, Ms. Feldman did not think this supposed prank was funny. Mr. Leaver's conduct constitutes indecent exposure in this and most jurisdictions."

Judge Hoffmeier's mouth flattened to a politically correct line of disapproval. Anne wondered if she could rescind her flirting.

"Your Honor, we think Ms. Feldman's testimony is admissible," Matt continued. "This is proof positive of the type of 'locker room' conduct that is encouraged at Chipster.com and at an increasing number of Internet companies. Sexual harassment suits are on the rise in the Internet companies because computer programming is so male-dominated. In fact, ninety-five percent of Chipster's programmers are male, between the ages of twenty-one and thirty-five, and none of the company's fifteen supervisors are women. This creates the raucous 'boys only' pattern of conduct, which permits conduct like Mr. Leaver's and Mr. Martin's to flourish."

"What about Ms. Murphy's point that this is a quid pro quo case and not a hostile environment case?"

"I agree with Your Honor that that is a hypertechnical argument. Sexual harassment is sexual harassment. And *Becker v. ARCO* notwithstanding, the law in the Third Circuit is not settled on whether evidence proving a hostile environment case can be admitted in a quid pro quo case."

Judge Hoffmeier rested his chin on his hand. "It does seem probative to me, especially considering that it is undisputed."

"I agree, Your Honor, and it is for the jury—not for any of us—to decide whether the corporate culture at Chipster is one in which sexual harassment is permitted. The defendant in the present case is the very CEO of the company, Gilbert Martin."

"Thank you for your argument, counsel," Judge Hoffmeier said with finality, and Anne couldn't tell which way he would rule. She couldn't take a chance on losing. The evidence would kill her case. Time for Plan B.

"Your Honor, if I may, I have rebuttal," Anne said, and Judge Hoffmeier smiled.

"The fighting Irish. Okay, counsel, but keep it short."

"Your Honor, in the alternative, defendant argues that even if the Court thinks the evidence is relevant, it should be excluded under Federal Rule 403 because of the danger of unfair prejudice. Imagine how distracted the jury would be if this evidence came in. Your Honor, we're talking here about *a naked man*."

On cue, the young man sitting behind Anne in the gallery stood up, stepped into the aisle, then unbuttoned his raincoat and let it drop in a heap at his feet. The man was sandy-haired, handsome—and buck-naked. The gallery let out a collective gasp, the court reporter covered her mouth, and the bailiff reached for his handcuffs, but Anne continued her legal argument:

"The image of a naked man commands instant and total attention. It is a riveting, galvanizing image, especially in a courtroom. If it's permitted, the jury will be so distracted—"

"What *is* this?" Judge Hoffmeier exploded. He was craning his neck and fumbling for his gavel. *Crak! Crak!* "Order! Order! My God in Heaven! Get dressed, young man! Put your clothes on!"

Matt sprang to his feet, pounding the table. "Your Honor, we object! This is an outrage!"

Pandemonium broke out in the gallery as the naked man grabbed his raincoat and took off, flapping his arms and sprinting down the center aisle and out of the courtroom doors, with the bailiff in hot pursuit. The gallery burst into spontaneous applause at his performance, and Anne decided on the spot to pay him a bonus.

Crak! Crak! "Order! I will have order in my courtroom! Settle down, everybody! Settle down!" Judge Hoffmeier stopped banging the gavel, and the redness ebbed from his face. He straightened his glasses and glared down at Anne. "Ms. Murphy, I cannot believe my own eyes! Did you arrange that ridiculous stunt?"

"Think of it as a demonstration, Your Honor. It proves my point that if a naked man enters the courtroom, all else stops—"

"Was that man *Mr. Leaver*?" Judge Hoffmeier's hooded eyes widened.

"No, he works for Strippergram. He sings, too, but the case didn't call for it."

"I object, Your Honor!" Matt was yelling, but Judge Hoffmeier waved him into his seat, never taking his stern gaze from Anne.

"Ms. Murphy, are you telling me you paid a *stripper* to come here today?"

"Who else would get naked for money?"

"Ms. Murphy! I could cite you for contempt

for this sort of thing! Send you to jail! My courtroom is not a peep show!"

"I'm sorry, Your Honor, but I couldn't think of any other way to show you. I mean, look around." Anne gestured at the gallery, now in complete disarray. People were half-standing and half-seated, laughing and talking among themselves, unable to get back in order. "See? The naked man is gone, but everybody was completely distracted by him. I was making a valid legal argument when he dropped his coat, but everybody stopped listening, including you."

Judge Hoffmeier bristled, but Anne went on.

"With all due respect, Your Honor, what just happened proves my point. If a naked man is on the jury's mind, they won't be able to focus on Mr. Martin, and he's the one on trial. They'll go into that jury room to deliberate, and a naked man is all they'll talk about. That's exactly what Federal Rule 403 was designed to prevent."

Judge Hoffmeier went speechless, and Matt simmered. The courtroom fell suddenly silent as everyone gazed, stunned, at Anne. She remained uncharacteristically mute, wondering if she could post bail with a Visa card. After a minute, Judge Hoffmeier sighed, nudged his glasses needlessly into place, and met Anne's eye.

"Ms. Murphy, I will not sanction this sort of foolishness in my courtroom. I maintain a relaxed atmosphere here, but you have evidently gotten the wrong message." The judge squared his shoulders in the voluminous robes. "I am therefore citing you for contempt, to the tune of $500. Thank your lucky stars I'm not locking you up for the weekend. But as I said, the Fourth of July is my favorite national holiday, and every American should celebrate our individual freedoms. Even Americans as absurdly free as *you*."

"Thank you, Your Honor," Anne said. As for the $500, she'd have to take it out of her personal savings, which would leave $17.45. She couldn't very well charge the client for keeping the lawyer out of jail. She was pretty sure it was supposed to be the other way around.

"And, Ms. Murphy, you're on notice." Judge Hoffmeier wagged his finger. "I will not tolerate another such display in my

courtroom next week, or any week thereafter. Next 'demonstration' like this, you go
directly to jail."

"Understood, Your Honor."

"Fine." Judge Hoffmeier paused. "Now.
Well. As for defendant's motion to exclude
evidence, I hereby grant the motion, albeit
reluctantly. I am loathe to reward Ms. Murphy's misconduct, but I cannot penalize the
defendant company for its lawyer's hare-
brained schemes. I therefore rule that Ms.
Feldman will not be permitted to testify at
the trial of this matter, and that there will
be no naked men in evidence next week,
either in word or deed. So ordered!" Judge
Hoffmeier banged the gavel, shaking his
head.

"Thank you, Your Honor." Anne wanted to
cheer, but didn't. She won. She *won!*

Matt rose briefly, with a scowl. "Thank
you, Your Honor."

"Now, Ms. Murphy, get out of my courtroom before I return to my senses." Judge
Hoffmeier got up and left the dais. "Have a
good holiday, everybody."

Anne stood up as soon as the judge had
left, felt a soft caress on her back, and
turned. Two lawyers in fancy suits stood be-

hind her. They were hot, successful, and evidently patronized the same custom tailor.

"That was amazing, Anne!" the one said, touching her again, though she didn't know him at all. He wore a practiced smile and a wedding band.

The other lawyer stepped closer. "Where'd you get that idea? And didn't we meet at—"

"Thanks," Anne said politely, but she didn't want to get picked up in federal court unless it was by Matt Booker. She peered past their padded shoulders at Matt, who was hunching over his briefcase, shoving papers inside. She waved, trying to get his attention, but his forehead was knitted with anger and he wouldn't look up. Then her view was blocked by the lawyers.

"How did you get the guts to do that?" the married lawyer asked, but Anne stepped around him.

"Matt!" she called, but he'd grabbed his briefcase, hurried down the center aisle, and left through the double doors. Anne didn't go after him. She couldn't apologize for representing her client. She couldn't say she was sorry she'd won. She stood there, suddenly aware that two suits were hovering over her, an entire gallery was gawking at her, and several reporters were rushing at her with notebooks drawn.

"Anne," the married lawyer said, in low tones. "I was wondering if you were busy tonight. I'd love to take you out to celebrate."

A reporter elbowed him out of the way, shouting questions in Anne's face. "Ms. Murphy, that was great! What a trick! What was the stripper's name?" The press glommed suddenly around her, like bees to a Pulitzer. "Did you think you'd go to jail?" "What did your client think about that stunt?" "Would you consider a photo shoot this week, for our 'up-and-coming' feature?"

Anne shoved her way back to counsel table for her briefcase and bag, answering none of the questions and ignoring all of the stares. She screened out the world around her, which left her feeling the way it always did, a little dead inside. But at least she'd won the motion, and she'd deserved to win. Even without any case precedent, Anne knew in her heart she was right on the law.

Mental note: Only a beautiful woman can understand the true power of a naked man.

2

Rosato & Associates, read the brass name-plate affixed to the sky-blue wall, and Anne stepped off the elevator into the air-conditioned cool of the empty reception area. Navy club chairs, a blue-patterned Karastan, and a glass table covered with a slick magazine-fan formed a corporate oasis after the heat and hubbub outside. Holiday traffic had already started, and Anne couldn't get a cab from the courthouse, so she had walked the twenty-five blocks in her Blahniks, which constituted cruel and unusual punishment. She kicked off her shoes and they tumbled over each other in a taupe blur.

"Faithless ones," she said, then went over and rescued them.

She tucked them into her briefcase and padded barefoot to the reception desk, which was also empty. The receptionist must have gone home early, and a quick glance around told Anne that the whole place had cleared out. It was silent except for the echo of laughter at one of the far offices, near the corner of the building. She knew who that would be.

She picked up the clipboard they kept on the reception desk and scanned the list of sign-ins and outs. Bennie Rosato had signed out all day in depositions, and Anne breathed a relieved sigh. She would have a lot of 'splainin' to do for the naked-man motion. The telephone rang on the reception desk, and she picked it up. "Rosato and Associates," she answered.

The caller was a man. "This is the *Daily News*, is Anne Murphy in? We'd like to ask her a few questions about—"

"I'm sorry, I'm not here." Anne let the receiver drop into the cradle, and when the phone began ringing again, pretended it was background music. She set down the clipboard and sorted through the WHILE YOU WERE OUT pink slips to collect her own, then grabbed her mail and FedExes from the black tray bearing her name. She padded, stuff in hand, to her office.

Sunlight poured through the window behind her chair, bathing her messy desktop in a too-white glare and illuminating the dust motes in the air, agitated by the slightly damp lawyer. Her desk sat flush against the left wall and above it hung wooden book-shelves stuffed with law books, thick copies of the Federal Rules, a couple of legal thrillers, and outdated Neiman Marcus catalogs full of clothes she deserved to own but didn't yet. Her office contained no photographs, and nothing hung on her walls except for her diplomas from UC Berkeley and Stanford Law.

Anne dropped her messenger bag and briefcase on a chair, her mail and messages on the desk, then walked to her chair and sat down. The laughter sounded louder now that she was closer to the source, the two older associates, Mary DiNunzio and Judy Carrier. They were hanging out in Mary's office, which doubled as their clubhouse.

She thumbed through her messages but her heart wasn't in it. She couldn't sit still. She felt jiggered up from her victory. She had called Gil on the cell to tell him about the win, but he hadn't answered and she'd left a message. She hadn't told him about the naked man, either; she'd wanted him to have deniability in case of her arrest. Now it would play out beautifully. She won!

Anne felt like celebrating. She heard the laughter again. Maybe she could take Mary and Judy out for drinks. She never had before, but why not? She had nothing else to do tonight except go to the gym, and she'd love to skip that for once. She worked out to burn off stress, but hated it so much it was stressing her. If this kept up, she'd have to go back to charging things.

Anne got up from her chair and walked barefoot down the hallway, toward the laughter. Its lighthearted sound was contagious, and her own smile grew unaccountably as she approached Mary's office and leaned in the door. "What's so funny, guys?" she asked.

The laughter stopped so quickly it was as if somebody had flicked the OFF switch.

"Oh, it was nothing," answered Judy Carrier, sitting on Mary's credenza. But her china-blue eyes were wet from giggling, and her unlipsticked lips still bore the trace of a smile.

Mary DiNunzio frowned from behind her neat desk. "Sorry if we were loud. Did we disturb you?"

"No, not at all." Anne's cheeks went hot. She should have known better. This law firm was worse than high school, and she felt like a D student crashing National Honor Society.

"How was court?" Mary asked. If she'd heard about the naked guy, it didn't show. Her expression was interested, if only politely. Her dark-blond hair had been swept back into a French twist, and she was wearing her trademark khaki suit from Brooks Brothers, in contrast to Judy, who flopped on the credenza in denim overalls, a white tank, and a red bandanna in her Dutch-boy haircut. These two were so different, Anne could never understand their close friendship, and had given up trying.

"Uh, court was fine." Anne's smile morphed into a professional mask. Mary had been filling in on Chipster, and Anne always sensed that they could have been friends, if things had been different. Like if they both lived on Pluto, where women were nice to each other. "I won, which is good."

"Jeez! You won?" Mary smiled. "Congratulations! How'd you do that? It was a tough motion."

"Hoffmeier just agreed, I guess." Anne didn't even consider telling them the story. It had been a mistake to come here. By here she meant Philadelphia.

Mary looked puzzled. "What'd he agree with? The cases weren't any help."

"Who knows? He bought the argument. I have to go, I'm really late. I just thought I'd say good-bye." Anne edged out of the office and faked a final smile. "Happy Fourth of July. Have a great weekend, guys."

"You probably have plans. Dates, right?" Mary asked, and Anne nodded.

"Yep. See ya."

"Tonight, too? Because I—"

"Yes. Big date tonight. Gotta go now."

"Okay, well, happy Fourth."

Judy nodded. "Have a good one."

But Anne was already out of the office and down the hall, padding quickly away. An hour later she was dressed in an oversized T-shirt, baggy shorts, and Reeboks, and standing in a practically empty gym, squaring off against a Life Fitness elliptical exerciser, a costly machine that simulates running for people who hate to run for free. SELECT WORKOUT, ordered the display, and tiny red lights blinked a helpful arrow that pointed to the ENTER button.

Anne hit the button, cycling through FAT BURN, CARDIO, and MANUAL, until she got to RANDOM, which resonated. RANDOM would place

huge hills in her path without warning. RAN-
DOM would keep her on her toes. RANDOM
equaled life.

She hit the button, grabbed the handles,
and started fake-running. The gym was deserted except for a muscleman on the
leg-lift machine, watching himself in the mirror, Narcissus on Nautilus. It was so quiet
she could hear the *humpa-humpa* of spinning music throbbing through the wall next
to her. She had tried spinning once, but you
had to do it with a class, which meant that
somebody, male or female or maybe both,
would hit on her. So Anne worked out alone
in front of the row of mounted TVs, looking
straight ahead and wearing earphones from
a Sony Walkman. The Walkman's batteries
were long dead; it was just a way for nobody
to bother her. She got her heart pounding,
watching CNN on mute and trying not to
hate exercise, CNN, or anything else about
her life.

She had won, after all.

The thought made her smile. A baby hill
rose ahead of her, and she fake-jogged up its
simulated incline, her eyes on the TV. Across
the bottom of the screen slid two stacks of
stock quotes, with their mysterious acronyms

and red and green arrows. There were lots of red arrows, pointing down. If Anne had money invested in the market she'd be worried, but she invested in shoes.

"Hi, Anne," said a voice beside her, and she looked over. It was a girl climbing on the exerciser next to her and selecting FAT BURN. The chick was too thin to need FAT BURN, but it was the only lie bigger than one-size-fits-all.

"Hi," Anne said, wracking her brain for the girl's name. The girl started walking at a leisurely pace, with her eyes focused at some imaginary point in the wall, and Anne finally remembered it. Willa Hansen. Willa was a brooding artist-type and she'd dyed her hair again, this time a normal human-being color. It was even a red shade close to Anne's.

"I like your new haircolor, Willa," Anne blurted out, after a minute. She gathered she was trying to strike up a conversation, but wasn't sure why. Maybe to prove she remembered Willa's name. Mental note: It is pointless to remember someone's name and not get credit for it.

"Thanks."

"How'd you get the blue out?" Anne asked, then wanted to kick herself. Somehow it sounded wrong. She'd always had a hard time talking to women. Men were so much easier; to talk to a man, all she had to do was listen, which they counted as the same thing.

"The blue came out right away. It was Kool-Aid."

"Huh?" Anne tugged out her silent earphones. Maybe she hadn't heard right. "You put Kool-Aid, the *drink*, on your hair?"

"Sure." Willa smiled. "Just add water."

Anne wasn't sure what to say, so she fake-jogged for a moment in silence. There were things she would never understand about her generation, and her experiments with haircolor tended to the more conventional. When she started practice, she dyed her hair Professional Brown, but it had proved futile. She'd remained Unprofessional, only with really boring hair, so she'd gone back to her natural Lucille Ball Red. She took another conversational stab. "I didn't know you could put Kool-Aid in your hair."

"Sure," Willa answered, strolling along in her T-shirt and shorts. "I used to use Manic Panic, but Kool-Aid works just as well. The blue was Blueberry, and to get rid of it, I just put Cherry on top, and my hair turned black."

"Blackberry?"

"I guess." Willa didn't get the joke. "Then I hennaed it, and it turned out kind of coppery."

Anne fake-scaled another hill and kept going. The lighted display on the treadmill told her she had fake-jogged for only 2:28, which meant she had approximately 3 years and 23 hours left. She let her glance slip sideways and checked Willa's display. Willa didn't have any hills ahead, which meant she lacked sufficient stress in her diet.

"What are you doing for the Fourth, Anne?"

"I have to hole up in my house and work all weekend. I have a big trial on Tuesday."

"Oh, that's right, you're a lawyer."

Anne felt the urge to tell Willa about her big victory in court today, naked man and all, but it would be pathetic. She didn't know Willa very well and they'd talked only a few times about their respective personal lives, or lack thereof. Like Anne, Willa lived alone and wasn't from Philly. Anne sensed that she had a trust fund, which was where the similarities between the two girls came to the proverbial screeching halt. "Do you have plans for the holiday?"

"Not anymore. I was gonna dog-sit this weekend for this couple, but they broke up."

"The couple?"

"The dogs."

Anne didn't ask. She was fake-puffing too hard anyway. "I didn't know you dog-sat."

"I do, sometimes, for fun. I love dogs. When I dog-sit, I use the time to sketch them." Willa strolled along on her machine. "There'll be a lot else to sketch this weekend, I guess. There's something called the Party on the Parkway, and fireworks at the Art Museum on Monday night."

"Oh, no. I live right off the Parkway." This would be Anne's first Independence Day in Philly, and she hadn't thought of it. How would she get any work done? Damn. Kilimanjaro loomed on her Life Fitness display. Another example of RANDOM. "I have to work this weekend. How am I gonna do that?"

"Don't you have an office?"

"Yeah, but—" Anne didn't want to run into Mary and Judy. Or worse, Bennie. Work would be okay if it weren't for coworkers.

"Offices suck, right?"

"Exactly."

"So why don't you take off?" Willa's saunter slowed to a crawl. Soon she would be going in reverse, and the gym would have to pay her.

"Take off?"

"Aren't you single?"

"Very."

"So go to the Jersey shore. I was on North Cape May once, and there's a national park there. Very quiet and peaceful. I got a lot of sketching done."

"Down the shore?" It was code for the Jersey shore. Everybody in Philadelphia vacationed in South Jersey. Unlike L.A., Philly wasn't a summer-in-Provence kind of town, thank God. "I suppose I could go."

Willa resumed her slow walk, and Anne fell instantly in love with the idea of a weekend getaway. What a way to celebrate her big win! She didn't own a car, but she always rented the same convertible, mainly to go food-shopping on the weekends. The manager at the Hertz in town usually saved it for her; it was a fire-engine red Mustang that would embarrass most pimps. She planned to buy it as soon as she got out of credit-card debt and hell froze over.

"Why not?" Anne said. "I could go away for the weekend!"

"Sure you could. Get crazy. Dye your hair purple."

"Or not." Anne giggled, her mood lifting. "But I could call a realtor. I'm lucky, maybe I'll get a cancellation."

"From some lawyer who had to stay in the hot city." Willa laughed, and so did Anne.

"Sucker."

"Totally."

Then Anne remembered Mel. "But I have a cat. I can't leave him."

"I guess I could sit for a cat. I like cats. I could sketch a cat."

Anne hesitated at the thought of letting a stranger into her house, since what had happened with Kevin. But Willa was a woman, and she seemed honest and, most importantly, not a psycho. Anne, who had never given a thought to going down the shore, now could hardly wait to get there. She could work like crazy, and she'd never seen the Atlantic Ocean. She was pretty sure she could find it. "Please, would you cat-sit for me this weekend, Willa?" she asked.

"Okay, I'll sketch the cat, and maybe even the fireworks. If you're near the Parkway, your place'll have a great view." Willa's walk slowed to a standstill. "You want to go now and beat the traffic? I'll finish my run on the way to your house. I can clean up at your place."

"Great!" Anne pressed the CLEAR button. "To hell with this! I'll run tomorrow morning on the beach, in the fresh ocean breeze! Or maybe I won't! Ha!"

Anne had scored both Mustang and seashore rental by the time she made it home, hurrying in gym clothes to her Fairmount neighborhood, which lay just outside of Philly's business district. It was a gentrified section of the city, characterized by art museums, the Free Library, and the family court, interspersed with blocks of colonial town houses with repointed brick facades and freshly painted shutters. Bennie Rosato owned a house in the area, and Fairmount was a quiet, safe neighborhood, which was all Anne cared about after her move east. Parking she could live without.

The house she rented stood three-stories high but was downright anorexic; only one-room wide, it was a cozy, two-bedroom trinity, which was what Philadelphians called houses with one room on each floor. Anne hit her front door running, ignoring the bills and catalogs spilling through the mail slot and onto the rug in the tiny entrance hall. She locked and latched the door, dropped her briefcase and purse on the living room floor, and tore upstairs with her gym bag.

"Mel! Mel! We won our motion!" Anne called to the cat, which confirmed for her she'd been living alone too long. She bounded into her bedroom and dropped the gym bag on the floor, startling into wakefulness the chubby gray tabby curled at the foot of her unmade bed. Mel flattened his ears in Attack Cat until he realized it was only her, then relaxed, blinking his large, green eyes slowly. Anne went to the bed, cupped his furry face in her palms, and kissed the hard, spongy pink of his nose.

"We won, handsome!" she said again, but Mel only yawned, his teeth bright white spikes. When he closed his mouth, the tips stayed on the outside, and he morphed into Halloween Cat. Mel was acting very scary today, and Anne wondered if he had his holidays mixed up.

"Mel, the good news is that we won. The bad news is that I'm going away, but you're going to be fine. You'll meet a very nice girl

who wants to draw your picture, okay?"
Anne gave him another quick kiss, but he
didn't purr, which told her he was worried
about being left alone with a total stranger
who dyed her hair blue. Mental note: People
project all sorts of emotions onto their cats,
and cats like it that way.

Anne gave Mel a final kiss, hurried to her
messy bureau, and pulled out clean undies,
two T-shirts, a denim skirt, and an extra pair
of shorts. She plucked her leopard-print
mules from the bottom of the closet, because they always made her feel festive and
she was celebrating.

"Did I mention that we won our motion,
Mel?" Anne asked, stuffing the clothes into
her gym bag. She'd shower at her new
apartment at the beach, though she hurried
into the bathroom, fetched her Kiehl's sham-
poo, conditioner, and grapefruit body lotion,
as well as her makeup in its *I Love Lucy* tin,
which bore a colorized scene of the road trip
to California. She couldn't leave without
Lucy or grapefruit moisturizer. That would
be camping.

"I'm outta here, Mel!" she sang out as she
hustled back to the bedroom, but Mel had
fallen asleep and didn't wake up even when

she stuffed the toiletries into the bag and zipped it closed, or even when the doorbell rang. It had to be Willa, and Anne slung the bag over her shoulder and scooped up the slumbering cat, who draped his stripy front legs on either side of her forearms and permitted himself to be carted downstairs. Sedan Chair Cat.

"Coming!" Anne called out when she reached the first floor and went to the peephole, just to be sure. The action was automatic at this point, even though Kevin was in jail a zillion miles away. She dreaded the day he got out, but that was two years from now. Standing on the front stoop was Willa Hansen, huffing and puffing in her workout clothes.

"Come on in!" Anne unlatched and opened the door, and Willa cooed the moment she saw Mel.

"Oooooh! Isn't he just so pretty!"

And Anne and Mel knew everything was going to be just fine.

Cars, minivans, and pickup trucks stretched in three lanes as far as the eye could see, with brake lights that formed dotted red lines. It was just another example of RANDOM, and

Anne resigned herself to not getting to the shore until way after dark. She put the Mustang convertible in park and leaned her head against the black headrest. The night air blew cool and blessedly free of humidity. The sky was deepening to a rich sapphire, the stars brightening slowly, diamonds in relief.

A blue Voyager minivan next to her had two kid's bicycles strapped to a rack on the back, their spokes laced with red, white, and blue crepe paper, and the rear compartment of the van had been packed with Acme grocery bags, folded sheets, and a Big Bird doll, his beak smashed against the smoked glass. Anne could barely make out the family inside, but here was evidence of them—kids bouncing on the seats, and a mother and a father in front.

She looked away and flicked on the radio, suddenly restless. She scanned but there was nothing on but oldies older than her and sports scores, which reminded her of exercise. She turned it off. The night fell silent except for the idling of three thousand minivans bearing happy families to the shore, undoubtedly poisoning the air of women refusing to be lonely in their Mustang convertibles. Anne plucked a can of Diet

Coke from the cupholder and raised it in a toast. "To carbon monoxide, and to me," she said. She took a sip of warm, flat soda, then got an idea:

She had won, and there was one person she could tell. She didn't stop to wonder why—for once didn't pause to observe herself observing herself—or to make even a single mental note. She was just going to do it. Just do it!

She set down the soda can and rummaged in her purse for her cell phone and little red address book, and opened both. She had to hold the address book up in the headlights of the car behind her to read it, and she thumbed to the M listings and found the phone number. There were five old numbers before it, all crossed out, and she didn't know if the most recent number would work. It hadn't for a few months, but it was all she had.

She pushed in the area code for L.A., then the phone number. It would be dinnertime there. The tinny rings started, one, two, three rings, with faint crackling on the signal. She waited for the call to be picked up, and despite the fact that she just had a slug of soda, her throat went suddenly dry. After a moment, the rings stopped and a mechanical voice came on:

"The number you have dialed is no longer in service. Please check your records . . ."

Anne felt her heart sink, a reaction she hated as soon as she had it, and gritted her teeth. She was determined not to be a victim, a wimp, or a total loser. So she let the mechanical voice drone away in a continuous loop and delivered her message anyway:

"Hi, how are you? I thought you might like to know that I won a very important motion today in court. I thought it up by myself, and it was a little crazy, but it worked. Other than that, I'm fine, really, and don't worry about me." She paused. "I love you, too, Mom."

Then she pressed End and flipped the cell phone closed.

3

Seagulls squawked over a greasy brown bag in a trash can, and dappled pigeons waddled along the weathered boardwalk, their scaly pink-red feet churning like so many wind-up toys. Saturday morning had dawned clear, hot, and sunny at the Jersey shore, and Anne had learned that the Atlantic Ocean looked exactly like the Pacific. Wet, big, blue, and moving a lot. Her idea of natural beauty remained the King of Prussia Mall.

She was finishing her morning run, having hated every step of three miles down the windy boardwalk, at fourteen minutes per. Okay, it wasn't the fastest pace, but Anne was sweating respectably through her big T-shirt and bike shorts. She was panting, too, but that was because her sports bra was cutting off her oxygen supply. Mental note: Satan exists and he works for Champion.

While Anne waited for her breathing to return to normal, she wiped her eyes behind black Oakley sunglasses and smoothed her hair back into its damp ponytail. A generous dollop of zinc oxide concealed her top lip. Other runners jogged by in smugly over-sized triathlon watches and brand-new Sauconys, their cushioned footsteps thundering on the old gray boards. There were so many more people on the boardwalk than when Anne had started her run. The Fourth of July weekend had evidently begun, and a family pedaled past in a rental surrey with a red-and-white striped awning. A few male runners broke stride to check her out on the fly, which was when Anne decided to go home to her little apartment and get to work.

She started to walk back, but the breeze was too warm to cool anything and she stopped at a newsstand on the corner for a bottle of water and a Philly newspaper. She bought both with soggy bills, stepped away from the newsstand, and was about to crack the white plastic cap to the Evian when she unfolded the newspaper, saw the headline, and froze.

LAWYER FOUND MURDERED, it screamed, and plastered underneath it was Anne's own law-school graduation picture.

Cheap inks colored her eyes the candy-coated green of M&Ms, and her hair was an orange-red seen only on hunting gear. A black band framed her photo, but the caption read simply, *Anne Murphy*.

She laughed, nervously. The lead story was evidently about her death, but she wasn't dead. Tired, yes, and retaining water. But not dead. It was obviously a mistake, a huge mistake. She opened the newspaper, but a gust of wind pungent with she-crab and diesel fuel whipped off the ocean, catching the pages like a sail. She defeated the unruly paper and read the lead paragraphs:

> Anne Murphy, 28, an attorney representing Internet company Chipster.com, was found slain at her home last night. Police have ruled the death a homicide resulting from gunshots fired at close range. Murphy was pronounced dead at Temple University Hospital at approximately 11:48 p.m. Friday night.
>
> Police were called to Murphy's home at 2257 Waltin Street when a neighbor reported hearing shots.

There was no sign of forced entry, and police have no suspects in the slaying at the present time.

Anne took off her sunglasses and read the paragraph again. Her sense of humor vanished. She had to be seeing things. It didn't make sense. Maybe the address was wrong? She double-checked it. 2257 Waltin Street. It was her house, but she wasn't dead. She wasn't even there.

Oh, my God. Suddenly her throat caught. She realized with a horrifying jolt what must have happened. It must have been Willa's body the police found.

Could this be? Could this really be? Was Willa dead? Anne's heart stalled in her chest. Her eyes welled up suddenly, blurring the busy boardwalk. She slipped her Oakleys back on with a trembling hand.

Kevin did this, whispered a voice in her head, a voice she'd thought she'd finally banished. *You know Kevin did this.*

She struggled against the voice and the conclusion, but she couldn't help it. Willa, dead? No! Anne needed to know everything, all the details. She reread the article, but it was only a summary of her legal career, with a group photo of the Rosato lawyers under the subhead A WOMAN'S TOUCH. It told her nothing more about the murder.

She couldn't wrap her mind around it. She held off panic vainly, like a hand raised against the ocean tide. What had happened? How could this be? She blinked tears from her eyes and ripped through the rest of the paper, but it was all Independence Day highlights: red, white, and blue sidebars about parade schedules and fireworks at the Art Museum. A cyclist with sculpted thighs eyed her as he sped past, followed by a trio of lanky runners, turning toward her as one. She tore back to the main story and read it over and over, trying to comprehend what had happened.

Kevin got out, but how? Why didn't they tell me?

Anne couldn't stop the voice, or the questions. Had the cops mistaken Willa for her? How? They didn't look anything alike. Willa had brown eyes, her nose was different, and she had no scars. Who had identified the body? Then Anne thought again. She and Willa were roughly the same height—both five foot five—and the same size, a six. Willa's hair was as long as Anne's, and her new haircolor was so similar.

Anne felt her heart wrench. Then she remembered that before she'd left, she had lent Willa her T-shirt from the office, the one with ROSATO & ASSOCIATES printed across the front. But so what? Anne didn't understand anything all of a sudden. The cops didn't rely on clothes, hair, or dress size to identify bodies. They used DNA, dental records, scientific methods, stuff like that, didn't they?

Kevin would know it wasn't me.

It didn't make sense. Or maybe he'd hired somebody? No. Never, not even from prison. He'd want to do it himself. She felt stricken. Who was killed in her house? Why did they think it was her? Her head throbbed. The newspaper itched in her hand. She didn't want to hold it a minute longer. She whirled around, dropped her water bottle, and collided with another runner, a middle-aged man who looked delighted to catch her in his arms.

"Excuse me, Miss," he said, then frowned behind glasses strapped on by thick red Croakies. "Are you all right? You're shaking so much—"

"I'm fine," Anne answered, breaking away. She stumbled to a wastebasket chained to the boardwalk rail and threw the newspaper into a nest of empty Budweiser cans and Fritos bags. Her knees went loose, as if somebody had kicked out the jambs.

She steadied herself against the trash can. Her heartbeat hurried out of control. The sun burned. The garbage reeked. Flies droned. A wave of nausea swept over her and she lurched away from the wastebasket, but she suddenly couldn't see anything around her. The sun bleached the people bone-white. The sky and clouds swirled together like boardwalk spin-art.

"Miss?" said a man's voice, and through the whiteness Anne could barely make out another man coming toward her. Then more, running to her.

The middle-aged man was saying something. The second man was in her face, his breath like coffee, and he gripped her arm and hoisted her. A third man pulled her other arm as if he were helping her to her feet, but Anne didn't think she had fallen. Their grips closed like handcuffs on her wrists. Her heart fluttered with fear. Her brain struggled to function. She had no protection. No gun, no cell phone. Not even a restraining order.

Adrenaline flooded her system. Her heart threatened to explode. She struggled against the men, twisting out of their grasp, shouting words even she couldn't hear. They backed off and stood stunned as Anne pulled herself to her feet, bit back the bile in her mouth, and fixed her gaze on the seesawing horizon. She stared down the sky until it righted itself. The sun resumed its position, and the clouds took their places. She grew steady, and the men surrounding her came back into focus as the volume came up:

"Don't try to stand, you're having a seizure! Are you diabetic?" "I'll call a doctor! I have my cell with me!" "Honey, can you hear me?" "Miss? What's your name?" "I'm telling you, she's dehydrated. She needs water, I have a bottle." "Here, let me help you up." "I'm calling 911!"

Kevin is back.

Fear cleared Anne's head. Chased her nausea and set her leg muscles twitching. Reminded her body of that most ancient of instincts. She took off, sprinting away without another word. The men would forgive her her bad manners. She was running for her life.

Her feet thudded on the boardwalk. Her thighs strained with sudden effort. The steel railing along the boardwalk blurred to a silver bullet. The Atlantic streaked to a choppy blue. Her breath came in ragged bursts. Her sneakers thundered on the boards, barely landing before she took off again.

She tore down the stairs to the empty beach, then raced toward the water. Hot sand sprayed from her heels. Sea air filled her lungs. A fishy chill cooled her cheeks. Her legs pumped hard, and she hit speed, then began to fly. A twelve-minute pace, then quicker, breathing easily, her heart squeezing and body functioning on its own now. She'd never run this fast, but fear fueled her.

Salt stung her eyes. The wind blew harder, buffeting her ears. Her Reeboks crunched on shards of seashells. She reached hard sand at the water's edge and ran in sea foam that splashed against the back of her calves. Water soaked her socks and shoes. She leapt over a broken bottle, its green glass glinting jaggedly in the sun, and hurtled forward, straight down the beach, parallel to the sea. She raced the horizon, flying into the distance until they both disappeared.

The sun burned high by the time Anne reached the clapboard duplex she was renting, and she chased up the weathered wooden steps to the second floor. She hit the front door with her chest heaving, her shirt and shorts so sweat-soaked she looked as if she'd gone swimming in her clothes. Her sneakers left blurry, sopping footprints on the splintery floorboards. Gritty, wet sand caked her ankles.

Her hands trembled as she fumbled inside her hidden shorts-pocket for the door key. Behind her came the carefree sounds of vacationers heading to the beach, chatting and laughing as they carried striped umbrellas on their shoulders. Their kids toddled along swinging plastic pails, and one boy rode a tricycle with a tiny American flag duct-taped to the handlebars. Anne unlocked her door and hurried inside, snatching her sunglasses off before her eyes had adjusted to the sudden darkness.

The apartment was a one-bedroom, its paneled walls festooned with hokey fish-netting, desiccated starfish, and a red plastic snow crab. Childproof fabric covered a cushy tan sofa flanked by white wicker chairs and end tables, with glass tops. Anne crossed quickly to the telephone on the end table. She couldn't believe Willa was dead. She snatched up the phone and punched in her own phone number, praying there'd be an answer.

She counted one, two, three, and four rings, then her answering machine picked up. She hung up quickly, not wanting to hear it, a sourness in the pit of her stomach. Was Willa really dead? Why else wouldn't she pick up? Where was she? She could be out, maybe running. But no answers came out of the blue, and the only sound in the still apartment was Anne's ragged breathing. She picked up the receiver and dialed her number again, just in case she had it wrong the first time.

Please, Willa, pick up. Again, the answering machine was the only reply.

Anne struggled to make her brain function, her fingers curling around the receiver. What next? Who would know where Willa was? Her family, but Anne had no idea where they lived. She didn't even know where Willa lived. Maybe Willa was just out. Maybe she wasn't dead. She couldn't be.

Anne's thoughts tumbled over one another in confusion. Okay, she didn't know where Willa was yet, but she had to tell the world she was alive. She thought of her own family, then skipped it. She couldn't find her mother to tell her, and she'd never met her father, a studio guitarist who had simply moved on before she was born. So much for that.

She thought of Gil and Chipster. Gil would need to know she was alive and that his case was going forward to trial on Tuesday. Chipster.com was on the line, and a jury verdict against it would kill a coming IPO, delayed once already. She picked up the receiver and called Gil's cell phone. Four rings, then five, then voice mail clicked on. She waited for his message to end, then the tone sounded and a mechanical voice said, "This service is presently accepting no more messages." The line went dead.

"Damn!" Anne pressed the button and tried again. Gil's voice mail must have been full. She listened again to the message and the aborted beep. She slammed down the receiver, her thoughts racing. God knows, there were plenty of other calls to make.

She picked up the receiver and phoned

the office. Somebody should be at work. Mary was taking a deposition for her today, of a witness in *Chipster,* and it was being held at the office at one o'clock. The call connected almost instantly: "You have reached Rosato & Associates," said the office answering machine. "We are closed until Tuesday, July fifth, in observance of the death of our associate Anne Murphy. Please leave a message and your call will be returned as soon as possible."

Anne hung up the phone, amazed. They had closed the office? They didn't even like her! She thought about reaching Mary on her cell phone, but what was her number? Anne didn't know it, but her cell phone did.

She hung up the living room phone and ran into the bedroom, where she'd pitched her temporary war room. The double bed had been transformed into a desk, sleep, and staging area; her thick Dell laptop sat open on its pillow-desk, and black binders filled with notes lay in a semicircle on the double bed. Her silvery cell phone, a Motorola Timeport, glinted in the sunlight streaming through the open window. She dove for the phone and flipped it open.

The screen was an opaque black. The

batteries had run out. In her hurry last night, she had forgotten to recharge it in the car. "Shit!" Anne shouted, slamming the cell into the mattress.

Kevin is out. Kevin is free. Kevin did this.

The thought momentarily paralyzed her. Last year, she had moved cross-country, to get as far away from Kevin Satorno as possible. She had met him at the supermarket at home in L.A.; he'd told her he was a Ph.D. candidate in history at UCLA. She had gone out with him once, a dinner date that had ended in a chaste kiss, but that single date had turned her life upside-down.

Afterward Kevin had started calling her all the time, talking marriage and kids, sending her gifts and red roses. Somehow he had gotten the idea that she loved him. At first she felt terrible that somehow she'd led him on, but she turned fearful when he began dropping in at her office unannounced and his ten phone calls a day grew to thirty. In no time Kevin began following her everywhere, stalking her.

She had gone to the authorities, where she learned about erotomania, or de Clérambault's syndrome, in which a person had the delusional belief that someone was in love with them. She'd gotten a restraining order as soon as she could, but it hadn't protected her the night Kevin attacked her at her door—and pulled a gun on her. It had been profound good luck that a passerby heard her scream, and Anne had moved to the East Coast to get safe and start over. Kevin had ended up in prison, but only for two years, on an aggravated assault charge. She'd put an entire country between them, changed her life and her job. Now Willa could be dead, because of her.

She closed her eyes in pain. But she opened them in anger. She was supposed to be calling the police to tell them she was alive, but first she had to find out if Kevin had been paroled. She grabbed the bedroom phone and called L.A. information for the district attorney's office. The DA who convicted Kevin might know where he was, but when she reached his office, his voice mail said: "The district attorney you have reached—Antonio Alvarez—will not return to the office until July fifteenth. Press one to leave a message, press two to return to the receptionist . . ."

Anne hung up, flipping through a mental Rolodex to remember who else was on the prosecution. It was reliving an awful memory; identifying Kevin in the police line-up, testifying against him, pointing him out as he sat at the defendant's table, which provoked his leaping up and lunging at the witness stand. She found herself shuddering despite the warm house, but a name entered her consciousness:

Dr. Marc Goldberger, the court-appointed psychiatrist who had evaluated Kevin and testified against him. The psychiatrist had explained to the jury about erotomania, and the graveness of the threat to Anne for some years to come. Most erotomanics were intelligent, well-educated, and resourceful enough to pursue the object of their obsessions for as long as a decade.

She snatched up the phone, called L.A. information again, and got the psychiatrist's office number. There was no answer, but she took down the emergency number that the answering machine gave her and called it directly. The call connected, and Anne recognized the sympathetic voice, like an echo in her memory. "Dr. Goldberger?"

"Yes, who is this?"

Anne was about to give her name, then stopped. He might be bound by privilege, and maybe he wouldn't talk to her if he knew who she was. "My name is Cindy Sherwood. I was a reporter on the Satorno trial, if you recall."

"I don't, I'm sorry. It's quite early in the morning, Ms. Sherwood, and on a holiday weekend. I don't speak with reporters and I don't remember being interviewed in connection with that case."

"Please, I was wondering if you had any information on the current whereabouts of Mr. Satorno. I am trying to do a follow-up story."

"As far as I know, Mr. Satorno is in prison. If you want to know more, speak with Mr. Alvarez, the district attorney."

"If you do happen to learn more about Mr. Satorno, would you please call me? The area code is Philadelphia, where I live now, since I got married." Anne left her cell number, and he was kind enough to take it down before they hung up.

She hung up the phone, thinking ahead, trying to keep her cool. If she lost control she'd be that girl racing down the beach, running scared. In a way, she had been doing that until this very minute, every day since she'd met Kevin Satorno, and she couldn't let that happen anymore. She was already getting a better idea.

She sprang to wet sneakers, but this time it wasn't flight, it was fight. She grabbed her briefcase and gym bag, and hurried to pack her papers and clothes. For the first time since she'd seen the morning newspaper, she was functioning. She had to get back to Philly, and find out if Willa was dead and who had killed her. And there was only one way to do it. If the world believed Anne was dead, then she was going to stay dead. *Play dead.*

For now, it was the only way to stay alive.

4

Half an hour later, Anne had turned in her apartment key to a puzzled realtor and was streaking toward the Atlantic City Expressway in the red Mustang. She had twisted her shower-wet hair into an up-knot under a white baseball cap, and its rounded bill rode low on her forehead. With the cap she wore a white T-shirt, the jeans skirt, and the leopard-print mules, because her sneakers were soaked. Her eyes were still puffy behind her Oakleys, from tears shed in the hot shower. She sensed they wouldn't be the last.

The Mustang zoomed along the highway, and she tightened her grip on the thick, padded wheel, sheathed in fake leather. The yellow spike of the speedometer jittered at seventy, then seventy-five. Traffic was next-to-nothing, because everybody was heading to the beach for the Fourth, looking forward to a sunny holiday weekend. Anne hit the Power button on the radio, found the

all-news station, and suffered through sun-
burn indexes, traffic reports, and ocean
temperatures until the hard news finally
came on. She cranked up the volume:

"Police still have no suspects or motive in
the shooting death last night of Rosato &
Associates attorney Anne Murphy."

Anne bit her lip. It was so hard to hear,
surreal and awful. Her alleged death was the
big news, and poor Willa remained name-
less.

"The Center City law firm of Rosato & Associates is offering a $50,000 reward for
information leading to the arrest and capture
of the person or persons involved. Anyone
with information is asked to call homicide
detectives at—"

It took Anne by surprise. She hadn't even
thought about a reward, much less that the
office would offer one.

"Stay tuned and we'll keep you posted on
developments as they occur. For in-depth
coverage of the story, visit our website at—"

Anne turned off the radio. A boxy Harrah's
bus blocked the fast lane but she accelerated to pass it. When she found open road,
she plugged in her cell phone and called her
house again. Still no answer. Then she

called Mary again. Also no answer. She declined to leave a *Hi, I'm alive* message and hit End. She would have to keep trying. When her speed went below eighty.

An hour later, having temporarily given up on raising Mary, she reached Philly. She got off the Expressway at Twenty-second Street and took a right toward the Benjamin Franklin Parkway, a six-lane boulevard that thronged with red, white, and blue activity. The Parkway was closed by a line of painted sawhorses, and traffic was being diverted.

Anne cruised to the corner, and a cop waved pedestrians across the street. She lowered the bill of her baseball cap. She couldn't afford to be recognized. The Mustang's engine idled, low on gas and superheated from the long trip, and she eyed the crowds crossing in front of its muscular grille. Families held hands as they headed to the Art Museum, where aluminum bleachers and temporary tents of parachute silk had been set up, and runners loped to the Schuylkill. Art students flung Frisbees to Labs in bandannas, and kids skipped down the gum-spattered sidewalk, flying Mylar balloons. Hot-dog steam scented the air, and vendors hawked American flags, Uncle

Sam hats, inflatable Liberty Bells, and T-shirts that read I GOT BANGED ON THE FOURTH OF JULY. Eeek.

Anne tensed at being back in the city. Her neighborhood began only five blocks from here, and she couldn't count the number of times she'd walked through this very intersection on the way to and from work, but now it didn't feel familiar at all. It had been changed forever, taken from her. If Kevin was free, she'd lost her chance to start over. And even so, she knew her loss was nothing compared with Willa's. If she really were dead.

The cop waved her ahead, and she looked down as she crossed the street under his nose. A wind from the Schuylkill River whipped down the wide boulevard, setting the multicolored flags of all countries flapping, rattling the chains that affixed them to the streetlights. A man crossing the street watched her as she drove by, and Anne pulled over and put up the convertible top. The cloth roof slid smoothly into place, and she felt safer with it covering her like a factory-installed security blanket.

She took off again, and in a few blocks— Greene, Wallace, then her street, Waltin— crossed the unofficial border into Fairmount.

She turned left onto Waltin and stopped at an unusually long line of traffic inching down its single lane. Out-of-towners, coming into the city for the celebration on the Parkway. Strangers, swarming over her street. Was one of them Kevin? Anne eyed them under her brim. None looked like him. She came to a stop behind a white Camaro. Her stomach tightened. Everything felt different now.

She scanned the block with new eyes. Rowhouses lined it, American flags hung from the second floors, and a gay neighbor flew his rainbow-colored flag with pride. The scene looked normal enough, though it was completely parked up on both sides, with only a few cars displaying the white residential-parking sticker. The sidewalk was crowded with people, but Anne didn't know if they were her neighbors because she didn't know her neighbors.

An older man walked a fawn-colored pug down the street, and the dog's curlicued tail bopped along, its rolling gait jaunty. She watched it with a pang, worrying about Mel. She craned her neck and peered down the street. The cat wasn't anywhere in sight. Her rowhouse stood midway down the block; its red brick had been newly power-washed and its oak door stripped of old green paint and shellacked a natural varnish. The usually chummy sight left her cold.

The traffic eased and the Camaro moved forward a car-length. Anne inched a few feet ahead, affording a closer view of her house. A piece of torn yellow plastic flapped from the top of her doorjamb. The sight pressed her back into the cushy driver's seat, a weight on her chest. It was crime scene tape. Willa had to be dead. It was only denial to think she wasn't. And Anne's home had become the scene of her murder.

She held back her tears. She had to know who did this; if it was Kevin. She had examined a few crime scenes in her time at Rosato & Associates, and she resolved to treat this scene like any other, even though she paid the rent. And Willa might have been murdered inside.

She drove ahead when the Camaro moved, her gaze trained on her house. There was no cop standing guard outside her front door, logging in official visitors, keeping out the curious, and otherwise preventing evidence from being contaminated. The absence signaled that the crime scene had been released. It was surprising. Cops generally didn't release a scene until the second or even third day.

The Mustang rolled ahead, and as she got closer, Anne noticed something else odd about her house. Passersby were lingering in front of her doorway, and when they moved on, she could see that on her front stoop lay a few cellophane-wrapped bunches of flowers. She looked out the window, puzzled. She'd guessed they'd been left for her, but she didn't have even that many friends. She squinted behind the Oakleys, trying vainly to read the cards from a distance. She couldn't help wondering if one was from Matt. Did he believe she was dead? Was he hurting for her today? She felt a twinge she couldn't shrug off.

HONK! A beep jolted her out of her reverie, and she glanced at her rearview mirror. A minivan driver, itching to let the kids out of the car. She rolled forward. She had to get into her house, but people were everywhere. She had to enter without being recognized. Then she had an idea.

Fifteen minutes later, Uncle Sam himself rounded the corner onto Waltin Street. He was wearing a red-white-and-blue stovepipe hat, a fake beard of thick cotton, and joke-sunglasses with superwide blue plastic frames—along with a jeans skirt, leopard-print mules, and a T-shirt that read HAPPY FOURTH FROM AN INDEPENDENT WOMAN! The outfit was completely ridiculous, but it was all the street vendors were selling, and fit in with the crowds of wacky tourists. Since she bought the stuff, Anne had already seen four girl Uncle Sams, one in Tod loafers.

She strode down the street and paused at the wrapped bouquets on her step. A dozen white roses lay on the top step, and she recognized the handwriting. Matt's. She reached for it reflexively, then caught herself. There wasn't time to dwell on it. She continued down the street until she reached the alley, where she slowed her step. She eyeballed the street behind the cartoon sunglasses. The coast was clear.

She sidestepped and slipped out of sight. The alley ran behind the line of rowhouses on her side of the street, and their backyards bordered it. Nobody ever used the alley for anything; there had been a flyer that circulated early this year, suggesting that the neighbors chip in and gate it for security reasons, but no one had bothered. It was hard to get Philadelphians excited about anything but the Sixers.

She scooted down the alley and almost fell on the moss-covered brick that sloped down toward a French drain, but grabbed a wooden privacy fence and righted her beard. She ducked low to account for the stovepipe as she hurried toward her house. She looked around for Mel, but the cat was nowhere in sight. He'd never been outside and even though he was chubby enough to survive without food for a while, she hated to think of him in city traffic. A dog started barking from one of the houses, and she darted toward the gray cinder-block wall, about six feet high, which enclosed her tiny backyard.

When she reached it, she slammed both hands on the scratchy blocks at the top, then boosted herself one, two, three bounces for a running start. She scrambled up the wall but stalled at the top, flopping on both sides like an Uncle Sam doll, then gritted her teeth and heaved herself over, landing with a hard bump on the unforgiving flagstone of her own backyard. Her mules flew off, and she gathered them up, otherwise taking inventory. She hadn't broken her legs, arms, or a nail, so she got up, dusted soot from her skirt, and crept to her back door. Getting into her house would be easier than getting into her yard.

Anne reached into her skirt pocket for the keys.

5

The smell that greeted Anne when she opened the door into her kitchen wasn't one she'd ever come home to. Strong, faintly metallic, and totally creepy. Suddenly she didn't know how professional she could be, after all. She couldn't stop thinking about Willa. She unhooked the big sunglasses from behind her ears and slid an eyepiece into the collar of her T-shirt. She glanced around the kitchen, trying to appraise it with an objective eye. It was so small, made from a corner of the single room that once constituted the entire first floor.

Cherry veneer cabinets ringed the room on three sides, the countertop was butcher block, and the sink was stainless steel, clean only because she'd been too busy to cook lately, meaning last year. One of the cabinet doors was partway open, and Anne peeked inside. It contained the usual glazed clay mugs, jelly glasses, and a wiggly stack of oversized coffee cups used for late-night Captain Crunch.

She considered the open cabinet. She didn't usually leave them that way, because she'd bonk her head on them if she did. Maybe Willa had. What had she taken? Anne peeked and realized what was missing almost immediately, because it was a souvenir. A pink mug with Lucy and Ethel in the chocolate factory, from "Job Switching." Episode No. 39, September 15, 1952. Anne knew all the *I Love Lucy* episodes by heart, but kept that as secret as her spending habits and several hundred other things. Where was her Lucy mug? Had Willa used it? Did it matter?

She scanned the room. No mug anywhere, and no sign of a struggle. Nor was there any fingerprint dust, the sooty grime left behind by mobile crime technicians. The cops evidently hadn't taken prints from the kitchen. It told Anne that the crime must have taken place elsewhere. She couldn't shake the smell, or the dread, but she willed herself to go ahead. She had to learn what had happened to Willa.

She walked into the dining room, reached by a narrow doorway to the right. The dining room wasn't much bigger than the kitchen, and there was a pine table against the wall on the left. Unopened Visa bills, offers for preapproved credit cards, and collection service notices sat stacked on the corner of the table, next to several Bic pens that Anne had personal knowledge did not work. Again, everything was as she'd left it, and there were no fingerprint smudges on the table or the two pine chairs that customarily sat catty-corner. On the rug near a table leg lay a catnip mouse with its gray fuzz loved off.

"Mel," she called softly, so the neighbors wouldn't hear. The cat would normally come trotting at the sound of his name, but this time he didn't. Anne felt like she shouldn't be thinking about her cat at a time like this, but she couldn't help it. "Mel!" she called again, but there was no answer.

She bit her lip. Had he gotten out? Was he alive? Had Kevin taken him? Hurt him? Anger drove her through another doorway, also narrow, and she scanned her living room. It was darker than the dining room and kitchen, the unhappy result of a northern exposure, and Anne was tempted to turn on a lamp but couldn't risk the neighbors catching Uncle Sam on a B & E.

Again, still no sign of Mel, or of a struggle. A brown sisal rug covered the floor, and a TV, stereo, and bookshelves sat across from a gray couch, which was flush under the windows against the north wall. In front of the couch stood a glass coffee table covered with dark fingerprint smudges, and she walked over to it. Black powder dusted the edge of the table, and in the middle of the smudge was a mug-sized circle. It must have been from the Lucy mug, and the police must have collected the mug for evidence. Anne tried to reconstruct the scene. Willa had probably been watching TV and drinking something. Where had she been killed?

The smell was thick here, and Anne looked almost involuntarily toward the entrance hall, separated from the living room by a door with a frosted-glass pane. The door hung partway open but the entrance hallway was dark. She stepped closer and peered inside. What she saw made her gag.

The entrance hall was an abattoir. Blood was everywhere, splattered across the dark-gray walls and drenching the gray wall-to-wall carpet with a horrific red-brown stain. The door was covered with blood, drying in uneven patches like the most awful crimson paint. Formless, dark-red bits of tissue stuck to the glass of the door and on the far wall. A jagged shard of bone had been driven into the far wall. A patch of scalp with bloodied hair still on it stuck grotesquely to the near wall.

Anne felt her gorge rise, but held it down and forced herself to objectify the sight. Her gaze found the faint chalk outline of the body, sketched thickly into the rug. The legs of the outline—*Willa's legs*—lay slightly apart and its feet lay close to the front door. The head—*My God, Willa*—lay straight behind it. It looked as if Willa had been shot as soon as she opened the front door.

Please God, the poor thing. Anne looked again at the blood on the rug. Most of it lay where Willa's head would have been, which suggested that she had been shot in the head. More precisely, in the face, if she had been killed when she opened the door.

Anne looked again at the outline and noticed something else on the rug. She stepped forward, squinting toward the door, trying not to breathe in the awful carnal smell. Next to Willa's body outline lay another chalk outline, on her left side, about a foot long. The smaller chalk shape looked blurry at a distance, then Anne realized what it was. A gun. Bennie had told her that cops always chalked a dropped gun. Had the murder weapon been left behind? The newspaper hadn't reported that. But they wouldn't.

She knelt down and examined the gun outline, covering her mouth with her beard, only partly because of the odor. Since the outline lay on the left side of the body, it would have been the killer's right side, and was only roughly the shape of a gun, with the handle nearest the door and the barrel slightly longish. It looked most like the outline of a sawed-off shotgun. Anne gasped.

Kevin's weapon of choice.

It was what he had used on her when he attacked her at the door. He had put it to her head, but, incredibly, the DA hadn't even charged him with attempted murder because he hadn't gotten a shot off. She shed her resentment to concentrate on Willa. It had to have been Kevin who killed her. He was right-handed and smart enough to know he was better off dropping the weapon at the scene than getting caught in possession.

Then she flashed on the newspaper article she'd seen this morning. It had said something about "gunshots" at "close range." She considered it. If Kevin had used a sawed-off shotgun and fired more than one shot at close range, Willa's face—her very features—would have been completely blown off.

Anne felt her stomach wrench but maintained control. The wound would have made the misidentification possible. And all of the circumstances would point to Anne as the murder victim; it was Anne's house and she would be expected to be in it. She and Willa had the same hair, were the same height and weight. And Willa was wearing her ROSATO & ASSOCIATES T-shirt. But Anne still didn't get it. Who had identified Willa's body? Was it somebody from the office? And one critical piece of the puzzle remained missing:

Why would Kevin kill a woman he knew wasn't me?

She scanned the entrance hall for an answer, trying to ignore the blood soaked into the dry wall, and her gaze traveled to the ceiling fixture. It was a cheap builder's-grade model with fake Victorian frosted glass, and was turned off. She couldn't remember the last time she'd used it. No one ever visited her.

She reached for the switch and flicked it, but the light didn't go on. Maybe it had burned out. Wait a minute. She couldn't remember ever putting a bulb in it when she had moved in. She was too short to reach it and hadn't bothered.

If the light had been out in the entrance hall, there would have been no illumination on Willa when she went to answer the door. If the living room light had been on, which it probably was at night—since Willa had evidently been sitting in the living room, watching TV and drinking something—the light from the living room would backlight her, at best. Willa would be a silhouette when she answered the door, and one that was the same size and shape as Anne. In Anne's shirt.

Anne gazed at the scene in her mind's eye, heartsick. It all made sense, now. Kevin had shot Willa, thinking he had shot Anne. He still might not know that he had killed the wrong woman. She had been right to play dead. She felt both relieved and horrified. But how had Kevin gotten out of prison?

Was it possible it wasn't Kevin? She rose bewildered from bended knee and stood staring at the spot, her thoughts coming around to Mel. Had Kevin taken him? Where could he be? Then she remembered a place the cat hid when the gas man came.

"Mel! Mel!" she called out, then turned around and hurried upstairs, into her bedroom. He wasn't on the bed but the louvered door to her closet lay partway open.

"Mel?" Anne ran over and slid open the door at the same moment as she heard an indignant meow. Mel had been sleeping among the Jimmy Choos and was stretching his front legs straight out.

"SuperCat!" Anne scooped him up, and his warm throat thrummed in response. She teared up at the softness of him, though she knew her emotions had only partly to do with his recovery. "Let's get outta here," she said, her voice thick. She left the room but the cat stiffened when they reached the top of the stairs.

"It's okay, baby," she soothed, but then she heard the sound of footsteps on the front stoop, outside her house. Then the metallic jiggling of the knob on her front door.

She stopped at the top of the stairs. Somebody was at her door. She edged backward, out of the line of sight.

Right before the front door swung wide open.

6

Anne stood in her second-floor hallway, scratching Mel to keep him quiet and listening to the shuffle of feet below. It sounded like a crowd, and she hoped it wasn't the mobile crime unit. She could hear the noises of holiday traffic coming in through the open doorway. Whoever had come in the door must have been standing in the entrance hall, where Willa had been killed. Then she heard a man's voice:

"It looked pretty clear to us, from the spatter pattern on the east wall, here, and against the entrance-hall door. Typical full-force spatter, from the shotgun. See, here, on the frosted glass? And the floor. The rug."

Shit! He sounded like a cop or a detective, and Anne drew away from the stairs, hugging Mel. As much as she wished she could go to the police and tell them everything, she would never do that again. They hadn't been able to protect her last time, and she couldn't forget the image of a steel gun-barrel pointed at her.

The detective was saying, "The young lawyer, Murphy, answers the front door. The shooter hits twice, two shots to the face. She falls in the entrance hall. The shooter drops the gun and takes off. He leaves the front door open. He's gone. He's outta there."

Upstairs, Anne felt vaguely sick and clutched Mel, for comfort this time. She had been right about the way it had happened, but it was so awful to contemplate. Poor Willa.

A woman spoke next. "He dropped the gun? This guy's no dummy."

Anne felt a start of recognition at the voice. *It's Bennie Rosato. What's she doing here?* She'd never been in Anne's house before, even though she lived less than five minutes away. But Bennie visited the crime scene in murder cases she defended. It was the first step in any investigation, to meet the arguments of the prosecution and build the defense case. So why was she here?

The detective again: "Yeh, he's good. Ballistics has the gun. They'll check it for prints, but that'll take days, given the holiday. Fourth a July weekend, we had to dig to get anyone at all. My guess is it'll turn up nothin'."

"I agree," Bennie said. "This guy had this planned. Perfect timing, perfect execution."

"No pun," added another man, with an abrupt laugh.

"*What* did you say?" Bennie demanded.

"That's not funny," chorused another voice, a woman's.

Another surprise. It was Judy Carrier. She must be down there, too. Judy had never come to Anne's house when she was alive; she had turned Anne down every time she asked her to lunch. And if Judy was down there, then so was Mary, because they were joined at the hip. Anne almost laughed at the absurdity. *Bennie, Mary, and Judy in my house? What provoked all this sudden interest in my life? My death?*

"I won't waste my time teaching you manners, Detective," Bennie said coldly. "Your apology is accepted. But I want you to know that Anne Murphy was in my care. She was my associate. She moved here to work for me and she was killed on my watch. I told her mother I'd take care of her, and I failed."

Told my mother? What? When? Anne was astounded. How had Bennie found her mother, much less spoken to her? And why? What was going on here?

"I'm sorry, Ms. Rosato—"

"Not sorry enough. Hear me—holiday or no holiday, you better find who murdered Anne Murphy before I do."

Upstairs, Anne felt stunned. Bennie was going to do *what*? *Why?* Anne could count on one hand the number of conversations she'd had with Bennie Rosato during the entire year she'd worked for her.

"Now, tell me you surveyed the neighbors," Bennie was saying.

"Last night and this morning. Nobody saw anybody running down the street from the house, or anything suspicious at all. Everybody was either at the Party on the Parkway, or out of town, avoiding the Party on the Parkway."

"May I have the specifics?" From below came the sound of papers rustling, and Anne guessed that Bennie was pulling out a legal pad, and the detective his notes. But Anne couldn't get over what she'd already heard. *Told my mother she'd take care of me?*

"Here goes. House number 2255, Rick Monterosso, not home, he's the neighbor on the east side. House number 2259, Millie and Mort Berman, neighbors on the west side, not home either. The couple across the street in 2256, Sharon Arkin and Rodger Talbott, the same. 2253, no answer at door last night or this morning, possibly out of town. 2254, the Kopowski family, out to dinner at Striped Bass. 2258, the Simmons, they were at the Parkway and didn't get home until after the murder."

"So both next-door neighbors were out. Who called 911 on the gunshots? If the door was open when he shot her, which it had to be, then the shots would be heard easily down the street. And it's not a big street."

"People musta thought it was firecrackers. We only got the one 911 call, guy named Bob Dodds, in 2250. I interviewed him last night, and that's all he knows."

"But you have at least the one good lead, don't you? Kevin Satorno, the stalker. If he's out of prison."

What?! How did Bennie know about Kevin? Anne almost gasped. She hadn't told anyone in Philly about him. She had wanted to put the past behind her when she moved here, and had kept him a secret. Nor had she breathed a word about Kevin in her interview with Bennie. She wanted the job and didn't want to seem like the kind of loser who dated psychos. So how did Bennie find out? Anne felt completely bewildered. Mental note: It's confusing to be alive after your own death.

Bennie was saying, "Given what I read in the court file, if Satorno is out, he has to be the number-one suspect. He tried to kill her once. He may have escaped and tried to kill her again. It's a no-brainer. I had the case file hand-delivered to you. Did you read it?"

"I read the file, of course," the detective replied, testy. "I called the DA in charge in Los Angeles. I'm waiting on the call back, but it's Fourth a July in California, too, Ms. Rosato. He's on vacation."

"They told me that, too, but they wouldn't give me his number in Hawaii. Do you have it?"

"I didn't ask. He's on vaca—"

"I don't get something. Kevin Satorno is a state prisoner in California. How hard can it be to find him?" Bennie laughed without mirth. "You're supposed to know where he is, at least most of the time."

Give 'em hell, Bennie. Anne felt heartened. She went to the banister and peeked over, with Mel tight in her arms. She could see Bennie standing in her living room, a tangle of long blond hair trailing untamed down the back of her blue workshirt, which she wore with faded jean shorts and beat-up New Balance sneakers. Her legs were superbuff from rowing, a sport Bennie seemed to like, despite the exercise required. At present Anne was revising her views on the woman, but not on exercise.

The detective was out of eyeshot, but Anne could hear him explaining, "If it weren't the weekend this would be easy. We know he was sentenced to twenty-four months and started out in L.A. County, but they transferred him a few times, and we're not sure where he ended up. He could be on parole."

"But you would know if he was paroled, or even escaped."

"Not yet. Paroled, we got the same problem as finding out where he's incarcerated. Gotta talk to the right people, and they're not in the holiday weekend. Escaped, it's still no picnic."

Bennie snorted. "I can't believe that. You can't even find out if he's escaped?"

"From the joint in California? Believe it. If some knucklehead gets outta state prison in any state, somebody has to enter his name in NCIC, the National Crime Information Center, outta Washington. Nobody knows nothin' 'til the name gets entered, and it has to get entered by a person, who has the time and is workin' the Fourth a July weekend." The detective paused. "Even if it gets entered, we get about a million of those teletypes a day. We never look through 'em, we don't have the time, or any reason to."

"Now you have a reason to."

"I got a gal goin' through them right now, but you have any idea how many we're talkin' about? There are 75,000 walk-aways in Philly alone, right now. And fifty of them are wanted for murder."

"What's a 'walk-away'?" Bennie asked. "What it sounds like?"

"Yeh. Fugitives at large. Bad guys, who walk away from work release or skip bail. Failures to appear, all wanted on bench warrants. This Kevin Satorno wasn't even locked up for murder, only ag assault. In the scheme of things, he's a nobody. And he's not even one of our nobodies. He's a *California* nobody."

A nobody? Upstairs, Anne felt sick. She knew Kevin had started out in L.A. County Jail but had lost track of him after that, too. She'd wanted to put the past behind her. Only it wasn't the past anymore.

"So what is the department doing to find Satorno, if he's out?" Bennie was asking, downstairs. "He clearly intended to kill Anne, and only to kill her. There wasn't even an attempt at robbery, and no evidence of rape."

"The department can't proceed on the assumption that he's out, Ms. Rosato. We don't have that luxury. It's not like we got the manpower. We got only forty uniformed cops total in the Center City District, twenty in the Sixth District and twenty in the Ninth. They got all they can handle with the holiday, that's why we released the scene. I can't assign them to look for a guy that may be locked up." The detective paused. "You wouldn't know if Satorno has contacted the victim recently, would you?"

"No." Bennie turned to her left, out of Anne's view. "Do you guys know? Carrier? DiNunzio?"

Anne peeked farther over the banister, and Mel stiffened. He didn't want to get anywhere downstairs, near the bloodstained entrance hall. She caught sight of Judy, in her well-loved overalls, a fresh yellow T-shirt, and a lemony bandanna.

Judy was shaking her head. "No. Sorry. I didn't know anything about Satorno until you told me today."

Suddenly, a hiccupy sob interrupted the conversation, a sound so emotional that it was almost embarrassing in public. Instantly Bennie turned around on her heels, as did Judy, just as a second sob came from the right, where Mary must have been. Anne couldn't help but hang over the banister, and the sight made her own throat catch with surprise:

Mary was weeping, making a petite, crestfallen figure sunk into Anne's sofa. She had buried her face in her hands, and her thin shoulders shuddered with sobs. Her hair was in disarray, and khaki shorts and sleeveless white shirt lacked their usual neatness.

"It's all right, Mary," Judy soothed, coming over and looping an arm around her friend. "They'll catch the guy, you'll see."

"I . . . can't think about that." Mary's voice quavered through her sobs. Her cheeks looked mottled and her neck blotchy. "I just can't . . . believe this happened. It's so terrible that . . . she was killed. The *way* she was killed."

Upstairs, Anne watched the scene, mystified by their reactions as well as her own. *Mary DiNunzio, who doesn't even know me, is crying for me. And, for some reason, I feel like shit.*

Bennie went to Mary and placed a steadying hand on her shoulder. "Mary, maybe we should get you back to the office."

"That's all right, I'm all right." Mary's sobs began to subside. Pain ebbed from her features and she held her palms against her cheeks as if to cool them. "I mean, there's blood everywhere. It's *her* blood!"

"I know, I know," Judy was saying, stroking Mary's back. "You want to wait outside? Why don't you wait outside?"

Bennie turned briefly to the detectives. "Maybe you could give us a few minutes alone," she said.

"Sure thing," they answered, in grateful unison. In the next minute, the front door opened again, a square of light reappearing on the living room carpet and the outside noise resurging. The detectives left and shut the door only partway behind them, and they stood on the stoop. In the next second, Anne smelled cigarette smoke wafting through the open front door. She moved closer to the landing, and her gaze returned to Mary.

"I mean, Bennie, do you see this?" Mary was stretching a small hand toward the entrance hall, and Anne could see the trembling of her fingers. "There's blood all over it. But we're standing here, the three of us, talking like it's a case or something. But it's *Anne* we're talking about!" Her voice rose, thinning out with anxiety. "Anne Murphy was *killed* here! Not a client, one of us! And she's gone! *Murdered!* Did you both forget that?"

Wow! Upstairs, Anne stood transfixed by the outburst. It was so unlike Mary to criticize anybody, much less Bennie and Judy, and they looked completely astonished.

Judy stopped stroking Mary's back. "We know it's her, Mary. We didn't forget that. We're here trying to figure out who did this, to bring him in."

"What's the difference?" Mary shouted. "We can find the guy, but it doesn't bring her back. She's dead, and you know what? We didn't know the first thing about her. We worked with her for a year and we never even got to know her. I dated Jack for two months and knew more about him!"

"We were busy," Judy said, defensive. "We were working. We had the Dufferman trial, then Witco. Maybe that's why you're upset, because of your breakup—"

"That's not it, it's *Anne*! It's *Murphy*, whatever she wants to be called. *Wanted* to be called."

"Murphy," Judy supplied, but Bennie was shaking her head.

"No, I think she went by that because I called her that. I think. She introduced herself as Anne, at her interview."

"Whatever!" Mary exploded. "It's *us*! We didn't make the time for her! We didn't even try. We don't even know her name. She told us she had a date tonight. Did she? Who was the date? Is he the killer? We don't even know! And now it turns out she had a stalker who tried to kill her last year, and who she even prosecuted! We never even knew that!"

Judy looked defensive. "Murphy kept it all a secret, she was so private—"

"What about the motion, Judy? She wasn't keeping that so private. She brought a *stripper* into court, and we had to learn it from the news! She probably wanted to tell us when she came to my office last night, but we cut her off!" Mary's eyes welled up again, but she blinked them clear. "We're supposed to be an all-woman firm, what a joke! We don't even support each other. What's the difference between us, anyway? Men or women, in the end we acted just like *lawyers*."

"You're just feeling guilty, Mare."

"I agree! I feel very guilty! And you know what, I should! You should, too!" Mary turned on her best friend, beside her on the couch. "You know what the truth is, Jude? You never liked Murphy. Anne. Whatever. You didn't like her at all. That's why you're not upset."

Whoa. Anne was shocked. She felt like she shouldn't be watching, but she couldn't help herself. It was such good gossip, the fact that it was about her was almost beside the point.

"I *am* upset!" Judy insisted, but Mary was out of control.

"You are not! That whole time I was out sick, you avoided her. She asked you out to lunch, you turned her down all the time. You didn't like her from the beginning. And you know why? Because she was so gorgeous! You thought she wore too much makeup, with the lipstick all the time."

They talk about my lipstick? Anne couldn't believe the irony.

"She did wear too much makeup!" Judy was going red in the face, too. "But that doesn't mean I'm not upset—"

"Why were we that way? I swear, it's some kind of biological thing, to compete with other women for men, even when there are no men around. It's sick! And when are we gonna rise above it?"

"It wasn't just her looks—"

"You thought she used her looks!" Mary erupted, pointing. "You said it yourself, Judy! That Anne never would have gotten Chipster if she weren't so hot."

Yikes! Upstairs, Anne couldn't believe what she was hearing. She wasn't supposed to know any of this and suddenly didn't want to. Kind of.

"Well, that much is true!" Judy finally shouted back. "How does a rookie get a case that big? The client knew her in law school? Gimme a break! You want to get real, Mary? Okay, let's get real. Gil Martin never would have hired Anne if she hadn't looked the way she did." Judy's head snapped around to Bennie, the bandanna flopping. "You had to wonder about it, Bennie. Why did Gil hire Anne, the youngest of all of us? The lawyer with the least experience? How many cases has she tried? One?"

But Bennie was already waving her hands, trying to settle the fight. "Calm down, both of you," she said, her voice even as a judge's. "Mary, you know, you're right. We all could have been more welcoming to Anne, and we weren't. We were busy—as Judy says—but that's no excuse." Bennie leaned over, squeezed Mary's shoulder, and gave her a gentle shake. "But blaming each other won't help Anne now. It didn't cause her murder."

"Can you be so sure?" Mary looked up at Bennie, her forehead creased with fresh grief. "Who knows what difference it would have made? If we had talked to her, taken her to lunch even once, maybe she would have told us about this stalker. Or if we'd been friends, maybe we would have been with her last night when he came. She'd be alive now, if we'd been together." Mary almost started to cry again, and even Judy was looking regretful.

"That's true," she added, her bandanna droopy. "That much is true."

I can't stand this. Anne couldn't watch them feel bad for nothing. First, she was alive. Second, not everything was their fault. She wasn't any good at women. She always had tons of dates, but no girlfriends. For as long as she could remember, she'd thought of herself as Lucy, without Ethel.

"I'm not pretending anything," Bennie was saying. "We did wrong by Anne, and we can all mourn her in our own way. For me, the best way is to find whoever killed her. I suggest you follow suit." She gave Mary a final pat. "I want to check out the back. You stay here, okay? Carrier, stay with her."

"I need a Kleenex." Mary rose slowly, her hand cupping her nose, and she looked around the living room. "Anybody see a box?"

Maybe I can tell them I'm here. Anne had to be able to get their attention without tipping off the cops. She eyed the front door. The detectives were outside, and something down the block was holding their attention. She decided to go for it. She shifted Mel to her right arm, tore off her red-white-and-blue stovepipe, and waved it wildly.

"Mary! Mary!" she called out in a stage whisper, but the women didn't look up. "Mary!" she whispered again, but Mary was preoccupied with her drippy nose and Judy was looking for the Kleenex. The detectives, apparently sensing that the sobfest was over, were heading back inside, the smoker flicking his cigarette butt into the gutter.

"There's no Kleenex anywhere," Judy said, checking the top of the TV. "There must be a bathroom, with toilet paper you can use. In trinities like this, it's usually up-stairs, at the top of the stairs."

The bathroom! Yes! It's here! Behind me!

"Good idea," Mary said, and headed for the stairs.

Without thinking twice, Anne turned, ducked inside the bathroom, and closed the door.

7

"Jesus, Mary, and Joseph!" Mary gasped, just before Anne clamped a firm hand over her mouth and backed her against the bathroom door. Mel's tail curled into a question mark against the small pedestal sink, where he'd been dumped.

"I'm alive, Mary!" Anne whispered. She yanked down the Uncle Sam beard. "See? It's me, Anne. I'm alive. I'm not dead!"

"Mmph!" Mary's reddened eyes rounded with shock, and Anne's hand pressed down harder.

"Shhh! I don't want the police to know."

"Mmmpu!" Mary shook her head, her eyes like brown marbles.

"I'm going to take my hand from your mouth, but don't say anything, okay? The cops can't know I'm here."

"Mmph!" Mary nodded vigorously.

"Don't be upset, okay?"

"Mmph!"

"Everything's all right."

"Mpphuo!"

"It's really me, and I'm alive." Anne removed her hand, and Mary started screaming.

"HELP! HELP, POLICE!!!!"

No! "Mary, shhhh! What are you doing!?"

"I saw you dead! On the table! You're a *ghost*! A *devil*!" Mary blessed herself in record time, and Anne looked around in panic. She could already hear shouting and footsteps clattering up the stairs. Loud, like clogs.

"Mare? Mare?" Judy shouted. "Is that you?"

"HELP! JUDY!" Mary hollered. "POLICE! ANYBODY! HELP! BENNIEEEEEE!!"

I can't believe this. "Shut up! I'm alive! It's me! It was my cat-sitter who got killed! See the *cat*?" Anne pointed behind her at the sink, where Mel's tail had straightened to an exclamation point.

"No, you're dead! I know it! I saw you! Dead, dead, dead! You had on your shirt! You were shot downstairs! Blood—"

"It was my cat-sitter, her name was Willa. I lent her the shirt!" Anne grabbed Mary's shoulders. "It wasn't me!"

"DiNunzio! I'm coming!" Bennie yelled, joined by the detectives.

"Miss DiNunzio? Miss DiNunzio?" They were almost at the landing, the voices were so loud.

Anne freaked. She'd run out of time. The damage was done. The doorknob was turning. She whirled around, jumped into the bathtub, and pulled the shower curtain closed just as the bathroom door swung open. Nobody would be able to see her through the shower curtain. It was opaque, a fancy flower print from Laura Ashley with a thick white liner. If it got her out of this, maybe it was worth the forty-six dollars. Mental note: Shoes, clothes, and makeup were allowed to be overpriced, but shower curtains had to prove themselves.

"Mary, Mary, are you all right?" It was Judy, alarmed.

"Miss DiNunzio!" It was the detective's voice. "What is it? What's the matter?"

"DiNunzio? You okay?" It was Bennie, who must have burst into the room and flung open the door, because the shower curtain billowed. "Why did you scream?"

Please, Mary, don't blow it. Anne held her

breath behind the curtain and stayed perfectly still against the white tile wall.

"Uh . . . I don't know," Mary answered, her voice shaky.

"But you screamed," Judy said, then laughed. "Oh, I see. The cat."

Bennie laughed, too. "A cat!"

The detectives laughed along. Everybody was *ha-ha-ha*ing. It was suddenly a bathroom party. "The cat startled you."

Mary, get a clue. They're feeding you lines.

"Yes, that's it," Mary said finally. "The cat. It surprised me. When I came in, it was sitting in the sink. Just like that. Sorry I screamed."

Jesus, Mary, and Joseph, Anne thought with relief, though she was hardly on a first-name basis.

"I guess Anne had a cat," Judy said. "The litter box is right there, under the sink. See?"

"I remember now," said the detective. "We made a note of the cat box last night, but we didn't find the cat. Well, here he is."

Excellent detective work. And the guy in prison is where?

"You should take him, Mare," Judy was saying. "He needs a home now. Can you have a cat in your apartment?"

"I don't know. I don't want a cat."

Judy scoffed. "Somebody has to take him, and me and Bennie have dogs. You had a cat once, didn't you?"

Take him, you idiot. I'm not dead, remember?

"Okay, I'll take him. Well, maybe we should go now."

"That's the spirit, DiNunzio," Bennie said, and the next sound was the opening of the bathroom door. "Maybe taking this cat is the thing you can do for Anne, huh?"

"Maybe," Mary answered, and the curtain ruffled again as the three lawyers, two detectives, and one confused cat left the bathroom.

Anne climbed out of the tub after she heard the front door close, then slipped out of the bathroom and hurried downstairs. She knew Mary would tell the others she was alive as soon as she had the chance. That meant Uncle Sam had to get to the office.

She slipped on her cartoon sunglasses and skedaddled.

Anne had parked the Mustang in the closest lot she could get, five blocks up Locust Street, so she had to hoof it past small shops, businesses, and a string of row-houses converted to architect, accountant, and law offices. She kept her head down but everybody thinking she was dead was a damn good disguise. Not to mention that the sidewalks were full of people dressed in green foam Statue of Liberty crowns, George W. Bush masks, and red-white-and-blue umbrella hats. Anne counted two more Uncle Sams, and they waved.

Locust Street was a tangle of traffic. Like most of Philadelphia, the street was wide enough to accommodate only a horse-drawn buggy, and permitted just one-way traffic. She had been told ad nauseam that Ben Franklin himself had designed the city, but she thought his famous grid led only to grid-lock. She looked ahead, down the street in front of the building that housed Rosato & Associates. The traffic bottlenecked there, because of news vans from ABC, Court TV, CNN, and the local networks parked illegally. Even at this distance Anne could see that re-porters, photographers, videocams, and satellite feeds besieged the office building. The press presence had more than doubled. Who would have guessed that a pretty lawyer being murdered before a sex trial was news?

Anne pushed up her cartoon sunglasses and plowed ahead. She scanned the street almost constantly. Kevin could be here. In a twisted way, he would want to be near her, even if she were dead. He might even want to catch a glimpse of Bennie. Or Judy. It worried her. Could they be in danger from Kevin? Not likely, but not impossible. She had learned from Erotomania 101 that the delusional often transferred their fixations.

She checked her watch. 12:30. The deposition was at one o'clock, but she didn't know how the press had found out about it. It wasn't public record, and she was sure Rosato & Associates hadn't leaked it. She hurried closer to the melee, lowering her stovepipe. Two blocks away, then one. No one should be looking for her, but a few of the reporters had come to know her from chasing her around on the Chipster. She pulled her red brim down. She had been worrying so much about Kevin, she hadn't focused on the fact that Uncle Sam would have to withstand media scrutiny, too.

Anne reached her office building and threaded her way through the crowd of media, keeping her eyes peeled behind the big glasses. Reporters sweated through their summer suits and TV makeup. She spotted one TV anchorwoman she knew and tilted her head down, checking her watch. 12:45. Tourists and onlookers thronged on the sidewalk, adding to the glut. She had to get going. She waded into the *thumpa-thumpa* of a rap CD and inhaled a puff of cigarette smoke.

Suddenly a cell phone started ringing, and it took Anne a minute to realize it was hers. Who could be calling? The whole world thought she was dead. She unlatched her messenger bag, withdrew her cell phone, and flipped it open. "Yes?" she said, keeping her voice low.

"Ms. Sherwood, this is Dr. Marc Goldberger."

"Yes, of course," Anne answered, surprised.

"I understand now why you were calling me. I just spoke with my supervisor. You weren't completely honest with me, Ms. Sherwood. If that *is* your name."

Oh, no. "I don't know what you mean."

"I think you do. Kevin Satorno escaped from prison a few days ago. Did you know that when you called?"

"Escaped?" Anne felt her heart stop. She

had guessed as much, but it terrified her to think it was really true.

"Are you going to tell me that you didn't know that? That it was just a coincidence that you called me today?"

Kevin is out. Kevin is free.

Anne couldn't reply. She couldn't speak. She pressed End and fought a frantic urge to crawl under something and hide. She didn't know what to do, except not panic. She forced herself to breathe until her heartbeat returned to normal. Suddenly alone in the noisy, smoky crowd, she looked up at her office building. It took her only a second to punch in the number on her cell.

Mary must have been waiting for her call. "Anne, where are you? Are you here?"

"Help!" was all Anne could say, then she got it together. "I'm right outside. Can you get me past security?"

"It's Herb, and we told him to expect a new messenger, dressed funny. You still wearing your beard?"

"Yes."

"I'm on my way down."

Thank God. Anne flipped her phone closed, suddenly eyeing every passerby. Her stomach tensed with fear. *There.* A blond man, with his hair Kevin's color and cut short, as if he'd been in prison. Anne was about to scream when the blond man looped his arm around the woman next to him. On his biceps was a tattoo that read *Semper Fi.* A marine, not an inmate. Not Kevin.

Anne wedged her way through the press and hurried through the revolving door to the building, which delivered her into the air-conditioned chill of a large marble lobby with restored plaster walls. She took a deep, relieved breath, but the mahogany security desk stood like a hurdle in front of the elevator bank. Mary may have called down to get Anne admitted, but there was still a chance the guard would recognize her, especially Hot and Heavy Herb. She had disguised her face but not her chest, which was all he ever noticed. Thanks to him, Rosato & Associates had the safest breasts in Philadelphia.

Herb's gaze zoomed in on her INDEPENDENT WOMAN as she reached the desk. "Hello, honey," he said, with what he hoped was a sexy smirk. He reeked of Aramis, and his navy uniform fit taut against his short, heavyset frame. He wore his pants with the belt buckled high, like Fred Mertz. "Why are you dressed like Uncle Sam, for a job interview?"

"It got me past the reporters, didn't it?" Anne kept her head down, pulled over the black spiral log book, and scribbled 36C on the solid line. "If I'm hired today, I don't want them recognizing me and following me everywhere."

"So why don't you take it off? You're inside now."

"I like the power."

Suddenly the elevator doors opened with a discreet *ping,* and Mary rushed out like the cavalry. She couldn't hide her smile. "Dressing for success?"

"You must be Mary DiNunzio." Anne extended a hand as if they hadn't met, just as a commotion began at the entrance, behind her. They turned around in time to see a familiar figure coming through the revolving door, with a group of people.

Oh, no. Now Anne was in real trouble.

8

Anne fled to the back corner of the elevator as Matt Booker stepped in with his clients, Beth Dietz and her ponytailed husband, Bill. On his right side stood Janine Bonnard, a pretty young woman in a gray Gap suit, who was being deposed today. Anne kept her stovepipe down and prayed Matt wouldn't recognize her, though he seemed so preoccupied he wouldn't have noticed if she'd been Godzilla.

She stole a sideways glance at him. Dark circles ringed his normally bright eyes, his broad shoulders slumped in a navy suit with no tie, and his thick hair wasn't neat enough for a deposition. She wondered if he was upset because of her. His briefcase at his side, he looked over at Mary.

"Mary, I'm so sorry about Anne," he said. Grief weighed down his usually confident voice. "Have you heard anything more from the police, since we talked? Don't they have any leads on who . . . killed her?"

Oh, jeez. Anne's face was on fire. She felt terrible, seeing him like this.

"Not yet," Mary said. "But they're working on it, I know."

"Please give my condolences to her family, and if there's anything I can do to help you . . . or the police, please let me know. Keep me in the loop, okay? I'd like to know what's going on."

"I will, thanks."

"I can't imagine who would do this. I just can't . . ." Matt's voice trailed off and he hung his head.

"None of us can," Mary told him, her face tight. Obviously, she didn't like lying as much as Anne did.

"Please give our sympathy to her family, as well." It was Beth Dietz, and her husband nodded.

"I will," Mary said. "Listen, I'm running a little late for the deposition. I have to get this new messenger started." She gestured quickly at Anne, who kept her head down. "Can you let me have an extra ten minutes?"

"Of course. Like I told you on the phone, I

would have agreed to move the dep back if you wanted to."

"Thanks, but it won't be necessary."

"Who will be trying the case, now that Anne is—"

"God knows."

Ping! The elevator doors slid open on the third floor. ROSATO & ASSOCIATES, read the brass letters on the wall, above the familiar rug, cloth chairs, and glass coffee table. Anne felt strangely as if she were coming back into her own life, but she couldn't risk lingering. She got off the elevator last and hurried out of the reception area, with her back turned to Matt.

Mary led Matt and his clients to one of the two conference rooms off the reception area and opened the door for them. "If you'll wait for me in there, I'll be right out. The bathrooms are on the left, and the court reporter's already set up inside. I'll be back in ten."

"Thanks," Matt said, and Mary scooted down the hall, right behind Anne.

"You're alive!" Mary bear-hugged a startled Anne, yanking her close to a linen blouse that smelled of Ivory soap and powdery an-

tiperspirant. Anne's Uncle Sam disguise lay discarded on Mary's neat desk, where Mel was sniffing her fake beard delicately. His coat looked silky in the sunlight streaming through the window, a fuzzy cat against smooth legal briefs. Lawyer Cat. Mary was beside herself. "I don't believe it! I don't believe it! This is so great!"

"Let her go before you kill her," Judy said from the door to Mary's office, but even she was smiling. Bennie stood next to her, grinning over a white porcelain mug that read JAVA DIVA.

"I'm so happy!" Mary segued into rocking Anne. "I'm so happy you're alive!"

"Is she always like this?" Anne asked as she swayed back and forth, and Bennie nodded.

"Yes, I've delegated all of my emotions to her. She has them for me, Carrier, and the entire Philadelphia Bar Association. It frees us up to bill time."

"This is so great!" Mary finally released Anne and stood in front of her tan credenza near the door. Her hair was still a messy ponytail and her brown eyes flashed with animation. "Tell us everything, girl! I thought you were a ghost!"

"There's no such thing as ghosts," Anne said, but Mary's forehead wrinkled.

"Of course there is."

Chick is a little crazy. Anne let it go and reached for Mel to give him a kiss hello. He greeted her with a where-were-you sniffing of the tip of her nose. Eskimo Cat.

"Tell us what happened, from the beginning," Bennie said. She eased onto the credenza with her coffee, and her smile faded. "I *identified* you, Murphy. I swear I saw you, dead, at the morgue. It was horrifying."

"But the face had to be—"

"It was, I could hardly bring myself to look at it. Your—or *her*—face was a mess, and there was cotton wadding from the blast, embedded where your eyes would have been. We all saw the body, but I made the ID, I signed the papers. I didn't think to question it. She had on your clothes, and her hair was red, even though it was covered with—"

Anne waved her off. "I get the picture. And I could see how you made the mistake."

"So, tell us what really happened," Judy chimed in quickly, eager to change the subject. She hopped up on the credenza and took a seat beside Bennie, dangling her red clogs. With her overalls she wore long silver earrings that swung whenever she moved.

How weird. The four of us together, in Mary's office. Anne knew it had never happened before, and they stood in the same office she had crashed only yesterday. She was having a hard time looking Judy in the eye, knowing what she felt inside, but the girl was so cute, with her face round as a circle, Campbell's-kid smile, and chopped-off crayon-yellow hair. Anne suppressed her resentment and let it rip. She told them everything, starting last year with Kevin, then fast-forwarding to Willa's murder, and how she had seen them at her house, then the call from Dr. Goldberger about Kevin's escape. She edited out her eavesdropping on their conversation, and if anybody realized she had overheard them, they didn't mention it.

Even Judy stilled as the story ended, her baby face positively colicky, but Mary looked shaken and grave. On the credenza, Bennie's gaze remained out the window, and her empty coffee mug hung from a thumb. She spoke first:

"I'm wondering about a critical assumption you're making, Murphy. You assume that the killer is Kevin and he meant to kill you, and I see why. The facts look like that, especially given his escape." Bennie looked at Anne directly, her blue eyes cutting like ice. "But it's at least a possibility that the killer isn't Kevin, and also that, whoever he is, he did mean to kill Willa."

Anne didn't get it. "Bennie, you said exactly the opposite to the cops. You said it was a no-brainer that it was Kevin."

"I didn't know then that Willa was at your house, so that changes the facts for me. It should for you, too." Bennie's eyes narrowed. "Was Willa seeing anyone? I assume she wasn't married, if she agreed to cat-sit for you."

"She was single, and I know she wasn't dating anyone."

"How old was she?"

"About my age."

"Where did she work?"

"At home, I think. She was an artist, she worked alone."

"She must have had friends, family."

"I guess so, but I don't know anything else about her, except that I think she lived off a trust fund. I know she's not from here, originally. She told me that once. I have no idea where her family lives or how to reach them."

"We have to find them. She was their daughter, their sister. They have a right to know she's dead. Where did she live?"

"In town, somewhere. I only knew her from the gym."

"You can find out where she lived, how hard can that be?" Bennie didn't wait for an answer. "Tell me about the last time you saw Willa. You said she ran to your house from the gym. Did she have anything on her? A purse or a gym bag? Keys? The police found no identification on her."

Anne flashed on Willa, huffing on her front step. "No. Her hands were empty."

"Do you need to show ID or a membership card to use your gym?"

"Yes." Anne finished the thought. "So Willa would have had to bring her ID and her purse with her, to get into the gym. It may still be there, with her keys, and the lockers are usually unlocked. I never leave my stuff there. I bring just my keys, membership card, and a dollar for a bottle of Evian."

"We'll follow up on that, too." Bennie paused. "Another thing. Did you really have a date last night? Was that true?"

Anne avoided Mary's eyes. "No date. I haven't gone out in a year. Kevin Satorno was my last date." She had to get Bennie back on track. "That's why I know Willa wasn't the intended victim. She was in the wrong place at the wrong time. It was Kevin and he wanted to kill me. He's been in prison, probably following my career, maybe even reading about me and Chipster. The Philly papers are online. And the sawed-off shotgun, the attack at the front door, everything is the same as before, in L.A. He's probably been watching my house since he escaped."

Bennie cocked an eyebrow. "Then why didn't he see you leave for the shore last night? Why didn't he see Willa come over?"

"Maybe he wasn't watching at that moment, and I didn't go until it was almost dark, a little after nine o'clock. I hung around, we talked a little and played with Mel. I lent Willa my shirt and a pair of clean shorts, since she'd come straight from the gym. What time did the murder take place, do they know?"

"About eleven o'clock, they think so far." Bennie mulled it over. "And your hallway light didn't work? How do you know it didn't burn out this morning, when you turned it on?"

"I never used it, not once. I doubt there's even a bulb in it." Anne kicked herself for not checking. "Bennie, I'm telling you, it was Kevin who came to shoot me last night, just like before, and I'm certain he thinks he killed me."

Judy was shaking her head slowly. "But Bennie could be right. It's at least a logical possibility somebody meant to kill Willa, for some reason. We know so little about her."

Mary shot her a sidelong look. "No, I think Anne is right. An attempt was made on her life, just a year ago. Kevin was the one who tried to kill her before, and he's escaped from prison. He's obsessed with her, he's a stalker. She's the much likelier victim. No doubt."

Eeek. Our first fight. Anne could feel battle lines being drawn. Mel chose her side, even though he had fallen asleep on Mary's desk. Loyalty Cat.

Bennie raised a hand like a traffic cop. "Hold on, let's table the discussion for a minute. There's another assumption I don't like, Murphy. If the killer is Kevin, why do you assume he's still in town? If he's a fugitive and he killed you, why wouldn't he just run? His job is done and he doesn't want to get caught. Any murderer would bolt."

"Not an erotomanic. That's not the way they think. Kevin views himself as linked to me, romantically, forever. It's all imagined, of course, but it's strong. He'll want to see where I worked, maybe even see you guys."

"I agree, stalkers are in a league of their own," Mary said quietly. Her brown eyes flickered, and she raked a dark-blond strand back with manicured fingernails. "You know, once I had a problem with . . . someone."

"Really, you?" Anne looked over in surprise, though she knew the statistics. Three out of every ten women will be stalked in their lives. So she and Mary did have something in common, after all. She just wished it were something good, like compulsive spending.

"My case was a little different, because I didn't realize I was being stalked. But I remember, you have to be careful how you deal with a stalker, and it's no win. If you go to the cops, it makes him crazy. If you don't, you're unprotected."

Right. It was so nice to finally be understood, and by somebody who wasn't court-appointed. "That's why I never should have gotten the restraining order against Kevin. It punctured his delusion that I loved him. It was the ultimate rejection, one even he couldn't deny, and it became a declaration of war."

"But you had every right to go to court!" Judy said, and next to her Bennie nodded.

"You did the right thing. You were trying to protect yourself."

Anne tried to explain. "Ten percent of women in abuse or stalking scenarios are killed right after they apply for a restraining order. In New York, they found one woman dead—with her restraining order knifed to her chest." She fell silent at the horrible image. "These obsessive types, they're different from normal murderers, if there is such a thing. That's why Kevin will stay in town. He'll want to be around me, to walk places I walked. To stay near me, even in death."

Mary shuddered. "I would bet this guy won't leave Philly before your funeral."

"True," Anne said, though she hadn't thought far enough ahead to a funeral. "But it's Willa's body in the morgue. What will they do?" They all looked at Bennie, since she always knew everything.

"The medical examiner won't release the body for two or three weeks, given the holiday and the backlog."

"Backlog?" Anne asked. The term applied to bills, not bodies.

"July Fourth, in the City of Brotherly Love? The fireworks are in the ERs. The medical examiner has a small staff, too. They'll do blood and DNA tests on Willa's body, but the results won't be in until next week, since the ID is unquestioned. If we don't say anything, it's possible that they'll release her body for burial, thinking it's yours." A pall fell over all of them for a minute, then Bennie continued. "We can't have that, for Willa's sake. We have to find Willa's family, and we have to call the cops, Murphy. Tell them that Satorno escaped and that you're alive. And that they have the wrong person reported dead."

"Absolutely not. I agree with you about Willa's family. We can find them and tell them, maybe convince them to work with us to find her killer."

"No, that's not tenable. Hear me out." Bennie held up a finger with the mug slung on it. "Kevin is a dangerous fugitive, and the cops can find him sooner than we can. They have the manpower, the resources, the expertise. They can put out an APB to all uniforms, contact the FBI, interface with the California authorities."

"You heard what they said, they only have *forty* cops covering all of Center City. They can't even cover my house. Besides, I trusted the cops once to protect me and almost ended up dead. They couldn't even charge Kevin with attempted murder, that's why he got so little time. I won't rely on the justice system. It almost killed me."

Bennie looked grim. "Murphy. You are in real danger from this man, and it's no time for amateurs."

"No cops."

"I don't agree."

"It's not your life."

Bennie didn't flinch. "Murphy, you mistake me. I own this law firm, and you are my employee. I am chargeable with your actions, which means that I am responsible for everything that happens here and everything that you do. Like hiring naked men, for starters." She couldn't find her smile. "I cannot have this information and not disclose it to the police. It approaches obstruction of justice. They're investigating the murder of the wrong person, and we have material information about the whereabouts of a major suspect." Bennie folded her arms, and Anne folded hers, too. Judy and Mary watched the showdown in silence.

"Bennie, if you tell them, I'm outta here."

"Child, if you leave, you're fired. And I tell the cops anyway."

Ouch. Anne had to get better at folding her arms or she was sunk. "Wait, I got an idea. How about we compromise? You tell the cops that Kevin's escaped, but *don't* tell them I'm alive. Then I get to play dead and keep looking for him. You get to tell the cops and let them get busy. This way we're all working to find Kevin, us and the cops!"

"No, it's too dangerous," Bennie answered, but she hesitated. "Let the professionals find Satorno. They know what they're doing."

"They can't even find him in jail! He's a nobody to the Philly police! You heard the detective!"

Mary nodded. "Like Anne says, none of us can judge her until we're in her shoes. Even I can't know what that's like. If it's her life at stake, we should do it her way, with her compromise."

Judy finally spoke. "I agree. Let's tell the cops he's escaped, but let's follow up, too. We run our own murder investigations all the time, parallel to whatever the cops are doing. This is nothing new, not to us."

Whoa. Anne glanced over in surprise, but said nothing. Judy's words clearly carried weight with Bennie, who was looking at the three associates with exasperation.

"But what do I tell the cops, girls? How would I know that Kevin has escaped if Murphy's really dead? She's the one who got the call from the shrink, not me."

"You'll figure it out," Anne answered. "You found my mother, didn't you? Go ahead, call the cops, but let me stay dead at least until Tuesday morning."

"Why Tuesday morning?"

"Tuesday morning I try *Chipster.*"

Bennie looked at Anne like she was crazy. "You can't think you're trying that case! No way will you be ready for trial with what's going on, and God knows it would be a miracle if the cops find Satorno that quick. Murphy, staging a full civil trial is a complicated thing. You have to postpone."

"I can't. Gil wanted to go forward, to stay on track with his IPO. In this climate, everybody wants funding and it's a coup to get it. If there's a hiccup of any type, the funding will take a pass. That's why we didn't settle the case in the first place—Gil wanted to be completely vindicated for his Board and the venture capital guys. If we derail the case now, he loses the IPO. End of Chipster."

"So don't postpone, but don't *you* try the case. Not with what's going on with Satorno. Be practical, Murphy!" Bennie slid off the credenza and onto her running shoes. "Look, I'll reshuffle some deps and try it for you."

"Thank you, but I want to try it myself." Anne felt surprised at the strength of her feelings, until she understood their source. "Kevin Satorno has taken quite enough from me. A new friend. My new home. My feeling of safety. My peace of mind. He's not going to take my job, too. It's my case and my client." She folded her arms again, at least mentally. "I call these shots."

Bennie sighed. "Okay, fair enough. You brought the client in, you make the decisions." She checked her watch. "Let's rock and roll. I have to call the cops. DiNunzio, you gotta take the dep. The court reporter must be threatening to leave by now. Murphy, you stay here, so no one can see you."

"Thanks." Relieved, Anne turned to Mary,

who was already getting up from her desk. "Mary, you know what to do, right? Get Bonnard to talk about the incident last May. You know, she claims Gil Martin hit on her, at a seminar they went to at the Wyndham. Gil says she's pissed because she didn't get a raise, and we can document that with the e-mails she wrote. Pin her down on the details, so we can try to predict her testimony at trial."

"Got it. It shouldn't take long." Mary went around her desk, collecting her notes and exhibits. "Feel free to use anything in the office, but stay inside, at least until the dep's over."

"Right." Bennie paused at the doorway, her hand on the knob. "And one last thing. You should know that I spoke with Gil last night. He was obviously upset about your murder, and so was his wife. How are you going to handle that? Are you going to tell them you're alive?"

"I was going to. I trust Gil. He'll keep it confidential." Anne felt Judy's eyes boring into her back. What was it she had said? *Gil Martin would never have hired Anne if she hadn't looked the way she did.*

"Can I make a suggestion?" Bennie asked. "Why don't you hold off on telling the client for now? You have to lay low, and with Gil thinking that I'm handling the case, just let it be for now. Think about it." Bennie opened the door and let Mary out. "And find out more about Willa, okay? We have to talk to her family. And I'm not convinced she wasn't the target. Get on it. Humor me."

Damn. So she hadn't convinced Bennie. Anne felt vaguely defeated as the office door closed, leaving her and Judy alone in the small, clean office. They looked at each other, then looked away. They didn't like each other. Anne didn't know what to say. *If I can't talk about lipstick, I'm fresh out of conversation.*

"Thanks for the support, with Bennie," Anne said finally, because that needed saying.

"No problem."

Okay, now go. "You don't have to hang with me or anything, Judy. I'm fine, and you probably have work to do."

"Nope, I'm good. My cases are nice and quiet. It's summertime."

"Then why stick around the office? You probably have something better to do, for the holiday. You have a boyfriend, don't you?"

"Yes, Frank Lucia, from the Lucia case. You met him, remember?"

No. "Sure."

"He went fishing for the weekend. I was just painting at home, when this happened. I'll stick around and keep you company."

GO AWAY! "Whatever."

The office fell quiet except for the crowd of media outside. The window overlooked Locust Street, and Judy turned toward it, gesturing. "Noisy out there," she said.

"Reporters."

"Let's go drop water balloons." Judy went to the window, but Anne hung back. It drove her nuts that Judy was trying to be nice to her. Mental note: Some feelings make no sense.

Judy turned and waved her over. "Come here, look at this. It's a zoo!"

Anne went to the window, of smoked glass, and looked out. A sea of people shifted and moved in front of the building, bigger than before. Reporters with microphones, tape machines, and notepads, and photographers with videocameras, print cameras, and klieg lights. A hot-dog vendor with a red-striped umbrella peddled lunch, and a young black kid handed out advertising flyers. Anne counted three Uncle Sams and one uniformed cop.

She squinted against the sun, scanning for Kevin. She wished she could start looking for him right now. He could be down there. It would make sense. The day was slipping away. The weekend was slipping away. She had lost enough of her life to that asshole. And he had killed Willa. Anne had to find him. To make him pay and to make herself, finally, safe.

"You're looking for him, aren't you?" Judy asked, reading Anne's thoughts, which annoyed her.

"Yes."

"What does he look like?"

"Why?"

"I can look, too. Two pairs of eyes are better than one. It's four eyes altogether. It's a lot of eyes." Judy grinned, and Anne was pretty sure she was kidding.

"Well, he's good-looking, for a psycho. He has pale blond hair and blue eyes, close together. His nose is long and sort of beaked, a little—"

"Wait." Judy held up a palm, turned from the window, and began ransacking Mary's desk. She stopped when she found a small pad of white paper and a sharpened pencil. "Start over, with his eyes."

"What are you doing?"

"I'm going to draw him."

"Why?"

"I understand things better when I draw them."

This chick is crazy, too. Maybe I wasn't missing anything.

"Start again, with the eyes—"

"They're blue." Anne went into a detailed description, surprised that she remembered as much as she did about Kevin's face. She had read that many stalking victims become obsessed with their stalkers, but she thought it was simply impossible to forget the face of someone who had looked at you with intent to kill. "Light blue, scary blue. And he has a weak chin, by the way. It goes back a little."

"Recedes."

"Totally."

"Got it." Judy sketched some more,

asked a few more questions, then, after ten minutes, flipped the pad over and held it up. "How's this?"

My God. The likeness was almost dead-on. It looked like Kevin's face emerging from the sketch. Right in front of Anne.

"You hate it." Judy's face fell.

"No! I mean yes! I hate it and it's him! Exactly. You are incredible!"

Judy turned the pad over, surprised at her own handiwork. "I never did that before, drew from words. Usually I only draw from life. Or pictures."

"It's like a composite! A police composite!" Anne came around and stood next to Judy, staring at the sketch. It was almost as good as a mug shot and was already giving her an idea. "Can I have it?"

"Sure." Judy handed her the pad. "Why?"

Eeek. "You really want to know?"

"Yes."

"It's a secret."

"I can keep a secret."

Anne didn't know if she could trust her; she didn't even know if she wanted to trust her. Judy might try to stop her, tell Bennie, or do something equally sensible. Anne had never confided in a woman she liked, much less one she didn't.

"Well? You gonna tell me?" Judy cocked her head, her silver earring dangling to the side, and on the desk, even Mel raised his chin, waiting for her response with interest.

Curiosity Cat.

9

Fifteen minutes later, Uncle Sam and her large, stuffed manila envelope were downstairs in the office lobby, being let out the service entrance by Herb, who held open the door to make sure her breasts left unharmed. "You got the job?" he asked. "Congratulations!"

"Thanks." Anne clasped the manila envelope to her INDEPENDENT WOMAN shirt like a lead shield.

"Hey, what's your name, honey? I checked the log but I couldn't read it."

Heh heh. "Samantha. I'll be back in ten minutes. Will you let me back in?"

"Sure. Knock. I'll be listening for you."

The mouth of the alley opened onto the cross street, around the corner from their office entrance on Locust. Crowds of tourists and other people were making their way down the cross street, going north to the Parkway, and the media was thronging south, trying to get to Rosato & Associates.

Anne waited until the foot traffic was at its densest, then flowed into the crowd as Uncle Sam, with sunglasses, beard, and a package tucked protectively under her arm. She had insisted on making the delivery herself, despite Judy's arguments to the contrary. Anne was the new messenger, after all, and this was something only she could do. She wanted to be down here in the crowd, in case she could spot Kevin. Any time she saw a blond head, she scrutinized the face. No Kevin. But she couldn't help but feel that he was here.

Anne walked toward Locust, craning her head to see if the hard-working kid on the corner was still there. He was, and his flyer supply was dangerously low, evidence that he'd been foisting junk onto the public with vigor. Sweat beaded on his brow, and he looked a lot younger down here, maybe sixteen. His hair was shaved into a fade, and he wore a heavy gold chain over his EAT AT BOBO'S T-shirt, which matched his flyers. *Damn*. Anne wished she'd thought of matching T-shirts to her flyers. Mental note: Law school is useless.

She slowed when she approached the teenager, giving the reporters and tourists a chance to flow around him. When she got next to him, she opened her hand. Inside was a hundred-dollar bill she got from the office kitty, and she flashed it. "You wanna pass some flyers out for me?"

"Sure, clown," he answered, taking the bill and the manila packet. He opened the brass fastener, slid one of the flyers out, and looked it over.

Anne couldn't help but read over his shoulder. They'd printed the flyer on red paper, and the top half was a copy of the composite picture Judy had drawn. The text they had written together:

CALLING ALL REPORTERS! HERE'S WHAT THE POLICE ARE HIDING FROM THE MEDIA!

Do you want the hottest lead in the Anne Murphy murder? Find this man!

He's shown above in a composite

drawing. His name is Kevin Satorno and he's the prime suspect in Anne Murphy's murder, but the police aren't telling you that yet. Satorno is Caucasian, age 29, about 6 feet tall, 175 pounds, with light blond hair and blue eyes. He has recently escaped from a penitentiary in California, where he had been jailed last year for aggravated assault, for trying to kill Murphy. Find him and scoop the competition!

Anne thought it was a beautiful flyer and a great idea. The press was as dogged as the cops and were aggressive by occupation. Why not turn the reporters to her advantage? Put them to good use? Get them working for her, instead of against her?

"Fuck is this?" the kid asked, with teenage scorn.

"It's a flyer. All you gotta do is give one to any reporter you see. TV, newspaper, anything. Anybody with a camera or a microphone. You got me?"

"How 'bout that shortie from Channel

Ten?" The kid nodded at a pretty woman in the press crowd. "She's *fine*."

"Fine is good. Hand it to everybody fine. Shorties and tallies. Knock yourself out. Don't be picky. I'll be watching you, and if you do a good job, I'll be back with more."

"I'm down." He waded into the crowd with the flyers.

Anne watched him hand them out, and in the next few minutes bright spots of red began blooming in the crowd, like a poppy field. One anchorwoman, orange-faced with TV makeup, paused to read the flyer, and a photographer was handing his copy to the cameraman beside him. Reporters were putting their heads together, and Anne began to hear snippets of conversation, everybody suddenly buzzing: "You think this's for real?" "You wanna take the chance it's not?" "News at Six will get on it, they got the staff." "Not this weekend! I wanted to be home by three. My kid's got T-ball, my wife's gonna kill me!"

Hope surged in Anne's chest, and she was about to go back to the office, according to plan. But then she saw him.

Kevin?

She stopped, breathless. A blond man in

the middle of the crowd was reading the flyer, his face lowered. He looked like Kevin. His hair was crudely shorn. He was Kevin's height. He wore a nondescript white T-shirt, and his shoulders were broad, with powerful caps. He was standing almost directly across from the office entrance, but he didn't appear to have press credentials. Anne waited for him to look up so she could see his face, but when he did, he turned away. She didn't get more than a flash of his features.

It's him, it's him, it's him. Is it him?

Suddenly the blond man started moving. He made his way through the crowd, a light patch in the crowd of black cameras. He moved like Kevin. Slow. Deliberate. In control. Didn't anyone notice he was the guy in the red drawing? *Was* he the guy in the drawing? She stood on tiptoe, watching him.

He's getting away!

He was leaving the crowd, calmly. Walking evenly, down Locust toward Broad Street, heading east and out of the action. She couldn't see the rest of the man's body, but he was doing what Kevin would be doing if he were handed that flyer. He would get away without drawing attention to himself. Anne was tempted to yell but she didn't want to blow her cover, not with the media surrounding her. She wasn't sure enough it was him. She shut her mouth, but she couldn't let him go. She knew what she had to do.

Stalk him. Stalk him back.

She took off, trailing the blond man toward Broad Street, leaving the media behind but picking up more tourists. Kids waved stiff American flags, fake colonial dames conducted tours with tiny megaphones, and teenagers stampeded past. Anne passed the new hall for the Philadelphia Orchestra and avoided families posing for snapshots on the sidewalk. Her heart started hammering. Her eyes trained on the blond head, moving away with purpose, heading east.

He stopped at a red light at the corner of Broad and Locust, and she picked up her pace not to lose him. She scooted to Broad and, as she got closer, she heard string music *plink*ing on the breeze, with the bass thumping of kettle drums. There had to be a parade marching down Broad, stalling the blond. His back was turned, and she caught a glimpse of his build. His triceps bulged under his T-shirt and a deep crease ran down his back. He was more muscular than the Kevin she knew, but maybe he had started working out in prison.

Anne heard the characteristic *ringa-jinga* of a summer Mummers string band, and a phalanx of harlequins in orange, magenta, and black sequins began to parade past. The costumes caught the sun in riotous color, and sky-high peacock feathers sprouted from their elaborate headpieces. The crowd burst into applause, except for the blond man pushing his way to the curb.

She wedged her way through people, toward the front. The music, clapping, and cheers got louder but she blocked it all out. The Mummers' string band surged in full glory, then strutted by. The crowd, finally permitted to cross, pressed forward, with the blond man in the lead, crossing Broad Street, then breaking into a casual run.

No! "Please lemme through. I gotta get through!" Anne shouted and took off after him, fighting the crowd. Everybody was trying to cross at the parade break, west to east and east to west, jostling each other out of the way. She stayed on her feet but when she reached the other side of Broad, she'd lost sight of him.

No! Where was he? Anne looked wildly

around. People were streaming toward Broad, and she ran the other way, sprinting upstream. Only an expert could sprint in Blahniks, and she qualified. When the crowd thickened, she jumped into the air to see him above the crowd.

There! Her heart leaped when she did. He was two blocks away! Straight down Locust, and he was taking a left, onto the cross street. She ran for it, confident that he couldn't detect her now that he'd turned the corner. She banged into only one man and apologized over her shoulder as she turned the corner. Then she stopped. Kevin was nowhere in sight.

Anne looked desperately down the street. A young woman was striding toward her, a block away. She would have been on the block when Kevin turned onto it. Anne straightened her sunglasses and hurried over to her. "Excuse me," she said. "I'm looking for my friend. He's tall and blond, but he wears his hair really short, almost shaved. Did you see him? I thought I just saw him come around the corner."

"Was he wearing a white T-shirt?"

"Yes!" Anne couldn't believe her good luck, and the woman pointed to the top of the street. A windowless storefront lay in the next block, and it appeared to be open for a very active business. A crowd flowed into the place from the sidewalk, and red, white, and blue balloons flew from a sign. "In there?"

"Yeah. He went inside, I think."

"Thank you!" Anne said. She almost hugged her, but remembered that she was Uncle Sam, so hugging strange women carried federal penalties. She caught her breath and made a beeline for the store.

10

Frankie & Johnny's, said the sign on the storefront, in funky black letters. The windows had been covered with plywood and painted black, and the large front door, also black, was nondescript. Anne slowed her step, and a man at the end of a group going into the place smiled back at her as she fell into step behind him and went inside.

Dance music blared from the pitch-black within, and the smell of sweat and cigarette smoke assaulted her nose. She recognized the song instantly, The Weather Girls singing "It's Raining Men." And when her eyes adjusted to the light, Anne saw that it was. The place was packed with bodies moving to a single beat, and all of the bodies were male. Shirtless, tank-topped, flag-shirted, and tattooed; they were all men, with only one or two women. She turned around and peered through the darkness at the crowd near the door. They were all men, too. She stood, rooted uncertainly to the spot. She was inside a gay bar, for the first time in her life. Mental note: New things are disconcerting at first, then stay that way.

She suppressed the strangeness and tried to find Kevin in the crowd. Where was he? Redheads, shaved heads, brown hair, baldies, and fades; she couldn't see the blond head for the darkness. The only illumination came from red, white, and blue spotlights roaming over the crowd, flashing with the *boom-boom* beat of the music. Everybody was moving, shifting, boogying, changing places. It was almost impossible to keep track of any one of them, and Anne couldn't see a thing for the darkness and smoke. Not to mention her sunglasses. Was Kevin really in a gay bar? He wasn't gay, not that she knew. He'd been fixated on her.

She lingered, confused. The bar had looked like a small storefront from the outside, but inside it was so much bigger, with a twenty-foot-high ceiling and a half-shell of a balcony that held dancing men and a stage. A long martini bar lined the room's right side, and affixed to an immense mirror behind the bar flickered a huge martini glass in hot-red neon. Anne used the mirror to try to find Kevin, but all it reflected was an anonymous, sweating throng of men.

Wasn't there a bouncer at the door? Everybody here was built like a bouncer. She peered through the cigarette smoke at men pouring into the bar. Behind them she spotted a muscle-bound man in a white tank top bearing the bar's logo. She wedged her way to him, breathing in the commingled odors of chocolate martini and Paco Rabanne. "Excuse me," she shouted to the doorman, to be heard over the music, "did you see a blond, tall, white guy come in here, just a minute ago? His hair is short and he's muscular. He was wearing a white T-shirt!"

"Yeah, plenty!" The guard cupped his hands around his mouth. "Why, he underage?"

"No, but I have to find—" Anne started to say, but the crowd came between them, dancing as soon as they came in the door and crossed the threshold. Her heart sank with the realization that Kevin could have gotten past the guard the same way she did, on the far side of a big group. Maybe someone else had seen him come in.

She made her way to the other side of the

packed entrance, where a lineup of flat-screen TVs mounted ceiling-height showed a Jennifer Lopez video on mute. Anne side-stepped to two men standing against the dark wall near the door, who were wearing matching white tank tops with jeans shorts. "Excuse me!" she shouted, and they turned to her, still moving to the *boom-boom*. "Excuse me, did you see a man just come in here, five minutes ago? About thirty, blond, tall, very muscular?"

"Don't I wish!" shouted one of the men, and they both laughed. Other men stood grouped around the door, all of them drinking and bopping to the music, which was segueing into Grace Jones's "I Need a Man." She approached the second group, but they hadn't seen the man. Neither had the third group. The fourth asked her if she wanted to party, and the fifth told her that her sunglasses were so Six Flags. She agreed, but like Grace Jones, she still needed a man. A blond man in particular.

She looked around. All she could see with any clarity at all was a bartender by the cash register, illuminated by a single pool of halogen. He also wore a white bar-logo tank top and was shaking a gleaming martini shaker.

She made her way through the crowd to the bar, which was packed, and finally got the bartender's attention. "I'm trying to find somebody, a blond man in a T-shirt. It's really important."

"Did you ask one of the Muscle Queens?" he shouted, and when Anne looked puzzled, he translated. "Security."

"I didn't see any security, I asked the doorman."

"Then try the manager, in the back office. He can help you." The bartender waved her off, responding to the clamoring customers, and she edged from the bar, made her way around the dance floor, and found an office, past the rest rooms. She knocked on the black door and laughed with surprise when it opened. The manager was dressed like Uncle Sam, too, but in a classy beard, real satin stovepipe, and a shiny blue jacket with fancy lapels.

"I'm jealous," Anne said. "You have the jacket."

"No, *I'm* jealous! You have the Blahniks."

Anne laughed. "But my sunglasses are so Six Flags."

"That's why they're great!"

Anne slid them off, feeling fairly safe with

him. He wouldn't recognize her and he certainly wouldn't hit on her. "Can I bother you a minute?" she asked.

"Sure, come on in." He ushered Anne into his office. He had a Madonna-type headset hanging around his neck, was about five foot eight or so, with silvering at his close-cropped sideburns, and he was slightly overweight. Mental note: Evidently not all gay men work out, which is to their credit. "What's your name?" he asked.

Uh. "Sam?"

"What a coincidence," he said, smiling, and she looked around quickly. The office was crammed with a gray metal desk and a file cabinet, a computer and an old monitor, adding machines, money counters, and a black matte safe with a silver combination lock. Invoices, correspondence, and inventory sheets sat in stacks on the desk; a large clock with manila timecards in slots hung by the door. It was another surprise. Anne had expected *The Birdcage* and was getting Cigna.

"I'm looking for someone who came in here about five or ten minutes ago." She liked the manager so much she decided to level with him, almost. "He's dangerous, a killer. His name is Kevin Satorno and he's escaped from a prison in California. I know it sounds kind of crazy."

"Not at all, unfortunately." The manager didn't blink. "We do get men released from prison. Parolees, ex-cons. Gay bars are magnets for all kinds of transients. It's a problem for us, and the community."

"Even if the man isn't gay? I mean, I don't think this man is gay."

"I love it. Nobody's gay but we somehow stay in business." The manager chuckled. "The cons that come in, not all of them are gay, they don't have to be. They come for the hustle, not the sex. If they're just out of the joint, they won't have any money. They hustle for drinks, cigarettes, a warm bed to sleep in. Or sometimes they pick up the customer, go home with him, and roll 'im."

"For real?" Anne asked, like a true Philadelphian.

"Sure. It's dark in here, and the cops don't exactly drop in for doughnuts. And my staff knows not to pry, all of us do. Too many people in the closet, you know. Each to his own, as long as he spends money." The manager's cell phone began ringing from a belt holster, but he ignored it. On separate black holsters hung a beeper and a walkie-talkie. "You're sure he's here, at the tea dance?"

Tea dance? Anne hadn't seen any tea at the tea dance, unless Stoli qualified. "Yes, I'm pretty sure. A woman outside saw him go in."

"What does he look like, this man you're looking for?"

Anne wished she'd kept one of her red flyers, but she hadn't known she'd spot Kevin. She rattled off a description, and the manager's eyes widened in alarm.

"Wait a minute," he said. "Light blond hair, almost platinum? Cut close, almost shaved?"

"Yes," Anne answered, excited. "You saw him?"

"No, but I heard about him. A friend of mine manages The Eagle, and he told me that some asshole took a swing at one of his customers last night. Broke his nose."

Anne's heart stopped. *Last night.* The night Willa was killed. "What time? What happened?"

"After midnight, this good-lookin' blond guy came in the bar. Everybody noticed because he was new. A queen sent him a few drinks, because he's into blonds, but when he went over to pick him up, the blond freaked out on him. Called him a faggot and hit him across the face."

"My God." Anne felt her chest tighten. Had it been Kevin? At only an hour after the murder, he'd still be jiggered up. Violent. "Did they call the police? Is there a report?"

"No. They threw the guy out, they took care of the queen, and it was over."

"No! Why didn't they call 911? A customer was assaulted."

"I don't know any bar that would. We sure wouldn't. We keep the cops out of here, we police ourselves. Especially this weekend. Holidays are pure gold in this business. We'll pay our rent on this tea dance, then we close up, clean up, and reopen again tonight. Hold on." The manager crossed to a shelf that held electronics equipment Anne hadn't noticed before; a VCR, another black box, and a small TV monitor, in black and white. It was a security system!

Her hopes soared. "You have security cameras here?"

"Sure do, for times like this. This is a multiplexer. We have three cameras in the bar and one on the door."

"I can't believe it!" Anne stepped over to the monitor. The TV screen was divided into four windows, with a time and date stamp on the upper right. The quartet of images was gray and shadowy, but she could see now that the lower right box was trained on the front door. The front door was opening and closing, and men were piling into the bar. It was hard to tell the true colors of hair and clothes, but the men's features were discernible, if grainy. "And you have a tape?"

"This is it. You say it was about five, ten minutes ago that this guy came in?" The manager hit the rewind button on the VCR, and the men on the monitor screen started flying out the front door of the bar. The time stamp in the top right corner ran backward. "Here we go."

Anne watched in nervous silence as the tape stopped rewinding and began to play. The front door kept opening and closing as men piled in on mute, obviously laughing and talking, in large and small groups. "He was wearing a white T-shirt."

"Honey, that's half the men in here. Watch the screen and tell me if you see him."

Anne bit her lip as a group of men dressed in T-shirts and tank tops boogied in. Suddenly a foursome burst in together, and the fifth, a man hanging in the back, had hair that made a white blotch on the grainy tape. Anne felt her heart seize. It was Kevin! "There! That's him!"

"Hold on." The manager hit the pause button, and the image froze on the screen. "Which is he?"

My God. He's here. Anne found herself pointing. A grainy face on the screen was clearly Kevin's. She'd found him. She couldn't speak for a minute, as the manager replayed the tape again in slow motion and stopped it at the best shot of Kevin.

"That him, in the Joe Camel T-shirt?"

"Yes!" Anne squinted at the screen. She hadn't noticed it because she hadn't seen Kevin's chest, but his T-shirt bore a small cartoon of Joe Camel over the breast pocket. "That's him!"

"I guess he's making the rounds, lookin' for a place to hide. I'll be damned if I'll let him hurt my people." The manager was already reaching for his walkie-talkie and withdrawing it from his holster. He pressed the Talk button on the walkie-talkie and rattled off a perfect description of Kevin in the Joe Camel T-shirt. "You read me, Mike? Julio? Barry? Call me as soon as you grab him. Good. Over."

"Let's go get him." Anne was already heading for the door, but the manager frowned.

"No, we stay here. My security guards will get him."

"I didn't see any security out there."

"They're there, and they know what they're doing. They're trained to deal with situations like this."

"Of course they are, and what do I know? I'll just stay here and wait." *Yeah, right.* Anne held on to her stovepipe, opened the door, and bolted out, leaving the startled manager behind.

"Wait! What are you doing?" he shouted after her. "I can't have you running around my bar, fucking up my tea dance!"

Anne found herself plunged into darkness again, but this time the manager caught up with her and grabbed her hand, less friendly than before. The two Uncle Sams tugged at each other until he gave up, evidently not wanting to make a scene. He began searching with her, moving them both quickly and expertly through the crowd, looking at everyone and talking into his Madonna headset, looped over the brim of his stovepipe.

Anne didn't see Kevin yet, but the scene in the bar had changed. Men stuffed the dance floor, but they weren't dancing, they were clapping at a show on the elevated stage. She looked up. BEST BUNS CONTEST, read a placard on an easel, and a row of semidressed men stood on the stage with their backs turned to the audience. They were dressed in only their underwear, a crazy-quilt of tiger print, stars-and-stripes, and zebra stripes, and a drag queen in red sequins was emceeing. She bumped her microphone against a tush in leopard print. "Give it up for Couple Number 1!" she shouted, and the crowd went nuts.

The manager and Anne searched for Kevin, eyeing each face, most of them turned to the stage. Security guards in black T-shirts with white STAFF lettering on the front prowled through the crowd, and the manager was talking into his headset.

"Let's hear it for Couple Number 2!" the drag queen shouted, and the clapping intensified. Stars-and-stripes trumped tiger print. It was a patriotic crowd. Too bad they couldn't serve in the military. *But where was Kevin?*

Suddenly the manager stopped, holding

his earpiece, then turned to Anne. "Head for the front door."

"Did we get him?" Anne asked, her heart leaping up, but the manager held fast to her hand and pulled her through the crowd to the front door. The doorman she had talked to before was there, and the manager gestured him over.

"Did you see him?" he shouted to the doorman.

"Joe Camel? I think I did. I told Julio, I think I remember him leaving about five minutes ago."

"You *think*? Did you or didn't you?"

"Yeah, yeah, I saw him."

"Never let that guy in again, and if he ever comes to the door, call me immediately and don't let him in." The manager turned to Anne. "Well, he's outta here. Sorry," he said, but she was already shaking her head.

"But, the doorman's not sure. Maybe he's wrong. I talked to him before, and he said he hadn't seen a blond man come in, and we know that's wrong."

"That was before I heard about the Joe Camel T-shirt," the doorman shouted defensively, but the manager placed a heavy hand on Anne's shoulder.

"Honey, he's my doorman, and he knows what he's doing."

No! "Why don't we go back to your office and check the tape? It would show for sure if Kevin left."

"No, it wouldn't. It sounds like he got out while we were playing it, and it doesn't record while it's playing. Now it's time for you to go." The manager escorted Anne to the door and opened it, just as the dance music started playing a campy version of "The Party's Over."

She would have protested, but she heard her cell phone ringing and she found herself outside the bar, blinking on the sunny sidewalk. She reached in her pocket for her cell phone and opened it up. She couldn't read the blue numbers in the sunlight. "Hello?" she said into the phone.

"Anne, Anne!" It was Judy. "Where are you?"

Uh. "I'm out!" *Of the closet?*

"Anne, hold on." There was silence on the phone, then a new voice came on.

"Murphy! Murphy! WHERE THE FUCK ARE YOU?"

Bennie Rosato, their own Muscle Queen. What to do? Anne didn't reply, but Bennie didn't seem to notice.

"Murphy! I don't want you out there! I can't believe you and Carrier made these flyers! Are you nuts? Come to the office, right now! Come in through the back! NOW!"

Damn! Anne couldn't bring herself to give up on Kevin, and she couldn't say no to Bennie.

Then she got an idea.

11

Fifteen minutes later, a cherry-red Mustang idled in an illegal parking space, pointing toward an unsuspecting gay bar. The car contained four women on their maiden stakeout: Bennie at the steering wheel, Judy riding shotgun, and Mary in the backseat with Anne. Bennie had driven over, but was delayed because the Mustang had been out of gas and they had to stop to fill up. The bar was closing its doors, and the tea dance had ended with no sign of Kevin. Anne had told Bennie and the others everything, but she couldn't leave without making sure he really hadn't been inside.

"I think I won't fire you yet, Murphy," Bennie was saying, in the front seat. A red flyer lay crumpled on the dashboard, presumably where she'd thrown it. "You either, Carrier. Because that would be too easy. It would be capital punishment instead of life in prison, and I'm philosophically opposed. You get my drift, girls?"

"You want us to suffer?" Anne ventured.

"Exactly. You, in particular."

Anne kept her eyes trained on the bar. Judy's and Mary's were, too. The black door of the entrance had been propped open, and men were leaving in droves. Some dispersed down the street or hailed cabs, but most lingered, laughing, chatting, and smoking in small groups on the sidewalk, enjoying the shade cast by the buildings. There had to be two hundred men that they'd seen leave, and Anne never would have guessed that they had all fit inside. The bar was a clown car for gay men.

Bennie continued, "There's only one rule at Rosato & Associates, and it's this—I'm the boss. I'm Bennie Rosato. I own Rosato & Associates. See? It rhymes."

Anne nodded again. No Kevin. *Damn!*

"Murphy, I tried to explain to you that I am chargeable with your actions, and it follows from this that nothing happens in my law firm without my approval. No employee of mine does anything insane without clearing it with me first. This is because I pay the salaries and bills, including but not limited to rent, light, water, casebooks, Pilot pens, and fresh coffee beans."

Anne's hopes were sinking. The sidewalks were full of naked chests, tank tops, and short shorts, but Kevin's Joe Camel shirt wasn't anywhere in evidence.

"I was trying to reach Detective Rafferty when I heard that my newest associate was in a gay bar dressed in an Uncle Sam outfit, trying to catch a psychotic killer. Imagine my surprise at the news." Bennie paused. "Not only were you supposed to be researching Willa Hansen, you were supposed to be *dead*. This leads me to believe that you missed the point of my earlier lecture. As I told you once already, Murphy, I was the one who identified your body." Bennie's voice caught abruptly, and the sudden silence got everyone's attention.

Anne checked Bennie in the rearview, and her eyes flickered with pain. Judy looked over, and Mary hung her head.

Bennie was clearing her throat. "The physical details aren't the point. Mostly what I saw, what all of us saw, lying in a very cold, stainless-steel drawer, is what Kevin Satorno is capable of, if it was him. He didn't just want to kill you, Murphy. He wanted to destroy you. He aimed right for your beautiful face and he blasted it to kingdom come. Given the opportunity, he will do it again."

Anne swallowed hard. It sounded as if Bennie had been worried about her. *Cared* about her. It was a new thing. "I'm sorry, I really am," she said, meaning it.

"Good." Bennie checked her watch, and Anne and Judy returned their attention to the bar. But after a minute, Anne became aware that Mary hadn't lifted her head and she did something she had never done with another woman; she reached over and held Mary's hand. Just then a familiar stovepipe appeared at the front door of the bar, schmoozing with a crowd of partiers.

"That's the manager," Anne said, watching. The manager was withdrawing a large key-ring from his blue satin pants and shooing everybody out of the way. Closing time, at least until they reopened. Then he went back inside the bar, presumably to lock the front door from the inside.

Goddamnit! "Maybe Kevin's hiding inside," Anne said, but even she didn't believe it. She met Judy's eye, and she looked almost equally bummed. Anne was feeling better about her since the red flyer. Almost.

"I'm sure they get everybody out before they close," Judy said. "So if he was still there, he's not anymore. I think we lost him, Anne. At least for now."

Mary raised a small, manicured fist. "Don't give up! We'll get him yet. He will feel the wrath of girls!"

Bennie waved the associates into silence. She opened her cell phone and made a call. "Is Detective Rafferty in yet?" she asked.

But Anne was already thinking ahead. Mary had given her an idea, when they had all met, earlier in the office. Anne would start working on it as soon as she got back to the office.

She could hardly wait.

Bennie and Judy were meeting with the detectives in a conference room, giving them the reconstructed details of the sighting of Kevin at the gay bar. Mary had left for Anne's neighborhood, to find any witnesses to what happened the previous night. Anne was sitting at her desk with Mel, making the last of her phone calls to set up Plan B. It had taken some doing, but she was pretty sure she could catch Kevin this time, especially now that she knew he was in the vicinity. She would have to tell the others about it, even Bennie, because she'd need their help. And she was trying to play well with others.

The office fell quiet except for the *shh-chunk* of the printer outside Anne's office, spitting out copies to further Plan B. Anne's gaze strayed to her office window, and the smoked glass reflected her latest incarnation. She couldn't run around forever as Uncle Sam, so she'd chopped her hair into a short cut and dyed it Rich Sable, #67 from Herbal Essences. The box promised a "rich, dark brown" but Anne didn't like being a brunette. It made her worry about her credit balances. Eek.

Mel sat upright on a stack of depositions, and Anne smoothed his whiskered cheeks. His green eyes elongated with each stroke, transforming him into the politically incorrect Chinese Cat. It was one of Anne's favorites. She felt mildly fresher, having showered at the office and changed into clean clothes from the firm's closet of spares; a khaki skirt from Banana Republic and a white T-shirt that read I MAKE BOYS CRY. She kept her Blahniks but wore no lipstick, caving in to peer pressure now that she had peers. Mental note: Progress brings its own downside.

Now that Plan B was almost in place, Anne wanted to find Willa's family, to notify them. But where to begin? She took a last sip of cold coffee and logged onto whitepages.com, an online phone directory. She typed in "Willa Hansen" and "Philadelphia" for the city, but the answer came back: **Sorry, no people match the phone search criteria you entered.**

Hmm. It meant Willa was unlisted. Anne felt her energy returning. It wouldn't make sense to search under Hansen, because she didn't know where Willa's family lived. Then she got another idea. She picked up the phone and called her and Willa's gym. A young man answered, and Anne tried the ditzy voice she'd heard on their solicitations: "Hi, I'm Jenny, the new massage therapist, in the spa? I'm the one who does the in-homes?"

"Jenny? I heard about you. It's Marc. Wanna do my in-home?"

"Ha!" Anne forced a giggle. "Hi, Marc. I'm calling because I'm on my way over to one of the member's houses, but I lost the sheet with her phone number and address. Her name is Willa Hansen. Do you have her info?"

"Sure." Keystrokes clicked on the other end of the line. "Willa Hansen lives at 2689 Keeley Street. The phone is unlisted, but she put it on her ap. You want it?"

"Please." He read it off, and Anne took it down. The address was across town around Fitler Square. She knew only because she got her hair cut near there, when she wasn't cutting it herself. "Do you have any other information about her in the computer? Anything in her member profile that would help me? I need to build up my client base."

"Let's see." A few more keystrokes. "Not much, Jenny. Her account shows she's a two-year member, but she never took any of the spinning, yoga, or cardio classes. She didn't fill out the member profile. She checked 'single' on her application, but she didn't sign up for any of the singles nights. She doesn't sound very friendly."

"Not at all." Anne couldn't avoid the irony. It could easily have been her own member profile. "Anything else? Anything at all?"

"Let's see, she rents her house and is self-employed. She didn't fill in the blank for her yearly income, but that was optional. She's a slow pay on the dues. I'm looking at her picture, we have it on file, but I don't remember her at all, and I've been here three years."

"Great. Gotta go."

"Listen, Jenny, I'm having a party on Monday night for the fireworks. If you—"

"Thanks but no." Anne hung up, thinking. 2689 Keeley Street. She had to get over there. Somewhere in the house would be something that would tell her about Willa's family and how she could get in touch with them. She would tell Bennie as soon as she got free. It would make Bennie feel better, but it was having the exact opposite effect on Anne. She was the reason Willa was dead.

"Meow," Mel said loudly. He was walking back and forth across the Chipster depositions, distracting Anne. She would need to memorize the deps for trial. It might do her good to work on the case and not think about Willa for now, or Kevin.

She edged Mel off the deposition of the plaintiff, Beth Dietz. Anne recalled Beth as reserved, with an engineer's superior air despite her mellow smile, hippie clothes, and ratty Birkenstocks. Beth was smart enough to fabricate her case and so was her husband. The courts had become the real-life version of *Who Wants to Be a Millionaire?* And the final answer was, everyone. Anne started reading:

Q: (By Ms. Murphy) Now, Ms. Dietz, you allege in your Complaint that Gil Martin forced you to have sex, during a meeting on September 15th of last year. Please tell me everything that happened in that meeting.

A: (Plaintiff) Well, I came into his office at about 8:15 that night. It was a Friday, and he asked me to sit down on this couch he keeps along the wall. I thought it was kind of weird, since his laptop was on the desk, and you can't work on a web application without a computer.

Q: I see. What happened?

A: I sat down and right away he put his hand on my waist. Near my breast.

Q: How close to your breast?

A: About three inches. On my waist. Then he slid his hand up my shirt and put it on my breast. I pulled away and got his hand out, like pushed it away.

Anne knew not a word of it was true. No way in the world would Gil Martin tussle on his couch with a programmer, with his board in the next room and his funding for a $55 million IPO at stake. Anne had known Gil from law school, and he was always headed for great things; good-looking, witty, with a sharp legal intellect, but a technical mind as well. It didn't come as a surprise when he quit after first year, started Chipster, and grew it into one of the front-runners in web applications. Along the way, he'd married his college sweetheart, Jamie. In the credibility contest that was *Dietz v. Chipster*, Anne knew Gil Martin was telling the truth. This Tuesday, she'd have to prove it. She read on:

Q: Is there anything else that he said, or have you told me everything?
A: He said he thought about me all the time. He said he wanted me to let him make love to me, I had to let him. That I had to let him because he was the boss.
Q: That's exactly what he said?
A: Exactly. I am the boss.

Boss? Anne kept thinking about the word. She couldn't imagine Gil using that word. It was so old-fashioned, she didn't know anyone who used it. Then she remembered. Back in the Mustang, on the stakeout, Bennie had said, *"I am the boss."* It was a fortysomething thing, not a twentysomething thing. What did it mean? Anything? Would it help? She returned to the dep.

Q: And what happened next?
A: He forced me to have sex.
Q: Right there, on the couch, in his office?
(Mr. Dietz stands up.) That's just about enough! She just answered the question, lady! Why do you have to make her say it over and over?
(By Ms. Murphy) Matt, please have Mr. Dietz take his seat and remain silent during the deposition.
(By Mr. Booker) Mr. Dietz, please sit down. Please.
Mr. Dietz: This is absurd! He raped her! He made her fuck him to keep her job! Could it be any clearer? You have to make her spell it out?

(By Mr. Booker) Bill, please!

Mr. Dietz: She loves getting this dirt! She wants to hear every gory detail so she can have a good laugh. Her and that asshole, Martin!

Plaintiff: Bill, please, it's okay. I'm fine.

Anne read it over again, flashing on the way Bill Dietz had morphed from hippie to psycho at the deposition, yelling in the quiet conference room. The businesslike Courier font of the deposition page, almost embossed on thin onion-skin paper, could never convey that he'd jumped enraged to his feet, stretched his full-six-two frame over the conference table and begun pointing, his finger almost poking Anne in the face. She had found it almost laughable when she took the deposition. Why was it bothering her so much now?

Of course. Kevin.

Anne was seeing the ponytailed Bill Dietz with new eyes. Finding abusive men everywhere. Still, she set the deposition aside and went to the accordion file for the Dietz deposition. She had deposed him for a day in connection with his loss-of-consortium claim, which meant that he was suing Chip-

ster.com in tort, for loss of his wife's com-
panionship and sex during the marriage. He
had kept his temper the whole time, answering even the most personal questions with a
cool demeanor. She opened his dep, just to
double-check:

Q: (By Ms. Murphy) Where are you employed at the current time?
A: I work at Chipster.com, a web applica-
   tions company.
Q: In what capacity?
A: I write code for various web applica-
   tions. I specialize in Cold Fusion, a
   computer language.
Q: How long have you been employed at
   Chipster?
A: Five years, since its inception. I was
   one of the handful of programmers
   who were there when Gil Martin
   started the company. It was just six of
   us, in his garage.
Q: And as such—I'm jumping ahead
   here—did you receive certain stock
   options, as part of salary?
A: No, I did not.
Q: Did any of the other programmers receive such stock options?

A: Three did. Basically, ones that Gil knew from his college days. He tends to go with people he knows. I didn't know him then, and neither did another guy, so we were on the outside.

Anne didn't like the sound of it. It read as if Dietz were resentful, which he hadn't seemed at the time, when he had merely stated it as a matter of fact. But there had to be resentment there; those stock options would make its founders millionaires when Chipster went public. Did it matter? Did it have anything to do with the bogus case for sexual harassment? Did it motivate it? Anne hadn't focused on Dietz before because his claim was derivative, frankly, bullshit. She'd had it dismissed under Third Circuit law, but she had taken his deposition before the dismissal, for free discovery. She thumbed through Dietz's deposition, to the core of the claim:

Q: (By Ms. Murphy) Now, Mr. Dietz, you allege that as a result of the sexual harassment of your wife, Beth, you and she experienced certain difficulties

with respect to intimacy in your marriage, is that right?

A: Yes.

Q: When did they begin?

A: When the harassment began. On September 15th.

Q: And how long did it last?

A: We are just now healing. The effects of
sexual harassment are like those of
rape. It takes the victim time to re-
cover, and to trust men again. And
Beth feels guilty, even though she
shouldn't, for what happened.

Q: And what exactly were the difficulties
in your marriage, caused by the alleged sexual harassment?

A: Beth withdrew from me. She kept
more to herself and became de-
pressed. She slept poorly, she lost
weight. She spent more time on-line,
four or six hours at nights and on the
weekends. She would be in the chat
rooms, role-playing or playing Internet
games, silly games. Popcap.com and
the like.

Q: Specifically, how did the alleged sexual harassment affect your sex life?

A: She became uninterested in sex, and the frequency of intercourse went from once a week to less than that a month. It became unsatisfying. For both of us.

Anne read the rest of the dep, but it didn't tell her anything more about Bill Dietz. But that wasn't all she had on him. She had served him with interrogatories and a document subpoena, routine in employment cases. She reached for that folder, opened it, and skimmed his answers to interrogatories. The opening questions were background, and her gaze fell on the third interrogatory:

HAVE YOU EVER BEEN CONVICTED OF A CRIME?
NO.

The veracity of the answers was attested to by Dietz's signature on the next page, but he wouldn't be the first person who'd lied in his interrogatory answers. He'd obviously lost control at the dep, almost violently. Had it happened before? Anne's gut told her it had, and she set the interrogatories aside, turned to her computer, and logged onto the

Internet, clicking onto one of the myriad snooper websites. Onto the screen popped a banner:

Check court records for liens, finances, and criminal convictions!

She typed in the name "William Dietz." It didn't take two seconds to get an answer:

Your search has revealed 3680 persons named William Dietz with criminal convictions.

Anne wasn't surprised. It was a common name. She couldn't begin to read each one, it would take until Tuesday. She narrowed the search geographically, to Pennsylvania. As far as she knew, Bill Dietz had been living here at least in the recent past. He had worked at Chipster for less than five years.

Your search has revealed 427 persons named William Dietz with criminal convictions.

Hoo boy. Anne checked her watch. 5:10. It was getting late. Still, what was the point? She had so much to do, and this was un-doubtedly a detour. She didn't even know why she was following up. So what if Dietz was violent? So what if he had a criminal record? So what if he only pretended to be a sensitive ponytail? Still. Anne flashed on the scene in the dep, on the rage in Dietz's eyes. She moved the computer mouse over the first five listings in blue, and clicked.

Eighty-two listings later, Bill Dietz still hadn't been convicted. Anne rubbed her eyes. This was stupid. She wasn't getting anywhere. She checked her watch. 6:05. Was Bennie still in with the cops? What was taking so long? Anne stretched, tense and frustrated. She was about to take a break when the door to her office opened a crack.

Bennie stuck her face inside the open door, her forehead creased with anxiety. "You're wanted in conference room D. Now."

"The cops? Is there a problem?"

"No, the cops are in C." Bennie snuck inside and shut the door behind her like a co-conspirator. "What's worse than the cops?"

"Brown hair."

"Think money."

"My Visa bill."

"Think like a lawyer, not a woman," Bennie said, but Anne was already on her mules.

12

"What's going on?"

"Gil Martin's here," Bennie answered. "Carrier's in with him."

"*What?* Gil? Here? Why?"

"Turns out that since you got killed, he's been having doubts about me trying *Chipster.* He came here to fire us. He seems to think I'm not up to it."

Anne almost laughed. She had tried ten cases to Bennie's thousand, and they had been in L.A., where even O.J. got off. "So, what did you tell him?"

"That he shouldn't worry, that I was up to speed. That we function as a team, a family."

"The family stuff never works," Anne said without thinking, and Bennie blinked, hurt.

"It doesn't?"

"All companies say it. It's never true."

"It's true for me. I mean it."

"Well, I believe it, but they don't. Other people don't."

Bennie still looked hurt.

"Okay, it depends on who says it."

"Well, anyway, young Gil ain't buying. We're toast. He's already contacted Crawford, Wilson, & Ryan. He knows people there, and he's also looking at Ballard, Spahr. First-rate firms. They're running conflicts check as we speak, and we both know what they'll say."

"What do you think I should do?"

"He's your client, make your decision," Bennie answered without rancor. "What do you wanna do?"

"I didn't even want *you* to try this case. You think I'll lose it to someone who's not even family?" Anne smiled, and so did Bennie. "No question. I'll tell him I'm alive. Swear him to secrecy. I want to keep this representation."

"I understand, but I'm not interested in killing you to save a client. Even if it wasn't Kevin who killed Willa, we know now that he's in the vicinity. Can you trust Gil to keep it quiet, that you're alive?"

"He'll keep it quiet."

"Okay. But I go first, to keep the cops in C." Bennie opened the door narrowly and checked the hallway. "Your client's in D."

"Thanks. By the way, I got Willa's address."

"Good job." Bennie slipped out the door, and Anne waited a minute, then left and hurried down the hall. She whizzed past the Deer Park cooler, watercolors of City Hall's Victorian facade, and endless rowing sequences, all of which looked like a skinny guy in a rowboat wearing a bad tank top. She reached conference room D, opened the door, and slipped inside quickly, closing it behind her.

Gil was standing with Judy and he was well dressed in a navy-blue blazer, pressed khakis, and Gucci loafers. His boyish face was lightly tanned, albeit showing signs of IPO strain.

"Hello, Gil. It's me, Anne," she said and looked at him directly. She didn't want to play with his emotions, and he seemed not to recognize her for a moment. His forehead knit and his sharp, blue-green eyes looked confused. He ran a quick hand through shiny brown hair, which fell expensively back into place. Anne managed an encouraging smile. "It's really me, Gil. I'm not dead. I'm alive. It's a mistake."

Gil looked like he wanted to laugh, but it

turned to something like a hiccup. "Is this a joke?"

"Maybe you should sit down." Anne gestured to the modern, tall-backed chair on the other side of the table, but Gil was already sinking into it, all six feet of him, slowly collapsing from the knees, like a house imploded from its foundation. He couldn't take his eyes from Anne's face, and she had to set him straight. "Gil, I'm sorry, it's all a misunderstanding. I mean, I wasn't killed last night, another woman was. Not me."

Gil looked uncertain, his smile cautious. "You're really Anne Murphy? Then tell me something only you would know, from first year."

"Okay, we met the first day of Contracts class, sitting next to each other alphabetically. Martin and Murphy. I memorized offer and acceptance, and you improved Game Boy."

"Ha!" Gil laughed softly, almost coming around. "It's you? I can't believe it. But . . . in the news, on TV, they said—"

"They were wrong. It's all wrong. The woman who was killed was taking care of my cat. The cops don't know I'm really alive.

Only we do. Now you. And it has to stay that way." Anne reached for the pitcher of water they always kept on the table, but it was off for the holiday weekend. Only the glasses remained, turned upside down on a pebbled paper towel. "You want something to drink?"

"Got scotch?" He smiled, and Anne did, too. Next to him, Judy rose without being asked and headed for the conference room door, but Gil was scrutinizing Anne so intently, she wasn't sure he noticed. She had to bring him down to earth, fast. She wasn't about to lose this representation. "Gil, the cops know who killed my cat-sitter and they're in the conference room right now, planning how to get him. They're going to arrest him any day, but all of this is beside the point." She leaned across the table, trying to engage him, and once they locked eyes, she held him. "I know this is a lot to digest, all at once. But what matters to me and to you is Chipster, and I intend to defend you and your company on Tuesday. I know the facts, I know the case inside out. You can't switch counsel now. You don't need to."

"You're really alive?" Gil kept raking his sandy hair with his fingers. "This is so . . . odd."

"On Tuesday, we'll tell the cops and pick a jury. But you have to swear to keep this secret for the weekend. Even from Jamie, okay? From everybody."

"I just can't get used to it. It's so fucking odd."

"Tell me about it." Anne had to defuse the situation. There was business to conduct. "I know who we want on the jury, I've prepared Beth's cross, because she'll be their first witness. In fact, I was just rereading the deps."

"But where *were* you, last night?"

"I went away to prepare for the case, in quiet. You know better than I do how the city gets on the Fourth. I wanted to think."

"And you didn't tell anybody? You didn't tell me?" Gil frowned. "What if I had to talk to you?"

"I didn't think you would, and you didn't." Anne flushed defensively. She didn't understand why the questions. Maybe it was the initial shock. "Besides, I remembered you told me you'd be at a dinner party last night, in the suburbs."

"I did. I was. I remember. You know what's really weird?" Gil laughed suddenly. "We sent you flowers! Jamie picked them out!

Lilies, a dozen. She felt so bad, when she heard about you. We saw it on TV. Did I say that already?" He laughed again, his discomfort plain, and Anne reached out impulsively to pat his hand.

"I'm sorry that you were upset, and Jamie." Jamie was an at-home mother, and the very definition of a softhearted woman.

"You say the cops know who did it?"

"Yes. But here's a question, and I know it sounds strange. In your own words, what is Bennie's relationship to me?"

Gil frowned. "Who?"

"Bennie Rosato."

"No, I mean, who did it? Who killed you— I mean, this other woman? She was in your house?" Gil seemed concerned, but Anne didn't want to get into this. She wanted him to stay on track.

"It's a long story and it's not germane to the case."

"But is the killer still out there? I mean, walking the streets?"

"Gil, forget it. The cops are working on it. They're professionals. Leave it to them."

"Ha! Right. Then how come they haven't figured out that you're not only alive, you're right across the hall?" Gil laughed, but it stopped when the door opened and Judy entered, closing the door behind her and bearing a clear plastic pitcher of water. She set it down and reached for a glass, which she filled with a *glug glug glug* and handed to Gil. Anne thanked her because Gil didn't, and made a mental note of the change in Judy. The flyer they'd made together had been a peace treaty. Okay, they weren't exchanging recipes, but at least they weren't mud wrestling.

Gil drank thirstily while Anne continued. "I don't want you to think for a second that we're not on top of this case, because we are. Mary DiNunzio, whom you met, covered today's dep beautifully, and Judy here has been helping out a great deal. Bennie knows more about trying a case, *any* case, than I ever will. You and Chipster are already in excellent hands. There's no reason to go anywhere else. So call off Ballard and Crawford. Tell 'em to sit back and watch how it's done." Anne smiled, which seemed to coax a genuine grin from Gil.

"I didn't really want to fire your law firm. You know that." He set down his glass. "I mean, I came to you for good reasons. We've known each other a long time, and you were always so"—he seemed to fumble for the word—"smart. Really smart."

"Thank you."

"I knew you'd work your ass off for me, and frankly, I wanted a woman to represent me. I thought it would help with the jury, on a sexual harassment case." Gil seemed to be talking aloud to himself, trying to get his bearings. "Also, you're so attractive, I knew you would get the jury's attention. And the media's."

"All of these reasons still pertain." Anne nodded, vaguely aware that Judy was bristling beside her. *He never would have hired her if she hadn't looked the way she did.* Well, here was proof positive. Anne hoped she was happy.

"I mean, I was trying to be aggressive in the company's defense. If you're going to hire a woman, hire an all-woman firm, right?" Gil spread his palms. "Do it in a big way."

"Of course. And you did." Though Gil had never articulated his rationale this fully, Anne wasn't stupid. He'd used the publicity to his advantage; he'd been accused of sexual harassment and had managed to come out looking like a feminist champion. But none of it worked, unless Anne won a jury verdict. "So let's talk about the case a minute. Answer my question. What is Bennie's relationship to me?"

Beside her, Judy looked nonplussed, and Gil shrugged. "Bennie Rosato? She owns the law firm, doesn't she?"

"Yes, but what do you call the person who owns the business?"

"Like me? The owner, I guess."

"Not 'the boss'?"

"I never say that. It's weird. Why?"

Of course. "Just a question. Now that you've gotten over the shock of me still drawing breath, how else can I help you? Is there anything you want to talk about? Has the media been driving you nuts?"

"This is kind of strange, don't you think?" Gil looked with renewed doubt from Anne to Judy and back again. "You're just going to pretend that this isn't happening? That some woman didn't get murdered? That this murderer, whoever he is, isn't out there?"

Anne felt stung. "Gil, I'm not pretending anything. I am simply handling both. Doing both. Multi-tasking."

"It's my company, Anne. My reputation." Gil's expression darkened. "The mutual funds are watching, the VC guys. I'm risking everything here. I have to win, I've guaranteed it to my Board. I can't go forward with less than a hundred percent from you."

"I understand that, and you have it."

"You're ready to try this case, even with this murder thing hanging over your head? It's a huge distraction, and now you're telling me you have to hide from the police—"

"It'll be resolved by the time of trial, Gil."

"If not?"

"That's not possible." Anne knew she was losing him, watching him edge backward on the seat of his chair.

"I don't know," he said after a pause. "I just don't know. It's good that you're alive—great, obviously—but it's strange. I can't let this get personal. It's business."

"Then think about your business, Gil," Judy interrupted, and Gil's head swiveled to her at the sharpness of her tone.

"What do you mean?" he asked.

"The whole world knows that Anne Murphy of the all-woman firm of Rosato & Associates represents you. They also know that Anne was brutally murdered last night. How will it look if you fire the girls when they're down? How's that gonna look to everyone, to the press, and to your potential stockholders? Or to the women who end up on your jury?"

Gil paused. "I can handle the press and the shareholders, and my lawyer can ask the jurors about that when we're picking them. He'll just make sure the ones who think like that stay off the jury."

"No, you can't," Judy said. "It's not a criminal case, where the jury gets vigorously screened for impartiality. Voir dire in a civil case is routine, especially in Judge Hoffmeier's courtroom. You came to us because we're women and it may be the reason you're stuck with us."

Gil's eyes glittered. "That's blackmail."

"That's litigation."

"Wait a minute," Anne broke in before it came to fisticuffs. "Listen, Gil. This is all news to you, my being alive, my trying the case, and it's a surprise. So why don't you sleep on it and we'll talk again tomorrow?"

"I don't know."

"Give me a day. You've known me a long time. I've done good work for Chipster, won almost every motion. We have them where we want them. If you want to fire me Sunday, you can. I'll turn over the files on the spot."

"Prudence is the better course," Judy added, as if she'd been a Republican all her life. In red clogs.

Gil looked from one lawyer to the other, his expression impassive. "I don't know."

"Don't decide now."

"There's one thing, Anne." Gil rose to go, smoothing out his khakis. "I tell Jamie everything. She's been with me every step of the way, from the beginning, even through the humiliation of this case. I'd like to discuss this with her, if I'm waiting a day. I trust her to keep anything confidential."

"No," Anne answered firmly. "Fire me now if you will, but don't tell another living soul."

Gil gave the table a brief knock. "Okay then, I'll call you tomorrow at nine."

"Try after my memorial service."

"Memorial service?" Gil asked, and even Judy looked over in surprise.

It was Plan B. Anne was throwing herself a memorial service, and she knew Kevin would find a way to be there. Then they could catch him, once and for all. "Yes, tomorrow at noon the office is holding a memorial service for me, at the Chestnut Club. It would be great if you could come."

Gil snorted. "You want me to come to a memorial service and pretend you're dead?"

"I'm sorry, it can't be helped. You can't stay away. The media will be there."

"Jesus, Anne." He walked around the conference table to the door, where he stopped. "Look, I'm not unsympathetic. I know you care about the case. But my priority is my company."

"Leave that to me," Anne said and pretended not to mind when Gil opened the door and closed it abruptly behind him.

As soon as the women were alone, Judy's eyes flared with outrage. "I hate that asshole!"

"Why?"

"Aren't you offended by what he said? That he hired you because you're a woman?"

Here we go. "Judy, I'm not naive. Companies hire black lawyers to represent them in race discrimination cases. Rapists hire women to represent them in rape cases. Everybody hires older men when they want authority."

"I know that." Judy raised her voice. "The question is, doesn't it offend you? It does me, even though I know it happens."

Go for it. Anne braced herself. "But that's

not what's really bothering you, is it? Because that's not exactly what Gil said. He said he hired me because I'm a pretty woman. Frankly, he wouldn't have hired me if I were an ugly woman, right?"

"Right." Judy reddened slightly.

"And we both knew that, you and me." Anne leaned over, leveling with her. "But you know what? It doesn't bother me, because I find it ironic. In my mind, I know how bogus my beauty—my alleged beauty—is."

"Bogus? What are you talking about? You're perfect! Your face, your body, even in your new haircut. Men fall at your feet. You look like a supermodel."

"I was born with a cleft lip, a unilateral cleft lip."

Judy looked like she wasn't sure exactly what that meant, and Anne sensed it would do her good to explain it, to say it out loud. She never had before, outside of a doctor's office. It was her dirty little secret. That, and the fact that she'd been rejected twice for an American Express card.

"My lip, right here"—Anne pointed to the left of center—"was split halfway up to my nose, at birth. It's the most common birth defect, and my case was relatively mild because the palate wasn't cleft, just the lip. The vermilion, the surrounding tissue, to be exact."

"Jeez."

"Exactly. My mother, well let's just say, didn't have the best of reactions. She was a pretty woman and she wanted a pretty baby. One she could make into a movie star." Anne refused to sound like a victim, so she shortened the story. "I didn't get the surgeries I needed—lip, palate, even gum—until I was past ten. It took seven operations to get me to look like this, and by the end I felt like a science project. So when something comes to me now because of the way I look, I just laugh inside."

"It must have been awful." Judy swallowed hard, and Anne shrugged.

"I can't take it back, my prettiness or my ugliness, and I wouldn't. I just know that the world changed when I got pretty, and you're right, lots of unfair advantages came to me. Men, clients. The manager at Hertz saves me a Mustang. The boy at the video store sets aside the new releases. Security guards at the courthouse run interference for me. I know how well I'm treated now, because I saw the difference. I'm a walking 'before' and 'after' picture. And I used to feel the unfairness, the resentment, and the jealousy. Like you do."

Judy's light eyebrows slanted unhappily.

"So I don't begrudge you your feelings, and you don't have to hide them from me. I feel more like you than me." The conference room fell so quiet, Anne could hear the rasp in her own voice. She had never spoken so intimately to anyone before, but she had to clear the air. "And I have a confession to make. I overheard you this morning, in my house, but it didn't come as a surprise. I know you don't like me. No women like me. I can't make a girlfriend at gunpoint."

Judy emitted a dry laugh.

"I just hope that you give me a chance, because now you know better. When you think of the clients, the men, the new DVDs, and the perks that my looks bring me, think of the rest, too. Like Kevin Satorno, who's trying to kill me. Beauty isn't a blessing, Judy, take it from me. It's a curse."

Just then the door to the conference room opened. It was Bennie, bristling with excitement. "Ladies, we're outta here. I just got a call from Mary."

"What about?" Anne asked.

"Your murder. Let's go."

13

Anne, in her white baseball cap and black Oakleys, Bennie, and Mary stood in the bright but tiny third-floor kitchenette. It had been converted from a corner of a bedroom by installation of a dorm-sized Kenmore fridge, a two-burner electric stove, and a baby stainless-steel sink. It smelled pleasantly of Lysol and home fries but was oppressively hot, despite the lateness of the day. A cheap plastic Duracraft fan oscillated on a countertop, to no effect.

Mary DiNunzio sat at the kitchen table across from Mrs. Letitia Brown, holding her hand. "Mrs. Brown, these are my associates, and they want to hear what you told me. About what you saw last night. Do you mind repeating it all?"

"Thas' no problem, I like some ladies visitin'." Mrs. Brown was seventy-seven years old, her black skin oddly graying and her eyes cloudy behind trifocals. Her glasses pressed into cheeks slackened by time, draped like velvety stage curtains around a steady smile. Gray hair sprang in thinning coils from her scalp, and she wore a flowered housedress with black plastic slip-ons. Anne knew she'd end up in shoes like that and she was actually looking forward to it. Mental note: Perspective sneaks up on everyone, in time.

Mary was asking, "So tell me again, what did you see last night, on the street?"

"I seen people, evabody playin, partyin'. I seen people goin' out, goin' to the Parkway, to the fireworks, the whole day people be comin' an' goin'. Plenty to see." Mrs. Brown waved a shaky hand toward the window over the kitchen table, of rickety pressboard. Thin Marcal napkins had been weighted down with heavy cut-glass salt-and-pepper shakers, so they wouldn't blow away in the breeze from the screen, clearly an abundance of caution. "Lots to see out this winda, better than the TV. In the day, I look at my stories, then I come over and look out the winda."

"And what about the house I asked you about? Number 2257."

Mrs. Brown wet her lips. Fine lines around

them led to a small, parched mouth. "I seen everythin' las' night, at the house you talkin' 'bout."

"Which house? Show us."

"That one, 2257. My eyes ain't that bad, I see the number." Mrs. Brown raised an arm and pointed to the window, and Anne followed her crooked finger just to make sure. It was Anne's own doorstep, just two doors down, on the same side of the street. Mrs. Brown's third-floor vantage point gave her a good, if parallax, view of anyone who came to Anne's door. Though Anne had never seen Mrs. Brown, Mrs. Brown had undoubtedly seen her.

"And what were you doing, last night?" Mary's voice was soft and even, uncannily matching the tone and cadence of Mrs. Brown.

"What I always doin', settin' here. Settin' here and lookin' at muh papers and muh pitchers and muh books." Mrs. Brown gestured happily to a lineup of children's school photographs, all girls with their hair neatly braided, and one older boy in cornrows and an Allen Iverson jersey. "These muh grandbabies."

"They're so cute."

"And this here's muh books." She reached for a stack of crossword-puzzle books and opened one only with difficulty. Printed on the soft paper was a large-size crossword puzzle, completed in shaky ballpoint. Anne eyeballed ten down "three letters for place to sleep." The blocks were filled not by BED but by QOP. She scanned the entire puzzle. Each block had been neatly filled with a letter, written in a jittery hand, but none of the letters formed words.

Mary looked back at Anne. "Her daughter and son-in-law live downstairs, with their two kids. They were out last night and weren't here when the cops canvassed. Mrs. Brown stayed home. She was upstairs the whole time, but the cops didn't know it."

Anne nodded. They had met the son-in-law downstairs. A chilly young man who evidently didn't like his mother-in-law enough to teach her to read, or even to come upstairs when a group of lawyers came to call. Plus they had central air downstairs, but only a single fan on the whole third floor. How could someone leave her mother up here like this?

"Go ahead, Mrs. Brown," Mary said, encouraging the woman with a nod.

"I was settin', lookin', an my daughter an my son-in-law, they all went out. An there was fireworks, above the roof. I seen the ones that made it high enough. Then there was a big noise, real big."

"Not firecrackers?"

"No. Gunshots."

"How do you know that?"

"I *know*. Mm-mm."

"Did you see somebody shoot the gun?" Mary asked.

"No, I was dozin' I think, jes a little, and my eyes, they come open"—Mrs. Brown opened her hands in front of her eyes, and Anne pictured her drowsy, sitting at the table on a stifling summer night—"and out I look and I seen that man."

"What man? Tell us everything you saw then."

"Young, pretty, white. Blond hair. His face all lit up from the house, from inside the house. 2257. I seen him and he let go of the gun, he sure did."

Anne's mind raced. *It was Kevin.*

"And God strike me if he wasn't cryin', cryin' like a newborn baby, like his heart was gonna break in two, and then he run, he run down the street, all the way, and I couldn't see him no more."

Anne couldn't breathe for a moment. She had always known it was Kevin, but this made it so real. At least Bennie would be fully convinced now.

"I seen that poor girl's feet, lyin inna door. She was wearin' sneakers and they were shakin', shakin'! Then all of a sudden, they stopped." Mrs. Brown's eyes welled up, and Mary gave her wrinkled hand a squeeze.

"If I showed you a picture of this man with the gun, could you say if it was him or not?" Mary reached into her purse for the red flyer, but Bennie stopped her with a hand on her shoulder.

"Don't do that. I don't want to take a chance of screwing up any photo array the cops show her. We got what we need."

Mary slid the red flyer back into her purse. "Mrs. Brown, thank you for talking to us. You've helped us very much. We want to call the police now. Will you tell them what you told us? They want to catch this man and put him in jail."

"Surely, I will."

Bennie was already flipping open her cell

phone. "Detective Rafferty, please, it's Bennie Rosato," she said, and she didn't have to wait long. "I'm here with a witness to Anne Murphy's murder, and she has described Kevin Satorno to a T. One of the neighbors. You want to pick up or shall we deliver?" Bennie paused. "Fine. See you at 2253 Waltin Street in ten minutes." She snapped the phone closed and turned to Judy. "Carrier, why don't you take our new messenger to the car and keep her company."

"Got it." Judy thanked Mrs. Brown and started to leave.

But something kept Anne rooted to the spot. Something bothered her about leaving the old woman alone. Something about a daughter who would desert her mother like this. Then she realized that for all she knew, her own mother was sitting in a stifling room on somebody's third floor, passing the time until she died.

"Whatsa matter, child?" Mrs. Brown asked, her voice kind, and she eyed Anne even through her clumsy disguise. Sunglasses, baseball cap, or lipstick, Anne had been hiding something as long as she could remember.

Everything. "Nothing, thanks," Anne answered.

She followed Judy through the remaining room on the floor, Mrs. Brown's bedroom, scented faintly of drugstore talc. It contained a saggy double bed covered by a thin chenille spread so neat that its worn white tufts lined up like monuments in a military cemetery. Over the bed hung a large wooden crucifix, and on the nightstand a doily runner, a small fake-Tiffany lamp, a yellowed Westclox alarm clock, and a worn Bible that left Anne with a thickness in her throat.

She hit the stairwell full of emotion she couldn't begin to sort out, much less express, exacerbated by the annoying *clop-clopping* of Judy's wooden clogs on the uncarpeted stair. By the time they reached the second floor, then descended to the first, which was air-conditioned and full of modern smells, Anne couldn't say goodbye to the son-in-law because she wanted to throttle him, even with the police on the way. She headed for the front door, opened it wide, and came face-to-face with a man about her age, standing on the front stoop, about to knock.

"Hello!" the man said, and grinned in a toothy way. He wore a tan Australian bush hat with one side pinned up, and a white Weezer T-shirt with loose jeans and black Teva sandals.

"Uh, hello," Anne replied, startled.

"I'm Angus Connolly. Sorry to disturb your holiday, but I was wondering if you've seen this man." He reached into his back pocket and handed Anne her own red flyer. "His name is Kevin Satorno."

Anne was so shocked she couldn't find her voice. Not even her inner voice.

"I was just wondering if you've seen this man. He's a suspect in the murder of one of your neighbors down the block, last night. Just two doors away." The man turned and pointed at Anne's house.

"Who *are* you?"

"I'm a reporter. With *City Beat*."

"*City Beat*?" Anne eyed him for a press pass but found none. "I've never heard of it."

"We're a free newspaper, and I'm trying to make a name for myself, me and my friends. We're investigating this murder and asking all the neighbors if they saw this man last night." He frowned. "Wait a minute, you do live here, don't you?"

"No, she doesn't," Judy answered, coming up behind Anne. "And she hasn't seen that man. But I know someone who has. She's right upstairs and she's about to tell her story to the cops, who will be here any minute. Looks like you got the scoop, dude."

"For real?" The man climbed the stoop, and at the same moment, Anne felt Judy's knuckle in the small of her back, nudging her out of harm's way.

"Go right upstairs," Judy continued. "Bennie Rosato's there, too. She'll answer any questions you have."

"Bennie Rosato? *The* Bennie Rosato? Oh my God!" The wanna-be reporter whipped a cell phone from the back pocket of his jeans. "I need a photographer fast," he was saying into it when he hustled inside the house.

"Go, go, go, girl!" Judy whispered, falling into step beside Anne, pushing her forward by her elbow. "You want the cops *and* the press to recognize you?"

"No, of course not," Anne said, but her heart felt so full. *What's the matter with me? Why am I acting like such a loser?* Tears came to her eyes, and fatigue washed over her. Maybe it was all catching up to her at once. She let Judy lead her down the street, hurrying her along, past her own house and the cellophane-wrapped bouquets on her front stoop. She looked over and stopped at the sight of one of them. A bouquet of daisies, wrapped by a white ribbon. It hadn't been there before. She bent down and picked it up.

"What are you doing?" Judy asked, between gritted teeth.

A couple passing by were scowling at Anne, their disapproval undisguised, but she couldn't speak. She stared down at the daisy bouquet. A pink card attached to it had been typed, as if the flower order had been phoned in. It read simply:

Love, Mom.

14

Bennie steered the Mustang through the city traffic, keeping an eye on the rearview mirror. By now Anne had learned enough about Bennie to know it wasn't the traffic that had her worried. Judy kept glancing back at her, and Mary was permanently affixed to her right hand.

"Don't worry, everybody, I'm fine," Anne said, though she sat in the backseat clutching her mother's daisies like a baby blanket. Mental note: You can know you're acting like a dope and still not be able to stop it.

"There's really nothing to worry about," Mary said, squeezing her hand from the seat next to her. "We couldn't have planned it this well. The cops will get Kevin's ID from Mrs. Brown, and the news will run the story tonight. It's probably all over the web already. Everybody in the city will be looking for Kevin Satorno."

"Yeah, Anne." Judy twisted around in the

front seat, the last of the day's light filtering through her sunny hair, her bandanna blowing in the wind. "The heat will be on him. They'll have Kevin in custody in time for us to take a field trip to the fireworks."

The Mustang cruised forward to a red light, and Bennie braked. "Only problem is, it may discourage him from showing up at the memorial service, if he's still a fugitive."

"He'll be there," Anne said, with absolute certainty. They were getting closer to catching Kevin, and Bennie's reaction to Plan B had been much better than she had expected, though she wasn't sure why. "He'll find a way to be there."

The Mustang idled in traffic, and Bennie tapped her finger on the wheel. "Let's think about that. How will he do it? Talk to me, Murphy. It was your idea."

"Well, I used to think he'd come as a guest, a mourner in some half-assed disguise, but now I'm beginning to wonder." Anne wondered if Bennie was just trying to engage her, but played along because it was such a nice thing to do. "Not with the cops and every reporter in the city, looking to make his mark. I'm thinking now he might try to come in another way."

"Like what?" Judy asked.

"I don't know. Maybe as staff of some kind?"

"Secret agent stuff." Judy smiled. "Yowza!"

"So, what's at a memorial service, ladies? Let's brainstorm." Bennie gave the car some gas. "We're having it at the Chestnut Club, in town. What staff will be there? Any?"

"Only the head lady, because it's closed." Anne had made the arrangements for her memorial service, posing on the telephone as a cousin from California. The Chestnut was one of the oldest eating clubs in Philadelphia, with two stories of dining rooms and waiters in white jackets with time-warp Nehru collars. "They subcontract out the catering. The lack of house staff will make it easier for Kevin."

Mary frowned. "How?"

"Well, Kevin is smart. It's not beyond him to anticipate that my firm would hold a memorial service of some kind, especially after you offered the reward. I took out ads in the Sunday papers, announcing the service, open to the public. He's got to see one of them and find out where it is, then maybe he'll get hired by the caterer or something."

"Really." Mary sounded almost respectful, and Anne knew the feeling.

"I know. My stalker is a genius."

"There'll be flowers," Judy offered, thinking aloud. "He might come as a flower delivery guy."

It sent a chill through Anne. "Very possible. Kevin's a red-roses kind of psycho. Sent them to me every day, a single one."

The Mustang accelerated down Race Street. "Here's how it'll go down," Bennie said, wind blowing blond tendrils into her eyes. "I'll backstop everybody, but we all need our own jobs. Carrier, you quiz the flower delivery guys. DiNunzio, you deal with the press. Don't let them in the service, but check their IDs anyway. Satorno may use it as a way to get close."

Mary nodded. "Got it."

"Thanks," Anne said, touched by their willingness to help. "I can cover food and drink. The kitchen staff is from Custom Catering. They were the only ones not booked this weekend."

"I'll help with the food," Judy chirped, and Mary laughed.

"There's a surprise."

Bennie glanced over. "Carrier, make sure

you get a list of the kitchen staff. Does that cover everyone?"

Anne tried to picture it. "Folding chairs, and a lectern. Microphones. I rented them all from a caterer the club uses. I'll check chair guys, too."

"Okay, that's it, I think." Bennie turned left onto Broad Street and steered south. The parade had gone but the street was still full of partiers, drinking beer and hanging out, waiting for dusk and the laser show. "The cops will be there, and I'll hire security. Rent-a-muscle guys, and we'll have Herb, too."

Anne cringed. "In case our breasts need protecting."

"Be nice, Murphy. He knows his stuff, and he was very upset when your chest passed on." Bennie laughed. "Ladies, it's almost dark and you're all ordered home to bed. Di-Nunzio, I'm dropping you off first, then Carrier. Murphy, you're staying with me tonight. You'll be safe at my house."

Anne looked up in surprise. She hadn't planned that far ahead. She couldn't very well turn Bennie down. She knew from the movies that sleepovers were a big deal with girlfriends. But she thought of Mel, alone in the office, and then, of Matt. She wished she could tell him she was alive. She wondered what kind of a night he'd be having.

"Agreed, Murphy?" It was Bennie, jolting Anne from her thoughts.

"Sure, yes. Thanks. But we have a stop to make first."

"My thoughts exactly." Bennie checked the rearview. "You're not too tired? You've had a helluva day."

"Not worse than hers," Anne said, looking out the window, as night came on.

Judy looked at Bennie, confused. "What are you guys talking about? Where are you going?"

Anne let Bennie answer. It hurt too much to say.

Fitler Square was one of Philadelphia's historic pocket-parks, a square block limned by privet hedge and wrought-iron fence, with tasteful wooden benches around a center fountain and newly refurbished brickwork underfoot. Fitler Square didn't get half the attention of Rittenhouse Square, which was roughly in the same city neighborhood, but Anne found Fitler more charming. It was out of the way of the business district, at Twenty-sixth and Pine, and any time she had gone past it in a cab, it was full of moms pushing strollers and toddlers dropping Cheerios or scribbling sidewalk pictures with chubby pastel chalks.

But the neighborhood, Willa's neighborhood, had been changed for her, too, and tonight the scene was different and felt strange. Fitler Square was almost empty, and the black Victorian gaslights that anchored the park's four corners flickered in the darkness, barely illuminating a couple on one of the benches, their arms around each other. The Mustang cruised around the square, looking for a space, and headed to Keeley Street. Anne edged forward on her seat as they rounded the block and pulled into a space at the end of the row.

Bennie parked and shut off the engine. "Got the purse?"

"Yes," she answered, taking Willa's purse from the seat between them. It was a striped cloth sack from Guatemala, and she had retrieved the purse from a locker at the gym, where Willa had left it last night. A quick check inside revealed that it contained no wallet. Anne figured that Willa, like her, didn't bring her wallet to the gym, because the lockers didn't lock. The little bag held only keys, sunglasses, and a bruised organic apple, and Anne felt funny carrying it as she fell in step with the taller Bennie and walked to Willa's house.

The night air was punctuated with the popping of distant fireworks, and the short heels of Anne's mules dragged on the sidewalk. Fatigue and emotion were catching up with her, but she set both aside. She owed this to Willa. It was awful that it had taken her all day to get here. She had to find Willa's family before the day was over, and tell them the worst news of their lives.

They passed 2685, then 2687. The rowhouses on the skinny back-street reminded Anne of Fairmount and were of the same colonial vintage; a lineup of attached brick homes, two-stories high and with a door flanked by two front windows, distinguished by the paint color of their shutters or the occasional clay flowerpot on the step. Anne's stomach tensed when they reached 2689. She opened Willa's purse for the keys, feeling terribly like they were invading the dead woman's privacy. Going into her purse. Entering her home.

"You want to wait outside?" Bennie asked, but Anne shook her head.

"No, thanks. I'm the one who owes her."

"Don't think about it that way." Bennie's tone softened, though Anne couldn't make out her expression in the dark. The only streetlamp was down the block. It would have been what Anne's own street looked like last night, when Willa opened *her* front door.

Anne fished for Willa's keys and inserted them in the lock until she found the one that clicked. She opened Willa's front door and stepped into the darkness. *Please God don't let there be an entrance hall.* A light went on suddenly, and she turned.

"You sure you're okay?" Bennie was standing behind her, one hand on a switch on the wall, and the other closing the door behind them with a solid *click*.

"I'm fine." Anne turned back and looked around. There was no entrance hall, and the light switch illuminated a white parchment sphere with red Chinese characters which hung over the small living room. But this was like no living room Anne had ever seen. Every inch of wall space was covered with a drawing. Skilled, detailed charcoal cityscapes had been tacked up, cheek by jowl, floor to ceiling. Sketches of storefronts in the Italian Market. Skyscrapers in the business district. The concrete lace of an Expressway interchange. The lights on the boathouses along the Schuylkill River.

"Wow," Bennie said quietly. "Look at these drawings. There must be hundreds."

"She was so talented." Anne tasted bitterness in her mouth. Kevin would have to pay for this. For taking Willa.

"Notice anything unusual about them, by the way?"

"Not really." Anne scanned at the drawings. "All of them are black-and-white, I guess."

"True, and there are no people in them."

Anne double-checked and saw that Bennie was right. The series of drawings of Fitler Square focused on the gaslights and the shadows they cast, or the intricate pattern of the wrought-iron fence. There were no babies, no mothers, no kids. A study of Rittenhouse Square depicted its statues—a frog, a goat—but none of the people who used the statues as meeting places. Anne wasn't immediately sure what it meant.

"I like art with people," Bennie said. "You've seen my Thomas Eakins prints of rowing."

"Sure." *Hate them.* "Love them."

"They're from the exhibition at the Art Museum. Did you see it?"

"Missed it." *But I've been to the Lucy-Desi Museum in Jamestown, New York. Does that count?*

Anne surveyed the rest of the living room. It contained no TV or VCR, only a sixties-retro sling chair in white, sitting in front of a cordless phone, a stereo system and stacks of CDs on a white entertainment center. It was more gallery than living room and contained no clues about Willa's family, but Anne couldn't help but linger in it, breathing in the faintest smell of dust and lead. It was all that was left of Willa, that and a misidentified body, cold in a morgue.

"Here we go," Bennie said, crossing to the telephone and picking up the receiver. "Here's a way to reach her family and friends instantly. They'll be on speed-dial."

"Good idea." Anne wondered why she wasn't thinking of this good stuff. She felt suddenly so passive, a half-step behind. "Maybe I should be the one to tell them."

"No, let me handle this. When my mother was alive, she was in the number-one spot. Actually she still is. I don't have the heart to take her off." Bennie pressed the first speed-dial button, listened into the receiver, then frowned. "No number in the first spot." She pressed the second button. "No number in the second spot." She pressed another button. "Strike three," she said, after a minute, then hung up the phone. "Evidently, Willa didn't set up her speed-dial. So there's nobody she calls all the time. That seems strange."

"Not really," Anne blurted out almost defensively. She hadn't set up her speed-dial either.

"Maybe not. Come along." Bennie touched Anne's arm. "There has to be something, somewhere, that can help us. Bills, correspondence, old birthday cards with a return address. Something that would tell us more about her, or where her family is. How old did you say she was, again?"

"My age."

"She's too young for her parents to have passed on."

"Right," Anne said, though she wasn't thinking that clearly. Maybe she was exhausted. Or maybe she just had no idea how families kept in touch with each other. She'd never gotten a birthday card from her mother. She wouldn't know her father if she ran him over with a car. She followed Bennie through the living room to the back of the house.

The layout was similar to Anne's, a combination dining room and kitchen fashioned from one room, and she could tell at a glance that it would reveal little, if anything, about Willa's family. Sketches blanketed the white walls here, too, and the oak table was bare except for a bouquet of dried flowers. The kitchen was perfectly clean, with Kenmore appliances that landlords always installed. The remarkable centerpiece of the room was a beautiful, cinnabar-red spice rack that had been mounted above the stove.

She stepped over to it, reading the hand-lettered names on the spice jars, which were so exotic she'd never heard of them, much less cooked with them: cumin, cardamom, turmeric. Willa must have been a wonderful, creative cook. Anne felt a terrible twinge, stepping into a life that was lost because of her.

"Maybe she has an office upstairs," Bennie said, turning away. "There has to be a place she paid her bills. We'll have better luck there." She left the room, and Anne followed her numbly. Bennie turned on a light over the stairwell and led the way upstairs. Sketches served as wallpaper all the way to the second floor, and Anne marveled at the hours it must have taken to draw all of the scenes.

At the top of the stair was a tiny bathroom that they skipped in favor of the bedroom, another completely unconventional room. A wall that would have typically existed between two bedrooms had evidently been taken out, leaving an L-shaped bedroom-studio. Sketches covered the wall, their subjects similar to the ones downstairs, but much larger here, as if this were the second floor of an exclusive gallery, reserved for private customers.

A pine double bed, whose canopy top had been draped with long, white sashes of silk, sat at an unusual angle against the front windows. Beside it was a plain white IKEA-type dresser and desk, covered with papers in neat stacks. Bennie made a beeline for the desk and when she reached it, turned on a black halogen lamp. Anne went over after her.

"No computer, that's unusual," Bennie said, but somehow it seemed to Anne like speaking ill, so she didn't say anything.

"Here's her bills." Bennie thumbed through a pile of envelopes as Anne watched. Visa, Philadelphia Electric, and Verizon; Bennie pulled out the Verizon bill, which was already open, and reached inside. "The phone bill. It'll have a record of her calls. Maybe we can find her family that way. She has to call them, even if they're not on speed dial." Bennie slid out the bill, flashing the familiar sky-blue, and they both skimmed the listings.

"Almost nothing beyond the basic charges," Anne said, recognizing it. The bill could have been a duplicate of Anne's own; they were even on the same billing plan. "She's on the plan where you pay by the call. It makes sense if you don't make a lot of calls."

But Bennie was already casting around for a telephone. "No phone up here. Jesus!" She slid her cell phone from her pocket, and flipped it open, and called the first number on the bill, which was local. She listened on the line, then hung up. "Taws, the art store, and they're closed. Read me the next number." Anne read it off, and Bennie called it on the cell, then listened. "The Philadelphia Horticultural Center, also closed. Wonder why she called them?"

"To sketch it?" Anne guessed, but Bennie was on a tear.

"Try the next." Bennie called the number as soon as Anne read it off, listened, then flipped the phone closed. "Fresh Fields. Gourmet foods. Shit!" She skimmed the rest of the bill and tossed it aside. "None of the calls are long-distance, to family."

Anne's gaze fell on a stack of correspondence on the desktop. Maybe there'd be a letter from Willa's parents. Obviously, Willa wasn't a computer jock. Maybe she grew up in a family of artists. Anne picked up the topmost letter, but it had a letterhead from Mether Galleries in Center City. It was dated last week, and she skimmed it:

Dear Ms. Hansen;

We are writing in the hopes that you will reconsider your decision not to let us represent your portfolio. We understand that you were one of the most talented students in Bill Hunter's class at Moore College of Art, and believe that we can help your art find wonderful homes, in addition to providing a substantial income for you. Please

contact us as soon as possible at the
above address.

Anne mulled it over. Mether Galleries was one of the fanciest in the city. Why didn't Willa want to show her wonderful drawings there? If she had a trust fund, she didn't need the money. But still. Why hide all this talent under a basket?

"No luck on the other bills," Bennie said, opening the top file-drawer of the desk. "You finding anything?"

"Not yet." Anne reached for the next letter in the stack. It was an earlier letter from Mether, and there were two others underneath it from galleries in SoHo. She glanced through the letters, but they were like the ones from Mether Gallery. Why hadn't Willa at least responded? "All these galleries want her art, but she won't sell it. From the looks of it, she doesn't even call them back."

"Nothing here." Bennie had opened the upper file-drawer of the desk and was rooting through a stack of correspondence and papers, narrating as she went along. "No family pictures or anything. No birthday cards. Just receipts from Taws and some from Anthropologie. She doesn't buy much at all. Here's a transcript from Moore College of Art." Bennie frowned as she read. "She was doing well, then there's no courses listed after the first semester. Too bad. She must have dropped out." Bennie set it down and opened the lower drawer, filled with manila folders. "Now this looks promising."

"What?" Anne replaced the gallery correspondence.

"Taxes, old check registers, and stuff." Bennie dug to the bottom of the drawer. "Here's a copy of her lease, and there's other legal papers."

"She mentioned a trust fund." Anne watched Bennie pull out a sheaf of papers and read through them, her mouth tightening like a rubber band. Anne got a bad feeling. "What's the matter?"

"She had an inheritance. Willa's family was evidently from Holland, Michigan, and her parents died there, two years ago. This is their will. It was probated there."

"No. Really?" Anne felt so sad, for Willa. About Willa. She held out her hand for the papers, and Bennie passed them over without a word. They were so cold and white, the paper stiff and unusually thick, folded in thirds. She skipped the boilerplate to the bequest, to see if Willa had any siblings. But the bequest referred only to "our daughter, Willa." Willa was an only child, and, with the death of her parents, alone in the world. Anne felt her eyes welling up, and bit her lip, but Bennie was already leafing through another set of stapled papers.

"It looks like the parents had an auto accident, from the executor's report. Extensive hospital bills were paid by the estate, for both of them. They died within a week of the accident." Bennie folded up the papers, then dug for more in the folders. "That's tough, on a girl so young. She must have come here to go to Moore, then her parents were killed and she dropped out. What a shame."

Anne wiped her eyes when Bennie bent over, rummaging in the drawer. She didn't want to explain her feelings to Bennie. She couldn't explain them to herself.

"It was a large estate, almost a million dollars. It's held in trust, wisely invested. I should give the trustee a call, at some point." Bennie was reading from something that looked like financial schedules. "If Willa lived carefully, as she obviously did, she'd be set for the rest of her life. That's why she didn't sell the drawings. She didn't have to."

No, it isn't, Anne thought, but didn't say. "So there's no family to notify," she said instead, and even those words caught in her throat. It was hard to hold back an overwhelming sadness. Willa lived alone, in a black-and-white world of her own, cutting herself off from everyone around her. The only color in her life was her hair, and that Anne couldn't quite explain. Willa had only her work for company and she didn't share even that with anyone. She led a completely insular life, and Anne sensed it had begun when her parents had been killed. It was a normal response to trauma, and an uncomfortably familiar one.

"Oh, well." Bennie returned the documents to the drawer and closed it. "I guess, at this point, I'm fairly convinced that nobody wanted to kill Willa Hansen. Given what we learned today and tonight, I think Kevin is the murderer and you the intended victim. I was wrong. Sorry about that, Murphy. You were right."

She was killed because of me. "No I-told-you-so here," Anne said, forcing a pat smile.

It was late by the time they got to Bennie's house, and Anne settled onto the warm dining room table, trying to shake her gloom and her fatigue. Bennie had gone to fix some dinner for her and to get Mel a saucer of milk. The cat crouched at Anne's feet while Bennie's golden retriever, Bear, snuffled up his fur with a wet nose, leaving slobbery patches in the cat's usually immaculate coat and misaligning his dark stripes. Anne's hand hovered protectively nearby. For the dog's protection.

"How they doin'?" Bennie called from the kitchen, just out of eyeshot.

"Oh, they're becoming fast friends!" Anne called back. Mel took a declawed swipe at Bear, which would remain their little secret. It did nothing to deter the dog, a hundred pounds of red fur with a pink tongue. Bear had been in constant motion, dancing around Mel when Anne first set him on the floor, then bowing in front of him to play, and finally pawing the air between them. She marveled that Bear craved such instant intimacy and attributed it to a disturbing lack of discretion on the animal's part. In other words, a dog thing.

"Is the cat okay?" Bennie called out again. From the kitchen came the *clink* of glasses, and in the living room Mel took another swipe with his paw, which Bear misinterpreted as an invitation to frolic. Anne was getting the distinct impression that goldens believed everyone really loved them, despite any and all evidence to the contrary. They could be the erotomanics of the dog world.

"Not to worry!" Anne called back.

"Two percent or light cream?"

"Two percent is fine!"

"I have a can of tuna, too."

"Great! Thanks!" Anne lifted the cat onto her lap before he blinded his new best friend. Mel settled into Sphinx Cat, and by the time Bennie entered the room with a tray, he looked completely innocent. He was scary-good at it.

"Here we go," Bennie said, setting the tray down on the oak table. The tray had a frosted-glass bottom, funky blue handles, and a price tag stuck to the side. $12.98, Michael Graves, on sale at Target. Anne was no sleuth but she figured Bennie didn't entertain much, and she'd heard something about Bennie breaking up with her live-in boyfriend. Mental note: You never can tell who's lonely just by looking.

"Thanks."

"Can this tiny thing feed this creature?" Bennie asked, holding up a white ramekin of milk.

"Sure. Just set it on the floor."

"No way. Not with a golden in the tri-state area. Food on the floor is fair game." Bennie set the ramekin on the dining room table, as Mel watched. "Murphy, you want to show it to him or something?"

"He sees it. He'll have some when he's ready."

"Amazing." Bennie rolled up the sleeves of her workshirt. Between it, her worn shorts, and her slightly grubby bare feet, she looked remarkably comfortable, not only in her own house, but in her own skin. "A dog never delays eating. See?" Bear's tail wagged like crazy and he was already sniffing the ramekin. He would have snorted it empty if Bennie hadn't leaned over and moved it out of reach. "I hope the cat doesn't wait too long to have some."

"Guaranteed that he will, for purposes of doggie torture." Anne stroked Mel's head and he purred. She reached for her soda and took a long, cold slug. "Thank you for the drink and the hospitality."

"I'm happy to do it." Bennie cocked her head so that a tangle of ponytail tumbled over her shoulder to her breast pocket. "I checked on what I have for dinner. Oranges and three eggs. Sorry, I haven't had the chance to go food-shopping, with depositions and the near-death experience of one of my best associates."

"I'm not really hungry. I usually have cereal for dinner."

"That I can cook." Bennie turned, headed for the kitchen, and returned with two tablespoons, two bowls, a half-quart of Wawa milk, and a box of Shredded Wheat, which she put on the table and sat down in the chair opposite Anne. Track lighting that ringed the room set a soft glow to her face and highlighted her blond hair. "Dinner is served."

"Great!" Anne said, though she usually avoided Shredded Wheat. The box remained on the table: squat, red, and remarkably smug for a breakfast food. Its long list of "Nutrition Facts" faced her, reporting alarming amounts of phosphorus, magnesium, zinc, and copper. Metal belonged in plumbing, not breakfast, but Anne reached for the cereal, fixed herself a bowl, and pretended it was Captain Crunch.

"So, let's review," Bennie said, swallowing. "You've survived a stalker who wanted to kill you, a client who wanted to fire you, and haircut by office scissors."

Anne managed a smile. "One of these things is not like the other." She took another bite of Shredded Wheat, which didn't taste bad because it lacked taste altogether. She glanced around the polished pine table for a sugar bowl, but it was completely bare except for the woven place mats of yellow straw. *Maybe that's what was in this cereal.* "May I have some sugar, please?"

"No," Bennie answered.

"Kidding?"

"There's no sugar in the house. No sugar and no TV. They're both bad for your health."

Anne thought this must be some form of insanity. *No Lucy? "No sugar?"*

"Ever hear of sugar blues?"

"Is it how you feel when there's no sugar in the house?"

Bennie smiled. "Forget it." She finished

another mouthful of Shredded Wheat. "You don't like sports, do you, Murphy?"

"I shop. It takes stamina. I train by eating Cocoa Krispies. Now *that's* dinner." Anne became vaguely aware that she was trying to make Bennie laugh, and wondered why that was so.

"I admire you, Murphy. I do."

"Me?" Anne almost choked, but it could have been the place mat.

"I think you're handling your situation like a champ. I've taken some heat in my time, but not like this. I'm proud of you. This is just awful, and I know how horrible you feel about Willa."

"Thanks," Anne said quickly, feeling her face warm. "I do appreciate everything that you, and the others, have done for me."

"No problem, but it's not over yet. Tomorrow is the big day. The memorial service." Bennie ate more cereal and washed it down with Diet Coke. "We will get this asshole. DiNunzio's tougher than she looks, and Carrier comes through in any clutch. They both do."

"I bet."

"But I have an apology to make, on their behalf and my own." Bennie paused, eyeing Anne directly. "None of us was welcoming when you first came to the firm, and it's my fault. I didn't take the time to get you assimilated. I didn't realize how important it was. None of us acted very well, and I'm very sorry for that."

"That's okay." Anne swallowed the thickness in her throat. She set down her tablespoon and vowed never to eat home furnishings again.

"No, it's not okay. I'm a good lawyer, but I see now I'm not a good manager. I'm not so good, I think, at making sure everybody is getting along, being happy. Working together. I usually make sure we win."

"Winning is good."

"Not good enough. Things fall through the cracks, and people. Like you."

"I wasn't so friendly—"

"The burden was on us. On me. You came to my city, to my firm. However you acted was understandable, considering what you'd been through."

No time like the present. "I have a question, Bennie. You knew everything about Kevin. About my past." She thought of her mother's bouquet of daisies. "How was that?"

"One of your work references told me about Kevin. That he'd tried to kill you, that you'd held up under extreme pressure and put him in jail."

"They're only supposed to verify term of employment," Anne said, surprised.

"They wanted you to get the job. They were trying to help you change your life. And when I heard the full story, it sold me. I knew you could take anything *I* could dish out."

Anne smiled. She really wanted to ask about her mother, but it seemed so awkward.

"The rest I researched. I have lots of friends in the criminal defense bar out there, and I asked around." Bennie sipped her soda, and the ice made a sound too festive for the conversation. "I remembered from the interview that you said you had no family. But you didn't say anybody had died. And there was no mention of a family or even birthplace on your résumé. So I had our firm investigator look into it. You know Lou, don't you?"

"You *investigated* me?" Anne tried not to sound too pissed.

"Sure, and I don't apologize for it. I can't have just anybody at my firm, and people don't spring from somebody's head. Everybody has a family, whether they deny it or not. Not just a family, a *context*. Like a word, with meaning in a paragraph." Bennie smiled over the rim of her glass. "And with some work, I found your context."

"My mother?"

"Yes."

"Not my father."

"No."

Anne felt her heart quicken. "Where was she, anyway?"

"Southern California." Bennie set her glass down. "That's all I should say. She asked me not to tell you, and I promised I wouldn't."

Anne held her features rigid. A knife of familiar anger sliced near her heart. "How nice of her."

"I am sorry. I respected her wishes, but I thought it was hurtful, too."

"I don't care enough to be hurt," Anne said quickly, and she sounded lame even to herself. She wanted to scream. How can a parent have this power over a grown child? Even the *worst* of parents?

"I think she wasn't very proud of herself, and that's why she didn't want you to know." Bennie paused. "There is a drinking problem, I gather."

"Meaning she was barely coherent when you spoke." Anne knew just how that conversation would go, and her face flushed with sudden shame. "She didn't ask you for money, did she?"

Bennie didn't confirm or deny. "My family is no model either, but I miss my mother every day. Well. We all make mistakes."

Anne's chest felt tight. "Has she contacted you, since then?"

"No, but I remind you. She left the flowers you've been driving around with." Bennie smiled softly. "Not that you care."

"I only had to die to get her attention. She phoned it in. The card was typed at the store." Anne stared at her leftover cereal and tasted a bitterness in her mouth that wasn't magnesium. "I don't even know how she got my home address."

"I told her," Bennie answered, and Anne looked up.

"*You*? When?"

"When I spoke to her last year, when you moved here."

Anne fell silent. *So it's not even like she follows me in the newspapers.*

"You wish I hadn't. I'm sorry." Bennie sighed. "We always wish our parents were better than they are. Bigger, stronger, richer. Better people, more reliable. But they're not, they're just not. Sometimes, the best course is to try to accept that, as truth."

"I accepted that a long time ago," Anne said, then hated the way she sounded. She pitied herself for pitying herself, and even more because Bennie was right.

Mental note: Maybe bosses became bosses for a reason.

15

Outside the second-story window, dime-store firecrackers popped and holiday lasers sliced the night sky, but Anne ignored it all in favor of the computer monitor. She sat at the workstation in Bennie's messy spare room, which contained old athletic equipment, a white Peugeot bicycle, and boxes of old files, which had been stacked on the skinny daybed against the wall before they had cleared them off. Anne would have gone to bed but she couldn't help finishing her Internet search of Bill Dietz's background. The top of the screen read:

Your search has revealed 427 persons named William Dietz with criminal convictions.

She had picked up reading the listings at 82, and she was already at 112. She still didn't know why she was doing it. She didn't know if she'd find anything and didn't know why it mattered. Only that she had looked into Bill

Dietz's eyes and remembered malevolence behind them. Evil masquerading as concern for his wife; abuse dolled up as protection, even love. She returned to the search.

At 226, Anne was in the zone of eliminating Bill Dietzes and taking a caffeinated pleasure in the accomplishment of a simple task. Click on a listing, read it, click on the next. It was easier than redrafting her opening argument or trying to guess which guise Kevin would take in his next incarnation. At 301, she'd still had no luck.

"Murphy, it's very late," Bennie said, from the threshold of the office. "You have to get to sleep." She entered with Bear behind her, his nails *click-clacking* on the pine floorboards. She wore a white terry-cloth bathrobe and her hair had been piled into an unruly topknot, but when she got closer Anne could see that her eyes were tinged with pink and vaguely puffy.

"What's the matter? You getting a cold?"

"I guess I'm allergic to cats. My face itches, and I can't stop sneezing."

"Oh, no." Anne felt terrible. "When did this start?"

"After dinner. I took a shower but it didn't help."

"Should I leave and take Mel?"

"No, you don't have anywhere else to go. Just keep him in the room. On the bright side, our eyewitness Mrs. Brown is all over the news. On TV, on the radio. The cops announced they're officially looking for prison escapee Kevin Satorno in connection with your murder. He's a wanted man."

"The wish of erotomanics everywhere."

"Which brings me to my next point. Since Satorno is on the loose, I wanted you to have some peace of mind. I can protect us, if need be. Don't freak out when you see this." Bennie stuck her hand in her bathrobe pocket and extracted something. Its silvery finish caught the light from the lamp.

"A thirty-eight special, huh?" Anne reached for the gun and turned it over expertly in her palm. Its stainless-steel frame felt cool, and the hatchmarks on its wooden handle were slightly worn, as was the gold-toned Rossi logo. She thumbed the cylinder-release latch and let the cylinder fall open into her hand. The revolver was loaded with five Federal bullets. She closed the cylinder with a satisfying click. "It's about ten years old. You musta bought it used."

Bennie cocked an eyebrow. "Yes. How do you know that?"

"These guns don't circulate much anymore. Rossi made 'em in Brazil. They were a bunch of guys who spun off from Smith & Wesson. That's why it looks like one." The clunky gun was a knock-off, but Anne didn't say so. She wouldn't like people saying bad things about her gun. She turned the revolver over in her hand, appreciating its heft, if not its style. "It's a good gun. Practical. Plenty of stopping power. Good for you." She handed it back.

"So you're not freaked."

"By a gun? Not unless it's pointed at me. I'm not a gun nut, but I bought one after Kevin attacked me. I own a Beretta thirty-two, semi-auto. Fits in my palm. Cute as a button. I don't even have to rack the slide to load it. It pops up, so I don't break a nail. A great girl gun." Anne could see that her boss was looking at her funny, so she explained. "I tried therapy, Bennie, but I sucked at it, and I'm not the support-group type. I went to the shooting range four nights a week. After a year I can kill a piece of paper, and I feel a helluva lot safer."

"My, my. You're an interesting girl, Murphy."

With a crooked smile, Bennie slipped the revolver back into her bathrobe pocket. "I want you to know the gun is here and it's loaded. We're safe. I'll keep it in my night table."

"Why don't you leave it with me?"

"That's not a good idea. Do you have experience with this type of gun?"

"Can Eakins paint by numbers?" Anne smiled, and so did Bennie.

"Just the same, I'll keep it in my night table." She turned to the computer monitor and scanned it with swollen eyes. "What's the point of this search, when you should be getting ready for bed? So what if Dietz has a criminal record?"

"I can use it on cross, for impeachment."

"True, but I don't know what that gets you. If it really matters, we can sic Lou on him, after the holiday. Bill Dietz isn't your enemy in *Chipster.*"

"I know. His wife is."

"Wrong. You're the lawyer. Your opponent is her lawyer. Matt Booker."

"Of course." Anne resolved instantly not to tell Bennie her feelings for Matt, and vice versa. "That's a given."

Bennie squeezed Anne's shoulder. "Do

me a favor and go to sleep. You're running on adrenaline, and you have a big day to-morrow. Now, good night." She turned and padded out, sniffling, with Bear *click-click-*ing after her down the hall.

Anne took a deep breath and resumed her search. She eliminated 302 through 397, hoping against all odds that this would be her Bill Dietz. She slowed just after 426, then clicked on the very last entry, feeling unaccountably as if she were rolling the dice. But the screen read only: **William Dietz, birth date 3/15/80, Cochranville, PA. Misdemeanor theft.**

"No!" Anne said aloud, without meaning to. There was nothing. Mel picked his head up quickly, his ears flat.

Anne felt suddenly lost. She had been wrong. Bill Dietz did not have a criminal record. He was just a jealous, protective hus-band who had committed no crime, not even a misdemeanor. She felt stupid, useless, and depleted of energy and emotion. Nothing was going right. She was too exhausted to think. It had been too crazy a day.

She got up, turned out the desk light, shimmied out of her skirt, and slid into bed, slipping under the covers in her T-shirt. In time, the house fell quiet except for a loud, breathy snoring from Bennie's bedroom down the hall. Anne assumed it was the dog, and hoped that she hadn't made Bennie completely sick. At the foot of the bed, Mel circled a few times, then curled against her covered feet, just like home. But it didn't feel like home. She could never go home again. She lay in the dark, feeling suddenly that she didn't belong anywhere, with anyone. She had lost whatever context she had. It was just as Bennie had said, with characteristic bluntness:

You don't have anywhere else to go.

Anne closed her eyes, trying to clear her mind, and in a minute the snoring from down the hall was joined by street noises. Cars honked, people laughed and yelled, fireworks went off. A party somewhere must have ended, or she just hadn't heard the noises before. She put the down pillow over her head but it didn't help. It wasn't her bed, and she missed her own pillow, with its woven photo of Lucy kissing Desi from "Redecorating the Mertzes' Apartment." Episode No. 74, November 23, 1953.

Anne flopped over and tried not to think

about her house, then Willa, who had died there. And her mother, whose daisies did nothing to scent the room. And Mrs. Brown, sitting all by herself with her puzzle books. And especially not Kevin, with his gun. Would they be able to catch him tomorrow, at the memorial service? They had to. After losing him today, it was her last chance.

An hour later, she still hadn't fallen asleep. She was jittery and anxious. She flopped back and forth, thinking of Matt. His flowers on her front stoop. The emotion in his voice at the office. The way he'd looked, grief-stricken. Would he come to her memorial service? She wished she could tell him she was alive, and she wished she could see him. She felt a politically incorrect need for a strong shoulder to cry on, a warm chest to burrow into. Anne loved men, and, before Kevin, she had dated a lot; fallen in and out of love a few times, and been very happy. Was Matt where she belonged?

Fifteen minutes later, Anne had dressed, closed Mel in her bedroom, and grabbed her messenger bag, which contained her cell phone and a borrowed revolver. It had been almost too easy to sneak into Bennie's bedroom and steal the gun from the drawer. The snoring had been the dog's, thank God.

She steered the Mustang through the streets of Philadelphia. She knew she was taking a risk being out, but it was calculated. She could protect herself, and her odds of seeing Kevin were slim to none. He'd be hiding from the cops, laying low, and still he had no reason to think she was alive. It was almost two in the morning, but the sidewalks were hardly deserted. Tourists club-hopped and walked in groups, laughing, talking, and holding hands. People carried brown bags with bottles inside or swung six-packs joined by plastic loops.

Anne cruised to a red light, eyeing the partiers on the street. No Kevin. The night was sultry, with a wildness in the air. Everybody was misbehaving, Anne most of all. Driving where she shouldn't be, for no justifiable reason. All bets were off. She pointed the Mustang toward the colonial part of the city and Matt's house. She had gotten the address from 411, but hadn't called ahead. Olde City lay east, centering on Independence Hall, where the Declaration of Independence had been signed. It would be the most crowded section of the city, now that Philly was throwing itself the nation's birthday party. She sped downtown, and soon colonial brick rowhouses covered with ivy were whizzing past the car window.

Anne could feel the summer night ruffling her short hair, and accelerated. She forgot about her mother and the *Chipster* case. Put distance between herself and Kevin. She felt like she did when she first moved here. Hopeful. Excited. Her heartbeat quickened. She drove around for a parking space and finally took an illegal one out of necessity; even at this hour of the morning, the holiday partied on. She cut the ignition and was about to go when she caught sight of herself in the rearview mirror. She had forgotten her lipstick. The stitch in the middle of her upper lip showed.

So be it.

She reached for her purse, removed the revolver, and stuck it in the waistband of her skirt, just in case. She slipped on her sunglasses and climbed out of the Mustang with a confidence that comes cheap with a concealed weapon. She walked a few blocks until she found Matt's house, a brick rowhouse like hers, only with older brick, a faded, crumbly melon color. The shutters

and door were black, and a light was on on
the first floor, shining through the blinds, so
he must be working late, as she had been.
She knocked on the front door and after a
minute, the outside light went on and the
door swung open.

Anne gasped when she saw Matt. "What
happened?" she asked, astonished.

16

Matt looked like he'd been punched in the face. An inch-long cut tore though his left cheek, jagged and freshly red, and underneath it rose a goose egg, almost swelling closed his left eye. He still had on his Oxford shirt, but it was spattered with tiny droplets of blood. His one good eye widened at the sight of Anne.

His lips parted in disbelief. He bent closer and peered into her face. "My God, you look like—"

"I am. It's me. Anne. See?" She took off her sunglasses, not wanting to linger on his front stoop. A couple on the street was already turning around. She didn't think they could see her, much less recognize her, but still. "Let me in, Matt. I'll explain inside. It was all a mistake. I'm alive."

"*What? Anne? A mistake? Alive?*" Matt stalled in confusion, so Anne took his arm and pressed him into the house, shutting the door behind them. A lamp was on in the living room, which had exposed-brick walls and a contemporary black couch and chairs. Yellow legal pads, Xeroxed cases, and documents with the Chipster.com logo covered the coffee table and buried a laptop. Matt's house was enemy headquarters, but Anne couldn't think of it that way. Or him that way, no matter what Bennie had said. He was bursting into a joyous smile at the sight of her, alive in the lamplight.

"My God! Anne, it is you! I see you! *Anne!*"

"Like my new hair?" she asked, flicking it with her fingers, but before she could fish for more compliments, Matt had gathered her up in his arms. He felt strong and solid, and relief flooded through her body, spreading warm as lifeblood. It was so good just to be held, even by someone who had never held her before.

"You're not dead!" Matt began laughing, with evident relief. He squeezed Anne tighter, his arms so long they wrapped almost completely around her. "I can't believe it! I'm not letting you go! I have you. I have you now!"

Anne hugged him back, letting her emotions come, and felt a tear slide down her cheek. She hadn't cried since her shower, which seemed like ages ago. She buried her face in the rough cotton of Matt's shirt, nestling against his chest. She didn't know if she belonged here, but she needed someone to lean on, and hadn't realized how much until this very minute.

"Tell me what happened. No, don't! Forget it. Don't talk, *I* want to talk. I have something to say. I've been regretting not saying it every minute since I heard you were dead." Matt released her and looked down at her, wiping wetness from her cheek with a warm thumb. "Don't cry, this is a good thing. What I have to say is—I love you, Anne."

Wow. Anne started smiling then, her tears ebbing away, and reached up for him, kissing him fully, in a way she'd wanted to for a long time. She could feel him reaching for her with his kiss, too, with the urgency of his entire body. When he released her, he eased her into sitting on the couch, and sat down next to her, brushing uneven bangs from her forehead.

"What happened?" Matt asked, managing a concerned expression despite a beat-up cheek. "This is crazy. You're *alive*?"

"First off, you can't tell anyone. This is the

worst-kept secret in the world, and I can't risk it getting out to Kevin. He thinks I'm dead."

"Kevin. You mean this guy they're looking for, on the news? Satorno? Is that why you changed your hair?" Matt listened while Anne told him the whole story, and when she had finished, he remained in stunned silence for a moment before he spoke. "You took a risk coming here. Why did Bennie let you?"

"She doesn't know, I snuck out of her house. You've been asking me out for a year, I figured it was time to say yes." Anne couldn't look at him without seeing his injury, and close-up it was worse than she thought. The gash rent his cheek and fresh blood filled the cut. He might even need stitches. Anne was an expert. "What happened to your face?"

"I can't tell you."

"Why not?"

"It's privileged."

"How can that be? A privileged fistfight?"

Matt waved her off. "Forget it. Why did the police think you were—"

"A privileged fight would be a fight with a client." Anne thought a minute and arrived at the answer with a start. "It was Bill Dietz! He hit you, didn't he?"

"He didn't mean it."

"That asshole, I knew it!" Anne flashed on the Bill Dietz listings. No assaults, except the one tonight on his own lawyer. So she had been right about the rage in Dietz. "Why'd he hit you?"

"This isn't confidential, so I'll tell you. But we have to observe certain boundaries here. He is my client."

"You're loyal to him? You should fire his ass!"

"It doesn't work that way."

Right. "Well, it should. So what happened?"

"We were at my office, after the dep." Matt paused again. "I hate to tell you this. It's not unethical, it's just stupid, and this is the beginning, where I tell you only the good stuff about me."

The beginning. Anne liked the sound of it. "Just tell me."

"Well, Bill said something I really didn't like, and no, I'm not telling you what it is, so don't start asking me"—he wagged his finger at her—"and I told him so. Then he told me not to talk to him that way, that I was only *his mouthpiece*, which is such a stupid term, and then he hit me. I still can't understand it." Matt touched his wound gingerly. "He didn't mean to cut me, but when he threw his punch, he had on a big college ring and that did it. He felt worse than I did. He apologized, and so did Beth. They offered to take me to the hospital."

"Oh, what a guy. A full-service client."

"The Dietzes are really nice people."

"The Dietzes are lying scum."

"No way. Gil's the liar."

Anne sighed. "Matt, you've gotten to be friends with them, and it's clouding your judgment. Dietz has issues. I wouldn't be surprised if he abuses his wife. Normal people don't have physically violent reactions. He socked you for something you said."

"It doesn't mean he beats his wife. He loves Beth. He would do anything for her."

"So would you, and you have. You're her lawyer—and his!"

"I don't know anybody who doesn't want to punch out a lawyer. And half of *them* are lawyers! Maybe you're the one who's gotten too close to your client. You just don't like the Dietzes."

"But they're extorting money from an innocent man. They're taking down his company and ruining his chance for IPO. Chipster is one of the most successful—"

"Anne?" Matt reached out and touched her arm. "Let's not talk about the Dietzes, or Chipster, anymore. I liked what we were doing before."

"Come on, what did Dietz say to you? Just tell me. I'm dying to know."

"No! I will *not* tell opposing counsel anything my client tells me!" Matt turned serious. "You're getting paranoid, and I don't blame you, but we can't keep talking about the Dietzes. Agreed?"

"You can't blame a girl for trying."

"I can and I do. And I'm still pissed about that stripper thing."

"You're less fun than I thought." Anne pouted as Matt's arms slipped around her shoulders. She sank deep into the couch's cushy pillows, then felt a hardness against her hip. *Oops.* "Hold on, wait a minute." She unclinched enough to extract the revolver from her waistband and set it on the coffee table on top of his scribbled notes.

"Jesus!" Matt edged away, shocked. "Where did you get *that*?"

"It's Bennie's."

"Is it loaded?"

"Of course. You can't shoot anybody if it's not." Anne edged over to Matt and touched his arm, but he kept staring at the gun.

"Does it have a safety?"

"What's a safety, big fella?" she whispered, planting a soft kiss on the good side of his face.

"A safety's the thing they have on guns so they don't go off."

"I'm kidding. It's a revolver, so it doesn't have a safety."

Matt recoiled. "Will it go off?"

"It can't. You have to pick it up, aim it at somebody you don't like, and pull the trigger."

"Well, point it away or something. I can't relax with it aiming at us."

"Fine." Anne took pity on him, reached over, and spun the gun so that its barrel had a clean shot at the entertainment center. "I think everything will be okay now, unless the gun decides to shoot your DVD player. Now, if you kiss me like you did a minute ago, I can forget about what a big baby you are."

"You liked that?" Matt grinned down at her, pulling her closer, and the part of his face that wasn't injured went soft. "God, you're so beautiful it's scary."

"No, not really." Anne pointed impulsively at her scar. "Attractive, huh?"

"So what? You got nothin' on me right now."

"That's it? '*So what?*'" Anne blinked, nonplussed. "I was a freak, at birth. I have a scar, and unlike yours, it's permanent."

"It's not a scar, it's a target, and I think it's not big enough." Matt covered her mouth with his, kissing her softly, then again, slowly, overcoming her shame with each kiss. She kissed him back, letting him lead her away from herself and her fears. She was careful with him, too, going slowly so she didn't hurt his wound, getting to know him better, with a deeper kiss.

She eased back onto a sofa covered with his papers and felt him pressing onto her, her body warm with his weight. She ignored the crackle of Xeroxed cases under her and didn't give a second thought to which precedent he was citing. She didn't even try to peek at his laptop screen later, when he reached over to turn out the lamp.

Mental note: Some people have to

choose between making love or making war, but lawyers can do both.

Nobody was on the sidewalk at dawn Sunday morning, and only a few light trucks and vans rumbled by, hauling ice, tables, and tents for the city's festivities. Anne hurried from Matt's house through the streets of Olde City, happy and reenergized, after a night with a man who loved her. She couldn't say she loved him yet, but she was very much in deep like, and it was a slippery slope.

She picked up the pace, keeping a hand near her messenger bag so the revolver wouldn't fly out. Okay, she wasn't a model of firearm safety, and she wasn't wearing underwear either. She hadn't had time to find it. She had gotten up early to get back to Bennie's, so she wouldn't be worried. Or discover that her rookie associate was sleeping with the enemy. Anne needed to cover her ass. Literally.

She hustled down the cobblestone sidewalk, breaking a sweat in the thick air. Philadelphians always said, "It's not the heat, it's the humidity," but Anne didn't agree. *It's hot, stupid.* She pushed up the sunglasses sliding down her nose and jogged the remaining two blocks to the street she'd parked on, slowing to catch her breath when she saw a line of cars she recognized from last night. She cooled down past a blue minivan, a white Mercedes 430, and a blue Ford truck, which was the last one at the top of the row.

Anne stopped, looking around in confusion. Dude, where's my car? There was no red Mustang on the street. In fact, there were no cars at all where the cars had been parked last night. Had they all left? Was she on the wrong street? She checked the green street sign. Delancey Street. Right. She had parked here last night.

She looked around for the Mustang but it was nowhere in sight. She turned on her heels and came face-to-face with a red-lettered sign that she hadn't noticed the night before, when she was in heat. It read: NO PARKING TOW ZONE. But it could just as accurately have read:

RANDOM.

17

Loser! Anne's heart sank. The Mustang had been towed! She cursed herself and her red roots. Her bad planning and her lack of undies. What was she going to do? She could go back and get a ride from Matt, but she didn't want to reveal her stupidity. Now she knew what he had meant, *"This is the beginning, where I tell you only the good stuff about me."*

Anne got another idea, a better one than parking a getaway car in a tow zone. Sooner or later a cab would show up, and until then she would start walking. It would take an hour to get to Bennie's house, walking from one end of town to the other, but it was in the no-choice category.

She started to hoof it, heading west, up Delancey, and taking mental inventory. The Mustang was a rental anyway, and she still had a cell phone and a knock-off Smith & Wesson. What else did a girl need? And even though the gray sky was lightening to a watercolor blue, she was reasonably safe. Kevin would still be hiding from the cops. There was only one problem: she'd never make it to Bennie's in time, now. What to do? Anne wracked her brain for a good lie, but came up empty, which worried her. Maybe the sex had sapped her superpowers. Disarmed, she'd have to tell the truth. She'd have to admit that not only had she committed high treason, she'd been too horny to read a traffic sign.

She kept walking and took her cell phone out of her purse, calling Bennie's home number. "It's me," she said, when the call connected.

"Murphy?" Bennie sounded sleepy. "You're calling me? Aren't you in your room, in bed?"

"Not exactly." Anne looked for a cab as she headed uptown. The street was littered with trash and paper cups from the night before. Plastic poppers lay popped in the gutter. "I'm so sorry, I thought I'd be home by now. I'm calling so you wouldn't worry."

"What shouldn't I worry about? Where are you?" She sneezed, and Anne cringed.

"Gesundheit. I'm sorry, really sorry. I'm on

my way." She bit her lip. This was a lousy way to repay Bennie's kindness. No wonder she never told the truth. It was hard. "I was at Matt's house last night. I'll be home in an hour unless I can get a—"

"Did you say Matt? Matt Booker? Why? Was it settlement talks?"

"Not exactly." Anne flushed, but maybe it was the heat, or the humidity. "I spent the night with him. I'm seeing him, Bennie. I think."

"*Matt Booker?* You're *seeing Matt Booker?* What? How long has this been going on?"

"One night. Look, I know it sounds terrible, but this is personal, not business." Then she remembered about Matt's injuries, and didn't know if she should tell Bennie. Would she be betraying Matt if she told? Would she be betraying Bennie if she didn't? And what about Gil? Mental note: There are many good reasons why you shouldn't sleep with opposing counsel.

"You and Matt Booker are *personal*? Are you crazy?"

"I shouldn't have done it, I know."

"He's plaintiff's counsel!"

"I was weak."

"God, I keep forgetting how young you

are!" Bennie shouted, then caught herself. "We'll discuss it when we see each other. But here's more bad news. I'm looking out my bedroom window, and the press has taken up residence in front of my house, waiting for me to come out."

"They weren't there last night."

"That's because they sleep at night, like you should have been. Bottom line is, there's no way you can get back in without you or the car being recognized."

The car is no problem.

"Meet me at the office," Bennie said, sternly. "Use the back entrance. We have to get ready for the memorial service. It's today, at noon. It would be nice if you attended. You're the guest of honor."

"I know. Sorry."

"Okay, see you at the office. Be careful."

"Don't worry."

Bennie harrumphed, then hung up.

Anne slipped the phone in her purse and hurried to the corner for a cab. None was in sight, so she kept walking. It was less than an hour to the office from here, and she headed for work, picking up a free tabloid from an open box on the way. It was *City Beat*, that paper she'd heard about, and its circulation must have been local only. THE FUGITIVE, read the headline, above a blown-up mug shot of Kevin, and Anne was thrilled. Everybody would be looking for him now, even regular citizens.

She read the story as she walked, and it was all her history with Kevin, with a sidebar about Mrs. Brown. She glanced up at the byline: *By Angus Connolly*. The gonzo reporter in the Australian bush hat had gotten his big scoop. She wished him luck, then tossed the paper into the nearest trash can.

Anne was sweating big-time by the time she got uptown and ducked the horde of reporters, TV cameras, and Nikons massing outside the office on Locust Street. She scurried back down the alley behind the office building, hid her breasts past Hot and Heavy, and finally escaped upstairs to the office and past the empty reception area to Bennie's office in the back.

Bennie's door was open, and Judy and Mary occupied the two chairs in front of her desk. The office was cluttered with law books, awards, and dark-red accordion files, and the lawyers were huddling over something Anne couldn't see. She called a guilt-ridden hello, and all three heads looked up at once. Mary and Judy smiled instantly, but Bennie shot her a look that said you-are-in-such-big-trouble, deep-shit-would-be-an-improvement.

"I'm so sorry to have worried you, Bennie," Anne said quickly, meaning it. She'd had ten blocks to think about what a jerk she'd been, and she'd concluded that as wonderful a man as Matt was, she didn't belong with him, not yet. Tuesday she'd be in court against him, and a man wasn't always the answer. Anne felt vaguely like an alcoholic who'd fallen off the wagon. Mental note: Men rehab sucks.

"We'll discuss it another time. We have work to do." Bennie's scowl seemed all the more severe because of her ersatz-mourning clothes. She wore a black suit with an off-white shirt and black pumps, and her curly blond hair had been tamed by a black linen barrette. "Someday in the future, I may accept your apology. Right now I'm taking it under advisement."

Sitting on the desk, Judy was smiling. "Have a nice time, Murph the Surf?" She had on a black cotton sweater with short sleeves and a funky black skirt, shin-length. With black fake-ponyskin clogs.

"Oh, stop, Jude," Mary jumped in. She looked like a friendly nun, in a plain black A-line dress. "I think Matt's hot, too, and you deserve to be happy, after what you've been through. And I trust you not to tell him anything about the case."

"Thanks," Anne said, but Bennie still wasn't smiling.

"By the way, I'll take my gun back."

"Sure. Sorry about that." Anne tugged the revolver from her purse, and Mary blanched.

"Is that really *a gun*?"

Judy jumped. "Is it *loaded*?"

"No," Anne and Bennie said at the same time.

Anne handed Bennie the weapon. "I only used one bullet."

"That'll be ten cents," Bennie said, and their eyes met in a temporary truce over the weapon. Bennie opened her desk drawer, placed the gun inside, and twisted the tiny key in the lock. She extracted the key and slipped it into her suit-jacket pocket. "No more gun. Everybody remain calm."

Judy shuddered. "I didn't know you had a gun, Bennie."

"Now you know everything. Favorite color is golden retriever, favorite sport is rowing, favorite hobby is winning cases. Pet peeves? Cats, no pun."

"How is Mel, I was just about to ask." Actually Anne had been afraid to.

"He meowed for you this morning. I wanted to shoot him but somebody stole my gun."

"Bennie!" Anne and the other associates looked horrified.

"Just kidding." Bennie plucked a yellow legal pad from her desk. "Okay, kids, we all have our jobs today, right? Carrier, you're on flower detail. You have your list of kitchen staff, right?"

Judy nodded, consulting a piece of notebook paper on Bennie's desk. "Most are women, so we're in good shape there."

"Make sure the only kitchen staff are the ones on that list, and you meet each one."

"Got it."

Bennie looked at Mary. "DiNunzio, you're press person, which is a big job. Satorno might come in with a camera hiding his face, or with TV makeup on. No press admitted. None at all. It's too risky."

"Right." Mary nodded. "Like we said, I

verify all press passes outside and call the cops if I find him, but don't alert him to it. And nobody gets into the service but attendees."

"Yes." Bennie glanced at her list. "Murphy, you handle the physical plant, the set-up before. You'll play the grieving cousin from California. What if your mother happens to show up? Are you prepared for that?"

"It won't happen, but if it does, I'll ignore her."

"Can you do that?" Bennie's lower lip buckled with doubt.

"Not a problem. I have years of practice."

"You think she'll recognize you?"

"No. Not with my new hair, and she hasn't seen me since college."

Judy and Mary exchanged looks, then Mary smiled. "Nobody will recognize you, not even your own mother, in the disguise we picked out for you." She turned to a red, white, and blue Liberty Place bag sitting on the floor. It was what they'd been rummaging in when Anne first walked in.

"What is that?" she asked, edging to the bag, but Judy held her arm and pressed her into her chair.

"Last night, we went shopping for your

bereavement outfit." Mary reached excitedly into the bag. "All the stores were open and there were tons of great Independence Day sales. Look at these shoes! Aren't they so cute?" She pulled a pair of black flats from the bag like a rabbit out of a hat.

Eeek. "Wow, they're great!" Anne lied, automatically. The habit came back to her easily, like riding a bike.

"Try them on!" Mary bubbled. "They're Superstriders, really comfortable. I wear them all the time. They wear like iron. I figured you were a size eight, like me."

"Good." Anne had never worn Superstriders in her life, but she kicked off her Blahniks and stepped into them. They had absolutely no heel and were made apparently of rubber, but they fit like Cinderella's slipper and felt better than mules ever could. She cheered instantly, maybe because her toes could move for the first time in years. "I can catch a killer in these babies!"

Mary nodded happily. "We also got you a dress. Judy picked it out."

"It's very cool." Judy crossed her legs on the desk. "You'll love it."

Anne looked up to see Mary holding up a dress, the requisite black, but otherwise utterly unconventional. It had a high neck, a dropped V-waist, and a winged collar. The skirt billowed past the knee and the material crinkled like crinoline. It was beyond fashion faux pas, it was well into Halloween costume.

"It's kind of dramatic," Mary said tactfully. "But Judy thought you'd like it. And it covers you up, like a good disguise."

Judy nodded with pride. "It's one of a kind. I got it in the crafts store. Slip it on, let's check the fit. It's not just a dress, it's wearable art."

Huh? "Art is good. I like art." Anne took the dress, slipped it over her head, and shimmied it down over her T-shirt and skirt. It fit in the waist, but its black skirt flowed to the floor like an oil spill. "We'll have to staple the hem, but it's perfect. Thank you."

Even Bennie was beaming. "You haven't seen the best part yet. The last, essential piece."

"More?" Anne looked over in fear, and Mary was holding up a black straw hat with a bigger brim than most beach umbrellas. She handed it to Anne, who set it on her head, impulsively tilted it to the side, and pivoted like a prom queen.

Bennie, Judy, and Mary broke into collective grins. "Wow!" Mary clapped.

"Awesome!" Judy said, then her face changed. "Oh wait, I almost forgot. You can't go without these." She reached into her pocket and extracted something that fit in her palm, then held it up. It was a pair of long earrings, with tiny, irregularly shaped red, black, and blue glass beads, in wild zigzag and swirling patterns. The beads caught the sunlight and glowed like fireworks.

"How beautiful!" Anne was amazed. She'd never seen anything like them and she'd shopped everywhere. "Where did you get them? The art store?"

"Not exactly. I made them for you. The beads are glass." Judy handed them over with a sheepish smile. "Welcome to Philadelphia, Anne."

Anne clipped on the earrings, touched. These women were so generous to her, each in her own way. They were trying to help her. They actually seemed to care about her. Her throat was suddenly too thick to permit speech, so she did what came naturally and threw herself into their arms, hat and all. "Thank you so much!" she managed to croak out, and her hug spanned three lawyers with some success. "You guys are the best!"

Mary hugged her back the hardest, then Judy, who laughed with surprise. But it was Bennie who patted her back and whispered into her ear: "Everything's gonna be all right, honey."

It filled Anne with a warmth she had never experienced. Mental note: Girlfriends are more necessary than underwear.

"Okay, ladies, it's showtime!" Bennie announced, breaking the clinch, and the three mourners sprang into action, with one lagging behind: Anne.

"Bennie, would this be a good time to tell you what happened to the Mustang?" she began.

18

The Chestnut Club was one of Philadelphia's grandest gray ladies, a Victorian mansion with a huge, paneled entrance hall, a sweeping, mahogany staircase, and a landing with an immense, stained-glass window depicting William Penn negotiating with the Native Americans. Their lawyer wasn't present.

Inside, Anne checked her watch, tense. 11:30. Half an hour before the start of the memorial service, and a few people were still arriving. It was a small crowd, which she'd expected; not because of the holiday or the shortness of the notice, but because nobody liked her until twenty minutes ago. She circulated among the mourners, her face artfully made up, her head bent under the wide-brimmed hat, with her sunglasses on. Nobody could *see* her, much less recognize her, and she was able to spy through the lattice weave of the straw.

She spotted a nice client on one of her

commercial contracts cases, Marge Derrick, another commercial client, Cheryl Snyder, and a lovely woman, Lore Yao, whom she knew from a benefit for the Free Library. The staff of Rosato & Associates appeared in force, and Anne wished she could have let them in on the secret, but Bennie had ruled against it. Kevin was nowhere in sight.

Anne walked to the front entrance of the club and looked outside. The press thronged on the street, now joined by on-lookers and holiday partiers. Photographers held their cameras above the throng, snapping away, and TV anchorpeople stood to the side, talking to videocameras. They spilled off the sidewalk into traffic, uncontained by too-few uniformed police and sawhorses. Still, no sign of Kevin.

She shifted her gaze to the four rent-a-muscle men Bennie had hired, mixing with the crowd in suits. They were dressed as lawyers, but the biceps straining their suit seams betrayed them. She spotted the Australian bush hat of Angus Connolly, and saw Mary circulating, checking press credentials, passes, and faces. Anne didn't see Kevin in the crowd. She felt a strong hand on her shoulder and looked over, startled.

It was Bennie. "Relax, Murphy," she said. "Everything's fine. The kitchen, the press, and the flowers are all taken care of, so far. Maybe you'd feel better if you came in and sat down."

Anne nodded, just as she spied Matt outside, in a dark suit and light-blue tie, breaking from the gauntlet of the press and climbing up the stairs. The swelling had gone down on his cheek, and her heart leaped at the sight, then hardened. Matt wasn't alone. Right behind him came Bill and Beth Dietz, dressed in black. Anne couldn't believe her eyes. Why had Matt brought them?

"Do you see this?" she murmured to Bennie, who clearly had, from her expression. Her mouth set grimly and her blue eyes had gone flinty. She took Anne by the elbow.

"Time to go inside," she said, leading Anne back into the entrance hall. "Get going. I gotta mingle."

Anne walked to the large room, as Matt passed her on the right without recognizing her, shepherding the Dietzes. Why would he bring them? For the press? He had to know it would upset her, either way. She kept her head down and her wits about her, then became aware of a man falling into stride beside her, looking right at her. It was Gil Martin.

It gave Anne a start. She had pushed Gil to the back of her mind, but she was in denial. This could be the day she got fired. There was no telling from Gil's expression, which was professionally grave. He wore a dark suit, a shiny Hermès tie, and a renewed tan. His hand touched her arm briefly.

"If this is you under the hat, we need to talk," he said in a low voice.

Damn. "Now?"

"Yes. Jamie's inside the service already. We only have a minute."

Anne led him past the staircase, a hall of old-fashioned wooden telephone booths, and toward the smoking lounge. Nobody would be in there; it was tucked away. She reached the room, pushed on the paneled door, and found the small room empty. She slipped inside, with Gil behind her.

"Gil," Anne said, beginning her opening argument. "I really think you should let me keep—"

"Stop." Gil squeezed her shoulder. "You don't have to convince me. I thought about what you said, about the case, and frankly, about the media. I bet on you before and I'm staying the course."

"That's wonderful!" Anne felt so grateful she hugged him, Victorian hat and all. But just then the door to the lounge opened with a loud creak, and Anne and Gil looked up from their embrace. Gil's wife, Jamie, was standing in the doorway in a black Chanel suit, shaking with anger.

"Here, too, Gil? Can't you keep it in your pants at a *funeral*? With me *in the next room*?" Jamie's pretty face was red, her lipsticked mouth contorted. "Who's this one? Forget it, I don't care! You promised, Gil! We made a deal!" She turned on her heel and left, letting the heavy door bang closed behind her.

Anne backed away from Gil, stunned. She tried to process what had just happened. She always believed Gil and Jamie had a good marriage. "What was she talking about, Gil? What deal?"

"I have no idea what she's talking about," Gil answered, his features calm and in control. "Jamie always thinks I'm having affairs, which I'm obviously not. Are we having an affair? No. She's just crazy."

"Bullshit!" Anne had been hit on by too many married men to believe him now. Had she been played? Had Matt been right? Was Gil the liar, not Beth Dietz? "Is Beth telling the truth? Did you force her to have sex with you?"

"Please!" Gil's blue-green eyes narrowed. "I never forced myself on anybody, I don't have to."

"You had an *affair* with her, then?"

"All right, fine. You're my lawyer, you have to keep it confidential, right?"

"Gil, tell me the truth!" Anne shouted, but Gil gripped her arm, angry.

"Shh, don't make a big deal. So what? Me and Beth had an affair, we were fooling around for months. But I didn't make her screw me to keep her job. She wanted to. She hates her husband. He's an abusive jerk."

My God. Anne edged away. What was true? Was it really a consensual affair? Dietz *was* an abusive jerk. Her thoughts raced, but Gil seemed superbly in control.

"There's no basis to the lawsuit, Anne. Beth filed it because I broke off the affair and she wanted to get revenge. My defense is the same as before. This changes nothing."

"It changes everything! I asked you more

than once if you had an affair with Beth, remember? You lied to me!" Anne couldn't believe how gullible she'd been. She'd believed him because she'd wanted to believe him. He was her client, her friend. "You told me you were insulted by the question! You made me feel like shit!"

"I didn't want you to know about the affair. I was embarrassed and afraid you'd tell Jamie. Or at least you wouldn't be able to hide it around her. But it still doesn't make any difference to the lawsuit. I'm telling you, I still didn't *make* her have sex."

"What deal did Jamie mean? What deal did you make?"

"She stays with me through the trial, then IPO. I want to be squeaky-clean. Besides, if she waits until after the IPO, she divorces me and gets ten million. If she does it now, she gets zip. Which would you choose? And she'll lie at trial if we want her to."

"We don't want her to!" Anne couldn't think fast enough. She didn't know this side of Gil. How could she have been so stupid? "I won't put Jamie on the stand to lie for you! And I won't put you up there either! I don't want your defense anymore. Find yourself another shill!"

"Oh, come on, don't be so emotional." Gil's tone was supposed to be soothing, but it disgusted Anne. He reached for her to calm her, and she pulled back. She couldn't wrap her mind around any of it. She had just kept the case of her career, only to find out she was defending a total sleazebucket. And she didn't have time to deal with it now. Kevin might already be out there. The memorial service would be starting any minute.

She turned on her heel, enjoying the rather theatrical swirl to her skirt, and walked out on her client without another word. She had no explanation for her behavior, now that she was a brunette. Mental note: Impulsiveness may not be related to haircolor.

She hurried down the corridor, past the entrance, and entered the service. The room was paneled, large and boxy, with rows of tan folding chairs in two blocks with a center aisle. Only the first three rows of seats were taken, and Anne took a seat in the back row, for the best view. She tried to get back in control. This was her last chance to catch Kevin. She searched every head, every set of shoulders in front of her. No Kevin. She checked her watch. 11:55.

The service was about to start. Where was he? Was he coming?

Anne checked the room. Judy and Bennie stood in the front, talking together off to the side, and Mary entered and joined them. Matt sat on the right side of the room, next to the Dietzes. Gil was seated two rows behind them, his head bent in an impression of a man with a conscience. Near him sat Detective Rafferty, in coat and tie, and his chain-smoking partner, whose back pressed heavily against the folding chair. The gathering seemed to settle as the last of the stragglers came in. Anne tried to ignore the fact that her mother couldn't be bothered to attend, her lover had betrayed her, her client had lied through his bleached teeth, and her psycho killer was still on the loose.

A flower deliveryman came in, and she watched Judy hurry to meet him at the door, check his ID, then wave him to the front of the room, where he set the flowers down with the few others: lilies, mums, and white sweetheart-roses. The white roses were a corporate gift from a client, and the other flowers were from various Center City law firms, and there was one from the gym. None was from friends, because Anne had no friends, and if that wasn't a graphic enough illustration, no one in the crowd was weeping or even looking mildly bothered.

She felt an echo of the same emptiness she'd experienced in Willa's house, looking at her black-and-white drawings. She didn't want to continue on Willa's path, closed up and alone, and it was where she'd been going. All around her was proof positive. She resolved on the spot to let her death change her life. But first she had to stop Kevin, once and for all.

Bennie was already at the lectern. "Good afternoon," she began, adjusting the black stem of the microphone. "I'm Bennie Rosato, and thank you very deeply for coming to this memorial service. Today we honor a young woman I greatly admire, Anne Murphy. I hired her a year ago, because she struck me as an intelligent, well-trained, and hardworking young lawyer. But, in truth, I didn't take much time to get to know her, this past year. It was my loss, and not hers."

Listening, Anne felt her mouth go dry. This wasn't the script they had discussed back at the office. Bennie had hated the idea of lying to the people, so she was supposed to keep her eulogy generic and impersonal. On the sidelines, Judy and Mary exchanged looks, and the office staff whispered to each other in their seats.

"But more recently," Bennie continued, "I have come to know Anne Murphy, and actually to love her. Her boldness, her courage, and her doggedness. Her resourcefulness, even her recklessness—"

Suddenly, a young man stood up at the far end of the third row. "Judy Carrier! Ms. Carrier!" he shouted. "Ms. Carrier! *You!*" He pointed to Judy, standing at the front of the room. "*City Beat* wants to know, Ms. Carrier!"

Bennie's lips parted in surprise, and Judy edged away, appalled. Anne didn't get it. Was it a joke? Who was this clown? The crowd turned to the young man, who kept shouting.

"Ms. Carrier, why were you in Anne Murphy's car the day *after* she was murdered? What do you have to say for yourself?" The man had leaped from his folding chair and headed straight for Judy before anybody knew what was happening, pulling a tiny digital camera from his jacket pocket. "*City Beat* wants to know!"

City Beat? It was the paper Anne had read on the way to the office. The one with that wanna-be journalist, Angus Connolly, with the bush hat. But this guy wasn't Angus Connolly, and what did he want from Judy, for God's sake?

Anne rose to her feet, watching in shock as he snapped pictures, advancing on Judy. Detective Rafferty jumped from his chair and lunged toward the reporter, as did his heavy-set partner.

All of a sudden a second man started yelling from the other side of the row. "Judy Carrier! Carrier! Answer our allegations! What were you doing with Anne Murphy's car? You killed Anne Murphy! *City Beat* has the story!"

What? Anne was stunned. Judy's eyes widened, her arms pinwheeled, and she tumbled backward into the flowers. Anne rushed to help Judy, but she saw Gil bolt for the exit with the Dietzes right behind. Matt and Bennie tried to get to the second reporter, who was charging toward Judy, brandishing something.

"Judy Carrier!" he shouted. "You killed Anne Murphy! We have the proof! *City Beat* has the proof! An exclusive undercover investigation!" He was shouting as Bennie grabbed him. Matt and two other men piled on, but the young man wouldn't stop yelling. "Confess! You had her car! We have the proof! You were driving her car the day after you shot her!"

My God! Anne froze on her feet, her mind racing. These amateurs thought Judy was her killer!

"You did it!" yelled the first reporter, as Detective Rafferty and his partner forced him to the ground. "You can't do this! We are the working press! We are the working press! We have rights! Constitutional rights!"

The service was thrown into pandemonium. People darted from their seats, tripping on chairs. Anne was pushed against the guests when a vivid flash of red at the door caught her eye. A dozen red roses, held by a deliveryman, his face visible over the roses. His hair was dyed matte-black, but his eyes, nose, and mouth were recognizable.

It was Kevin.

"Stop him!" Anne screamed above the din, but Kevin vanished in the next instant. "Stop him! Stop that man!" She yelled but her voice got lost in the uproar.

"No!" she screamed again, then turned around and took off after Kevin. She wouldn't lose him this time. Not again, never again. She threw herself into the people hurrying toward the exit. Cops charged into the room, blocking her way. She grabbed the short sleeve of one, trying vainly to get his help.

"Officer, I need you. Come with me!" But the cop was already past her and reaching for the handcuffed reporter being hauled off by the detectives. She'd have to do it herself.

"Move! MOVE!" Anne shouted at the people running from the room. She found open road for a brief instant, then pressed her way into the hallway, trying to see Kevin over the fleeing guests. Suddenly someone in front of her got pushed back, and Anne almost fell. Someone trounced on her hem. Her hat and sunglasses got knocked off. She looked wildly around, jostled this way and that. Kevin was nowhere in sight. She had lost sight of him. *Not again!* She felt like crying, like screaming. Tears of frustration sprang to her eyes.

"Hey!" she yelped as she was shoved from the side, then felt herself falling backward. She grasped for someone's handbag on the way down but the woman yanked it away. The next thing she knew she had hit the carpet and was in danger of being trampled. She covered her head with her hands and tried to roll away, with flower petals sticking to her hands and face.

Red rose petals.

Anne opened her eyes and squinted through the moving feet. Red petals lay scattered everywhere on the carpet. They had to be from the red roses Kevin had been carrying. He must have run out with them, then dropped them. Black pumps blocked her view and the spike heel of a dress sandal almost speared her in the ear. Ahead, an empty glass vase rolled on its side. Beyond the vase lay a white paper of some kind, bright against the blood-red rug. A small card, the kind that came with flowers. Kevin's card.

Anne crawled forward on her elbows, risking life and limb. The heavy rubber sole of a wingtip almost stepped on her nose, but she kept an eye on the card. A straight pin affixed it to a headless rose. If she waited until everyone was gone, the card could be as torn up as the bouquet. She got kicked in the ribs by indeterminate footwear and winced in pain.

She was only three feet from the card, then two. The card lay just out of reach. She stretched out her hand but a stack heel crunched down on her index finger.

"Yeow!" she cried, and took one final lunge.

19

The interview room at the Roundhouse, Philadelphia's police headquarters, was as full as a stateroom in a Marx Brothers movie, but far less funny. Detective Rafferty stood against the wall, jacketless, his striped tie loosened from the melee at the Chestnut Club. His partner sat next to him, hunting-and-pecking on an antique typewriter. It read Smith-Corona in script and sat atop a laminated wooden table against the wall. Except for a few chairs, including a steel Windsor bolted to the floor, there was no other furniture in the tight, airless shoebox of a room. It was a dingy green color, scuffed beyond belief, reeking of stale cigar smoke. Judy and Mary stood off to the side, near a smudged two-way mirror, while Bennie stood at Anne's elbow, acting as her counsel.

Anne occupied the steel Windsor chair. "No, I'm not dead," she said, which really seemed sort of obvious. Or maybe it wasn't. Her forehead bore a girl version of Matt's goose egg, and her ribs hurt from being kicked around the carpet. Two buttons had been torn from her art dress, and her stapled hem had fallen. On the plus side, she still had her beaded earrings and something else she treasured, tucked into her bra.

"So the body in the morgue, it's Willa Hansen's?" the detective asked.

"Right."

"She has no family."

"No immediate family."

"What about your family? You don't want them to know you're alive?"

"I haven't seen my mother in a decade. I never met my father."

"Well, well." Detective Rafferty rubbed his chin, where a five-o'clock shadow was beginning to sprout, even though it was only three in the afternoon. "We woulda figured this out by Wednesday, when the tests come back. Misidentifications happen, but we have procedures to prevent it. The holiday weekend screwed us up." Rafferty looked at Anne. "You pretended to be dead?"

Anne was about to answer, but Bennie

clamped a hand on her shoulder. "I'm instructing her not to answer that, Detective."

"Oh, Christ! Why, Rosato?"

"'Cause I'm a good lawyer," she answered. "Ms. Murphy has volunteered to speak with you only because you were about to question Judy Carrier in connection with her murder. Now we all understand that Ms. Murphy is not dead, and that Kevin Satorno shot Willa Hansen believing she was Ms. Murphy. Kevin Satorno is still your shooter, Detective. Find him."

"I do have a few more questions for Ms. Murphy, who intentionally deceived us as to her whereabouts, which constitutes obstruction of justice. As does your conduct, by the way, and those of the other ladies here."

Bennie didn't bat an eye. "That's not exactly the law, but I've no time to teach it right now. My client is happy to answer your questions, when I let her. Ask away."

The detective returned to Anne. "Run this by me again, Ms. Murphy. You rented the Mustang on Friday night, July first. Late Friday night, you were erroneously reported murdered. Then Judy Carrier drove the car around on Saturday and stopped for gas, using her credit card. July second."

"Yes." Anne tried not to look at Judy, who had to be kicking herself. It had happened when they'd gassed up. RANDOM, RANDOM, RANDOM.

"Then Ms. Carrier left her credit-card receipt in the car, and it's dated July second."

"Yes."

"Then you parked illegally on Sunday morning, and the car was towed."

"Yes." Now Anne was kicking herself.

"The rental contract was found in the car, identifying the Mustang as rented to you. The gas receipt with Carrier's name on it was also found, dated the day after your supposed murder. Are we all clear on the facts?"

"Yes. But how did these jerks get the receipt?"

"They were tipped off by the tow yard, who called one of them when the car came in." Detective Rafferty consulted his skinny notebook. "The yard owner called Angus Connolly because he wrote the story in *City Beat*. The yard owner sold him the information, photocopies of the rental contract, and the gas receipt. He also contacted the *Na-*

tional Enquirer and *Hard Copy*." Rafferty looked over steel-rimmed reading glasses at Anne. "Do you have any information relating to that, Ms. Murphy?"

"No."

"So all you know is that you're alive?"

"And that Kevin Satorno will kill me if he finds out."

Rafferty was shaking his head. The heavy-set partner was typing slowly. The newest line of the white interview sheet rolling out of the typewriter read KILL ME IF HE.

Bennie pressed on Anne's shoulder to quiet her. "We're asking you for one more day, Detective. Just one day, then you can go public with it. The world still thinks Anne's dead. Let's let them keep thinking it for one more day. If you release this information, you'll lose any chance of catching Satorno and you'll place my associate in jeopardy."

"I don't see what difference one day will make." Rafferty couldn't stop shaking his head, which Anne didn't take as a good sign.

Bennie leaned over. "It won't be July Fourth weekend, that's the difference, and it's all the difference in the world. Like you said, the tests wouldn't be delayed if not for the weekend. Later, you'll free up personnel. The holiday will be over, the traffic will settle down, and everybody will be back to work. Think about it, Detective."

Rafferty stopped shaking his head.

"When the world finds out that Anne is alive, the story will explode. Especially after the debacle at the memorial service, with her colleague accused of her murder in front of everyone. *Hard Copy*, Court TV, CNN, all the networks will pour into town, if they haven't already. You really think you can handle that kind of deluge today, with two uniforms on duty?"

"We have more than that."

"Not much, and consider, it's the Fourth of July celebration, in the city that gave birth to the nation. All eyes are on us, Detective. You really want Philly to look bad right now? What will it do for the department? You really want national attention focused on the fact that the department didn't notice the mistaken ID of a murder victim?"

Rafferty started to listen, and Anne knew Bennie was throwing anything against the wall that might stick, a time-honored tradition among trial lawyers.

"Detective, we all agree that Anne Murphy

was doing nothing but trying to save her own life, and hide from a man who had tried to kill her in L.A. You really want to charge her with obstruction, Detective? You really want to take this woman and hang her out to dry, for all the country to see, *on Independence Day, in Philadelphia*?"

Rafferty groaned. "You saying the women's groups gonna be on me now? Why does everything have to be 'woman this, woman that'?"

"It's not a woman thing, it's a victim thing."

"I'm not a victim," Anne blurted out, and Bennie said:

"Shut up."

Rafferty was shaking his head again. "I don't like being threatened, Rosato."

"Neither does Anne Murphy, and neither do I. All I ask is one day, one lousy day. I'll turn her in on Tuesday morning, and we'll break it to the press together. Hold a news conference, all of us making nice. Safeguarding victim's rights, after we catch the bad guy."

Rafferty's gaze slid toward his partner, who had stopped typing at FINDS OUT. "What do you think, Beer Man?"

Anne didn't need an explanation for the nickname.

"Tuesday isn't one day from now," the partner said. "It's Sunday, so Tuesday is two days."

Bennie didn't hit him. "It's right after the holiday weekend. Tuesday morning, bright and early."

Rafferty looked like he was thinking about it. "I don't know if I have the authority to do something like this."

Anne opened her mouth to say *Bullshit*, but Bennie buried strong fingers in her shoulder. "Let me talk to your captain, then," Bennie said. "Let me make my case."

"Can't. He's in the emergency room at Temple. Broke his ankle in a softball game."

"The lieutenant then. I'll talk to him."

"He's down the shore, at his house in Longport for the weekend."

"The inspector?"

"He's at PAL parties, for the neighborhood kids. He goes to thirty of them today. Sack races and roasted marshmallows. Fireworks, the whole thing."

"Only you and me working today, huh?" Bennie shrugged. "Then I guess you have the authority, Coach."

"Maybe."

"The real question is, what are you gonna do with those clowns in stir, those so-called reporters?" Bennie frowned. "I want them charged. They ruined our chance to catch Satorno and they attacked Carrier. Murphy almost got stampeded because of them."

"Right," Judy added. "And now everybody in the city thinks I'm Anne's killer."

"Don't come cryin' to me." Rafferty gestured at Anne and Judy. "You girls brought it on yourselves. You sent out the flyer. You whipped up the media, you told 'em to go get the big scoop. You shoulda known that you were gonna get legit reporters—and knuckleheads like those kids—all riled up."

Judy looked down, and Anne's fair skin turned pink. Unfortunately, the detective was making sense. Anne was happy she didn't have to speak for herself, for once. Mental note: Nothing wrong with the term "mouthpiece."

"That doesn't excuse what those two men did, Detective," Bennie answered, angry. "What is this, trial by tabloid? If they had evidence relating to a murder, gas receipts and such, then they should have turned it over to you."

"Like you did?" Rafferty snorted. "You had knowledge that Murphy was alive. Did you call us?"

"Please. I wasn't trying to make money, or get famous. I was trying to protect my employees, which is hardly the same thing, and we did call you in time. If you're not going to charge those two assholes, you'd better keep them away from me." Bennie was almost spitting-mad. It was like having a mother grizzly for a lawyer.

"Cool it, Rosato. They're kids. The one with the jungle hat, he's cryin' like a baby." His high forehead creased deeply. "The real question is what you're gonna do for me, if I let your girl stay dead."

"Anything. Almost."

"This is what I want." Rafferty turned and pointed a finger at Anne. "No more amateur cop, you. We got the resources. We got the expertise. We got a homicide-fugitive squad, joint with the Feds, and they're all over it. We link up with all the states, all the networks. We're the cops, you're not, get it? So, no more, young lady!"

"Agreed." Anne didn't add, *But I flushed him out with a bunch of flowers.*

"No running around, no funny hats, no

happy horseshit, understand?" The detective shifted closer, and his pantleg slid up, giving Anne a glimpse of an ankle holster holding a dark-handled revolver. A .38 caliber Smith & Wesson, not a knock-off. She wished she had one of those babies, but knew it wasn't the right thought at this moment.

"Yes, sir," she said.

"This is for your own good, Miss Murphy. Fugitive apprehension is a dangerous business. If I catch you outta line one more time, I'm lockin' you up. Got me, counselor?"

"Understood," Anne said. She did understand. Next time, she wouldn't get caught.

The detective eyed her warily, then Judy and Mary. "You read me, ladies?"

"Yes, sir," said Mary.

"We'll be good," said Judy.

"We got a deal?" Bennie asked, but she already knew the answer.

Half an hour later, the lawyers were running the media gauntlet outside the Roundhouse, barreling in mourning clothes through reporters, cameras, videocams, shouted questions, and klieg lights. Bennie broke the throng with a strong arm, clutching Anne's elbow. Judy and Mary flanked them like a moving offensive line.

Anne had kept her head down, wearing Judy's sunglasses and a canary-yellow PAL baseball cap they stole from a desk in the squad room. They'd made it to the curb, grabbed a cab, lost the newsvan that gave chase, and ended up back at Rosato & Associates, piling into Bennie's office. Anne had been in here so rarely she couldn't help looking around when she was supposed to be off with the others, making the requisite coffee.

Overstuffed tapestry-covered chairs in tones of pink-and-claret ringed Bennie's desk, and the desk chair was of cherry wood, covered with buttery, burgundy leather. The rug was a nubby Berber, and the office was even more cluttered than Anne's, with law books, papers, case files, and exhibits cramming the bookshelves and covering the large desk and countertops. Certificates and awards from the federal and state bar associations and civil liberties groups blanketed the walls, and Anne wondered if she'd receive even one of those awards in her career. But first she'd have to live long enough. She made it her business to do so. The secret in her bra would help. Not *that* secret, the *other* secret.

"Our luck has to get better, doesn't it?" Judy breezed into the office and handed Anne a cup of coffee, which she accepted with thanks from her somewhat bedraggled colleague. Judy's black skirt and clogs were drenched with flower water, and she'd lost an earring in the melee. The remaining silver teardrop dangled from her ear and it caught the sunlight as she took the seat next to Anne. "We agreed in the coffee room, the memorial was a fiasco."

"I'm sorry, Judy," Anne said. "I hate that everyone will think you're a murder suspect, even for a day."

Judy waved it off. "The cops will make a statement that I'm not under suspicion." Bennie and Mary came into the room bearing coffee, and took their seats, Bennie in her cozy desk chair and Mary next to Judy.

"But nobody will believe it," Anne countered, and Mary's face went red.

"I should have checked for pocket cameras."

Bennie shook her head, taking a sip of coffee. "He was posing as a guest, they both were, and we never thought to search the guests. We weren't worried about the press, we were worried about Kevin." She took another quick sip. "And I should have thought about the rental car, when you told me it had been towed. Everybody keeps the papers in the car, they're temporary registration. I just didn't think of it."

"Me neither," Anne said. "Look, let's not get crazy over it. It's nobody's fault. It's just one of those things that happen." She thought about explaining RANDOM, then decided against it. It would make her look ditzy, like memorizing most of *I Love Lucy*. Okay, *all* of *I Love Lucy*. Then she remembered her conversation with Gil and his admission of his affair with Beth. She couldn't keep it from them. They were all on the same side now, and girlfriends didn't keep secrets, Anne knew from TV. "Guys, there's something we should discuss," she began, and told them the story. When she had finished, the women were uniformly stony-faced.

"The man is a slimeball," Judy said.

"A pig," Mary said.

"A liar," Anne said.

"A *client*," Bennie said.

"Not anymore. I told him to get another lawyer," Anne shot back, and Bennie set down her coffee mug in surprise.

"Oh, really?"

"Damn straight."

"You're fired."

Ouch.

"I'm kidding, but you shouldn't have done that."

"Bennie, Gil lied to me. For almost a year, over and over. You think I didn't cross-examine Gil about Beth Dietz? I'm not that naive."

"Then get over the fact that he lied to you. Clients lie. *People* lie. They want others to think better of them than they are."

Anne squirmed even on the soft chair. "He cheated on his wife."

"Since when do you have standing to assert that? You her lawyer? This a divorce action?" Bennie's blue eyes flashed. "You're a very smart girl, Murphy, so think analytically. Reason it out. The man is right when he says that it changes nothing, in terms of his lawsuit. And you're right when you say you don't put him or the wife up on the stand. I won't have you suborning perjury."

"I should tell him to go to hell."

"No, you have no business speaking that way to a client. I'm sure he knows you were only blowing off steam. What you do now is tell him how to win this lawsuit, because that's what he's paying you for. Strike that. *Me* for. Even better." Bennie grinned, but couldn't coax one from Anne.

"So what do I do, Bennie? How can I win this case? Matt is totally right. He has the facts."

"Matt's a genius," Judy said. "A legal genius. He's Louis Brandeis with hair, Earl Warren with muscles, Felix Frankfurter. With a frankfurter."

Bennie and Mary laughed, but Anne was trying not to. "Forget I said that. Leave Matt out of it, okay?"

Judy giggled. "Anne, when we said to beat his pants off, we didn't mean it literally."

Anne pretended to ignore her. "Bennie, what do I do? Not with Judy, who is completely hopeless, but with Gil."

"Now it gets interesting." Bennie picked up her JAVA DIVA mug again. Everyone in the office knew who it belonged to. "He tells the truth."

"A novel defense strategy," Judy interjected, but Bennie had had better practice at ignoring her.

"You put him up, and he says there was an affair, but that it was consensual. You get all the details from him, like how they got together, how it all happened. Times they met, what they did. See if there are any cards she sent him, any notations of their meetings on calendars, any time they went to hotels or restaurants. You want evidence that it was an affair. You will *prove* it was an affair, and you'll win."

Anne shuddered. "Sounds ugly."

"It is." Bennie nodded. "Ask Clarence Thomas."

"I still believe Anita," Judy said.

"You know what's really interesting about this development?" Mary asked, and they all paid attention, because she usually left it to others to advance legal theory. She cleared her throat. "What's interesting is what Matt knows. In other words, has his client lied to him, like Anne's client lied to her? Does Matt think the affair was consensual or forced?"

"Forced," Anne answered quickly. Too quickly, she realized, because the others were watching her. They wanted inside information. Pillow talk. Maybe this was why you weren't supposed to share pillows with opposing counsel. "I don't think he'd bring the case if he knew it was a lie."

"Really?" Judy asked. "Plenty of lawyers would."

"Not him," Anne said, but everybody was too kind to question her. She had a feeling she would be questioning herself anyway. And she was still wondering why Matt had brought the Dietzes to her service.

Mary nodded. "I'm sure you're right, Anne. But another issue is why Beth Dietz filed the suit."

"The affair was over and she was pissed," Anne answered. "Revenge. That's what Gil thinks anyway. He said so."

Bennie stood up and stretched. "Okay, kids, we have a lot going on. The key thing right now is for us to keep Anne safe until the cops pick up Satorno. Here's what we do—"

"I'd love to get showered, changed, and get back to work on *Chipster*," Anne interrupted. She was thinking of the secret in her bra, and she still had no panties. She was having definite lingerie issues. "Can I go back to your house and get cleaned up, Bennie?"

"No. I don't want you out of my sight. You can use the office shower, like you did before, and we have plenty of clothes here."

Damn. Anne had to execute her new Plan B and she couldn't let Bennie in on it. The boss would never agree, after that meeting with the cops. "Please, the clothes here scream fashion mistake. I'll be safe. Mary and Judy can come with me. They'll be my bodyguards."

"You can use my apartment, if you want," Mary said. "I can lend you some clothes. We're about the same size."

Judy finished her coffee. "I'll watch them both, Bennie," she offered.

"So can we go, Mom?" Anne asked.

Bennie looked dubious, but this time it was Anne who already knew the answer, and they left the office, sailed down the elevator and out the back entrance, sweltering in black. Anne waited until they had all squeezed into the sweaty backseat of a cab and were five blocks from the office before she reached into her bra.

And the three girls went after Kevin Satorno.

20

Schwartz's Flowers, read the sign outside, and the dark-haired sales clerk was so harried that she barely looked up when the empty shop was invaded by three lawyers in black. She had a cordless phone crooked under one ear and was tapping away on an old keyboard at the computer/cash register. "We're closed," she said, hitting the Enter key. "I didn't have a chance to turn the sign over yet, but we're totally closed."

"I just have a question or two," Mary replied, planting herself at the counter. The girls had agreed by process of elimination that she'd do the questioning; Anne couldn't draw further attention to herself, Judy was already in the news, and Mary needed assertiveness training.

The clerk only grunted in response, taking an order over the telephone, and Anne took the opportunity to glance around. The store was a single room, square like a corsage box, and the air smelled floral and vaguely refrigerated. The floor was of green indoor-outdoor carpeting, and potted plants ringed the room. Against the walls sat stainless-steel display cases of Gerber daisies in orange and gold, tall iris in characteristic blue, white gladioli, carnations sprayed pink, and long-stemmed white roses. Despite their beauty, Anne felt a dark shiver.

Kevin had been here.

Her eyes fell to the counter cluttered with ribbon snippings, a leftover clump of baby's breath, and a stray fern. Next to the cash register sat a rack of small gift cards, many of which bore preprinted messages: With Sympathy, Thinking of You, For a Speedy Recovery. Anne spotted a plain white card like the one she'd recovered from the floor at the Chestnut Club and had tucked in her underwire. She plucked the new card from the rack and turned it over in her hand while the sales clerk, behind the counter, hung up the phone.

"We're closed, honest," the sales clerk repeated. Her eyes were a hazel brown, catching the light that streamed in the storefront window facing her, and her makeup had worn off. She wore a white T-shirt and jeans under a tall, white apron with a green FTD logo on it. Her nameplate read RACHEL, in kelly green. "I'm already cashed out for the day. I can't sell you anything."

"I don't want to buy anything," Mary said. "I'm looking for a man named Kevin Satorno, who brought or delivered red roses to a memorial service today. You either employ him or he picked them up here and brought them himself. Can you help? I won't take up much of your time."

"His name is Satorno? I can tell you he doesn't work here." Rachel smiled. "You gotta be family to work here. If he's not a Schwartz, he's not an employee."

"So you know all the delivery people?"

"They're all family."

"No temps?"

"You can't be a temporary Schwartz."

Mary smiled. "Okay, that's a great help. So, that means he bought roses here and delivered them himself."

"Whatever." The cordless phone rang, and Rachel picked it up. "No, Twenty-second Street! Twenty-second Street! *Not Twenty-third!*" She hung up. "My brother is a complete idiot. This is the bad thing about a family business. Your family."

"Were you working here earlier today and yesterday?"

"Yes. I'm the Schwartz who can count. My brother hates math."

"This man bought a dozen red roses here, today or yesterday. He delivered them with a card from this shop. He looks like this." Mary pulled half of the red flyer from her purse and showed it to Rachel. They had decided it was almost as good as Kevin's mug shot and didn't tip off that he was wanted by the cops, thus avoiding any pesky questions. "He's white, tall, young, and good-looking. He has blue eyes, and his hair used to be pale blond, but he's since dyed it black. It was either blond or black when he came here. I know it's not overly helpful, but it's all I'm sure of."

"Either way, his face doesn't look familiar." Rachel handed the flyer back.

"You don't remember him?"

"No way. Do you have any idea how many people have been in this store over the past two days, buying red roses? Everybody orders red for July Fourth, for entertaining and such. It's red-white-and-blue time. I can't keep anything red in stock." Rachel gestured at the display case. "See that iris? It's gorgeous but it'll rot there. July Fourth is almost as bad as Valentine's Day."

"I see. Do you keep records of what people order, when they buy?"

"Sure. I fill out an order for the sale, even walk-ins, if that's what you mean."

"Does it contain any personal information, like name or address?"

"Sure, I ask everybody for name, address, and phone number, but not everybody wants to give it. They don't have to legally, but we ask anyway, for the mailing list." Rachel looked defensive. "If it's really busy though, I don't always get a chance to write out the order. I just fill it and give 'em the flowers. Drives my dad nuts."

Anne was already eyeing the counter for the order forms.

"This Satorno," Mary continued, "may not have used his real name and he may have even used a fake address, but he bought a dozen red roses here either yesterday or this morning. Do you have any way of looking him up, seeing if he had an order? We need to find him. It's really important."

"Find his order?" Rachel wiped a dark strand of hair from her damp brow. "Listen, I'm sorry, but I have to close and I have a shitload to do before I leave. You know how long it would take to go through the orders for red roses? They're not even sorted and they're all mixed in. I wasn't going to deal with it until Tuesday."

Anne kept looking for the order forms. Behind the counter, next to a multicolored ribbon rack, sat a series of gray loose-leaf notebooks that contained catalogs, then she struck gold. Order slips. Some were stacked on an old-fashioned spike, but most were in disarray. She nudged Mary, whose gaze had already located them.

"Rachel, I know you're busy, but we can help. If you'd let us look through the order forms, maybe we could find him. With the three of us, we could look through them in no time, and we'd leave the orders sorted for you. You wouldn't have to do it on Tuesday. We could do it while you closed up and we'd be finished right away. Your dad would think you're a star."

"No, sorry." Rachel shifted her weight behind the counter. "I'd like to, but I can't."

"A woman's life depends on it. She's about your age, and but for the grace of God—"

Anne stepped forward. "My life," she said,

surprised at the desperation straining her voice. "Please, we won't keep you, I swear."

Rachel looked at Anne, and sighed heavily.

Half an hour later, the sign on the door had been flipped to CLOSED, but anyone looking through the storefront window would have seen three women in black, standing on the far side of the counter in front of three stacks of order slips. Mary, Judy, and Anne were each paging through the weekend's slips, but so far no red roses had been sold to a Kevin Satorno, anyone with the initials K.S., or any other aliases he would have used.

At least one that Anne could imagine. She had only ten orders left and she was already feeling it was a fool's errand. Kevin would never leave his real name or a real address. He was a fugitive and he was smart. But she wanted to be thorough and she tried not to be discouraged. There were two other piles. "How you doing, Mary?" she asked. "Any luck?"

"Not so far."

"Don't give up!" Judy said, but Anne could see her pile was down to five orders. No way was there an order for Kevin. It was a waste of time. She couldn't face it. If they didn't get him now, when would they? At her funeral? How many fake ceremonies could they stage? She returned to her receipts. Invoice # 00547, Invoice # 00548, Invoice # 00549.

Anne sighed. That was it. No more orders. She fought back tears of frustration. "Somebody please tell me that they found his order," she said aloud.

Mary bit her lip. Her stack had been searched and turned over. "No Satorno. No name here even remotely suspicious. Just a bunch of orders for red roses and red, white, and blue carnations."

Judy was examining her last invoice. "Lots of roses, none to him. Most of these orders were bought by women, but he wouldn't have gone that far with an alias." She turned to Anne. "Maybe we should just take all the red-rose orders and go to each house that's listed, regardless of name."

Anne shook her head. "No. He'd leave a fake address. Why wouldn't he? I bet he walked in, paid in cash, got his flowers, and walked out."

Rachel came from the back office, her apron gone and her hair swept back by a headband made from a leftover ribbon. She held a Hefty bag full of trash. "I'm all done locking up out back. I even cleaned out the delivery vans. Did you find him?"

"No," Anne answered, dejected.

"I'm sorry. If I could think of another way to help you, I would." Rachel logged off the computer at the counter, then unfolded the Hefty bag and snapped it open. "I only have one chore left, then I really do have to go. My family expects me at a barbecue."

"Sure, I understand," Anne said. She was wracking her brain. What else could they do? Should they go to the houses? Check if the addresses really were fake?

"My brother's already there, and my parents." Rachel reached under the counter, pulled out a large wastebasket painted with flowers, and hoisted it with one skinny arm. Anne grabbed the Hefty bag by its yellow drawstring and held the other side open for her, having nothing else to do but cry. "Thanks," Rachel said, with a grateful smile. "My brother always leaves the trash for me. Pig."

"Thank you for trying to help." Anne held her side of the Hefty bag while piles of silver flower-wrap, green tissue, and plant material tumbled inside, followed by a discarded catalog and soggy paper towels. Then she saw it. A plain white card. *I love you*, it said. Or did it? White freesia buds buried it like an avalanche. Was Anne seeing things? Wasn't that a card, like the one he'd delivered to the memorial? Wasn't that Kevin's handwriting?

"Wait!" Anne shouted. She shoved a hand in the trash, attacking it like a madwoman, shifting through the papers and cards and ferns. "Did you see? I thought I saw another card Kevin wrote."

Mary came over. "Like the first? Another one?"

Judy reached for the Hefty bag. "In the trash?"

Anne rooted around the trash, fishing for the card. "Can I dump it, please? Please? Rachel, please? I'd owe you so big-time, I swear."

Rachel half-smiled. "Sometimes I hate this job."

"I'm sorry, I really am. It's just that I saw something he wrote." Anne took the bag and dumped it on the floor, shaking it empty. She knelt down beside the filth and started sifting.

Mary held up the plain, white card they'd brought with them. "It looked like this, and says, 'I love you.' That's all."

Rachel took the card from Mary's hand, examining it. "This looks familiar to me. I remember this. I don't remember the guy, but I remember the cards."

"Cards?" Judy asked. "What do you remember? Cards? Plural?"

"Cards!" Anne almost cried, half-listening as she went through the trash. Rosebuds, daisy petals, gum, cigarette butts, and inventory sheets went flying. There was the card! She picked it up and held it high. "'I love you,' it says." Then her eyes fell on another card atop the trash. *I love you.* Again, in Kevin's writing. "Look at this! There's more!" She searched. *I love you I love you I love you I love you.* Four more cards, all in Kevin's hand. Then another. "There's five of them here! Wait, six!"

"My God," Mary said, hushed, and Judy bent over the trash pile and started looking.

"Here's another!" Judy said, finding a white *I love you* card. "I don't get it. They all say the same thing?"

"I thought that was a little weird!" Rachel exclaimed. "It's coming back, now. This dude wrote the card at the counter, which a lot of people do, but he wrote it over and over. At first, I thought it was so cute. He wanted it to be just right. I made a joke but he didn't laugh. He kept writing them over and over. Is *he* the guy?"

"Yes!" Anne was arranging the cards in a line on the counter. Eleven cards lined up like a dotted line. *I love you I love you I love you I love you.* "So, where is his order?"

"Oh, no. I was mad busy. He must have been one of the ones I didn't fill out." Rachel's face clouded. "He must have come at the worst time. I didn't have a chance, I just wanted to make the sale and not hold anybody up. That's why I don't remember his face, I guess."

"No address?" Anne's heart went through the fake-grass floor, but she didn't want to make Rachel feel bad. Kevin had probably planned it that way so he wouldn't be recognized, or maybe he just got lucky. "He wouldn't have left a real address anyway. Did you see where he came from?"

"No. I'm so sorry." Rachel looked so crestfallen, Anne reached out and touched her arm.

"It's all right. Did he drive or was he on foot, do you know?"

"I don't know, but you can't park around here. He must have walked."

"Do you recall how he paid?"

"Cash, I think. Yeah, cash." Rachel screwed up her cute nose. "It is weird to write the same thing so many times, isn't it? I mean, some people mess up or get obsessive, but not like that."

"He's more obsessive than most." Anne found a laugh, and suddenly Rachel brightened.

"Wait! I remember, he left his pen! He left his pen! He was writing so many cards and he was so happy when he got a good one, and then I made the joke and noticed him, and he got pissed off. He walked out so fast he left his pen. Does that matter?"

"I doubt it, but let's see." Anne couldn't help but feel excited, and Rachel was already grabbing the tall white pen-and-pencil holder.

"I put it in here. His pen, with the others." Suddenly she dumped the cup on the counter. Pens, pencils, a screwdriver, and an Exacto knife clattered onto the clean surface and started rolling around. There had to be thirty pens; red, green, blue, and white, piled like a child's pick-up sticks. Then Anne noticed something about the pens.

"They have logos! Maybe they'll say

where they're from." Anne scooped up a navy ballpoint, twisted it, and read the imprinted letters out loud. "'Property of The Best Grandpop in The World.'"

Judy was reading a purple pen she'd found. "'Claritin-D 24-hour.'"

Mary squinted at a black pen. "'Ace Appliance.' I use them!"

Anne grabbed a white pen, read it, and felt a jolt like electricity surge through her system. She thrust it into the air, and it shot up like a Roman candle. "We got him!"

21

Anne was surprised to discover that a lime-green VW Beetle could be almost as much fun as a Mustang convertible. Okay, not really, but she was so excited that they were finally going to get Kevin that she was trying to convince herself. Judy was driving her car, Mary was in the passenger seat, and Anne bounced along on the cloth-covered back bench as the VW chugged its way up the incline of the Ben Franklin Bridge. Mental note: Any vehicle with daisies in the dashboard is not a muscle car.

Anne rolled the white pen from the florist's between her fingers. It was a cheap plastic ballpoint with gold-toned letters that read DAYTIMER MOTEL. Underneath was the motel's address and phone, in Pennsauken, New Jersey. It had been the only motel or hotel pen in the pencil cup at Schwartz's, and Anne was praying that Kevin had found a room at the Daytimer. The Beetle reached the top of the bridge and slowed behind snaky lines of traffic.

"Uh, oh. People still going down the shore," Judy said with a sigh. She had rolled up the sleeves of her blouse and let her left arm dangle out the window. "I was hoping everybody who was going had gone already."

"Damn." Anne edged between the two front seats and assessed the traffic through the funky windshield. "This looks bad. How long will it be, do you think?"

"Not too long," Judy answered. "There's a line to the toll booths, but they're not taking tolls this direction, so it'll move along."

"It's enough time to call Bennie," Mary ventured. "I have my cell. Maybe we should."

"No," Judy and Anne answered in unison, and Anne was liking Judy better and better.

"Don't back out now," Anne said, to a worried Mary. "We settled this. We'll call Bennie as soon as we see that Kevin's checked in at the Daytimer. Why bother her if it's a dry hole? If this isn't the pen he left? We're just taking a chance that he's at the Daytimer, and it's a remote chance, at best."

Judy nodded. "Anne's right. Also Bennie would never let us do this, and why shouldn't we? It's fun! We get to play hooky! Isn't it so cool up here?" She waved her arm against a clear blue backdrop of sky and a soaring arc of expansion bridge, but Anne couldn't stop thinking about Kevin. They were back on track, after losing him at the service. She would get him yet. She was so close she could shoot him.

"It's smart of Kevin to stay in New Jersey, isn't it?" she asked, idly. "It gets him out of town and takes the heat off."

Judy agreed. "Plus, it raises a jurisdictional question with the Philly police. Requires co-operation with the FBI, which is problematic."

Mary covered her ears. "We shouldn't be discussing this. This is wrong. We're going against Bennie. She'll fire us." She uncovered her ears and turned to the backseat. "Murphy, let's talk about the case. *Chipster.* You have to make a new opening argument, now that you're going to tell about the affair."

"You're right," Anne considered it, then reached into her purse, snapped the phone open, and hit speed-dial for Gil. "Here we go. Everybody be quiet."

"No fart noises, Mare," Judy warned. The VW stopped next to a gigantic billboard for Harrah's Marina, in which a woman drove a steamboat as big as an ocean liner. Sequined letters glittered, I'LL TAKE YOU THERE. The call was picked up.

"Gil, it's Anne." She cupped the phone around her ear to keep out the traffic noise.

"Anne, where are you? Are you okay? I was so worried about you, after what happened at the Chestnut Club."

Right, that's why you haven't called. "Listen, we need to discuss your new defense. Meet me tonight, at the office at seven and bring any evidence you have of your affair with Beth."

"Evidence? Like what?"

"Cards, letters, anything." Anne flashed on *I love you I love you I love you*. Weird how parallel the relationships seemed. "Cards from flowers. Hotel receipts, phone bills, calendar notations. Any writings at all that show your relationship with Beth was consensual, not a quid pro quo for continued employment. We're not going to hide the truth. We're going to prove it."

"Anne, no! I don't want that public, not now."

"It's the only way you'll win. We have to preempt any argument Beth may have, any proof of a sexual relationship."

"She has nothing! I never wrote her any- thing. You think I'm stupid?"

Don't answer. It's not good client relations. "They have Bonnard, the French woman. She's already testified at her dep that you forced her into sex, so they have pattern and practice. We're moving to exclude it but the judge won't rule until next week, and he'll probably let it in. If they come at us, you're dead and so is Chipster."

"But I didn't force her! I didn't force any woman! I did have a thing with Janine Bon- nard, but—"

Oh, great. "I know, you've been fooling around for years. That's our defense. It isn't pretty, but it isn't illegal. We'll talk when we meet. Just bring the stuff. I have to go."

"What do I tell Jamie? That I'm going to humiliate her in public?"

You did that already. "Tell her I want her at that trial every day, in the front row. And when I put her up, she's going to tell the truth. Testify about the pain your affairs caused her, but say that you wouldn't force sex on anyone. Your philandering will win this case, Gil. Your pattern and practice is cheating, not harassment."

"That would be awful for Jamie, and for me!"

"No, it will be awful for you, but I have a feeling Jamie would love to tell her story, and she just may save your sorry ass. She'll be a counterpoint to the plaintiff, and the truth of what happened comes out best through her, because it's so obviously against her interest to admit. The jury will see that you've been punished, and go for the defense."

Gil sounded distinctly unhappy. "Anne, I have to think about this."

"We'll talk tonight, after I see what you got."

"Does this mean you're still my lawyer?"

"See you tonight." Anne snapped the phone closed, feeling uneasy. She'd liked the case so much better when she believed in Gil. Now she knew the truth.

Judy met her eye in the rearview mirror. "Traffic's starting to move," she said. "It's a sign."

"Let's go get 'em," Anne said, and Mary managed a cautious smile.

Fifteen minutes later the VW was zipping through the toll booths and negotiating

Admiral Wilson Boulevard, which didn't show the Garden State to great advantage. Its four lanes snaked through strip bars, liquor stores, then more strip bars and liquor stores. Sometimes the scenic wonder was interrupted by another casino billboard or a strip bar that called itself a gentleman's club. Anne felt confident that no gentlemen went there. The VW took a left, then a right, winding past tire warehouses, an auto body yard, and a stop for the PATCO speed line, a monorail tram that took commuters over the bridge into Philadelphia. After getting lost a little, the Beetleful of sweaty lawyers finally found themselves in the parking lot of the Daytimer.

It was a small, tawdry motel that looked like it had been built in the sixties, with a low-slung sloping roof at the entrance, which was meant to serve as a carport. The glass over the front door was covered by security bars, and to its right flickered a neon sign that read VACAN Y. As disgusting as the place was, it was all Anne could do not to run in. "I can't believe we're here. We got him!"

Judy pulled into a space facing the entrance and cut the ignition. "Whoa," she said, looking over the curved hood. "Take a look at this layout. I like it."

Anne boosted herself up and realized immediately what Judy meant. The motel had been designed as a short, straight line, like a hyphen set parallel to the parking lot, and it consisted of two floors, so that its two decks of numbered rooms were in full view of the lot and street. "We can see all the doors, and when he goes in and out."

"Hey, check out the license plates." Mary was eyeing the parking lot. "They're all out-of-state. Connecticut. New York. Maine. Virginia. That's funny. There's nothing to see around here, no tourist attractions."

"It's a cheater motel, dufus," Judy said knowingly. "Out-of-staters come here to cheat, probably traveling salesmen and people like that. The locals don't come here to cheat because if they do, they'll be seen."

Anne hung over the front seat. "That must be how Kevin got the room here on the holiday weekend. The business trade is down because of the Fourth. Even the cheaters stay home." The more she thought about it, the more sense it made. "And he's close to the PATCO speed line, between Philly and Jersey, if he stays here. That must be how he gets back and forth to the city, since he probably doesn't have a car."

"Look!" Mary exclaimed, pointing up, and they did. A short, older man dressed business-casual was leaving a room on the second floor. Next to him sashayed a much younger woman in red hot-pants and matching platform shoes. "Is that a—"

"Hooker," Judy supplied.

Anne was disappointed it wasn't Kevin, but Mary gasped.

"Is she a hooker? An actual *hooker*?" Mary couldn't stop watching the couple as they strode past on the top balcony, the woman's hips rolling expertly as she walked. "I never saw a real hooker before."

Anne was intent on getting Kevin. "So now what do we do? We have to find out if he's registered here, and if he's in."

Mary watched the entrance. "I wonder if we should call Bennie, or the cops. Let them take it from here."

"No!" Anne and Judy answered, again as one.

Anne leaned toward. "Don't worry. We don't know anything yet, not for sure, so we shouldn't call Bennie. And which cops would we call? The Philly police have no jurisdiction in Jersey, like Judy said, and we don't know anybody in the Jersey police. I wouldn't even know where to start."

"It's an FBI matter," Mary said, biting her thumbnail. "We'd start there."

Judy looked over. "Mare, what're we gonna do? Call 'em up? Hello, FBI?"

"Yeah, I guess," Mary answered, but there was little conviction in her voice.

"I don't think he's in there," Anne said, eyeing the motel. Nobody was going in and out of the front entrance. The place looked sort of empty. "We know Kevin was in Philly at noon, at the memorial service. My guess is he's still there, in town. Watching my house or the office, or hanging out in a gay bar until the excitement from the memorial service dies down. Planning his next move. A fugitive would want to stay mobile, so he can react as the situation changes."

"This sounds dangerous." Mary turned around, and Anne could read the fear straining her brown eyes.

"If he's not in there, there's no danger. We're not going to try to take him down ourselves, anyway. We go inside, see if he's registered, then call the cops. That's the plan." Anne's resolve strengthened.

"This is me, planning. Right before your very eyes."

Judy grinned. "It doesn't count as planning if you do it when you need it, Anne. It has to be in advance, like premeditation."

Anne was dying to get inside that motel. "Okay, so we have to find out if he's registered. Otherwise we're waiting out here for no reason."

"How do we do that?" Judy asked, turning to Anne. "He wouldn't be registered under his real name."

"We can describe him to the clerk, like we did to Rachel. Maybe the clerk will remember something."

Judy shook her head, so her lone silver earring dangled. "The clerk won't tell you, or let you see the register. He's not supposed to, and I bet he won't, at a cheater place. Especially to a woman. You could be the guy's wife."

"What if I paid him? I could slip him a twenty, or even a fifty."

"That only works in the movies. This is New Jersey."

Anne began to smile. "I have a better idea."

"Is the FBI involved?" Mary asked.

"Quite the contrary. But first, somebody has to go shopping. Mary, you're elected. Take the car. Cherry Hill Mall is less than ten minutes away. Judy and I will stay here, so we don't miss Kevin if he comes back. We'll hide in some car, if one is open." Anne twisted around, scoping out the surroundings. "Or maybe in that gas station. If Kevin comes back, we call the cops right away."

"What's your idea?" Mary asked. "And why do I have to go shopping? I just went shopping!"

"This is what happens when girls fight crime," Anne answered. And, as politically incorrect as it was, nobody even tried to deny it.

An hour later, three women emerged from a chartreuse VW Beetle and wobbled in red platform shoes across the gritty asphalt parking lot of the Daytimer Motel. Heavily made-up, they wore red satin hot-pants and midriff tops covered with blue-and-white stars. They were supposed to be hookers, but Anne thought they looked like an X-rated women's gymnastic team. Either way, they were sashaying a step closer to finding Kevin.

"I don't see why we had to dress all the

same, Mare," Judy grumbled. She was a large-boned, strong girl, but looked surprisingly slender in her midriff and hot-pants. Makeup added years to her face, so she looked almost postpubescent. "I don't think real hookers dress alike when they go out on . . . jobs. Or whatever they're called."

"It saved time to get three outfits the same, and it's a Fourth of July theme." Mary's ankle collapsed, but she righted herself. She cut a curvy, compact figure in her outfit, and the hot-pants made her short legs look longer. Her hair was pulled back into a ponytail, and her lips were a crimson red, expertly applied by Anne, who'd had to make them all up. Mary hadn't resisted the hooker makeover. "Besides, it's better for the plan."

"It's a dumb plan," Judy said.

"It's a good plan," Mary said.

"It's an awesome plan," Anne said. "At least the hot-pants are cooler than the black dresses." She wasn't a midriff fan, especially since she was still retaining water, but she was in love with the platforms. "Stiletto heels and ankle straps. I *love* ankle straps. They look like a pair of Bruno Maglis I saw once, for ten times as much."

"Watch out, *a curb*!" Mary shouted, like the lookout on the *Titanic*. The paved curb to the entrance of the Daytimer Motel loomed straight in their path. "*Curb!* Dead ahead!"

"Heads up!" Judy warned.

"Don't look down!" Anne advised them. "Hold hands and go for it! On the count of one, two, three!"

"Wheee!" They held hands like paper dolls and jumped onto the pavement. "We did it!"

"I *love* these shoes!" Anne said, exhilarated, and Mary giggled.

"I like being tall, even if I can't walk."

Judy grimaced as they reached the motel's front door, and she grabbed the smudgy glass handle. "Shopping for clothes, talking about clothes, wearing new clothes. Catching a psycho killer can only pale in comparison."

And the hookers hobbled inside.

22

There was no lobby in the Daytimer Motel, only a small paneled room with a fake-wood counter that blocked access to the elevators beyond. Folded brochures, improbably for Amish country, flopped over on a metal rack next to an old tan computer, a dirty telephone, and a stack of free newspapers called *Pennysavers*, their ink so black it came presmudged. The man behind the counter was pushing eighty years old, with greasy glasses, dark eyes, and a stained, white, polo shirt. His grizzled beard enveloped a fleshly leer that appeared the moment Anne walked in the door, leading her cadre of Fourth-of-July prostitutes.

She swiveled her hips as she approached, making the most of the distance to the counter, then leaned over and flashed the clerk an ample view of her stars and stripes. "I'm looking for a man," she purred. "Me and my friends, that is, we're looking for a man. We were told that he'd be staying here."

"He's a lucky man," the clerk said, sneaking a peek.

"Oh, he's very lucky." Anne batted her eyelashes prettily. It wouldn't have done much for Matt, but he wasn't old enough to remember Betty Boop. "We're sort of a present, for July Fourth. Sent by some friends of his, from his college frat. They wrote the man's name on a card, but I lost it. Silly me."

"Poor you."

"So the only way we can find this frat boy and give him his . . . gift is for you to help us. So will you? Help us?"

"Please help us," Mary murmured, flirting backup.

"If you don't help us, we'll get fired." Anne pouted. "A girl's gotta make a living, you understand? We can't get fired. That would be awful."

"Terrible," Mary added.

Judy leaned over. "Then we'd have to go to law school."

The clerk *heh-heh-heh*ed, his lips newly wet. "Sure, I'd be glad to help youse, all a youse. But how'm I gonna find the guy, if you don't know his name?"

"We know a little what he looks like. He's young, with real short hair, and he's kind of tall. Maybe six feet, kinda muscle-y. He's got blue eyes, and he's white. He has either black or blond hair, I forget. He likes to change it around, like a rock star or somethin'. He checked in recently, no more than a week ago at the most. He mighta gone out today."

"Got it." The clerk was already typing away on a dirty gray keyboard, checking an ancient 286 computer. His eyes went back and forth slowly as he read the screen, and he popped the Enter key with a dirty fingernail. "He's staying here, ya think?"

"Yes, we think so." Anne nodded, as did the others. *So say we all*, said the nod.

"Come on, honey." Suddenly the clerk stopped hitting the key and looked skeptically around the monitor at Anne. "You're lying about the frat boy, aren't ya?"

Anne tried not to look nervous. "Well, why do you ask?"

"'Cause the man you described, he sounds like this guy in 247, but he's no frat boy. He checked in five days ago. His hair was blond, but from the cut, I'd bet a million bucks he just got outta prison, not college."

"Really?" Anne's heart gave a little jump, in platforms. It had to be Kevin. "Maybe that *is* the man we're supposed to party with. Maybe the guys who hired us just didn't want to say. Not that I'd hold it against him, if he served his time and all."

"That's how I feel." The clerk clicked backward on the computer, then pointed at the screen. "Here he is. The name Ken Reseda ring a bell?"

"Yes!" Anne answered, with excitement she couldn't hide. Kevin was born in Reseda, California, she remembered from his file. Ken Reseda had to be Kevin Satorno. "That's him. Aren't you so smart!"

"Well, I don't know." The clerk smiled under his grizzle. "I can spot an ex-con a mile away. You'd be surprised what you learn, people-watchin'. I see plenty here. Been in the hotel business twenty-five years. I own the place, you know."

"I assumed. It's so well-run."

"And homey," Mary added.

Judy leaned over. "It's the fucking Ritz."

Anne suppressed her smile. "So, do you happen to know if Mr. Reseda is in or not?"

"I wasn't on this morning, but I'll check." The clerk looked at the old-fashioned wooden cubbyholes behind him, then turned back. "His key ain't there. You were right. He musta went out this morning."

"Oh, that's okay. Maybe you wouldn't mind giving us a key for Mr. Reseda's room and keeping it our little secret? So we can surprise him when he comes home?"

"I think we can arrange that, my dear," the clerk said, with a wink. He reached behind the counter and took a duplicate key from the cubbyhole.

"And could you ring his room if he gets back while we're in there?" Anne knew they were taking a risk, but nobody could be convinced to stay behind in the car as a lookout. "We'll need a little warning if he shows up, so we can . . . get ready."

"Powder our noses," Mary said.

Judy leaned over. "I have to build the cage."

"Okay. Here's the key, and I'll make the call, if I see him." The clerk held the key just out of Anne's reach, with lecherous grin. "Any chance I'll get a *gift* from youse girls in return? I got a good ticker, still."

Anne laughed it off, or tried to. "I'm not your type."

Mary chuckled in support. "I'm too expensive."

Judy leaned over. "I sue people for fun."

The man's leer evaporated, and he handed Anne the key with a nervous glance toward Judy. "She's a little freaky, isn't she?" he whispered.

"*Super*freak," Anne assured him, and they teetered to the elevator bank.

The tiny elevator was waiting, open, and the girls didn't start bickering until they were stuffed inside it with the doors closed. Judy pushed a freshly moussed curl from a mascaraed eye, looking wounded at Anne. "You told him I was a freak!" she said, hurt.

"All I did was play along so we could get past the desk." Anne couldn't wait to get upstairs, watching the broken floor-number change to two, but Mary looked increasingly worried.

"Are we really going up there alone? Shouldn't we call Bennie first and tell her? We said we would."

"Relax, it's an empty room," Anne said. "Also, she'll stop us."

"I'm not in love with this," Mary said, but Anne grabbed her hand as the elevator doors rattled open.

"Come on, we'll be fine." She found herself on a covered balcony with a vending machine set against white stucco walls, gone gray with grime. Anne led them to the right because there was no other choice. The balcony had a view of the motel parking lot, the gas station, and a tire dump. "Let's go."

"I'm no freak," Judy muttered, tottering behind. "I don't want to be a freaky hooker, I want to be a normal hooker."

"Then why'd you say that thing about the cage?" Anne checked the room key on the fly. It was stamped 247. They were at 240. Kevin was so close; at least his room was. Their platforms scuffed on the gritty tile floor as they clomped past 240, 241, and 242, with Judy still pouting.

"I don't know. My feet hurt."

"Well, I'm sorry if I libeled you. I really am." Anne couldn't fuss with Judy, not so close to Kevin's room. Her stomach felt tight.

Mary brought up the rear. "He liked you the best, Jude. I could tell, from the way he looked at you."

"You think? He said I was a freak."

"That's how I know," Mary said. "Men love freaky chicks. Crazy, freaky chicks. This is why I can't get a date. I'm too Catholic."

Judy lifted an eyebrow, and Anne fell silent when she reached the door. She slid the key inside the lock in the doorknob and opened the hollow door, her heart starting to hammer. Even though Kevin wasn't supposed to be here, she opened the door slowly. She felt suddenly loathe to enter his room, his world, his mind. When the door swung open, Judy appeared beside her and Mary filed in behind, surveying the bizarre scene:

The room was small, with a bathroom to the immediate left, but all of the furniture was covered by papers. There were clippings from newspapers, tabloid headlines, written notes, cards, even stacks of photographs. It looked as if it had snowed inside the room, dropping a white blanket on a saggy double bed against the wall and a cheesy desk with a portable TV on a metal stand. Exacto knives and a Scotch-tape dispenser lay strewn on the thin, worn brown rug, along with snippings of newspaper.

Anne felt instantly as if she had seen the room before, then realized she had. She flashed on the pictures of Kevin's bedroom at his L.A. apartment, which were shown at his trial, exhibits A through whatever. His motel room was a replica of his L.A. bedroom; pictures, clippings, photos of Anne had littered the place, along with maps to her house and her office, with places where she ate and where she shopped encircled. She felt now as if she was stepping into one of the trial exhibits, and the realization momentarily stalled her. *It was happening all over again.*

Mary closed the door behind them, hurried to the window, and moved the sheer curtain aside slightly. "I'll stay here and look out, in case he comes back."

Judy walked past Anne to the bed. "What is all this stuff? Legal papers?" she asked, picking one up. "They are. Here's the last brief we filed in *Chipster.*" She flipped through it in surprise, then set it down in favor of the others. "These are all of the papers filed in the *Chipster* case. Copies of the initial complaint, the answer, even the evidentiary motions, and the complete docket sheet. This is as good a file as ours, and all of it public record."

Anne willed her feet to move and crossed

to the papers littering the desk. Newspaper clippings about Chipster.com lay scattered over the Formica surface, each one carefully razored from the paper. NAKED MAN AP-PEARS IN COURT, read one subhead, and Anne winced. She sifted through the articles, and it was as if Kevin had scoured all the newspapers; he had all the sidebars on Rosato & Associates and the features on the individual lawyers, as well as the Dietzes. Anne picked one up. It had been printed in color, from the web. How had Kevin managed that? She shoved the clippings aside and buried beneath was a laptop, hooked up to a Hewlett-Packard printer. "Hello. Add receiving stolen goods to the record, ladies."

Judy had moved farther up the bed and picked up one of the papers. "Look at this. It's a map of the city with streets circled on it." She turned on a cheap lamp by the bed and studied the map. "Anne's house, the office, the courthouse. Weird, but true."

It sent a chill through Anne. "I don't want to live through this again." It came from her heart, speaking out of turn.

But Judy looked up, the map in her hand falling in jointed sections. "I'm not sure this is about you anymore," she said, her face grave under her exaggerated makeup. "Beth Dietz's house in Powelton Village is also circled here, and there's a notation on a circle in the middle of Fifteenth Street. It reads, 'Beth eats lunch here.'"

"What do you mean?" Anne went over to the bed, where Judy was holding up a photo of the Dietzes leaving the courthouse after a pretrial motion.

"There's lots of photos here of Beth. Even one from a website that helps people find their high school classmates. He must have researched her and gone in under a fake name."

"I know that website," Anne said, scanning the newspaper photos. "You're right. There are almost as many of Beth Dietz as of me, and he used that site to research me, too."

Judy was about to set a photo down on the bed when she stopped in mid-arc. "Oh my God, look at this." She picked up another photo of Beth Dietz and showed it to everyone. This one had a red heart drawn around her face.

Anne froze. She had forgotten until this minute. "He used to do that to my pictures."

Judy turned. "What's going on, Anne? Is

he in love with Beth now that you're dead? It looks like he's switching over or something."

"Erotomanics do transfer their obsession." Anne felt a shudder start at the base of her spine, then inch up. "If he thinks he killed me, he may be letting me go. Maybe he's going to start stalking Beth Dietz now."

"So he's in love with her."

Anne nodded. "Yes, but that's not the nature of de Clérambault's. It's the reverse, remember? What's happening now is that Kevin is an erotomanic, so he believes that Beth Dietz is in love with him."

"But she's married," Judy said, puzzled, and Anne tried to explain the inexplicable.

"No matter, he's delusional. No reality destroys the delusion, except for a restraining order. And we know the Dietzes don't have the best marriage in the world. Maybe Kevin knows that, too. He watched me for a long time before he asked me out. I didn't find that out until the trial. He'd been stalking me for months without my knowing."

"Can this happen even if they never met?" Judy asked. "I mean, I doubt that Beth Dietz ever spoke to Satorno."

"Again, it makes no difference. It was an erotomanic who stalked Madonna, and

Martina Hingis. And Meg Ryan. The man who killed that TV actress, Rebecca Schaeffer? He had de Clérambault's."

"That's so scary," Mary said. She came over and patted Anne's shoulder, but Anne wasn't sure whether she was comforting her or drawing comfort from her.

Anne surveyed the scene, knowing the implications for Beth Dietz as clearly as if she were clairvoyant. It would start with e-mails, visits, then roses, notes and cards, phone calls and gifts, and surprise knocks on the door at all hours of the day and night. And it could end with a gun. Anne struggled to compose herself. "As long as Kevin Satorno is at large, Beth Dietz's life is in danger. The question is, what do we do about it?"

"We tell the police," Judy answered. "No question."

"We also tell Beth Dietz," Mary added. "No question."

Anne held up a hand like a traffic cop. "Correction. We make sure the cops tell Beth, and I'll tell Matt, too. I still play dead until Tuesday. We don't need Kevin enraged right now, for my sake or for Beth's."

"Agreed," Judy said, and Mary was shaking her head.

"This is strange. We're going to save Beth Dietz's life, and she's suing our client. The line between good and evil is shifting."

"Yeah, it's funny," Anne said, though she knew it was just the RANDOM part, from her fake-jogging. "As relieved as I am that Kevin may be letting me go, I still wouldn't wish him on my worst enemy."

Judy smiled. "You know what that makes you, Murph?"

"A fool?" Anne guessed.

"A hooker with a heart of gold," Mary answered, and they all laughed.

Minutes later, the lawyers had closed the door to Kevin's motel room and were scuffing down the corridor and piling into the elevator. Mary flipped open her cell phone, as they'd agreed, and pressed in the office number. "Bennie, guess what?" she said. "We found Kevin's apartment. He's at the Daytimer Motel in Pennsauken under the name Ken Reseda."

The elevator was so tiny, Anne could hear Bennie yelling, "HOW DO YOU KNOW ALL THAT? YOU'RE SUPPOSED TO BE TAKING CARE OF MURPHY! WHERE IS SHE?"

Mary cringed. "We're all together, and it's kind of a long story. We called you as soon as we were sure it was him. We think he started stalking Beth Dietz. You wanna call the cops or should we?"

The elevator opened onto the first floor as Bennie shouted, "WHERE ARE YOU, DiNUNZIO? TELL ME YOU'RE NOT IN JERSEY!"

"Me? Where am I?" Mary tottered past the reception desk. "Uh, at a car wash?"

Judy burst helpfully into car-wash noises. "*Ppppshhhhhh! Pssssshhhhh! Ssshhhhhhh!*"

A car wash? Anne couldn't believe it. It was the lamest lie she'd ever heard. It was the lamest lie in the bar association. She was almost embarrassed to be in its presence. These girls were crying out for her expertise, but now wasn't the time for a lying lesson. She handed the room key to the surprised desk clerk on the way out. "Thank you for your help," she breathed, in character.

"Why you leavin'? Reseda ain't back yet."

"He's a superfreak," Anne answered, and wiggled out the door behind the others. She would have asked the clerk not to tell Kevin they'd been there, but he'd be arrested as soon as he hit the lobby.

She finally had him.

23

There was almost no traffic heading into the city, and the Beetle zoomed up the steep slope of the Ben Franklin Bridge, carrying three happy hookers. Wind blew off the Delaware River, setting everyone's moussed hair flying, and Anne felt almost high as they sped to the top of the bridge.

They had done it. They had found Kevin. He would be arrested, tried, and imprisoned for good. The nightmare would finally be over for her, and for Beth Dietz, who didn't even know it had started. For Willa, there would be mourning and justice. Tomorrow would be Monday, the Fourth of July. There would be fireworks and ketchup bottles that burped. And Anne was beginning a love affair; one that felt like the real deal, as they said in Philadelphia. She smiled inwardly, with only one regret. "I wish we could have stayed and seen him get arrested."

Mary's hair blew crazily around. "Me, too,

but Bennie wanted us out, pronto. It wasn't safe for us to stay. She called the cops on the other line and they're on their way. And we have to be back at the office, for you to meet with Gil. We're already late."

"Also we could have gotten arrested for indecent exposure," Judy added. As she drove, she wiped off her makeup with Dunkin' Donuts napkins.

Anne leaned over the front seat. "I wonder how they'll get him. I guess they'll stake out the motel undercover, so he's not warned when he comes back."

"Right." Judy accelerated. The car reached the tippy-top of the bridge, laying the entire city at their feet. The skyline shimmered, festive for the Fourth, with the spiky towers of Liberty Place outlined in red, white, and blue neon, and the tops of Mellon Center bathed in red lights. Stray fireworks launched from the Philly side of the waterfront, and one ersatz comet streaked into the twilight, trailing glitter.

Anne couldn't stop worrying. "Tell me they'll catch him, Judy."

"They'll catch him," Judy answered. "He's smart, but not that smart. They'll get the Philly and Jersey cops, even the Feds all over it. They'll face Bennie Rosato if they don't."

Anne felt reassured, almost. "But a zillion things can go wrong. I wish we could have stayed. I'd feel better. That closure thing."

Judy caught her eye on the rearview, then switched to the outside lane as they raced toward the city. "When they catch him, it'll be all over the news. Bennie said she'd call us on the cell as soon as they had him in custody."

Mary turned around. "You will be free, Anne. Really free of him."

"Wahoo!" Judy yelled, and Anne smiled.

"I guess you're right. It's just so hard to believe." She breathed in the fresh air off the Delaware, but Judy was rooting around on the floor of the car while she drove, causing the Beetle to veer out of its lane at the edge of the bridge. Alarmed, Anne grabbed the hand-strap to keep from falling. "Judy, what are you doing?"

"Watch this, ladies!" Judy sang out. She stopped rooting around, stuck her hand out the window, and hung her red platform shoes out by their ankle straps. They twisted in the wind as the car hurtled toward the city. "I'll be free, too!"

"Judy, don't do it!" Anne shouted.

"Stop! No!" Mary yelled, but it was already too late.

"Good-bye, cruel shoes!" Judy yelled, and flung the platforms out the window and into the air. The shoes split apart like booster rockets and seemed to soar into the sky for a moment, then, realizing they were mere footwear, plummeted in a final arc over the side of the Ben Franklin Bridge and fell a few hundred feet into the Delaware River.

"You killed them!" Anne said, but Judy was laughing her ass off.

Mary peered out the back window. "You didn't have to do that, Judy. They were perfectly good shoes."

"They sucked!" Judy yelled. "My only regret is that I didn't get to see them drown. Like Anne, I have no resolution, no closure."

Anne found herself laughing, her spirits light. "Bet it sounded a lot like a car wash," she said, and burst into car-wash noises. *"Ppppshhhhhh! Pssssshhhhh! Ssshhhhhhh!"* Judy joined her and in two minutes there was spit all over the VW dashboard.

Mary couldn't help but smile. "I'll never teach you guys anything," she said, but she was drowned out by a spray of hot wax as they slid down the bridge and into the twinkling city of Philadelphia.

"Anne!" Gil exclaimed as he entered the conference room at Rosato & Associates. He looked Anne up and down, studying each star on her breasts, then his gaze lingered on her hot-pants and platforms. "Goddamn! You are so hot! And the shoes are totally—"

"Please," Anne said, her face as red as her pants. They'd been so late to the meeting, she hadn't had time to change. Mental note: Don't dress like a whore to meet clients who cheat.

Gil couldn't stop grinning as he eased into a chair opposite her. "I can't get over it. Look at you, woman! You are so damn beautiful! You always were."

"Right. Thanks." She sat down in front of her legal pad to restore some sense of legitimacy, and noticed that Gil, in sports jacket and tie, was carrying a manila envelope. "You have the evidence of the affair? Great. Can I see it?"

"It's in my pants." He laughed, but Anne didn't. Was he coming on? Why was he talking like this? He never had before. She didn't like the way he was smiling at her and she could smell faintly that he'd been drinking.

"You come from a barbecue or something, Gil?"

"Or something. A party." Gil seemed to forget about the envelope on the table between them, its shape reflected on the polished surface. "I have to tell you, it's been really terrific working with you, Anne. You've been terrific."

"Thank you."

"You're a great lawyer. You're so—" he seemed to stall, waiting for the right word, "gutsy. Tough. Ballsy. For such a beautiful woman." His eyes flashed. "And so very beautiful. I've always thought it, ever since law school."

"Great." Anne let him babble while she reached for the envelope and slid it toward her. She didn't have time to waste, and she felt antsy and nervous. They still hadn't heard from the detectives about Kevin's arrest. Bennie and the others were sitting by the phone. She held up the envelope. "May I open it?"

"Sure!" He waved it off. "You know, me and the guys, you remember the guys, from the poker group in the dorm?"

"Sure. Played poker." Anne had no idea what he was rambling about. She unfastened the little brass brad and reached inside the envelope.

"We all were so hot for you. I had this picture of you, the one from the pig book. I always thought you were the most stunning woman I ever saw in my life."

Anne fished around in the envelope but there was no paper inside, only something thin and sharp.

"I knew you didn't go for my type. Computer geek. B.A. in engineering. I was smart, but you were way out of my league. Well, you're not anymore. I'm fairly successful, no?" Gil waved a raised fist. "Geeks rule!"

But Anne was only half listening, because there was nothing in the envelope except a CD. She pulled it out and held it up. Its silvery surface caught the overhead light in wiggly rainbow stripes. She flipped it over, looking for a label. Was it music, or some type of stored data?

"I'd really like it if you'd come work for me, Anne. I'm offering you a big job, a big, big job as general counsel at Chipster. Pay is three hundred grand to start, plus stock options. When we go IPO, you'll be worth millions."

Anne held up the CD. "What is this?"

Gil grinned crookedly. "You answer me first. When do you want to start? Me and you can take Chipster onward and upward!"

"You've been drinking."

"Guilty as charged!" Gil held up a hand. "So you wanna be my GC? 'Cause I wanna be your boyfriend."

Anne's stomach turned over. "Gil, focus a minute." She sent the CD spinning across the table like a flying saucer. "I'm trying to win a case for you, despite your best efforts to screw it up. First, you lie to me about your affair with Beth Dietz, then you bring me a CD when I ask you for evidence. What gives?"

"You don't need to win the case for me, Anne. I already won it for myself. The CD *is* the evidence, my love."

Anne ignored the "my love" part. Gil was only embarrassing himself, and it was the Glenlivet talking. "How is a CD evidence of an affair?"

"It's not, but it's evidence, all right. It's proof."

"Of what?"

"Of wrongdoing. Of theft. Of corporate espionage." Gil picked up the CD with difficulty and looked through the hole in the center, peeking out with one blue-green eye. "Boo!"

"Gil, what are you doing?"

"You underestimated me, Anne." He set the CD down, suddenly serious. "You thought that I had screwed up—as you say, interesting choice of words—but I never really do that. I cover my tracks. Plan all my moves. You have to, to be successful in e-business, you know. The competition is killer. On the bleeding edge, you can't be the one who bleeds."

"So what's on the CD?"

"Okay, well. Let me take you back a minute, to our corporate annals. I started Chipster with a few good men—sorry, good-lookin'—and one of them was Bill Dietz."

Anne remembered, from rereading the dep the other day.

"Dietz came a little later, from another web company called Environstar. Dietz was smart and he worked hard, put in the hours, and he had good ideas, for an asshole. Above all, he wrote good code."

"Okay."

"Chipster took off, and we developed our product, our web application, partly on the code he wrote. But a year down the line, Dietz told me he'd stolen the base code from Environstar." Gil held up the CD. "This is the code he stole."

"Did Environstar prosecute?"

"No, they had stolen code to start their own company. Everybody steals in software, mainly because it's never finished, it just goes through about three hundred versions, from 1.0 to 37.9, and people change jobs, over time. But that's not the point. This is about me, not Dietz. Be a smart girl and tell me what I did next."

Anne thought a minute. Last week she would have had a different answer, but she was looking at Gil with new eyes. And learning to plan—in advance. "You did nothing. You used the base code, developed it, and made a fortune. You shut up about its origin and you grew your company."

"Yes! God, and so smart, too! A whip!" Gil hunched over the desk. "I like women with brains. I'm not like the others."

No, you're worse. "Why didn't you give Dietz any stock options?"

"Because he came later, and he wasn't a

founder, technically. And I didn't have to keep him."

Anne was catching on. "No, because you'd found out about the stolen code. So you had something on him. If he left you, you'd expose him."

"I love it when you talk dirty. Do you talk dirty, Anne? I have often wondered about that, late at night." Gil leaned even farther over the table, but she stood up and walked around the back of her chair, really sorry that she was half-naked.

"Gil, what does the CD have to do with the *Chipster* case?"

"It will make it go away. I didn't have it before, but I finally paid off the right pro-grammer. Now I have the proof I need. Bye-bye Beth, hello IPO." Gil licked his lips. "I called Dietz directly after we spoke today. I told him to tell his wife to call off the dogs or I'll go public—with the CD." He laughed, but Anne was struggling to get up to speed and avoid attempted rape.

"If you expose him, you're liable too, maybe even criminally."

"He won't call my bluff, he's too scared. I can afford the hottest lawyer in town. He can't afford dick."

Anne ignored it. "But how does that get rid of the lawsuit?"

"Beth doesn't know he stole the code. They met after he came to Chipster."

"How do you know she doesn't know? Maybe he told her."

"No, she never would have sued me if she'd known, it was too risky. And she would have mentioned it during our little affair, but she didn't. Now he'll tell her the whole truth and nothing but, and she'll understand that suing me for revenge was not a good idea."

Anne blinked. "Gil, you won't win now. She'll just drop the suit. Withdraw it."

"No, no, no." Gil wagged his finger, rising from his seat. "Not what I want. Not what I asked my old friend Dietz for. I want the suit to go forward and the plaintiff to have a sudden memory loss. Trial amnesia, when she takes the stand. Then I want you to kick her lousy ass, get me my jury verdict, and restore my good name, so I look good to my Board. Not just settle. *Win*."

"You mean she'll deep-six her own lawsuit? Like a fighter, who throws a fight?"

"Exactly. Well put. God, I'm so glad you're

not dead. Be my GC and wear that tiny little top. Also the shoes. The shoes are—"

"I won't do it!"

"Okay, you win. No tiny top. Ha!"

"Stop, it, Gil. You're not funny." Anne shook her head. "No, I won't try a sham case. I won't play a role, or pretend. I won't do it."

"You have to. You can't withdraw from the case this late." Gil walked to one chair, then the next, closer to Anne. "We're both riding this rocket, and it's going up, up, up, baby."

"How do you know Beth will do it?" Anne asked, suppressing a tingle of fear as Gil moved closer, around the table.

"I don't for sure, but she will. The smart money's on Bill. He's the brains of that operation. She's just the pussy." Suddenly Gil lunged across the chairs, his hands reaching awkwardly for Anne's stars.

"That's it, get out!" she shouted, ducking away from his grasp, around the table and toward the door. "Get out!"

But Gil seemed not to have heard her. "And boy, did Dietz have some choice words to say about you! He said, 'I'm thrilled that little cunt is dead!'"

"I don't want to hear it!" she shouted, but her thoughts were racing. It must have been what Dietz and Matt had fought about. Why Matt had gotten slugged. *Her*. Anne flung open the door to the conference room. "Get out now!"

Gil tripped on a chair leg and caught the back of the chair, trying to right himself. "Dietz told his lawyer. They even got into a fight over it. Dietz said he would have shot you himself, for what you were doing to wifey. This is the man whose side you're taking against me."

"Get out! All I have to do is yell, and my friends will come running."

"Don't shoot!" Gil threw up his hands, and just then the conference doors flew open. Standing in the door was a furious Bennie, and Anne was hoping she was furious at Gil, not her.

"Get out of my law firm, Mr. Martin," she ordered, her mouth tight.

After the women got Gil into the elevator, down the alley, and outside into a cab, they recovered in the reception area while Anne told them the whole story of the CD and what Gil had done. They listened, draped over the soft navy chairs and loveseat.

Judy had changed into her denim overalls and Mary was still in her hooker outfit, but barefoot. Her platform shoes formed a vaguely pornographic mound on the Oriental rug.

"This is an interesting situation, very interesting," Bennie said, when the account was finished. She crossed one muscular leg over the other, in her shorts. "By the way, you're fired."

Anne hoped she was kidding again. "Have we heard anything about Kevin? Have they arrested him yet?"

"Rafferty said they're still staked out at the Daytimer. There's nothing to do but wait. They'll pick him up as soon as he gets back. Rafferty will call right away."

Anne wasn't liking this at all. Gil gone crazy and still no Kevin. "What about Beth Dietz? Did the cops tell her?"

"Rafferty said he would and we'll know for sure as soon as he calls back."

Anne sighed, flopping into a chair across the glistening glass coffee table. "What do I do now? How do I defend *Chipster*? Do I defend *Chipster* at all? The man is a pig!"

"A slimebucket," Judy said.

"A liar," Mary added.

"A client," Bennie said firmly, and Anne looked over.

"I'm having a déjà vu, Bennie. We had this conversation once already."

"I guess we'll keep having it until you understand it, Murphy. Your obligation as a lawyer is to represent your client fully and to the best of your ability. To say nothing false and to elicit nothing false. You have to be his advocate."

"But he grabbed my stars!"

Bennie seemed unfazed. "I'll try *Chipster* if you can't fulfill your ethical obligation to your client. Gil Martin is still and ultimately a client of my law firm."

"It was the earrings that drove him wild," Judy added.

Bennie waved everybody into silence. "Murphy, you gonna defend him or do I take over?"

Anne hated the sound of it. It was no-win. "I'll keep the bastard."

"Then do it and do it well. Fact is, we really don't know if Beth Dietz will go along with this scam or not. She may not."

Anne nodded. "If they have a lousy marriage, she may not care if her husband gets ratted out. This lawsuit is her chance to get Gil back for breaking up with her, and she may not give it up."

"Unless Dietz makes her," Judy said somberly. "He may threaten her. We know he can be violent."

Mary looked grave. "I wouldn't like to be responsible for someone getting a beating. Especially her. She's got enough problems now, with Kevin after her."

Bennie frowned. "You wouldn't be responsible. He would, and so would she. Beth Dietz gets no sympathy from me for staying with an abusive man. She's suing my client, and however much of a jerk he may be, I'm on his side. I'm sworn to it, and he's paying me for it."

Anne snorted. "Didn't you just throw him out of the office?"

"I draw the line. He hit on one of my associates. That is *not* happening on my watch. Keep your eye on the prize—the trial."

Anne considered it. "So we really don't know which way she'll go."

"Right," Bennie answered. "You have to be ready for whatever they throw at you. Just like any good trial lawyer, you'll have to think on your feet. You can do it. You have been for the past two days, and very well. With only one minor slip in judgment."

Anne said it before Bennie did: "Matt."

Everyone's gaze went instantly to Anne, three pairs of intelligent eyes in various stages of makeup. Mary's were full of understanding; Judy's slightly amused. But Bennie's had a clear-blue frankness that set Anne squirming. "You're not seeing him tonight, I hope," she said.

Oh, no. Anne had to fish or cut bait. Matt had left two messages on her cell phone, asking her to stay with him. She had returned one, telling him to tell Beth about Kevin. Truly she wanted to crawl into his bed, wrap his long arms around her, and feel safe and protected. Could she admit to any of these feelings in front of everyone? Was it even their business? All of a sudden she had both—girlfriends and a boyfriend. Mental note: Once you actually get a personal life, it's hard to live it.

"I'm not seeing him tonight," Anne said. It was the right thing to do. Or not to do. "I'm educable. Young, but educable."

Bennie glowed. "An excellent decision,

narrowly avoiding disbarment. You're learning, girl."

Anne took a bow. "But where can I spend the night? I mean, I can't stay with you, Bennie. I have to get Mel out of there before your nose explodes. I guess I could find a hotel."

"That wouldn't be safe." Mary got up from her chair with a new enthusiasm. "I know a great place to hide you. Our safe house!"

Bennie brightened, too. "An excellent idea! Why didn't I think of it?"

Judy clapped, jumping to her feet. "Perfect!"

Anne was bewildered. "Where are we going? What safe house?"

"You'll see," Mary said. "But we can't go dressed like this. We'll be killed."

That's safe? Anne thought, but Mary came over and took her by the hand.

24

It was dark by the time Anne and Mary reached the squat rowhouse somewhere in the redbrick warren that was South Philadelphia. They opened the screen door with its scrollwork D in weathered metal, and Vita and Mariano "Matty" DiNunzio flocked to them, hugging and kissing them, clucking and cooing like a pair of old city pigeons. Anne barely had time to set down the Xerox-paper box containing Mel in front of a worn couch. On the front windowsill sat a yellowed plastic figurine of the Virgin Mary, watching over the street from between two tiny, crossed flags, one American and one Italian.

"Come in, girls! Come in!" Mary's father was saying. He grabbed Mary, hugged her like a Papa Bear, and rocked her back and forth, all at the same time. "Oh, I love my baby girl!" He was a short, bald, seventysomething-year-old in a white T-shirt, dark Bermuda shorts, and a black belt that was superfluous except that it matched his slip-on slippers. He smiled with joy as he held Mary, and his brown eyes melted like Hershey's chocolate behind steel-rimmed bifocals. "Our baby's home! Our girl! Look, Vita, our baby, she's home!"

But Mary's tiny mother had wrapped herself around Anne and was caressing her cheek with a papery hand that smelled vaguely of onions. "You are Anna? *Che bellissima!* Such a beautiful girl! More beautiful than your picture!" Mrs. DiNunzio was about her husband's age, but an Italian accent flavored her English, so the word "picture" came out "pitch." "*Madonna mia,* she has the face of an angel, Matty! Look at this one! The face of an angel!"

"Wow. Jeez. Thanks." Anne's spirits lifted instantly, her energy surged, and she couldn't stop smiling. She even loved her new name. It was great to have people throw a party just because you walked in the door. Anne hadn't felt this good in a long time, maybe twenty-eight years. Mental note: I want to be Italian.

"She's such a beauty, it's a sin! God bless!" Dense trifocals magnified Mrs. DiNunzio's small, brown eyes, and her thinning, white hair had been teased into an elaborate coiffure and stuffed into a pink hairnet. Cotton strings from the hairnet straggled down her nape, and she wore a flowered housedress and a full-length flowered apron. But Anne wasn't playing fashion police. She was too busy being hugged and breathing in a pleasant, if peculiar, combination of Spray-Net and sweet basil. Mrs. DiNunzio stopped stroking Anne's cheek and stepped back from her, marveling. "You look like inna movies! Like actress inna movies or TV. Look, Matty, she—"

"She's a beauty, all right!" Mr. DiNunzio agreed, hugging Mary. The DiNunzios talked over each other and nobody seemed to mind. "A princess, she looks like! We'll take care of her. We'll take care of them both!"

"Nobody's gonna hurt you in my house!" Mrs. DiNunzio said, staring up at Anne with suddenly wet eyes. Mary had told her parents about Anne's situation, and Mrs. DiNunzio was practically crying for her. For a split second, something else flickered in the older woman's magnified eyes, then it disappeared. "God bless! You stay with us, everyting gonna be all right!" She squeezed Anne tight, trembling with a sympathy that seemed ironically to strengthen her frail frame.

"Thank you," Anne said again, which was stupid, but Mrs. DiNunzio appeared not to hear. Her eyes had darkened abruptly, and fierce little wrinkles deepened her brow under the pink hairnet.

"You work also for *Benedetta Rosato*! That *witch*, she's a no good!" Mrs. DiNunzio wagged a finger knotted at the knuckle. On the way over, Mary had told Anne that her mother had arthritis, from years of sewing lampshades in the basement of this very house, her childhood home. Mary's father had been a tile setter. And they both hated Bennie. "So much trouble she makes! Guns! Crazy men! Benedetta Rosato, is her fault! She no take care of my Maria! Or you! She no—"

"Ma, please don't start." Mary emerged from the clinch with her father and looped an arm around her mother. "Let's not get onto Bennie, right? Like I said on the phone, Anne can stay in my room, in Angie's bed—"

"Okay, okay. Atsa no problem." Mrs. Di-Nunzio patted Anne's cheek, her anger vanishing as suddenly as a summer thunderstorm. "Is ready, the bed. Clean towels, clean sheets, all clean onna bed, everything ready for you. First we eat, then go to bed. Welcome, Anna!"

"Thank you." *Time number four?* What else was there to say when people were so nice? "Did Mary tell you? I have a cat, too."

"Okay, a cat! I like, a cat!" Mrs. DiNunzio peered behind Anne, and Mr. DiNunzio was already shuffling over to the box and opening the top flaps. Mel popped his head out with an unhappy meow, and everybody laughed. Mrs. DiNunzio clapped her hands, then clasped them together in delight. "*Madonna mia!* How pretty, the cat!"

"What a nice kittycat!" Mr. DiNunzio lifted Mel from the box, letting the cat's back legs hang awkwardly until he finally gathered them up and cuddled Mel against his chest. "Vita, look, he's a such nice cat." Mel meowed, working the crowd with Love Cat, and Mr. DiNunzio beamed, his teeth denture-even. "See, Vita? He likes us."

"He's a nice cat, he likes it here!" Mrs. DiNunzio smiled, her head wobbling only slightly. "Welcome, Anna's cat!"

Mr. DiNunzio kissed the top of Mel's sleek head and looked over at Anne. "What's his name?" Anne told him, but he frowned, wrinkling well past his forehead. For a minute, she thought he hadn't heard her, but Mary had told her he was wearing his hearing aids nowadays. They sat snugly in his somewhat furry ears. "Mel?" he asked. "Is that a good name for a kittycat, Anna? I never heard of naming a kittycat a people name, like Joe. Or Dom." His tone wasn't critical, just honestly confused, and now, so was Anne.

"I didn't name him. I got him with that name from the shelter." Anne smiled. "It's kind of a stupid name, now that I think about it."

"How 'bout we call him 'Anna's cat,' then?"

Anne laughed. She and Mel had evidently been rechristened. "You got it."

"Come on, Vita. Let's get Anna's cat some milk," Mr. DiNunzio shuffled out of the living room, holding Mel. "Come, girls. Anna. Come and get something to eat. Did you eat, Mare?"

"No, not yet. Feed us, Pop. We've been here five minutes already." Mary hugged her mother out of the room. "Whatsa matter, Ma? You stop loving me?"

"Don' be fresh!" her mother said, with a

soft chuckle. She turned and grabbed Anne's hand, and they passed through a darkened dining room and entered a small, bright kitchen, hot with brewing coffee and steaming tomato sauce. Mrs. DiNunzio made a beeline for the stove and began stirring the sauce with a split, wooden spoon, and Anne came up behind her.

"You need some help, Mrs. DiNunzio?" she asked, catching a whiff of the pot. The richness of cooked tomatoes and garlic made her realize how hungry she was. She couldn't remember the last time she'd eaten and she'd never had home-cooking like this. The tomato sauce was thickly red, with bumpy meatballs bobbing below the surface and hot sausage curling at the ends, churned up by the gentle stirring of the wooden spoon. Anne tried to guess the recipe but it had to be genetic.

"Sit, sit, Anna!" Mrs. DiNunzio waved her off with a spoon covered with steaming sauce, and Mary grabbed Anne by the arm.

"Don't even think about helping, Anne. She'll hit you with the nearest utensil. She's very territorial, my mother. It's *her* kitchen, right, Pop?"

"Right, baby doll. Soon as I do this, I sit

down too." Mr. DiNunzio had gone to a photo-covered refrigerator for a waxed carton of milk, which he poured into a saucer and set down on an ancient linoleum floor in front of Mel. The cat started lapping away. "Cats, my wife trusts me with. Everything else, she feeds. Go, sit, Anna."

Anne was about to say thank you for the fifty-fifth time, but settled for "I give up," as Mary sat both of them down at the table, of Formica with gold flecks. A heavy amber-glass fixture was suspended on a gold-electroplated chain over the table, white refaced cabinets ringed the small room, and faded photos of several popes, Frank Sinatra, and a colorized John F. Kennedy, hung on a wall. On a thumbtack was a church calendar with a huge picture of Jesus Christ, his hair brown ringlets against a cerulean-blue background, and his eyes heavenward. Mental note: Start worshiping something other than shoes.

"Anna, Maria. Is ready, the coffee." Mrs. DiNunzio set the sauce-covered spoon on a saucer, then lowered the gas underneath the pot. She took a dented, stainless-steel coffeepot from the other burner and brought it to the table, where she poured it steaming into Anne's cup, then Mary's and her father's, who was sitting catty-corner.

"Thanks, Mrs. DiNunzio. This looks awesome." Anne sniffed the aroma curling from her chipped cup and tried to remember if she had ever seen coffee perked on a stove. It seemed like making fire with twigs. Everyone else took his coffee black, but Anne mixed in cream and sugar from the table, then sipped the mixture. It was hot as hell and even better than Starbucks. "Wow! This tastes great!" she said, in amazement.

"*Grazie!* Drink!" Mrs. DiNunzio went back to the stove, set the coffeepot, and returned to the table, easing into her seat. She didn't touch her coffee, and her brown eyes had clouded with concern. "So, Anna, the police, they look for this man? He wants to hurt you?"

Mary shot Anne a let-me-handle-this glance. "Yes, Ma, but soon it will be all right. Don't get all worried," she said, but Mrs. DiNunzio ignored her, gazing at Anne with an intensity that couldn't be chalked up to country of origin.

"I see trouble. You have trouble, Anna. Big trouble." Mrs. DiNunzio leaned over in her chair and reached for Anne's hand. "Your trouble, you tell me. I help you."

"Tell you what?" Anne asked, uncertain but touched nevertheless. She'd never felt so cared for, so quickly. It was as if Mrs. Di-Nunzio had been waiting for her, to help her. But her trouble wasn't anything that Mrs. Di-Nunzio could help with, unless she owned a bazooka. "My trouble is this man, Kevin Satorno. The police will get him. They'll call as soon as they've arrested him tonight."

"No, no, no." Mrs. DiNunzio clucked, as if Anne had misunderstood. "Not him, he's a no trouble."

"Ma," Mary broke in. "You don't have to know everything. It'll just upset you. We're handling—"

"Shhh, Maria!" Mrs. DiNunzio hushed her daughter with a raised index finger, and even the last trace of a smile vanished. "*Madonne?* you have trouble. Yes, Anna. It hurts your head. It hurts your heart. Yes. This I see. This I know."

Anne didn't know what to say, except that, truth to tell, she did have a bad headache. And lately she had begun to think her heart would never be right.

"Argh!" Mary's forehead dropped theatrically into her hands. "Ma, don't embarrass me in front of the other kids. I'm trying to make a nice impression here."

"Mare, this is something you don't interfere." Mr. DiNunzio rose suddenly and picked up his coffee cup. "If your mother says Anna's got 'em, then she's got 'em. Now let's get outta here. This is between Anna and your mother. Your mother, she knows. She'll help Anna."

I need help? Anne felt vaguely alarmed. The mood changed quickly in the kitchen. Mrs. DiNunzio turned suddenly grave. Mr. DiNunzio was escaping with his coffee, and Mary was on her feet, too. Even Mel stopped drinking milk and dropped to his Alarmo Cat crouch over the saucer.

Anne turned to Mary. "What's happening, Mary?"

"My mother has superpowers. She's her own action hero, with X-ray vision. She thinks you need her help and she can help you, so, just go along with it. Let her do what she wants to do."

"What does she want to do?"

"You'll see. This is an Italian thing, grasshopper. You must never reveal it to the outside world." Mary patted her shoulder. "We all took a vow of silence, the entire race, except for Maria Bartiromo, who I still don't believe is Italian. No Italian girl can understand the stock market. It's against nature. We're not built that way."

What? Anne laughed, mystified. She looked over at Mrs. DiNunzio, who squeezed her hand like a doctor bracing her for bad news. "Mrs. DiNunzio, what—"

"Anna, you got the overlooks. Somebody *hate* you. He wish *evil* on you. You have *malocchio*!"

"Mal*whate*o?" Anne asked.

"*Malocchio!* Evil eye!"

Mary was following her father out of the kitchen. "Yes, she's serious, Anne, and this is South Philly, the land of spells and curses. But don't worry. My mother knows how to take off the evil eye. The prayer was passed to her on Christmas Eve by her mother, who was also a superhero. Just go with it, and please don't tell her there's no such thing as ghosts. She owns a wooden spoon and she *will* use it."

"I have *the evil eye*?" Anne asked, incredulous. *I don't have the evil eye, I have a stalker.* "Mrs. DiNunzio—"

"No worry, I take away," Mrs. DiNunzio said, with another hand squeeze, which was surprisingly firmer, more oncologist than GP. "I make better for you, Anna. This I do for you. Now."

Were these people nuts? "Mrs. DiNunzio, it's very nice of you, but there is nothing you can do about this man." Mental note: Maybe I'll stay Irish.

But Mrs. DiNunzio had gotten up from the table and was already at the sink, running water from the tap into a clear Pyrex bowl. She turned off the faucet, took a gold tin of Bertoli olive oil from a shelf over the stove, and brought both back to the table, where she set the bowl and olive oil down between them. Then she took her seat, her eyes faraway behind her thick trifocals.

"Mrs. DiNunzio—"

"Shhh!" Mrs. DiNunzio held up a hand, then looked at Anne, her gaze softening. "You have *malocchio*. This, I know. *Vide!* Watch!" Mrs. DiNunzio picked up the tin of olive oil and poured three gimlet-hued drops in the bowl of water, one on top of the next. A large drop floated for a moment on the water's surface, and Mrs. DiNunzio watched it intently. The warm kitchen fell quiet except for the occasional popping of the tomato sauce on the stove. "Wait, Anna."

"For what? The oil?"

"*Si,* if you have *malocchio,* the oil, it goes apart." Mrs. DiNunzio pointed at the bowl, and the oil split into two drops, edging away from each other. "See? *Malocchio!*"

What is this, Italian Chemistry? "Mrs. Di-Nunzio, water and oil will always separate—"

"Anna, you have *malocchio* very bad. You have trouble, inside, yes?" Her eyes were so kind, and her soft voice so concerned that Anne couldn't help but feel the truth behind her words, despite the silly bowl of spreading Bertoli.

"Okay, I admit it, I have trouble," she found herself answering, low so Mary couldn't hear, if she was lingering in the dining room.

Mrs. DiNunzio was pointing at Anne's lip, directly at her scar. "I see you have, *come se dice?*" Her forehead wrinkled with concentration.

"A cleft lip."

"*Madonna mia!* A gift from God!"

"A gift?" Anne blurted out. "It's a curse!"

"No, no." Mrs. DiNunzio waved her finger between them, slowly. "God, a gift, he give you. You are so beautiful, Anna, that people, they will be jealous. They will *hate* you. God knows this. This is a gift from God, and you must thank him."

I'll get right on that, Anne thought. She couldn't imagine a God who would give a cleft lip to any kid, much less one with bright-red hair. Why? To make sure nobody would miss it?

"Shhhh." Mrs. DiNunzio squeezed her hand. "Close your eyes, Anna. I'm gonna help you. Let me help you. Nobody gonna hurt you no more."

Anne couldn't bring herself to close her eyes. It was absurd, wasn't it? There was no such things as ghosts, or the evil eye.

"Close your eyes, Anna!" Mrs. DiNunzio ordered, and Anne found herself doing as she was told. She closed her eyes and in a minute focused on the warmth of Mrs. Di-Nunzio's hand on hers. Breathed in the wonderful smells of the garlic and onions. Eased into the softness of the plastic pad on her chair. Listened to the percolating of the tomato sauce. In the next minute, Mrs. Di-Nunzio was mumbling softly in Italian, in a cadence regular and calming. Anne couldn't understand the words and she didn't try. In the next minute she felt a warm fingerpad, slick with oil, on her forehead.

"What are you doing?" Anne whispered.

"Shhh! I make sign of cross. Three times. Shhhh!" Mrs. DiNunzio resumed her chanting, presumably lifting the spell of the evil eye, and Anne would have laughed at the absurdity of it, except that she couldn't help but listen to the motherly tones of Mrs. DiNunzio's voice and loved the warmth of the oil spreading across her aching forehead. She felt somehow blessed to be in this kitchen, which was a remarkable conclusion for someone who didn't believe in God, the evil eye, or even mothers.

"Open your eyes, Anna," Mrs. DiNunzio whispered, with a final squeeze of her hand.

Anne did as she was told and looked at Mrs. DiNunzio, whose dark eyes drew her in like a loving embrace. She held Anne's gaze like that for a minute, and squeezed her hand across the table without speaking.

"All better now, Anna," Mrs. DiNunzio announced, after a moment. But it didn't sound like a question and didn't seek confirmation. In the next instant, Mrs. DiNunzio was reaching around her own neck for a long gold chain Anne hadn't seen before, tugging it from behind her apron and lifting it over her head and pink hairnet. It was a gold necklace, and Mrs. DiNunzio handed it across the table to Anne. "Anna, you take. For you. Take."

"No, Mrs. DiNunzio!" Anne didn't get it. The woman was giving her jewelry now? It was a longish gold chain with a fourteen-carat gold charm swinging at the end. "I can't possibly take it. I can't take your necklace from you."

"Take! Take! See!" Mrs. DiNunzio caught the charm and showed it between gnarled fingers, fingerpads still glistening with olive oil. The charm gleamed in the light and was shaped like a wiggly pepper. "Is for you! A *cornu,* a horn. You take! For protect you, from the *malocchio!*" She handed it to Anne, who pressed it back.

"No, I couldn't, really."

"Take! Is gift, from me. From me to you, Anna!" Mrs. DiNunzio's tone grew almost agitated. She dropped the necklace on the table in front of Anne, where it landed with the tiniest jingling sound. "You need, Anna! You must have!"

"Mrs. DiNunzio, I can't—"

"TAKE IT!" Mary shouted from somewhere in the dining room, and Mrs. DiNunzio smiled.

"I can't, Mary!" Anne called out.

"TAKE IT OR SHE WON'T LET US BACK IN!"

"Please, take!" Mrs. DiNunzio reached across the table, picked up the necklace, and slipped it over Anne's head with finality. *"Perfetto,* Anna. Now you stay safe."

"Thank you so much," Anne said, overwhelmed. She looked down at the gold chain, glinting in the kitchen light, and held the oily horn in her palm. She didn't really understand how a charm could keep away the evil eye, but she felt so touched that Mrs. DiNunzio had given it to her that she couldn't keep the wetness from her eyes.

"MY COFFEE'S GETTING COLD!" Mary shouted, and they all laughed.

"Okay, Maria!" Mrs. DiNunzio called back, smiling with obvious relief. "All better now. No worry now."

Mary came in, clapping. "So you kept it! Good for you. Now you have Italian insurance. The Prudential has nothing on us, do they?"

Anne blinked the tears away, and when she found her voice, could say only one thing: "You're lucky, Mary. You know that?"

"I certainly do." Mary came over and gave her mother a kiss on the cheek, and behind her, her father shuffled into the kitchen, bearing his coffee cup.

"How's your headache, Anna?" he asked, and Anne had to think a minute. Actually, she didn't feel anything. Her head was amazingly clear.

"It's gone!" she answered. It was the truth, and no one was surprised but her.

"Anne, wake up," Mary was saying, her voice loud in Anne's ear. "It's morning. You have to wake up. Anne?"

Anne didn't open her eyes. She was so sleepy. The pillow was so soft. Her tummy was awash with spaghetti, sweet sausage, and chianti. She wasn't getting up.

"Anne, Anne!" Mary was shaking her gently, insistent. "Wake up, it's important."

Anne opened an eye and took in her surroundings. The bedroom was small, clean, and spare, the walls creamy white. High school Latin trophies and religious statues cluttered a white shelf. A square of sunlight struggled through a lace curtain. It must be morning. A night table sat six inches from her nose, and on it glowed the red numbers of a digital clock. 6:05. Anne moaned. "It's so early."

"Wake up! You have to see this!" Mary's tone was urgent, and she held up a copy of the *Daily News*. "Look!"

"What?" Anne started to ask, but the question lodged in her throat when she saw the headline. Her eyes flew open. She took the newspaper and sat bolt upright. "This can't be true!"

"It is. I called Bennie and it's all over the web. She'll be here in five minutes."

"Maybe it's just more lousy reporting? Gonzos at work?" Anne blinked at the front page in disbelief. Her headache roared back. Then, with a bolt of fear, she remembered. They'd fallen asleep around two o'clock, after calling Bennie for the tenth time, to see if Kevin had been taken into custody. "Didn't Bennie call last night, about Kevin? Didn't they arrest him?"

"No. The cops never got him. He never came back to the motel. He's still out there.

That's what I'm trying to tell you, you're in danger now, Anne. We have to get you out of here."

Anne couldn't take her eyes from the newspaper. She flashed back to the tabloid from the first morning, when this had all started. But today's headline was even worse. She read it over and over:

MURPHY'S MOM: "NOT MY DAUGHTER!"

Underneath the headline was a photo of Anne's mother. And she was standing in front of the city morgue.

25

The commissioner's private conference room at the Roundhouse was large and rectangular, and contained a long walnut table with a single piece of polished glass protecting its costly surface. An American flag stood furled in one corner behind the head of the table, and in another corner Anne recognized the blue polyester flag of the Commonwealth of Pennsylvania she'd seen in state courtrooms. Air-conditioning chilled the room, but it could easily have been her emotions.

Ten high-backed leather chairs sat around the table, reflected in fuzzy shadow on its shiny surface, and Anne, Bennie, Mary, and Judy took seats in the ones on the left, across from Deputy Commissioner Joseph Parker, Detective Sam Rafferty, his partner, and a young black man in a suit, who introduced himself as a lawyer from the city solicitor's office. The city lawyer shook hands all around and began taking notes on a fresh legal pad as soon as he returned to his seat. Anne reminded herself it wasn't a war, despite the battle lines on opposing sides of the table, the lawyer making notes in anticipation of litigation, and the woman entering the room and quietly taking a seat at the head of the table, the putative plaintiff, one Terry Murphy. Anne's mother.

No doubt it was her, though Anne hadn't seen her in so long. She seemed shorter than Anne remembered, perhaps five two, and years of pills and alcohol had destroyed a woman once lovely enough to attract dozens of men and entertain fantasies of movie stardom. Her cheeks looked sunken, her skin withered, and the blue of her eyes seemed watered down, especially in contrast with too-thick liquid eyeliner. Her mouth was enlarged by coral lipstick, and she wore a matching melon-colored T-shirt with a scoop neck and white cotton Capri pants, with white Tod knock-offs. Something about the shoes made Anne sad.

She watched her mother shake hands with the police brass, extending a small hand with frosted fingernails. Her mother nodded in a wobbly way, as if she'd gotten out of her umpteenth stint at rehab, and her shoulder-length hair had been newly colored jet-black to hide the graying of its dark red. She shook Bennie's, Judy's, and Mary's hand, not looking at Anne until the last.

"Hello, Anne," her mother said, her voice thin, but Anne didn't reply, because she didn't know where to begin, and once begun, would never end.

The deputy commissioner cleared his throat. "Ladies and gentlemen, let me first welcome our guests, and thank them for coming down here on the holiday to discuss this subject, which I know is important to all of us." He was black and heavyset, balding, with dark, kind eyes and a soft smile. An unfortunate neck wattle hung over the tight collar of his stiff white shirt, which Anne gathered was worn by top cop brass, if his stripes, gold-eagle pin, and police-shield tie tack were any indication. The deputy commissioner continued, "The commissioner wishes he could be here, but, as you may know, he is out of the country."

"In Ireland, I had heard that," Bennie said, and Anne sat back against the cold leather. She was happy to let Bennie run the show, because it was clear from the jump that nothing meaningful was going to take place here, and for all of her newfound self-control, Anne was embarrassed at being in the same room as her mother.

"Most important," he continued, "permit me to apologize to Mrs. Murphy, here and now, for the judgment exercised by Detectives Rafferty and Tomasso. After an investigation, which I assure you is ongoing, it has come to my attention that these detectives may have permitted certain false information about your daughter's whereabouts to persist uncorrected. For that, and for any undue pain this may have caused you, Mrs. Murphy, we, as a department, are heartily sorry."

Terry Murphy nodded graciously, but that didn't stop the apologies, which Anne knew were for the record and rendered solely on the advice of counsel, undoubtedly higher up than the one taking notes at the table. They knew that under the circumstances, Anne's mother could sue the city and department for emotional distress and collect big-time. Only Anne knew that her death didn't cause her mother any distress at all.

"I assure you, Mrs. Murphy, that these detectives have excellent records of service to the department, Homicide Squad, and city. Their actions were taken not only at your daughter's request, but also in the sincere and reasonable belief that they were protecting her from further harm. You do understand that, I hope, Ms. Murphy."

"Yes, of course," her mother said, nodding again, and Anne detected a trace of a pseudo-English accent as bad as Madonna's. *Nice touch, Ma. Is that the acting part?*

The deputy commissioner smiled his nice smile. "However, it remains true that the detectives' actions were unorthodox, certainly, and also against police procedure, though they were undertaken in all good faith. We will be meeting with the press later today, to make clear our position in this matter. You should be aware, Mrs. Murphy, and we will tell the press, that we as a department are considering taking disciplinary action against the detectives for their actions."

Detective Rafferty bowed his head slightly, a gesture that showed the sincerity that her mother lacked, and Anne was moved to speak.

"If I may, Deputy Commissioner Parker," she said, raising an index finger. "As you correctly point out, Detective Rafferty and his partner took the actions—" she shook off the police speak and started over—"they kept quiet about the fact that I was alive because I begged them to, and to help me protect myself. I think it showed excellent judgment on their part, in addition to a really good heart."

"Thank you," the deputy commissioner said, and the city lawyer scribbled furiously. Rafferty looked up, a slight smile creasing his face, and Anne smiled back.

"I would hope that the police department would take no disciplinary action against either of these detectives. If the department would like me to submit a statement to that effect, for your purposes or for submission to the press, I would be happy to do so."

"Excellent, that would be most appreciated," the deputy commissioner said, and the city lawyer thought it was Christmas. Anne knew he'd send a follow-up letter as soon as he got back to his office, bearing the computer-generated signature of the City Solicitor and confirming her offer. The city and the department had just gotten a free release, but that was fine with Anne. She'd be damned if her mother would make a penny off of her alleged death, when she hadn't bothered to show up for her alleged life.

Bennie was nodding in agreement. "Anne's analysis is exactly correct, and my firm would be happy to state as much in a separate letter, if you wish."

"A letter from Bennie Rosato, *supporting* the police?" The deputy commissioner chuckled softly, his heavy chest moving up and down.

"Credit where credit is due, sir." Bennie smiled and leaned over the glossy table. "Now that we're done with that, tell me what the department is going to do to catch Kevin Satorno."

"We have assigned every available man to the search, and coordinated with the FBI and authorities in New Jersey. We remain staked out at the Daytimer. How did you find Satorno, by the way?"

"It doesn't matter now," Bennie said dismissively. The deputy commissioner didn't press her, evidently in return for the nice letter she'd offered to write, like a referee's compensatory call. "But can you offer Ms. Murphy any protection at all? We're sure that Satorno will be stalking her, to finish what he started, both on the West Coast and here."

"At this point, there's not much we can do. As a policy matter, we don't usually assign personnel to an individual victim of crime, and we're severely short-handed today, because of the Fourth." The deputy commissioner paused. "But when we free up somebody after the holiday, maybe we can put a car at her house or office."

"That may be too late. She needs protection now. Don't you have anybody, in a department this size? I can't believe there's nobody. What if a VIP came into town?"

"Unfortunately, there are already plenty of VIPs in town. We do have a Dignitary Protection Squad, but they're already deployed. The Secretary-General of the U.N. is getting an award today, and half of Hollywood is arriving for the fireworks ceremony at the Art Museum tonight. There's not a soul to spare." He turned to Anne. "Ms. Murphy, if you want my advice, the best thing for you to do is to take a vacation out of town, until we apprehend Mr. Satorno."

Anne had expected as much. "Thanks, but no. I have to work, I have to live. I'm trying a case tomorrow. I can't go hide out, and I wouldn't anyway."

The deputy commissioner looked sympathetic. "Then use your common sense, which I think you have in abundant supply. Leave the police work to us, Ms. Murphy."

"I understand, sir." Anne rose slowly, her hands leaving fingerprints on the table, and Bennie and the others took their cue from her, rising from their seats. "Then, if there's nothing more, we should probably get to work."

The other side of the table rose, too, led by the deputy commissioner, who eased his girth from his chair. "We won't keep you. Thank you for coming and we'll call you the moment we have Mr. Satorno in custody. If you want an escort through the media outside in the parking lot, I can have my driver accompany you."

Anne looked at Bennie, who answered, "That's okay, thanks. What time is your press conference?" She headed for the door with the other lawyers, and Anne trailed behind.

The deputy commissioner hustled to open the heavy, paneled door. "In two hours, and we're taking the same tack. I'm telling them what I just told you. With your permission, I will restate your position." He waited for Bennie's nod, then glanced at Terry Murphy, who remained seated at the table. "Mrs. Murphy isn't yet sure of her position, but she has kindly agreed to attend the press conference with us."

Cameras, lights, attention? "Why am I not surprised?" Anne muttered, but her mother heard it and turned in her seat, her face an almost-professional mask of pain.

"Honey?" she called out. "Can we talk, for a minute?"

But Anne was already gone, walking out the door without looking back. Just as her mother had, a decade earlier. Returning the favor felt good, and bad, but Anne had something better to do. Like save herself.

The women trooped down an empty hall to the elevator, piled into the cab and rode down without a word, at first. Anne felt everybody's eyes on her, and appreciated it. They cared about her. They worried about her safety; they worried about her emotional state. Bennie, Mary, and even Judy were her true friends now, and she was theirs. But that meant they wouldn't be able to go with her any longer. She couldn't endanger them.

The elevator doors opened onto the ground floor, and they got out. Anne could see the media mob thronging in the parking lot, through the glass double-doors of the entrance. They extended all the way to the sidewalk, but she wasn't unhappy to see them anymore. They were going to help now. But not with flyers, with something better.

"Get in wedge formation, girls," Bennie said, taking the lead and gathering the associates behind her like baby chicks. Then she looked back and frowned. "Murphy, where's your hat and sunglasses?"

"In my pocket." Anne patted the hat and sunglasses, rolled up together. "I've worn my last disguise. I'm going as myself from now on."

"No, you're not. Put them on. Now."

Mary touched Anne's arm. "Anne, you should get in disguise. Otherwise you'll be all over the TV and the news. The way you look now, your new haircut and color."

But Anne had already broken formation. She hurried to the double-door before anybody could stop her, and on the other side, the reporters were already clamoring for her. Shouting questions. Shooting pictures.

"Murphy, no!" Bennie shouted, but she was too late.

Anne was heading out into the sunlight.

Alone, except for a really good idea.

26

"I DO NOT BELIEVE YOU DID THAT!" Bennie was yelling at Anne from the passenger seat of Judy's Beetle, and her voice reverberated in the well-advertised dome of its interior. Judy was driving and they zoomed up the Parkway, heading uptown to the office, on Bennie's orders. "Do you have any idea what you've done, Murphy?" she kept yelling. "Now Satorno will know what you look like!"

"I'm sorry, I guess I wasn't thinking," Anne said and hoped Bennie believed it. She'd have to sell it better. She shot for a bad impression of herself. "I'm so tired of letting Kevin run my life. I wanted to be myself for once."

"THAT WASN'T VERY SMART, WAS IT?" Bennie was hollering so loudly that Mary and Judy cringed in stereo, but that didn't stop her. "You wanted to be YOURSELF? News flash—YOURSELF is the girl he wants to kill, and he knows he's gotta find you before the holiday's over and the cops get more than three people on it! YOURSELF is gonna get dead, if you keep this up! Are you nuts, Murphy?"

"Can we stop somewhere?" Anne wiped her bangs back with a fraudulent weakness. "I feel kind of carsick."

Mary offered her a half-bottle of water. "You want something to drink?"

"No, thanks, but I'm really queasy. My head feels so light." Anne listed to the left, channeling Lucy's fake illness in "Lucy Gets a Paris Gown." Episode No. 147, March 19, 1956. "Can we just stop a minute?"

Bennie twisted around, her hair blowing in her face. "You have to stop, Murphy? We'll find you a place to stop, so I can get out and yell at you better!" A minivan full of kids waving tiny American flags went by, and their mother was screaming at them from the passenger's seat, too. "I have had it with you! Pull over, Carrier! Now!"

"Bennie, take it easy," Judy said. "She's sick."

"Now!" Bennie ordered. The Beetle lurched to the next light, then swerved to the curb, where Judy pulled up, braked with a jolt, and cut the ignition. She opened her door and got out, and Bennie flung open her door and climbed out. "Everybody outta the pool! Now!"

"Thanks, guys," Anne said faintly. She climbed out of the car slowly, giving herself time to scope out the scene. They had parked near a small triangle of sparse city grass, next to the street. A grimy wooden bench sat in the middle of the patch of land, which was littered with cigarette butts, broken bottles, and torn bits of red-white-and-blue-striped streamer. Bennie was standing by the door, fuming.

Excellent. Anne would have to act quickly. It was a corny plan, but it worked for Lucy in more episodes than she could count. Anne screwed up all the red-headed courage she could muster, walked over to Judy, and stopped dead in her tracks, pointing in mock horror over her friend's shoulder. "Oh, my God! Judy, *that's Kevin!*" Anne yelled out. "Right *there!*"

"*Kevin? Where?*" Judy wheeled around instantly, and Mary and Bennie did, too.

In the next second, Anne grabbed the car keys from Judy's hand, scrambled back into the Beetle, slammed the key in the ignition and twisted it on, then hit the gas and took off. The Beetle fishtailed wildly, the driver's door banging against the hinges, but Anne managed not to fall out as she took off and zoomed away, toward the Expressway to the Parkway. She checked the rearview mirror. Bennie was already a receding figure on the green patch in the distance, and Mary and Judy stood with her. It worked! Mental note: Lucy Ricardo would have been a great lawyer.

Anne hit the gas, hoping they'd understand. She cared too much about them to bring them any further. She had already gotten Willa killed. She couldn't bear it if anything happened to one of them. She steered the Beetle uptown.

An older man in a station wagon glanced over at her, obviously annoyed that she was speeding, but she gave him a carefree wave. She intended to draw as much attention as she could today, to be as public as possible. To be noticed, *seen.* The newspapers had her picture and they'd run it soon, footage from outside the Roundhouse. People would start recognizing her. They would report more sightings than Elvis, ask her questions, create a buzz. Her whereabouts throughout the day would become known, which was all according to plan.

Anne intended to celebrate the Fourth of July in the City of Brotherly Love in the most public and obvious fashion ever, because she had no doubt that, at some point during the day, Kevin would find her. She was tired of running away from him and refused to do it even for one more day. She would let Kevin catch her. Then she'd catch him back.

She switched lanes, breathing easier. She was doing the right thing. It was the only way to bring this nightmare to an end. She would use herself as bait. If she didn't, she'd be running for the rest of her life. Scared, and in danger. She wouldn't move again. She would stand her ground, flush Kevin out, and nail him herself. Bennie and the girls would never have let her do it, that's why she had to do it alone. Well, not completely alone.

She took a turn toward Arch Street, heading up to her house, slowing in the increased traffic. It grew more congested the closer to City Hall she got, clustering around the Tourist Center and the Party on the Parkway. She made her way west, took a right onto Twenty-second Street, then a left, joining the line of traffic to her neighborhood and eventually turning onto Waltin Street.

Police sawhorses sat at the curb of the street, bearing a white sign that read BLOCK PARTY TODAY 3–5 P.M. Anne vaguely remembered a form she'd gotten for the block party, but she hadn't bothered to send in the money. The party must be today. Odd that they'd be holding it despite her murder. Mental note: If people celebrate when you get killed, it's time to make a few changes.

She fell into line behind slow-moving cars and SUVs, taking the time to look out the window and let people see her. She reached the top of her block and proceeded onto it, remembering when she'd walked it in the Uncle Sam stovepipe. Was that only two days ago? It hardly seemed possible. When she was five houses from her own, then four, she could see the yellow crime-scene tape still flapping in the breeze. People passed by on the sidewalk, stopping curiously, then moving on, not letting the ugly notion ruin their holiday.

She double-parked in front of her door, blocking traffic. How better to get some attention? She hoped all her neighbors would look out their windows and see her. Kevin could be in the area, betting she'd come back to the house. She had to get inside. She flung open her door and jumped out of the truck, causing a man in a white TransAm behind her to lean on his horn.

Anne gave him a happy wave. "Be just a minute!" she called out, and she fumbled in her purse for her keys and bounded to her stoop. It still had a few bouquets, withering in their cellophane. She didn't linger to look at any of them. She tore off the crime-scene tape, slid her key in the lock, then steeled herself to go inside.

The front door swung open, permitting the acrid stench of dried blood to greet her, but Anne ignored it and closed and latched the door behind her. *He is going to pay, Willa.* She hurried through the entrance hall without looking around, then darted upstairs and ran to her bedroom. She rushed to her closet, listening to the blare of angry honking outside her bedroom windows, from the backed-up traffic.

Anne opened the louvered door, reached for the top shelf, shoved aside a stack of winter sweaters, and fumbled around for the Prada shoebox. She found it with her fingertips, scraped to get it down but ended up batting it to the ground, the lid coming off. She knelt down and moved the white tissue-paper aside, and there it was, nestled safe and sound.

Her little black semi-auto, the Beretta Tomcat. It was a sleek little gun of Italian design, the Armani of handguns. She lifted it from the box, feeling its heavy, deadly heft in her palm. She pushed the grooved button in the handle and slid out the magazine. It smelled of gun cleaner and was fully loaded. She pressed the mag back, clicked the safety into place, and slipped the tiny gun into her purse. She was about to run downstairs when she thought of something. She couldn't run in Blahniks and she'd need to run. Why not think ahead, for once? She rooted in the bottom of her closet, found a pair of red canvas espadrilles, and slid into them. Then her eye fell on her summer dresses, hanging in the closet.

Why not? She'd be more recognizable in her own clothes, and for the first time in her life, she knew just what to wear. She tore through her clothes, sliding each work dress and suit along the hanger with a screech. There it was, way in the back. The dress she'd worn on her first and only date with Kevin. She hadn't worn it since, but something had prevented her from throwing it out. It was a part of her history. Now it would be a part of her future. She stripped, slipped the white picot dress from the hanger, and shimmied into it. The sleeveless skimmer felt cool, and she suppressed the bad memory it carried. She dropped the Beretta into its front pocket, because she'd be freer to move without her messenger bag. She went to her dresser, grabbed some cash in case she needed it, and headed out.

Honk! Honk! It was a hornfest out there, and Anne hurried downstairs. She hated going through the entrance hall again, and flung open the front door so fast that she startled an old man on the sidewalk. He looked vaguely familiar in his gray shorts, white T-shirt, and black socks-and-sandals combo, and he was walking a fawn pug, tugging mightily for such a tiny dog.

The old man's eyes widened, his cataracts ringing them with a cloudy circle. "Miss Murphy! You're alive?"

Anne came down the steps and steadied him by his arm, its biceps slack with advanced age. "I am, sir. Did you see the newspaper? It was an awful mistake. I was just out of town."

"Well, how remarkable! You know, I live next door to you, in 2259. My name is Mort Berman." Mr. Berman's head shook slightly. "I was so sorry to hear that you had been killed! You were such a nice, quiet neighbor. We felt funny holding the block party, but we thought we'd do a sort of memorial to you. And now you're alive! Will you come?"

"Thank you, Mr. Berman, I will." Horns blared from the line of traffic, and the man in the white TransAm was flipping Anne a very aggressive bird, moving his middle finger up and down. She hoped Mr. Berman couldn't see. "I'm sorry, I really have to go now. Happy Fourth!"

"See ya at the block party!" he called back, as Anne jumped inside the VW and shifted it into gear.

Her thoughts moved a lot faster than the traffic. She checked the Beetle's purple-and-red clock. 9:48. It was early. Good. She was one step ahead of Bennie, and Kevin, too. The newspapers wouldn't have published her photo so soon after she'd left the Roundhouse, but there was still a lot she could do in the meantime. She sensed Kevin wouldn't make his move until dark, because it would be safer for him, but she could let him get a bead on her before then. Anything could happen once she put herself in harm's way. At least now she had the Beretta for protection. And the gold charm necklace Mrs. DiNunzio had given her. She'd be ready for him and any other hobgoblin.

Come out, come out, wherever you are.

Anne hit the gas and took a left, heading west. She knew where to look for Kevin, so that he could find her. Twenty blocks later she was there. Powelton Village was a city neighborhood that lay between Drexel University and the University of Pennsylvania. The architecture was decidedly different from Center City; instead of the brick row-houses that marked Philly's downtown, there were large, detached Victorian houses made of stone, with slate-shingled turrets, funky gothic parapets, and arched porches. Their gingerbread trim had been painted in whimsical Cape May colors. Some of the large houses bore signs with Greek letters, and Anne assumed they were frat houses from nearby Drexel University and Penn. She took a left past the row of frats and then a right onto the street.

3845 Moore. She had remembered the address from the answers to interrogatories. It was where Beth and Bill Dietz lived. Anne had never visited the home of a plaintiff before, but Kevin had never started stalking anyone else. There was a chance that he'd be here, watching Beth's house, and if he was, Anne wanted him to see her. Maybe she could do some good, too. She had thought about calling ahead, to see if it was okay for her to come, but there'd be too much 'splainin' to do, and she didn't want to ask for permission she wouldn't get.

The Beetle cruised up the street, and she inched up in the driver's seat with anticipation. Tall, narrow houses lined the street like books on a shelf. American flags hung from the arch on the porches, and the smell of barbecued hamburgers blew from the backyards, but the streets were less busy than downtown. If Kevin was stalking Beth Dietz, he'd have a harder time finding places to hide. And so would Anne.

She found a space near the Dietzes' and parked legally, taking it as a good omen. Maybe she'd have some luck and draw fire. She got out of the car, walked down the street slowly in case Kevin was watching, and found the right house. It was made of large, dark stone and stood three-stories high, apparently only one-room wide, and had a green-painted porch with no flag. The porch's gray floorboards had warped, and its plank edges were crooked as bad teeth. She walked to the front door and knocked under its four-paned window.

It was opened after the second knock by Beth Dietz. She wore jean shorts, an embroidered peasant blouse, and a shocked expression on her pretty face. "I read you were alive, but seeing you—" she stopped in midsentence, her blue eyes astonished. "Well, I mean, what are you doing here? You represent Gil Martin. You have no business being here, and my husband will be home any minute." She glanced worriedly up the street, tossing back long blond hair, and Anne formed the instant impression that she was nervous.

"I know this seems inappropriate, but I came to talk to you about Kevin Satorno, not the case."

"Please. You have to go. My husband is on his way." Beth started to close the door, but Anne stopped her.

"Did the police tell you that Kevin Satorno is stalking you? Did Matt?"

"No one's stalking me. I would know if someone was stalking me."

It struck a chord. Anne had felt that way, too. "No, he is, and you have to take him seriously. He believes you're in love with him, and the cops don't understand how to deal with him. I'm worried—"

"Oh, please." Beth scoffed. "You're worried about me? You've spent the last year making my life miserable." She tried to close the door again, but Anne shoved her espadrille in it.

"Have you had a lot of hang-ups on your phone? Don't change the number, it takes away his outlet. Get a second phone line and leave an answering machine on the first. And save the tape, for evidence." Anne could see Beth hesitate for just a second, and was surprised to find herself softening inside. She and Beth were both women in the same predicament, even though they were at odds in the lawsuit. And she didn't judge Beth for having an affair; Bill Dietz would have driven any wife away. "I know it seems weird, but we have a lot in common. It's very possible that Kevin's watching us both, right now."

"Look, you know that my husband doesn't like you, especially after our depositions. You should really go. Our lawyer will be with him, you can talk to him." Beth glanced worriedly down the street, and Anne realized she was more worried about her husband than Kevin.

"Matt is with your husband? So, he told you about Kevin Satorno."

"They went out for a minute, for more charcoal. Please, go."

"Let me in, just for a minute. We're both in danger."

"Please, please go!" Beth's gaze remained fixed at the end of the street, then her eyes flickered with fear. Anne looked over her shoulder. A black Saab was cruising toward the house, and Beth let out a low groan. "Now he'll see you leave."

"If that's your husband, I'll talk to him, too. I can explain—"

"No!" Beth pressed hard on the door and almost slammed it on Anne's fingers. "Don't you see? You're just making it harder for me!"

Anne felt torn. She had no right to be here, but she didn't like a woman being bullied when her life was at stake. "Kevin is out there, Beth! He'll be looking for me today. And for you."

Suddenly Anne heard the loud slamming of a car door on the street and she turned in time to see Bill Dietz double-park the Saab and rush out of it, his long ponytail flying. He was alone; Matt wasn't in the car. He took big strides on long, thin legs and reached the front porch in no time.

"Oh, no," Beth moaned, and Anne edged backward. She put up her hands almost reflexively as Dietz charged toward her and bounded to the front door.

"Mr. Dietz, Bill, I can explain—"

"Anne Murphy!?" Dietz shouted. "Who the fuck do you think you are, coming to our house?" His chest heaved under a thin yellow surfer shirt, and his deep voice thundered. "You're dead, you're not dead? You like to play games, fuck with people? What is your problem?"

Anne's mouth went dry. "I'm here to talk with your wife and you about the stalker, Kevin—"

"What, you haven't hurt her enough? Hurt both of us? What *is* this? Are you crazy, or just a bitch?" Dietz raged in Anne's face, his skin tinged redder than it had been at the deposition.

"I'm trying to help Beth—"

"Oh, it's 'Beth' now? You didn't call her 'Beth' at her deposition! You called her a *whore!*"

"Bill, no, please!" Beth pleaded from the door. On the sidewalk, a mother with two young children hurried them past the house, avoiding the scene.

Anne stood her ground, wondering how much of his rage was because of the CD. Dietz was trapped and he knew it. The trap had been set by Gil, not her, but she couldn't say that. Anne was getting angry. "I never called her anything and I'm not here about the lawsuit! I'm here because—"

"I don't give a shit why you're here! You're a manipulative bitch! You're fucking Matt! Screwing my lawyer, that's rich! Using him to get to us! You can fool him but you can't fool me, you little whore!"

"What?" Beth asked in a whisper, and Anne's face went hot.

Matt had told Dietz. She felt ashamed, betrayed, driven to respond. "I'm not using Matt, and he never let—"

"*You're* the whore, not my wife! You think I'm gonna take that shit from him—or you? I fired his ass, and I'm reporting you to the state bar! I'll have you both up on charges! Now get the fuck off my property!"

Oh no. Anne's mind was reeling. She didn't see Dietz's hand coming. He cuffed her across the face. Her cheek exploded in pain. She stumbled backward and grabbed the porch railing to keep from falling down the stairs.

"Bill, no!" screamed Beth, clutching her husband at the front door. "Stop! Come inside!"

"Get out of my sight!" Dietz bellowed, shaking Beth off.

Anne scrambled to her feet. She thought of the Beretta but would never go there. She bolted from the porch and ran.

27

Anne dashed down the sidewalk to Judy's car. Her breath came raggedly and her knees had gone weak. She looked behind her. Dietz wasn't chasing after her. The porch was empty and the front door was shut. Beth must have coaxed her husband inside. Still Anne jumped into the car and fumbled for the keys, slamming them into the ignition despite the wrench in her shoulder.

She turned on the ignition, hit the gas, and tore out of the parking space, with one eye plastered to the rearview mirror. A block away, she reached for her cell phone, flipped it open, and pressed in Matt's cell number.

Come on, Matt. Pick up! But the ringing stopped and a mechanical voice came on. "The Verizon customer you are calling cannot be reached . . ." Anne sped away from Moore Street as the beep sounded.

"Matt, call me on the cell!" she shouted

into the phone. "I just had a fight with Dietz. Why did you tell him about us? I heard he fired you. Call me as soon as you can." She hit the End button and tossed the phone onto the seat. She didn't breathe easier until she was two blocks away and the rearview mirror was filled by cars driven by normal people.

Anne's heartbeat slowed, but her shoulder hurt and her cheek stung. She checked the mirror. Her cheekbone was swollen and puffy, but the skin wasn't broken. She felt angry, frightened, and bewildered. At a stoplight, she tried to reconstruct what had happened. Matt had told Dietz about their night together, in a moment of what? Honesty? Conscience? Closeness? She shook her head as the light turned green. Lots of plaintiff's lawyers got friendly with their clients, but this was ridiculous. Mental note: Men may be better at intimacy than Dr. Phil thinks.

Anne pulled up beside a minivan flying the American flag from its antennae and played out the scenario. Dietz was trying to deep-six the lawsuit because of the CD, but Matt didn't know that. So Dietz must have taken the opportunity, when Matt told him about their affair, to fire him. Now Dietz would come home, tell Beth the news about Anne and Matt, and blame it all on them. How could she have let herself get in this position?

Anne cruised behind the minivan and switched the air-conditioning up to MAX, letting it blast away at her stinging cheek. She remembered Kevin. He could be watching, waiting, listening. Fear shot through her but she willed it away. She had to draw Kevin out or she'd never catch him. She searched the street but she didn't see him; then again, she wouldn't. Then it struck her: If Kevin had overheard that scene on the porch, he learned that Anne had been sleeping with Matt. The news would enrage him and place Matt squarely in jeopardy. Anne's thoughts raced. Matt was stranded in West Philly without a car. Where had he and Dietz gone? What had they bought?

She gunned the engine to the end of the block, then crossed onto the next. It was a residential neighborhood, with not a store in sight. A young mother with two kids stood waiting to cross the street, and Anne called out, "Do you know if there's a convenience store around here? One that sells charcoal?"

"The minimart at the gas station. Up five

blocks, then take a right. They'll have charcoal, if they're not out of it already."

"Thanks!" Anne waved them across and
followed the directions to the minimart. A
bright-white building with gas pumps and a
bustling parking lot in front. Matt wasn't outside, but Anne pulled in, switched off the
ignition, and jumped out of the Beetle. She
hurried into the store, past a pyramid of
Kingsford charcoal. She looked around
quickly, but no Matt. If he had been here,
he'd gone. She was about to head for the
exit when she spotted a ratty black-and-
white TV set on a counter behind the
register, and the image on the TV screen
stopped her.

It was her mother, standing with the
deputy commissioner. It must be the press
conference. Anne screened out the noise in
the store and leaned over the counter toward the TV.

"In answer to your question," her mother
was saying, "I am overjoyed that my daughter is alive, and I won't be filing a lawsuit
now or at any other time against the police
department, the city, or the medical examiner's office."

Anne blinked in surprise. Her feet itched

to go, but she stood on the spot as if rooted. *Her mother, turning down money?*

Off-screen, one of the reporters was asking, "Mrs. Murphy, why weren't you called to identify your daughter's body?"

Anne held her breath for the answer.

Her mother bent her head and, when she looked up, her eyes were teary. "I wasn't called to identify Anne because she had no idea of my whereabouts. I have made some terrible mistakes in the past, but the biggest one was abandoning my daughter, long ago."

Anne was amazed at what she was hearing. She wanted to go, she wanted to stay.

"As terrible as it sounds, it took the report of my daughter's death to make me realize what I had lost, in her. I have an opportunity that many parents don't get—a second chance. I only hope she'll let me set things right. Anne, if you're out there, please know how sorry I am for what I've done." Her mother looked into the camera with a new earnestness.

Anne felt her chest tighten. "*Bullshit,*" she heard herself saying reflexively, and the cashier looked at her sideways.

Anne hustled for the exit, running away

from the TV, trying to forget the image. It was too little, too late. For as long as she could remember, her mother had blamed her addictions on casting directors and small-time agents who didn't recognize her talent. Anne had grown up shuffled from baby-sitter to neighbor to stranger, moving through a series of apartments, and usually finding herself alone, doing her homework in front of a television. It wasn't so bad. In her mind, she lived at 623 East 68th Street, in a modestly furnished New York apartment, with one wall of exposed brick, painted white, and a fireplace mantel that held two Chinese figurines, a clock, and an occasional pack of Phillip Morris cigarettes. Her mother was Lucy Ricardo, her father a handsome Cuban bandleader, and they were all very happy until little Ricky came along. Nobody needs a little brother.

Anne jumped into the Beetle and twisted on the ignition, but couldn't shake the memories. Her mother hadn't even cared enough to get her the operations she needed to fix her cleft. It had been a stranger who had done that; a neighbor who'd been a nurse had taken it upon herself to apply for the free surgeries, at a teaching hospital. In truth, Anne's mother had never been there for her. Anne had cobbled together school and federal loans to fund college and law school, and she'd be repaying them the rest of her life. Her heart hardened to bone. She pulled out of the space and took after Matt.

Anne sized up the situation. She was considering driving to Matt's house, but it would take too long to get there, given that it was the heart of the historic district, and then she might lose Kevin. She checked her watch. 1:15. The sun was high and hot, people were everywhere, and the city was alive with Fourth of July festivities. She decided to get back on track and keep leaving a public trail, so Kevin could find her.

An hour later, Anne had parked the car illegally, but not in a tow zone, and was threading her way through the crowds on the Benjamin Franklin Parkway, brushing her tiny bangs off her forehead, showing her scar, enjoying the freedom of going without disguise or lipstick.

"Hey, aren't you that girl they thought was dead, that lawyer?" asked a man in a red Budweiser hat. He was holding a little girl's hand, heading with the crowd to the Party on the Parkway.

"Uh, yes." Anne introduced herself and shook his hand, pleased that her picture was getting out, and he smiled like he'd met a celebrity. She hoped he'd spread the word and she was caught up in the flow of people. Workmen hoisted a plastic banner that read DOLLAR-A-HOAGIE on a huge white tent on Eakins Oval, and she paused to call Matt on his cell, house, and office phones. Still no answer. She didn't see Kevin but she didn't lose hope. The smell of grilling hamburgers and chicken kebabs wafted through the air, and she dug out some money. Anne felt like everybody else on the Fourth of July, killing time until it was dark and the fireworks could begin. She checked her watch. 3:15. Time for the party.

Anne slowed her step as she reached her block, which had been closed to traffic with blue-and-white police sawhorses. Waltin Street was packed with people, at least sixty adults, children, and pets, mingling in the dappled sunshine under the leafy maple trees. She eyed the crowd for Kevin. He could have seen those BLOCK PARTY 3–5 P.M. signs. He could be watching her, waiting for his chance. She didn't worry about drawing him here; he wasn't a danger to anyone but her. She wedged her way around a saw-horse at the top of the block, where an elderly man wearing a spotless polo shirt and pressed slacks was apparently checking IDs.

"Ms. Murphy, no need to prove you live on our street," he said, his face lighting up when he saw her. "I recognize you! I saw you on TV!"

"Thank you, Mr.—"

"I'm your neighbor Bill Kopowski. I live in 2254, with the red shutters. There." He pointed. "Nobody knew whether to hold our party, but we went ahead. My wife Shirley and I were concerned, you should meet her!" Kopowski reached with a shaking hand for an older, plump woman standing next to him, and she turned around, her aged eyes lighting up when she saw Anne.

"Oh, my goodness, it is you!" Mrs. Kopowski exclaimed. She wore a beige linen dress with a necklace of amber beads.

"Yes, hello," Anne said. She extended her hand, but Mrs. Kopowski reached out and swept her into her arms, pulling her close into her soft bosom. She smelled like Shalimar and lavender soap.

Heads in the crowd started to turn to

Anne, as neighbors surged toward her, chattering and chuckling. "Ms. Murphy!" shouted a middle-aged man in a madras shirt and Bermuda shorts. "We haven't met, but I live across from you, in 2258."

"Hi—" Anne started to say but was interrupted by a woman in a blue foam crown.

"Anne Murphy! Anne Murphy! You're not dead! I saw your mother in the newspaper. It was moving, very moving!"

"I see that, too!" another neighbor called out in accented English. He was an Asian in a red-white-and-blue T-shirt. "On TV! She look just like you! You call her, she love you!"

Everyone started calling to Anne, asking so many questions she couldn't begin to respond, and she felt someone clapping her on the back. She turned, startled, but it was another smiling neighbor, thrilled that she was alive, worried that such an awful thing had happened on their street, wanting to know the details. In no time the crowd had completely absorbed her, taking her in like the neighbor she'd never been, welcoming her with open arms and warm beer. She understood for the first time how many people are affected by even a single murder, and how profoundly it had shaken everyone on the block. The whole time she scanned the crowd for Kevin and if he were among them, she hadn't found him yet. She was worried about Matt, and curious where Bennie and the girls were. Sooner or later they'd find her, and she hoped it wasn't before she flushed Kevin out.

"Ms. Murphy, Ms. Murphy! A few questions please!" A man called from behind Anne, and she felt her back shoved rudely. She turned and banged into the lens of a videocamera. A reporter popped up beside the camera, a beefy man in a white T-shirt and jeans, his potbelly hanging over a gold belt buckle. "Ms. Murphy," he asked, rapid-fire, "what's the real story on Kevin Satorno? Any comment? Ms. Murphy?"

"I'm not going to answer any questions," Anne said, trying to get her bearings. The press was here. It made sense that they'd come to her street. This crew had lucked out in finding her. Had she lucked out, too?

"Come on, come clean. Is it true you were engaged to Satorno?" The camera lens trained on Anne, and her neighbors looked on in annoyance. An older man she recognized as a retired chemist was wedging his way toward the reporter, wagging a bony finger at the camera.

"You're not invited here, sir," he called out, his voice quavering with age. "It's residents only. We have a permit. How did you get past Mr. Kopowski? He fought at The Bulge."

Mr. Berman appeared beside him. "Are you reporters? You don't live here! Better get out, before we call the cops. One of you knocked the flowerpot off my front step yesterday!"

But Anne was thinking of her plan. "Hey, buddy," she called to the reporter, "why don't you ask me what I'm going to do next, now that I'm not dead? Like they do after the Superbowl?"

"She's going to Disneyworld!" Mr. Simmons, another neighbor, chimed in, and neighbors behind him closed in, encircling the reporter and cameraman.

"Yes, ask her what she's going to do next!" Mr. Monterosso called out.

Another yelled, "Yes! Print some good news for a change!"

A third neighbor cried, "You won't show that on TV, will you? You never run anything nice, even on the holiday."

The reporter turned to Anne, chuckling. "Okay, Ms. Murphy! What are you going to do next? Are you going to Disneyworld?"

"And leave Philly on the Fourth of July? No way!" Anne answered into the camera, knowing it would be aired for Kevin to hear. She thanked God that Bennie hated TV. "Tonight, I'm going to celebrate the country's birthday, Philly-style! Eat a hoagie at the Dollar-A-Hoagie tent, then watch the fireworks at the Art Museum! Happy Fourth, everybody!"

The neighbors cheered loudly, laughing and hooting, and Mr. Berman wielded his cane like a drum major. "Now, Mr. Reporter, you have your story! Go print it! *Vamoose!*"

"Yeah! Get outta here! You don't live here! Waltin Street residents only!" Mrs. Berman shouted, and a teenager, the tattooed daughter of a psychology professor, started chanting.

"Waltin Street rocks! Waltin Street rocks!"

"Waltin Street rocks! Waltin Street rocks!" the neighbors all began to chant, blasting the reporters and cameraman away with the power of their voices, singing out as one.

"Waltin Street rocks, Waltin Street rocks!" Anne chanted loudest of all, yelling at the top of her lungs, no longer so Kevin Satorno would hear it but because it made her feel good and happy and a part of a very special group, one that inhabited a block that formed one of the many blocks in the historic grid that built the United States of America. Ben Franklin himself designed the grid, she remembered with a new pride. Mental note: Patriotism is really about belonging, and Anne belonged right here.

But now it was time to get busy.

28

The sun was still high but glowing a late-day orange, scorching a slow descent through the sky. The air had grown oppressively humid, making Anne's dress stick to her skin. She picked trash up off her street and from between parked cars, and stuffed it into a large Hefty bag, eyeing each person who walked by. She didn't see Kevin and couldn't help but feel increasingly tense.

She kept an eye out for him as she helped her neighbors gather bottles for recycling, fold up aluminum picnic tables, and Saran-Wrap an awesome leftover pasta-and-pepper salad. They all dragged the police sawhorses away from the top of the block, only reluctantly opening to the rest of the city the enclave that had been Waltin Street. Foot traffic increased, spilling into the street as everybody streamed to the Parkway to get the best spaces to watch the fireworks. They carried beach chairs, rolled tatami mats, and spare bedspreads. One kid trailed his father carrying a set of lighted brown punks, tapers that scented the air with their distinctive acrid smell.

She checked her watch. 7:15. Time was hurrying along and taking her with it. She had seen a schedule of July Fourth events on the Parkway, starting with a "celebrity reading of the Declaration of Independence," then the Dollar-A-Hoagie sale, which ended at nine o'clock with the fireworks. She figured she would linger on Waltin a while longer, then head over to the Dollar-A-Hoagie tent, where Kevin would know to find her. It was almost time.

She bent down and picked up a smashed cellophane wrapper of Cherry Nibs, then put it in the trash bag, and, as she leaned over, felt the weight of her Beretta in her pocket. She had almost forgotten about the gun in the rush of good feeling generated by the block party. She began having second thoughts. Was there any other way? No. *If this doesn't end tonight, it will never end. Not until I'm really dead.* She stowed the trash in the bag and was moving on to a discarded paper cup when her cell phone rang.

She stuffed the bag under her armpit, dug

in her other pocket for the phone, and flipped it open to see who was calling. Matt's cell phone number glowed on the screen in bright blue digits. She hadn't answered Bennie's many calls, but this call she'd take. She pressed Send. "Matt?" she asked, lowering her voice. "Where are you? I've been trying—"

"I got your messages." His voice sounded anxious. "How are you? Are you okay?"

"Fine, fine, really." Anne cupped a hand over her free ear to hear better, and left the noisy street. She told him briefly about her debacle at the Dietz house, omitting the assault-and-battery part. No need to heighten his already heightened protectiveness. "Why did you tell Dietz about us? That was our business!"

"I had to. I called Beth and told her that Satorno was stalking her, but she didn't take it seriously, so I went over. I think it was because Bill wasn't buying it. He has a lot of influence with her."

"Duh."

"I had to tell Bill what happened to you, to make him believe it. He asked me how I knew so much, and I told him. I had to, or she'd be in danger."

"I'm so sorry," Anne said, chastened by the explanation. Between his client's safety or his own representation, Matt had made a choice she admired. How could she have been angry at him? "I feel awful that you got fired. What are you going to do?"

"Clean up the file and hand it over. I think they'll use Epstein now. Watch out, Anne. The good lawyers are coming."

"Bullshit." Anne bit her lip. "Can I help, or have I screwed things up enough already?"

"No, you didn't do this. I did. I admit, I needed to lick my wounds after he fired me, and I wished I'd talked to Beth alone, but it's okay now. He was my client, too, and he always speaks for Beth. You're the one I'm worried about. Bennie called my house, saying you had given them the slip. She's looking for you. She went up to your street to find you and there's a block party, but some old guy wouldn't let her in. Even Mary couldn't sweet-talk him, or Judy."

Anne smiled. Mr. Kopowski took no prisoners.

"She even called the cops, told them to look out for you. Where are you, Anne? You shouldn't be alone, not with Satorno still loose. I want to see you, to be with you."

Anne couldn't let that happen. She'd involved enough people in this nightmare. "I'm fine, Matt. I don't need my hand held." People flowed past her on the sidewalk, her neighbors waving good-bye as they left for the fireworks.

"This guy is a killer," Matt was saying. "He could be stalking you right now. Where are you? I hear people in the background."

"I'm in a cab, I'm on my way over to your house, right now. Just stay there and wait for me." It was a good idea, and would keep him in place until she caught Kevin. "I gotta go. Hear that beep? I'm low on batteries."

"I don't hear a beep. I'm worried that you're going to do something crazy. Bennie said you own a gun. Is she right?"

"No, guns are scary. They go off by themselves, did you know that? There's the beep again. I'll be over as soon as I can. The traffic is a mess. Wait there for me!" Anne pressed the End button, and suddenly another message popped onto the phone screen. ONE CALL UNANSWERED, read the blue letters. Probably Bennie again, but it could give a clue as to where she was. Her last two calls had been from her cell, and a mobile Bennie threatened Anne's plan. She dialed for her voice mail, then listened.

It was Gil, not Bennie. "Anne, I'm really sorry for what I did last night." His words sounded slurred and sloppy. "I never shoulda tried to, you know. Jamie's thrown me out, and I was wondering if I could see you tonight, you know, just to talk it over . . . oh, shit! Willya look at that! I'm in the bar on the corner of Sixteenth and the Parkway, you know the one, and I'm watching you on the TV right now! Damn, you look awesome! I love your—"

Disgusted, Anne deleted the message, then hit End, troubled. Gil was only five blocks away and he'd seen the footage about the Dollar-A-Hoagie tent. She could only hope he wouldn't interfere. She hit the Power button to shut the phone off, then slipped it back into her pocket. She glanced up at the sky, which had grown darker. The sun had dipped below the maple trees, flat rooftops, and loopy antennae. Its dying rays flooded the sky with a fierce orange. It was time to get started.

Anne removed the trash bag from under her arm, closed the drawstring, and set the bag down with the others, near the front of the alley. She couldn't help noticing it was the same alley that she'd scooted down in her Uncle Sam stovepipe, not so long ago. She took off for the Parkway, pausing as she passed her house, with flowers still on the stoop. She knew what lay beyond her front door and flashed on the blood spattered on the entrance hall. The obscenity of the murder. The stench of death. Willa had died there, and now her killer would be brought to justice. Anne bowed her head, then slipped off into the twilight.

She joined the crowd flowing to the Parkway, scanning the people as she walked, remembering the details of Kevin's newly dark hair and the shape of his head, watching for even the least sign of him. God knew what he'd be wearing. Something that blended in. She looked around. There were three hundred flag T-shirts in the moving crowd. Anne scooted along to catch up and check out as many as she could. None of them was Kevin.

She kept walking, slipping her hand inside her pocket for the Beretta, to reassure herself. She headed with the crowd onto the Ben Franklin Parkway, where the rowhouses disappeared. Eight lanes of the boulevard opened onto a sky washed with hazy pinks, aquamarine blues, and the most transparent of amethysts. Dusk settled, hard to discern, visible only in contrast to bright spots of unexpected light; the red glowing tip of a lighted cigarette, the hot pink of a child's neon bracelet, a white pool of flashlight borne by a sensible older couple.

The geometric skyline of the city had been colored red, white, and blue for the holiday. The lighted sign at the top of the Peco Building read HAPPY FOURTH in a continuous loop of dotted lights. The night air was filled with talk, laughter, and babies crying, and the breeze scented with insect repellent and domestic beer. To Anne's right was the Art Museum, the immense Grecian building usually bathed in tasteful amber spotlights, now colored a gaudy red-white-and-blue, with lasers that roamed the night sky. The huge limestone staircase that Rocky Balboa scaled in the movie was hidden by a massive temporary scaffolding, a stage of stainless steel, and panels of stage lighting. A warm-up band played on the stage, their electric guitars twanging through the speaker system mounted on the trees.

Anne checked her watch. 8:00. It was almost dark. She was running late. She picked up the pace as she crossed the Parkway's baseball diamond, set up for kids' T-ball but now covered with blankets, collapsible chaise lounges, and the citizenry of Philadelphia, eagerly awaiting fireworks. She picked her way through the vendors dispensing sodas, hot dogs, cotton candy, funnel cakes, and Mr. Softee. Anybody who wanted a hoagie for dinner would already be thronging across the street at the tent, and Anne made a beeline for it, as a drum solo thundered through the loudspeakers and reverberated in the night air.

She crossed the street with difficulty, as the crowd began cheering the band off, wanting the celebrities who were going to read the Declaration of Independence. A million people were expected at the fireworks and it was almost impossible to make it through the shoulder-to-shoulder crowd. Anne kept her hand on the Beretta in her pocket and pressed past people's sweaty backs and chests, making her way across the Parkway to Eakins Oval, a circle of grass, gardens, and fountains that fronted the Art Museum.

The reading of the Declaration of Independence was starting, and, even in the street accent of a rap star, its words remained beautiful: "When in the course of human Events, it becomes necessary for one People to dissolve the Political Bands which have connected them with another, and to assume among the Powers of the Earth . . ."

Anne craned her neck above the crowds to see where she was going, getting a bead on the dark statue of George Washington on horseback. He rode at the center of the largest circular fountain on Eakins Oval, flanked by two smaller circular fountains squirting red-, white-, and blue-lighted water. The white plastic canopy of the huge Dollar-A-Hoagie tent was right behind it, and mobbed. Damn. How would Kevin find her in that mob? And could she really draw a gun in a crowd? Maybe this hadn't been the best plan, but there was no changing it now. She could handle the gun and keep the safety on. Kevin wouldn't know better, and it would make sure no one got hurt.

A young movie actress was saying, with microphone feedback, "We hold these Truths to be self-evident, that all Men are created equal, that they are endowed by their Creator with certain unalienable Rights, that among these are Life, Liberty, and the Pursuit of Happiness—"

Anne took heart. More beautiful words had never been written. She had the right to happiness, to liberty, to life. She had a great job, a nice neighborhood, girlfriends, and a new romance. She was entitled to all of these things, and Kevin was taking them away. She navigated around a family on their blanket, steadying their little boy with a palm on his warm head, then kept going, stumbling on kicked-off sneakers and shoes in the darkness, parting the crowd, at a celebrity-struck standstill.

A Broadway actor was launching into, "But when a long Train of Abuses and Usurpations, pursuing invariably the same Object, evinces a Design to reduce them under absolute Despotism, it is their Right, it is their Duty, to throw off such Government, and to provide new Guards for their future Security."

Damn right! Anne was protecting her future security. The hoagie tent lay less than fifty feet ahead, and she checked the crowd for Kevin as she barreled through it. It wasn't easy to see, now that night had fallen. The only lights came from the old-fashioned gaslights near the fountains on the Oval and the intermittent lasers sweeping the sky.

A blond starlet was mustering colonial outrage: "The History of the present King of Great-Britain is a History of repeated Injuries and Usurpations, all having in direct Object the Establishment of an absolute Tyranny over these States. To prove this, let Facts be submitted to a candid World. He has refused his Assent to laws . . ."

Anne plowed her way to the tent. Toward Kevin. He had refused to assent to laws, too. She just couldn't live this way any longer. She felt unhinged and jittery. Exhausted and adrenalized from the last few days. She had a funny taste in her mouth, and wetness appeared under her arms and on her forehead. Her knees felt loose but she powered forward.

A distinguished Academy Award winner was saying, "He has obstructed the Administration of Justice, by refusing his Assent to Laws for establishing Judiciary Powers . . . ."

The litany of injustices resonated, and the fact that they had been perpetrated by the King of England was only a technicality. Anne was going to rectify injustice. Catch the bad guy and put him away forever. Get

justice for herself and for Willa. And now, for
Beth.

"Excuse me, sir," Anne said to a man in
her way, picking up speed, fueled by increasing anger through the packed crowd.
She looked for Kevin but didn't see him. He
was out there, she knew it. She could sense
him, a dark vibration. She held her head high
so he could see her.

Thirty yards, then twenty. The hoagie tent
lay right ahead. Anne started to hustle, un-
daunted by the crowd, jostling people in her
path. She could hear the chatter at the
hoagie tent. Smell the tang of spices and
fresh processed meats through the cigarette
smoke and beer.

She reached the line at the end of the
hoagie tent, took her place, and tried to
arrange her face into a happy mask, so she
could look like she was having fun. She kept
her hand cradled around the Beretta and
squinted through the laser beams at the
crowd. She had a better vantage point in the
line at the tent. Everybody was facing the
stage and the celebrities, gawking, pointing,
and taking pictures. She eyed as many faces
as possible, studying their features under
Phillies caps, foam crowns, deelyboppers,

and American-flag hats. Nobody was moving except for the people hurrying to the hoagie tent.

The Declaration continued: "We, therefore, the Representatives of the UNITED STATES OF AMERICA, in General Congress, Assembled, appealing to the Supreme Judge of the World for the Rectitude of our Intentions, do, in the Name, and by Authority of the good People of these Colonies, solemnly Publish and Declare, That these United Colonies are, and of Right ought to be Free and Independent States . . ."

The line shifted forward, but Anne couldn't see under the dark tent. When was the end of the Declaration of Independence? She should have known but she didn't. The fireworks would start right after. When would Kevin make his move? Her heart began to pound. She felt exposed, vulnerable, even in full view of everyone. Where were the cops?

The line went forward, moving fast, and Anne could finally see under the tent. An army of people, maybe fifty, were dressed in white uniforms and paper bifold hats with Stars and Stripes, and they were handing out hoagies as fast as they could, collecting the dollars in exchange and stuffing them into a barrel to be donated to Children's Hospital. Two cops stood behind the barrel, their arms folded in their short-sleeved summer uniforms. Great!

The Declaration sounded as if it were concluding. "And for the support of this declaration, with a firm Reliance on the Protection of divine Providence, we mutually pledge to each other our lives, our Fortunes, and our sacred Honor."

The crowd clapped and cheered wildly. The cops turned around and clapped, and the hoagie line burst into applause, becoming agitated now, anticipating the fireworks, wanting to get their sandwich and hurry back to their blankets. The noise was deafening, but the fact that everyone was clapping at once helped Anne. Because over there, across the sea of heads, stood a lone man who wasn't clapping. Her gaze shot immediately to him.

He was tall and wore a dark T-shirt. She recognized the shape of his head, even though he had shaved off all of his hair. His shorn head shone skull-white in the gaslight. His expression was determined, his shoulders muscular and pumped. He turned suddenly toward the tent, and a stray ray of blood-red light sliced his face, illuminating it.

The man was Kevin Satorno. And it was time for Anne's own personal Declaration of Independence.

29

Boom! A white chrysanthemum burst into bloom and faded to a sparking skeleton as the first fireworks went off in the night sky over the Art Museum, and the crowd oohed, aahed, and clapped. The explosion reverberated in Anne's heart but she kept her eye on Kevin, so she wouldn't lose him. His shaved head turned toward the hoagie tent. He was looking for her.

Anne suppressed a shudder and slid her hand into her pocket. Her fingers found the Beretta's grip, now warm with the heat of her body. She willed herself not to be afraid and edged out of the line, going to her right, so that the line lay between her and Kevin. Everyone was looking up at the fireworks, except for him. She could see him as he faced the line. She would have to come up from behind him.

Fireworks shot hissing into the air, their launching convulsive, soaring to the heavens, where they exploded into glittery red, white, and blue sprays. They left searing white lights suspended in the air like incendiary fairies and detonated with a thunder that sent little kids covering their ears.

Anne was on the move. She walked behind the line slowly, so she didn't lose Kevin or draw his attention in her white dress. It stood out at night. Thank God she had found him first. *Ca-shoosh! Ca-shoosh!* Fireworks went off with cacophonous screeching. Howling curlicues of red, green, and blue spiraled into the firmament. The colors tinged the faces around her, then they'd fall again into darkness.

Anne reached the tent and continued around the back. People stood still, transfixed by the show in the sky. Kevin was turning his head, scanning the line for her. His eyes narrowed to slits. His mouth flattened to a grim line of purpose. She felt her heart pounding.

She checked the cops' position. They stood stationed at the cash barrel to her left. She thought about running to them right now and pointing Kevin out, but she wasn't sure she could convince them fast enough, before he ran off, or maybe hurt somebody.

She had a better idea. She'd come up from behind, stick the gun in Kevin's back, then move him toward the police and away from the crowd, so nobody would get hurt. As soon as she had flanked him successfully, she'd yell for help. General George Washington, riding his bronze horse not fifty feet away, would have been proud.

Ca-shoosh! The air smelled of smoke. Cinders fell like blackened snowflakes. Anne snuck around the tent and got a bead on the back of Kevin's head. She had him now. She was directly behind him, with only the rapt crowd in between. She picked up speed and moved through the crowd. Closing in at thirty feet. Then twenty. Ten.

Anne's blood drummed in her ears. She gripped the Beretta's handle so tightly its hatchmarks imprinted on her palm. Her hand was shaking but she ignored it. *Boom!* Firework palm trees in green glitter waved in the air, and the crowd laughed. She was so close to Kevin she could count the bumps on his scalp. A group of rowdy teenagers partied between them, wearing blue football jerseys and waving Heinekens and show-off cigars.

Bang! Bang! Fireworks like red pom-poms flamed overhead and their red glitter dissolved to hearts glowing in the sky. The teenagers cheered, raising green bottles of beer, and Anne threaded her way through them. Their cigar smoke blew toward Kevin, wreathing his head.

Her stomach steeled. Her heart seemed to stop. She felt oddly like someone else, someone braver than herself. She inched the Beretta from her pocket.

Pow! Pow! A wolf pack of white lights detonated in a frenzy that got the teenagers hooting in her ears. Anne had almost passed them when Kevin moved away and started walking toward the tent. Even better. She'd have him where she wanted him, closer to the cops. The two uniforms remained at the cash barrel, their blue caps silhouetted in the light from the tent. It was time. *Go.* She drew her Beretta and held it at her hip.

"Hey, gorgeous, where you going so fast?" asked one of the football players. He sidestepped into her path, blocking her view of Kevin.

"Move, please!" Anne started to go around him, but he grabbed her arm and spun her around so quickly she almost dropped the gun.

"What's your hurry, honey? Dontcha wanna watch the fireworks with me?"

"Leave me alone!" Anne wrenched her arm free and rushed frantic around him.

But Kevin wasn't standing where he'd been a moment ago. She looked around wildly. He had disappeared. Only the crowd was facing her; men, women, and children looking up at the fireworks. Had she lost him? *No!*

Anne plunged into the crowd around the tent. She couldn't lose Kevin, not now. She searched the mob but he wasn't there. Had he gone on the other side of the line, like she had? She let the Beretta slip back into her pocket.

Ka-BOOM! Ka-BOOM! Silvery streams sprayed all over the sky, as if heaven itself had sprung a huge leak, as the fireworks segued into the finale. *Ka-BOOM! Ka-BOOM!* The sky erupted into rapid-fire explosions, like a war zone. *Ka-BOOM! Ka-BOOM!*

Anne hurried to the tent, looking everywhere for Kevin. His shaven head, his black T-shirt. People stood riveted, cheering. No Kevin. She wanted to scream with frustration. She thought fast. Time for Plan B. She had lost sight of Kevin, but she would *not* lose him. She turned and looked for the cops, to tell them. They'd call for backup; he couldn't be far.

Suddenly Anne was grabbed from behind and her right arm wrenched up behind her. Something sharp cut deep into her back. She was about to scream when she heard a hot voice at her ear, against her cheek.

"Don't scream or I'll drive a hunting knife through your heart." It was Kevin.

Anne froze with fear. Her shoulder seared with pain. The knife dug into her back. She wanted to scream but he'd stab her on the spot. She couldn't reach her gun with her left hand. Even if she could, she couldn't shoot in this crowd. She didn't know what to do. Her heels left the ground as Kevin lifted her up by her arm and propelled her forward, away from the tent and the police. The knife sliced between her ribs. Anne struggled to think through her terror.

Kevin cranked her arm up farther. "You're coming with me. You won't get away from me this time. You're mine, now. Finally."

Tears of fright sprang to her eyes. He was breaking her arm at the shoulder. The fireworks erupted into their high-decibel finale.

BOOM! BOOM! BOOM! The sky was a canopy of white lights, smoke, and thunder. Anne prayed to God it wasn't the last sight she'd see.

Kevin put his cheek close to hers, driving her forward with the knife. "You bitch, I dreamed of you every night. I looked at your picture every minute. I wrote to you, called you, bought you gifts. Flowers, jewelry, poems, candy. I gave you everything I had. I was devoted to you, dedicated to you."

Anne tried to make sense of what was happening. She had to survive. The knife-point drilled into her back, now hot and warm with blood. Her blood.

She tried not to panic as Kevin hurried her through the crowd to the street, shoving her toward the apartment buildings and the grove of trees and bushes at the dark edge of the park. Nobody was around. Trees blocked them from view. Maybe she could reach her gun. Get off a shot without hurting anybody else.

Kevin's breath grew heated. "I loved your face. I loved your body. I loved every inch of you. I would have done anything for you. Anything, Anne."

Ka-BOOM! Ka-BOOM! Kevin was taking

her past the bushes. Heading around the back of an apartment building toward the Expressway. Anne could feel the weight of the Beretta in her pocket. It banged into her thigh. Could she wrap her hand across her body?

"You played me, you fucking bitch!" Kevin's voice shook with pent-up rage, unleashed. "You threw me away! You sent me to prison! You know what that's like? You know what I went through in there? Because of you, you fucking bitch! I hate you! I hate your fucking guts!"

Anne blocked out his words; they paralyzed her. She had saved herself from him once before. She could do it again. She forced herself to wait for the right moment. It would come. She would get the gun.

Ka-BOOM! Ka-BOOM! Red, white, and blue lashed through the leaves of the trees.

"I'll love killing you, Anne. Love every single fucking minute of it. I'll make it last forever. It'll be the best sex of your life."

Anne felt a bolt of sheer terror. Kevin was forcing her toward a deserted stretch by the Expressway, strewn with trash and litter. They were almost at the back of the building. Nobody to see them here. Her eyes filled with tears. Her gut told her this would be her last moment on the planet. She had nothing to lose. No one here to get hurt but her. She reached for her pocket but Kevin pressed the knife into her flesh, stabbing her with the tip. She let out a desperate cry no one could hear. "Help!"

Ka-BOOM! Ka-BOOM! Ka-BOOM!

"Anne? Anne! Is that you?" shouted someone, not far behind them.

"Help!" Anne screamed again, just as she felt Kevin's body torque toward the sound. She seized the opportunity and twisted enough to reach her left pocket. She grabbed the Beretta. Kevin was too distracted to notice.

Anne struggled in his grasp, holding the Beretta against her leg, waiting. She was a good shot, but not good enough to shoot over her shoulder. She disengaged the safety with her thumb, pressing it down. She couldn't hear the solid *tik* she knew it made. The Beretta was loaded and ready to fire.

The man's voice called again, right behind them. "Anne! Anne, are you okay?!" It was Gil! He must have come from the bar, looking for her.

Ka-BOOM! BOOM! BOOM! Fireworks detonated like bombs.

"Gil!" she screamed, but Kevin was already turning toward him, relaxing his grip. Anne felt the knifepoint ease from her back, wet with blood. She seized the chance to leap from Kevin's hold, spin around on her heel, and aim the gun at him. "Hold it right there!" she screamed. "I'll use it, I swear."

But Kevin was already lunging at Gil with the jagged hunting knife. Gil caught Kevin by the wrist, pressing him backward. The two men struggled back and forth. Anne aimed for Kevin, but he was moving too much for her to fire. She couldn't take the chance and shoot Gil. Fighting men were different from a paper target.

"Anne, shoot him!" Gil shouted, but the men kept struggling, turning this way and that. She stepped closer to the fight to get a better shot, but suddenly Gil reached out with a desperate hand and grabbed the gun from her. Kevin came at him, brandishing the knife, and reached Gil just as the gun went off, a flame of red-orange firing from the snub barrel, the report lost in the fireworks. Then another, and another, from the semi-automatic.

BOOM! BOOM! BOOM!

Anne screamed. Kevin's neck exploded in blood. He dropped backward onto the ground, crumpling like a straw man. She hurried to Kevin. He lay sprawled on the ground, his legs bent crazily, his body motionless. His mouth hung agape, his eyes stared open but unseeing. Blood squirted red from where his Adam's apple used to be, spurting into the air with his pulse, falling back on his face like a grisly fountain. His throat emitted a hideous, gurgling sound.

"No!" Anne heard herself scream without knowing why. Hot blood spattered her dress and drenched her hands and arms. It was no use calling 911. One look at Kevin told her he was dead.

"It's all right now," Gil was saying, over and over, his hand on her shoulder.

But Anne heard him only as if he were far away, and tears she couldn't begin to explain poured down her cheeks.

30

At the interview room of the Roundhouse, fluorescent lights on the ceiling cast harsh shadows that hollowed out the faces of those assembled. Having given her statement, Anne sat numbly in a bare side chair, her white dress puckering with drying blood in gruesome polka dots. Her back stung where she had taken five stitches over the knife wound, but she'd been so disoriented at the hospital that she hadn't even washed her hands. They lay apart in her lap, blood-stained and recoiling from each other.

She was relieved that her nightmare with Kevin was finally over, but she couldn't help wishing it hadn't ended with such an awful death. Her shoulder slumped with exhaustion; she felt drained and spent. Her head hurt so much she couldn't begin to parse her complex knot of emotions. She knew she'd be doing that for the next few days, if not years.

Judy and Mary stood behind Anne's chair like a hastily dressed girl army, their faces drawn and saddened even by a war won. A bruised Matt hovered near Anne, with an arm on her shoulder, as they all listened to Gil finish giving his statement to a grave Detective Rafferty. The heavyset Detective Hunt-and-Peck did the typing, and everyone pretended that Deputy Commissioner Parker, who leaned against the wall in a crisp uniform with his dark arms folded, always attended such occasions.

"I saw that he had Anne," Gil was saying, seated in the steel chair bolted to the floor. "He had his hand in her back. I thought he might have a gun, or a knife." Bennie stood behind him, her head cocked as she listened. She was representing Gil in the investigation, since Anne wasn't permitted to, as a witness to the shooting.

SAW THAT HE, typed the detective, and Detective Rafferty leaned forward, his elbows resting on his legs. He was still dressed in a suit, but his tie was loose and the knot hung off-center. "And you knew it was Satorno, how?"

"We went over this," Gil said, tired. His seersucker sports jacket had been torn, the lapels stained by Kevin's blood. Anne was fairly sure that the police wouldn't charge Gil with anything, even involuntary manslaughter, not with Bennie on defense. But it wasn't a certainty. Anne didn't want to see Gil indicted for saving his own life, and hers.

Bennie tapped her client's shoulder. "You should probably repeat your answer."

"Okay, I'll say it again. I knew it was Satorno because I'd seen his photo on the TV and in the newspapers."

"You remembered the way he looked from the mug shot?"

"Of course. I took an interest. He tried to kill my lawyer, my friend. When they ran his photo, I checked his features. I did the same thing with the Unabomber, didn't you?"

"I see." Rafferty rubbed his chin, grizzled now. "And how is it that you happened to be there at the time, Mr. Martin?"

"Be where?"

"At the hoagie tent."

"Well, I was at a bar farther down the Parkway. East, I should say. Chase's Taverna, okay? Celebrating the holiday."

"You were alone?"

"Yes," Gil replied. "My family was at home."

Anne noted that he wasn't volunteering any background about Jamie throwing him out, but that wasn't police business anyway.

"Talk to anybody at the bar who'd remember you, Mr. Martin?"

"Not really. A blonde drinking Cosmopolitans, but I don't know her name."

"Try to pick her up?"

"Does it matter?" Gil shot back, drawing a disapproving look from Bennie.

"Maybe," Rafferty answered.

"Okay, yes. I tried to pick her up." Gil offered his wrists. "Cuff me."

Off to the side, Anne was starting to wonder about Gil. Picking up a blonde right after Jamie threw him out? Trying to hit on Anne? The affair with Beth? At some point, she'd advise Gil to get some counseling, but that would be after *Chipster.*

"How about the bartender?" Rafferty was asking.

"I didn't try to pick her up."

Rafferty didn't laugh. "I didn't know she was a woman. I meant, would the bartender remember you?"

"Yes. Her name's Jill. Jill and Gil, that's how I remember. Yeah, we talked. She would remember. We laughed about the name thing."

"Then what happened?"

"Then I saw Anne on the TV over the bar, and she said where she'd be, at the hoagie tent around nine o'clock. So I went there. When I got there it was so crowded, I knew it was too crazy to even bother, so I left. When I was heading back to Center City, I just happened to see her. Her dress was white and it caught my eye. Then I saw what was going on."

JILL AND GILL, typed the heavyset detective, and Rafferty gave a sigh that had a final ring to it, then glanced at Bennie. "Ms. Rosato, of course I'll have to discuss it with my superiors, but I doubt that we'll be charging Mr. Martin with any crime."

"That's the right result, Detective," Bennie said. If she'd been worried, it didn't show. She put a hand on Gil's chair. "Mr. Martin understands the dangers of ordinary citizens trying to save lives, however well-intentioned their efforts may be. He won't be doing it again." Bennie acknowledged Deputy Commissioner Parker. "Sir, again, you've handled this matter with professionalism and sensitivity, and we'll be happy to appear at the press conference tomorrow."

"Thanks. You'll be escorted past the feeding frenzy outside. My driver and the commissioner's driver will take you all home. The conference is at ten o'clock tomorrow morning, here. The inspector will be back by then."

"I'll be there." Bennie glanced toward Anne. "Ms. Murphy can't be, she has a court date."

"I know, I read the newspapers," the deputy commissioner said, with a sympathetic grin at Anne. "Ms. Murphy, if you need a doctor's note for that judge, you got one from me."

"Thanks." Anne managed a smile and rose from her chair on surprisingly wobbly knees, and Detective Rafferty met her eye.

"Aren't you forgetting something, Ms. Murphy?" he asked, and after a second, Anne realized what he meant. He was holding his hand out, palm up. "It's not as if you have a carry permit."

"Oops." Anne reached into her pocket, pulled out the Beretta, and surrendered it to the detective. She guessed she wouldn't be needing it anymore, but she felt funny without it.

Rafferty raised an eyebrow. "When did girls start carrying Berettas in their dresses?"

"When they leave their purses at home," Anne said, which coaxed the first smile she'd seen from the detective. "Does this mean no weapons charges? You're cutting me a break?"

"Only 'cause you're Irish," Rafferty answered, smiling.

Matt took her arm gently. "Let's get outta here," he said, and Anne let him guide her to the door with the others, breathing a sigh of relief.

It was finally over. All of it. She'd never have to worry again, never have to look over her shoulder. She didn't need her gun. Kevin was gone, really gone. She felt shaken, but finally safe.

Downstairs in the lobby of the Roundhouse, surrounded by wood-paneled walls and glass cases displaying old squad cars, they all milled around before sorting themselves for departure. Anne went first to Gil, giving him a hug. "I don't know how to thank you for saving my life," she said, surprised to find Gil get a little misty, too.

"Don't think anything of it." His cockiness had vanished, replaced with a genuinely happy smile. "I'm just lucky I was there."

"No, I am." Anne reached next to him for

Bennie, hugging her like the mother she never had. "Thank you so much for everything," she said, and Bennie hugged her back.

"I'm glad you're safe."

"Sorry I ran away from you."

"Don't remind me." Bennie cocked an eyebrow in mock-offense. "And don't tell anybody I fell for that look-over-there crap."

Anne laughed, and Judy and Mary filled in, with Mary throwing open her arms to hug Anne. "The love continues," Mary said, giving Anne a big squeeze. "I'm so happy for you, and so happy you're okay."

"Give your parents my regards," Anne said. "And I'm there for dinner next Sunday, to return my evil-eye necklace in person."

"Done!" Mary said, hugging her again. "Hold it hostage until they return the cat."

Anne laughed, about to wipe wetness from her eyes when Judy swept her up in a death-defying hug, then backed off.

"Still got your earrings, I see." Judy grinned, pleased.

"Of course I do. I love them." Anne felt overwhelmed that she'd found such good friends in Mary, Bennie, and even Judy, but she was feeling much too emotional to say so. That would be something else she'd have to attend to, in the very near future.

Matt looped a proprietary arm around Anne, with a smile. "Thanks, Bennie. All of you. For taking such good care of her."

But Gil, at the edge of the hugging, was looking from Anne to Matt and back again. Anne caught his hard eye, with a start. She had forgotten. Gil didn't know about her and Matt. *Oh no.* She felt terrible, especially now, after what he'd done. She faced her client. "I'm sorry, Gil. You didn't know this, but I've begun seeing Matt."

"No, I didn't know." Gil's mouth was tight.

"I swear to you, I haven't let it interfere with the case." Anne felt her cheeks flame with embarrassment. She could feel Bennie's eyes upon her, with little sympathy. She had to make a choice on the spot. She thought of Matt's choice, made the same day. "I am sorry. If you want to hire another lawyer, you can. We can get a continuance, and given the events of tonight, it wouldn't look strange to your Board."

Matt cleared his throat. "Gil, for the record, Anne didn't compromise her representation of your company in any way."

Gil ignored him, but found a smile for

Anne. "Anne, I wouldn't fire you now, not after what you've been through for this case, and I know you won't let your personal relationship affect you. This is business, and you're still my lawyer."

"Thanks, I won't let you down," Anne said, taking a deep breath. She wondered if Gil's decision was based on what he'd told her about the CD, and she couldn't begin to focus on what would happen at the trial tomorrow, not with blood drying on her hands. It was time to start over. She found herself feeling an urge she hadn't felt in a long time. "I want to go home," she heard herself say.

"But it's a crime scene," Mary said. "Come with me. My parents would love to have you again, and Anne's cat is there. You can even stay there until you find a new place."

Bennie blinked. "Or come over my house. Keep the cat at Mary's. I'll make you cereal."

Judy laughed. "Mine's the only place you haven't stayed. Don't you want a change of pace?"

Matt squeezed her close. "Anne, come back with me, to my house. You don't want to be at your place, not after what happened there."

Anne looked at Matt and the others, ringed around her, their expressions reflecting concern and love. Her future was beginning, and they would all be a part of it. But as grateful as she was, she knew where she really belonged.

"Thanks but I want to go home. To my house, on Waltin Street."

And her words matched her thoughts exactly, for once.

31

It wasn't an hour later, delivered by a speeding squad car, that Anne was home, dressed
in jeans, a pink tank top, and yellow Playtex
gloves, yanking the stained wall-to-wall carpet from her front-entrance hall. She should
have been sleeping or preparing her opening argument, but she couldn't do either.
The rug reeked of blood and pain, and she
wanted it *out.* She had already gotten up
three sides, with only the last remaining, the
front right corner. She gritted her teeth,
closed her eyes, and tugged harder, and the
rug surrendered suddenly, sending her
backward onto her butt.

"Argh!" she grunted from the floor. Her
shoulder, back stitches, and butt hurt, but
she got to her feet, dragged the rug into the
living room, and flattened it. She tried not to
look at the bloodstains, so she wouldn't
start crying again. She had cried in the

shower when she first came home, then she had steeled herself and gotten to work.

She dropped to her knees and rolled up the rug, then snapped open a Hefty bag from the orange box on the coffee table and stuffed the rug inside. She picked it up and was about to take it outside to leave it at the curb for pickup, but she stopped herself. It wouldn't be respectful. It wasn't trash. It had Willa's blood on it. It felt substantial in Anne's arms, like a human body. Without knowing exactly why, she set the bagged rug down on the floor.

She swallowed the lump in her throat, stood with her hands on her hips, and surveyed the entrance hall, now illuminated by the fixture above. Bloody streaks had dried a cakey brown on the wall and the entrance-hall door. The baseboards were stained, and thin wood slats bordered the floor where the rug had been stapled down, but there were no stains on the hard wood. Plan B was to wash and paint the walls in the hall. She couldn't leave them this way, not even one night. Cleaning the entrance room would be gruesome and awful, but it had to be done. For Willa. And it was cathartic, already making her feel better, bringing to an end this awful part of her life. Anne got her second wind and suspected it was heaven-sent.

She went to the kitchen and took off a Playtex glove long enough to grab a handful of Captain Crunch, while she filled up the blue Rubbermaid bucket in the sink with a brew of Lysol, Pine-Sol, Comet, and hot water. Fizzy suds formed quickly as the water rose, floating the thick pink sponge, and she turned off the tap, grabbed the bucket, and returned to the living room, flicking on the stereo on the way, a classical station. It would suit her mood and her task.

A lone Spanish guitar came on, playing acoustic. Anne's thoughts went to her father, the guitar player she'd never met, then to her mother. She wondered idly when she'd see her again, *if* she'd see her again, but suppressed the tiny tug in her chest. The TV appeal had given her pause, but her past was over. She had to go forward with the rest of her life. It was time to start over starting over. She sloshed to the entrance hall with the heavy bucket.

She put the bucket down and let the guitar music soothe her as she got down on her knees and reached for the steaming sponge. When she bent over, the little Italian charm popped out from her tank top, swinging on Mrs. DiNunzio's gold chain, and she tucked the necklace away with a smile and started cleaning the wall. The dried blood turned briefly red again when it made contact with the hot sponge, bringing up that carnal smell. Her stomach turned over, but she kept at it, washing streak after streak, thinking of Willa, and blinking away the tears that inevitably came. Anne had gone through three full buckets of sudsy water, a bottle of Lysol, and several Kleenexes when the doorbell rang.

Anne stopped, startled still. Her heart fluttered in her chest. The last time that bell had rung, a killer had been at the door. The ringing echoed through the apartment, quiet except for the guitar playing. She told herself she was being silly. There was nothing to be afraid of, anymore. Kevin was dead; she had seen him killed with her own eyes, and the sight, though it had brought her no satisfaction, at least brought her safety. Right?

The doorbell rang again, and Anne dropped the sponge into the water and stood up to look in the peephole. It was Matt! Everything was all right. She really was safe.

She undid the chain lock in a hurry and

opened the door onto the warm summer night. Matt was standing on the stoop wearing a black Dave Matthews T-shirt, jeans, and a smile, and holding his briefcase flat, like a tray. On it, he balanced a bottle of merlot and two wineglasses. Anne couldn't help but feel happy to see him. "What are you doing here?" she asked.

"I couldn't sleep and I knew you wouldn't be. You said you were starting over, so I brought you a housewarming present." Matt plucked the wine bottle off the briefcase tray and gave Anne a quick peck on the lips, then followed it up with a warm, deeper kiss she didn't resist, even though her gloves were dripping suds.

"Wow. Come on in," she said and closed the door behind him as he crossed the threshold and tiptoed over the wet floorboards in wonderment.

"Are you cleaning?" He winced only slightly when he smiled, since the residual swelling from his goose egg had subsided.

"Yep. I just finished washing." Anne appraised her handiwork, but couldn't deny the darkness that still stained the white wall in many places. "With two coats of white paint, it'll be back to normal."

"Sure it will." Matt set the wineglasses on the floor just outside the entrance hall, then slid a corkscrew from his back pocket and sat down on the floor. "I can't believe you're doing this yourself. You could have hired a service or something. I thought you'd be getting ready for trial, planning how you're going to kick ass."

"Nah, this is more important." Anne stripped off her wet gloves and draped them over the side of the bucket.

"*What*? What happened to the girl who would do anything to win, including hire a stripper?" Matt laughed as he unwrapped the metal seal from the top of the merlot, then inserted the corkscrew and extracted the cork with a festive *pock*. "Don't tell me you've changed."

Anne thought a minute. "Hell, no!"

"Praise be." Matt grinned and handed her an empty wineglass. He poured them both some merlot, then set down the bottle and raised his glass in a toast. "To you, and to your not changing. Ever."

Anne raised her glass. "And to you—"

Brrng. Brrng. It was the unmistakable ringing of a cell phone, and they both reflexively went to their holsters, but Anne had left her cell in her purse in the living room. Matt unholstered his phone. "Rats," he said. "Just when you were going to tell me how great I am."

"You'd do it better," she said, as he flipped open the cell phone and answered it. She watched his blue eyes light up.

"Oh, really? Okay. Relax. I understand, we'll discuss it. I'll be right over," he said, then snapped the phone closed excitedly. "That was Bill Dietz."

"Anger Management Boy." Anne sipped her wine. The thought of Dietz killed her mood and she took a bigger sip. "What did he want?"

"To see me. He said it was important. I think I may be getting my old job back." Matt took a swig of his wine and was already getting up, and Anne felt happy for him. Sort of.

"Dietz assaulted us both. Why do you like him so much?"

Matt looked conflicted. "He just told me, he's sorry he pushed you. He lost his temper."

"Oh, that makes it okay." Anne took a gulp

of merlot. It tasted terrific. She couldn't remember the last time she'd eaten and was starting not to care.

"I'm sorry to run out on you. I have to go over to the house."

"See ya, wouldn't wanna be ya." Anne took a final gulp, draining the glass. "If you become opposing counsel again, then we're over until the trial ends. I'm a brunette now and we're not as loose as redheads."

"Oh, all right. Be that way." Matt leaned down and gave her a quick good-bye kiss. "Will you be okay? You seem okay."

"I'm more than okay." Anne poured herself another glass of merlot and hoisted the bottle, channeling a tipsy Lucy Ricardo. "'The answer to all your problems is in this lil ole bottle.'"

"Vitametavegamin!" Matt said with a smile, and Anne couldn't believe her ears.

"You know Vitametavegamin?" she asked, astounded. "From 'Lucy Does a Television Commercial'? Episode No. 30, May 5, 1952?"

Matt laughed. "I don't know the dates, but I know the episodes. The chocolate factory, stomping the grapes, crushing the eggs, baby chicks, Teensy and Weensy, you name it. My mother was a Lucy freak, too."

"I think I'm in love," Anne said, meaning it, and Matt blew her another kiss before he opened the door and hustled out, leaving her with a bottle of merlot, a bucket of suds, and a tingle of hope.

She got up, relatched the chain, and began to collect the gloves, sponge, and bucket to get ready for painting. She was working only five minutes when the doorbell rang again. Ha! Matt must have forgotten something. Maybe the rest of her toast? Maybe another kiss. A random firecracker exploded somewhere with a distant *crak*! It had been that way since she'd gotten home.

"Coming, Matt!" she called out, getting up to answer the door. She undid the chain lock without checking the peephole because she knew it was Matt.

But when she opened the door, it wasn't Matt.

32

On the front step stood Beth Dietz and she looked like she'd been crying. "Can . . . I come in?" Sobs choked her voice, and she was trembling in shorts and her peasant blouse. "Bill and I, we just had a big fight about that stalker, Kevin. I heard on the news, he's dead."

"Sure, come in. We should talk about it." Anne instantly felt terrible and ushered Beth inside, closing the door behind her and latching the chain-lock reflexively. But when she turned around, Beth had stopped crying and was pointing a black handgun at her.

My God. It took Anne a second to process. Then she opened her mouth to scream.

"*Shut the fuck up!*" Beth was already pressing the gun into Anne's chest, shoving her back against the door. The gun was cold and hard. The barrel drilled into her sternum, leaving her gasping.

"What are you doing, Beth?" Anne asked, hoarse. She tried not to panic. She went weak in the knees. She could barely look over the deadly gun into Beth's eyes, red with spent tears.

"When did you start sleeping with Gil, Anne? I want to know!"

"Beth, please, put down the gun." Anne's tongue still tasted of wine, but its effects had vanished. "If you want to talk about something, we can talk about it. But not with a gun—"

"Don't you *dare* tell me what to do!" Beth bellowed, her fair skin mottled. Her blond braid was in disarray, her lips trembling with anger. "Tell me when you started fucking Gil! It was *you* he wanted all along!"

"No, never." Anne shook her head in disbelief. She flashed on the scene in the conference room, when Gil was drunk. Then the call on the cell phone tonight. "I never felt anything for Gil. I never did anything—"

"Liar!" Beth screamed. "He used to talk about you all the time, and when we broke up and I filed suit, he went and *hired* you!" The gun bored into Anne, making her breathless with fear.

"No, please—" Tears sprang to Anne's

eyes. She imagined the bullet tearing into her, ripping flesh and heart. She flashed on her entrance hall, drenched in blood. She knew just what it would look like. She'd be shot to death in her entrance hall. The horror had come full circle.

"I loved him and you took him from me!" Beth shouted, her features contorted with fury, spitting into Anne's face. "He didn't mean anything to you! I was going to leave Bill for him, but it was *you* he wanted! And you're already on to Matt! Bill was right about that, you are a *whore!*"

Anne struggled to regain control. She had to do something. She tried to think.

"I was here Friday night!" Beth ranted. "I wanted to kill you for what you did to me, and I did, *I killed you!* But it turned out it wasn't you at the door! And now Gil saved your life, I saw it on TV! *Now he's more in love with you than ever!*"

Anne's brain jolted with the revelation. Kevin wasn't the murderer. It was *Beth* who had killed Willa. Her thoughts raced. Kevin must have been watching Anne's house that night. He had seen Beth shoot Willa and he thought she'd shot Anne. He must have come over, picked up the murder weapon in shock, then dropped it. *My God.* It was Beth, all along!

"This time you're going to stay dead," Beth said evenly. "Bye-bye." She raised her gun and aimed it point-blank between Anne's eyes.

"No!" Anne screamed and whipped her arms upward into the gun. *Crak*! the gun exploded in a deafening report.

"You bitch!" Beth roared, enraged.

"Help!" Anne screamed and shoved Beth to the floor, bolting past her for the staircase. She took the stairs two-by-two as a second gunshot rang out. *Crak*!

"Help! Somebody! Please!" Anne screamed as she tore up the stairs. Where was she going? What would she do? She had no gun, she'd turned it in. Was there time to dial 911? She had a phone in her bedroom. She hit the second-floor landing with Beth running up the stairs behind her. She swung around the landing for the lighted bedroom before Beth could get off another shot.

"Help!" Anne screamed but nobody came. Where were her neighbors? Mr. Berman? Mr. Monterosso? All of them?

She tore down the hall and into her bedroom. She darted to the desk for the phone but it was too late. Beth was coming down the hall, running toward the bedroom. Anne grabbed her thick laptop from her desk, spun on her heels, and flung it at Beth's face. It landed with a resounding *thwack*, then fell to the rug.

"Aargh!" Beth's hand flew to her nose. *Crak*! The gun went off with an ear-splitting sound. Flame flared from the muzzle. Anne felt the heat of a bullet whizz past her cheek. The thought terrified her. Beth bent over, cupping her nose. Blood poured through her fingers.

Anne ran for her life. She bolted from the bedroom screaming, streaking for the stairwell and downstairs for the front door. In the next second Beth was after her, her footsteps hard on the stair.

Anne raced to the front door. She couldn't make it in time. She'd be shot undoing the chain-lock. She'd have to fight. She looked around wildly. The rolled-up rug in the Hefty bag. Perfect!

She snatched the rug off the living room floor and swung it like a bat at Beth's waist just as she hit the living room, raising her gun. The rug smacked Beth full-force. She doubled over, jarring the gun free. It fell to the living room rug, and Anne dove for it. She had it aimed on target by the time Beth straightened up, bleeding profusely from her nostrils and still howling with fury.

"You won't shoot me!" Beth shouted, spitting blood.

Anne found herself shaking with rage. She hadn't shot Kevin, but she couldn't get off a clear shot then. She could now. She looked down the barrel of the gun, an old Colt revolver. No safety. Ready to fire.

Anne felt a surge of adrenaline. She could kill Beth. She *should* kill her. She should blow her face clean off. It seemed suddenly like a very good idea. The best Plan B Anne had had to date. No Lucy episode to cover this one. It was real life. She moved the site down, training the revolver between Beth's blue eyes.

Anne flashed on everything Beth had put her through. She had just tried to kill her, she *would* have killed her. She had killed Willa. It must have been why Kevin was stalking her, not because he was in love with her, but because he knew she'd killed Anne. And she thought of Willa, her murder still unavenged, her lifeblood staining the walls.

Anne looked numbly at the gun in her

hand. Then her gaze fell on something else. The Italian charm, twinkling around her neck, outside the tank top. It reminded her of Mrs. DiNunzio. The fragrant little kitchen. The percolating coffee. It reminded her of friendship, of family, and of love.

Anne's fingers tightened on the smoking gun.

And she made her choice.

33

The fifth of July, a Tuesday morning, dawned clear and cool, the temperature hovered at a civilized seventy degrees and with no humidity. The sky over Philadelphia had a crystal-blue clarity, bringing the glitzy, metallic skyline into crisp focus. The sun was still low, lingering behind the skyscrapers, sleeping in after a busy holiday weekend of Uncle Sam stovepipes and red platform shoes.

The city was going back to work, collectively recharged. Boxy, white SEPTA buses barreled down streets that had been closed to traffic yesterday. Green-shirted employees of the business district speared cups and paper bags from the gutter. Storefronts rolled up their security cages on chattery, greased chains. People strolled to work a little late, wearing clean shirts with fresh tans, holding briefcases they hadn't opened over the weekend. Many of them, like Anne, carried a folded newspaper under an arm.

FOURTH OF JULY FIREWORKS! read her *Daily News* headline, a special edition. Anne would have preferred CASE CLOSED, because the *Chipster* trial wouldn't be going forward. Matt was at the courthouse, filing a notice of withdrawal. It would have been difficult to maintain a lawsuit with the plaintiff in custody for murder one.

Anne walked with her head held high, on taupe Blahniks. She wore a linen suit the color of buttercream with a white stretch T-shirt. She was feeling almost normal again, except that normal now meant no sunglasses, no lipstick, and a scar. And she was going in late to work because she'd dyed her hair back to its original color. Mental note: Life is too short to be anything but a redhead.

Her step was strong and lively as she strode the last block to work, down Locust. Part of her happiness was her clothes, but most of it was her new idea. The very thought buoyed her even as she floated toward the sea of cameras, reporters, and newsvans outside her office building. Uniformed police, eight of them, managed to keep the press from blocking traffic, and Anne smiled at the irony of the sight. It was more cops than she'd seen all weekend.

A reporter on the fringe of the crowd recognized her first and started running toward her. "Ms. Murphy, how did you catch the killer?" "What was Beth Dietz's motive?" "We want the exclusive!" Other reporters started turning around, and camera lenses swung toward Anne. "Ms. Murphy! Anne! Over here!" they all started calling, and flooded toward her, breaking away as a mob.

Anne brandished her folded *Daily News* and met the throng. "No comment!" she said, waving them off as she plunged into the crowd. "I have no comment!"

She pushed through the crowd to the clicking of motor drives and the whirring of videocameras, but her way was blocked by a TV reporter until a beefy hand came around the reporter's body and offered Anne an assist. She looked up gratefully, and at the other end of the arm was Hot and Heavy Herb, in full dress uniform.

"Outta the way, everybody! Outta the way!" he shouted, and he ran interference, leading Anne to the entrance of the building, where he ushered her in ahead of him and followed through the revolving door. He escorted her into the lobby, laughing and wiping his brow with a folded handkerchief. "Whew! Those guys are nuts!"

"Thanks for rescuing me," Anne said, meaning it. She was in such a good mood, she was happy even to see Hot and Heavy, who was grinning down at her with more amusement than lechery for a change.

"So, Carrot Top, it was you, that new girl?"

"Yes, it was me, and I'm sorry. I didn't mean to lie to you."

"Are you kidding?" Herb waved a hand, chuckling as he walked her to the elevator, which was open on the ground floor. "I'm just glad you're alive. I like you, kid." His voice sounded genuine, almost fatherly.

Anne entered the elevator cab and pressed the button. "Thank you, I'm flattered," she said, and the elevator doors slid closed, carrying her upstairs.

The elevator doors had barely opened again when the receptionist leaped from the front desk and started hugging Anne, and the other secretaries and paralegals flocked to her. "You're alive! You're really alive!" they chorused, and Anne, who was growing happily accustomed to having girlfriends, knew exactly what to do: hug back, get misty, then go shopping.

But when the receptionist released her, her teary eyes looked worried. "Anne, Bennie wants to see you. She has a new case. She's in C."

"A new case? No, you're kidding!" Anne looked with dismay at the closed door to the conference room, off the reception area. "I don't want to work! I want to hug and hug."

The receptionist frowned. "You'd better go in. Judy and Mary are in there, too, waiting for you. The new client's in conference room D. Something's up."

"A lawyer's work is never done," she said, with a sigh. She bid all her new gal pals good-bye, headed to the conference room, and opened the door.

Bennie, Mary, and Judy were seated around the polished conference table, in front of clean legal pads and Styrofoam cups of fresh coffee. Anne had seen them only a few hours before, back at the Roundhouse when Beth was arrested, but they looked as jazzed up as she felt, alert and businesslike. Bennie wore her khaki suit, Judy a T-shirt and blue denim smock, and

Mary a silk blouse with a Talbot's navy suit, her hair in a French twist.

"You really want me to work?" Anne asked, and Bennie smiled easily as she came toward her.

"Good morning," she said, hugging Anne briefly. "You get any rest?"

"For two hours, yeah. Mel says hi."

"I miss him." Bennie smiled, and Mary and Judy came over, exchanging hugs, but the air felt tense despite the warmth and familiarity of the group. Bennie obviously had an agenda, but Anne had one of her own.

"Before we start, I have an idea," she said. "Can I go first? It can't wait."

Bennie hesitated. "Okay, what is it?"

"Sit down, everybody. Especially you, Bennie. You'll need to be sitting, for this. Here's the deal," Anne began, as all three women took their seats. "Well, I remember from the radio the other day, when you all thought I was dead, that you were offering a reward to whoever found my killer."

"Yes."

"The firm was offering $50,000."

"Yes, sure."

"Well, as you know, *I* found my killer, Beth

Dietz, and last night I turned her in to the authorities and she was arrested."

"So you're saying what?" Bennie asked, and Mary and Judy looked equally uncertain.

"I want the reward. I want to donate it to a crime victims' group, in Willa's name. I think the money would make a nice memorial to her, and do a lot of good. Maybe even help prevent the Kevins of the world."

Bennie nodded. "Fair enough. Done. That's a very good idea."

"Aren't you going to fight me?"

"No."

"It's a lot of money."

"It sure is."

"It comes out of your pocket."

"Understood." Bennie's eyes darkened. "You may not have thought about this, but you may also want to use part of the money for burial expenses and the like, for Willa."

"No, thanks." Anne's throat caught suddenly. "I've already decided. I'll be doing that myself, and setting up a memorial service for her. It would be nice if you all could come."

"We will," Bennie said quickly.

Judy nodded. "Of course, we will."

"We'll help with the service," Mary said.

"Thanks." Anne patted the table, to dispel her sadness and get herself back to business. "Now, what's going on? I hear we have a client waiting."

"Yes, I know you'd love to relax, but it can't wait." Bennie rose at the head of the table and cleared her throat. "We have a new client, in trouble. Big trouble."

"Murder?" Anne asked, but Bennie held up a hand like a traffic cop.

"Not that bad, but close."

"Civil or criminal?"

"Civil." Bennie nodded. "And I have to tell you, this client is liable. Absolutely liable. In other words, guilty. Very."

Anne sighed. "Why don't we ever get the easy cases?"

"We're too smart for the easy cases."

"Also we look hot in platforms," Mary added.

"You maybe." Judy scowled.

Bennie waved them into silence. "Now, getting back to the case, our client is guilty, but the transgression occurred a long time ago. There may be a defense in there somewhere."

"The statute's run?" Anne asked, meaning

the statute of limitations, and wondering in which jurisdiction the client lived and what he did wrong.

"Not on this, but there are very interesting facts, ones you should know about and should be brought to light."

Anne didn't get it. "What did he do?"

"You have to get the facts. Investigate and understand everything about the situation. You know how to prepare a case. The client's waiting for you, in D."

"It's my client?"

"Most definitely. You couldn't have handled this case before, but you can now. I think after all you've been through, you've got the experience, the maturity, and now the perspective. Things come to us when we're ready, sometimes. Take the next few days off and spend some time with it."

"Really?" Anne rose, grabbing a clean legal pad from the center of the table. "Like a working vacation?"

"Absolutely." Bennie smiled. "In fact, you know that place you rented down the shore, to get ready for *Chipster*? I rented it for you. It's yours this whole week, and we're bringing Matt down for the weekend. It's all set up. A romantic weekend, just the five of us."

"Really?" Anne squealed, and Bennie laughed.

"Really. By the way, have you ever dealt with anybody who was guilty before?"

"Gil, sort of. I hated that."

"Well, here's the key. Clients come to us the way they are, and we don't have the luxury of choosing them. They're like family that way. So when you meet a new one, don't judge, just listen. Understand?"

"Yes."

"You can ask questions, and you can certainly doubt, but you may not judge. Lawyers don't get to judge, only judges get to judge. Get it? It rhymes. Now get thee to a conference room!"

"Thank you so much, Bennie." Anne went around the table to give her another hug, then went back toward the door and opened it. "I'll stop by your office after I'm finished."

"You do that," Bennie was saying, as the door closed. Anne hurried through the reception area to conference room D and opened the door. There, looking very small, at the end of the table, sat her mother.

Her fake black hair had been pulled back and she wore a simple blue dress with only a discreet brush of neutral lipstick. She

squirmed slightly in her chair, resting a manicured hand on the table's surface, and her
eyelids fluttered as if she were ashamed.

You should be ashamed, Anne thought.
She was too surprised to say anything.

"I came here this morning, to see you,"
her mother said. Her voice was halting, and
her British accent had disappeared. "But
your boss, Bennie, she asked me to wait in
here. She said if she spoke to you first,
maybe you would see me. She's very kind."

"You don't know her." Anne wanted to
wring Bennie's neck, until she remembered
her words. *Don't judge, just listen.*

"I was hoping maybe I could speak with
you, before I went back to L.A. I don't expect anything of you. I was just hoping we
could speak to each other, one last time.
And you should know, I've been clean and
sober for five months and ten days now. I
even have a job at the center. A real job, that
pays."

*Clients come to us, and we don't have the
luxury of choosing them. They're like family
that way.*

"If you want me to, I will leave now," she
continued. "I have a ticket on the next flight.
It's at three this afternoon."

You couldn't have handled this case before, but you can now.

"I just didn't want to leave without saying good-bye. And, hello."

Anne felt something come free deep within her chest. Something she had been withholding, but wasn't ready to acknowledge. She remembered Mrs. Brown, alone with her crosswords, and Mrs. DiNunzio, surrounded by her family and food. Anne knew there was a connection, but was too shaken to puzzle it out right now. She found herself sinking into a chair and automatically setting the legal pad down on the conference table in front of her, as she would in a meeting with any new client.

"So we can talk awhile?" her mother asked.

"Yes," Anne answered. She eased back in the chair, ready to listen. After all, she was trying to start over starting over. Maybe this was a good place to start. Over. "Please, begin at the beginning," she said.

And so, they began.

Acknowledgments

There are no rules about writing acknowledgments, and my personal survey says that every author does them differently. Because I think of acknowledgments as a special thank-you, in the past I have thanked my readers here. But I've come to think that it's my readers who should get the ultimate thank-you—the dedication. And now they have. *Courting Trouble* is dedicated to my readers, for giving me their support and loyalty, for coming to book signings when there are so many other demands on their time, and for sending me notes and e-mail offering thoughts, encouragement, and even, occasionally, criticism. Books connect us, and my reader is always in my mind when I write each sentence, each word. My readers know that, and return it a thousandfold. So my deepest thanks go to you, dear reader. For your dedication, I offer mine. On page one, and every page thereafter.

Thanks to the wonderful gang at HarperCollins—to the great Jane Friedman, expert in both style *and* substance, and to Michael Morrison, Cathy Hemming, and now, Susan Weinberg. A huge and very emotional hug to my beloved editor Carolyn Marino, and another hug to gal pals Tara Brown and Virginia Stanley. Thanks, too, to Jennifer Civiletto, for all her help.

Heartfelt thanks go, as always, to the lovely Molly Friedrich and amazing Paul Cirone of the Aaron Priest Agency, for their enormous help and guidance in improving this and every manuscript. And love to Laura Leonard, who keeps me laughing every day and works so hard on my behalf.

Thanks to the many experts who helped with *Courting Trouble*; their advice was critical, and anything I did with it was my mistake. Thank you to my dear friend Jerome Hoffman, Esq., of Dechert, for his legal expertise and creative imagination, and to Allen Gross, Esq., for all of the above. Thanks to Art Mee, my genius detective-by-the-sea, and to Glenn Gilman, Esq., of the Public Defenders Office of Philadelphia.

Thank you to the kind people who have generously contributed to some very important charities, in return for having their names used as characters in this novel. I could never have made them villains, for they are too kind: Lore Yao (The Free Library of Philadelphia), Marge Derrick (Thorncroft Therapeutic Riding), Crawford, Wilson, & Ryan (Chester County Bar Association), Rodger Talbott & Sharon Arkin (scholarship program at California State University, Fullerton), and Bob Dodds, for the Miami Valley, Ohio, Literacy Council, via book maven Sharon Kelley Roth of Books & Co.

Thanks and love to my husband and family, and to Franca Palumbo, Rachel Kull, Sandy Steingard, Judith Hill, Carolyn Romano, Paula Menghetti, and Nan Demchur, et al. You prove how important girlfriends are. And thanks to my brother Frank, who lent his good humor and his gayness to a scene herein, and to my mother, who can get rid of the evil eye *over the telephone.* You think I make this stuff up?

A final thank-you to Lucille Ball, to Lucy fans everywhere, and to my own personal Lucy fan, who reminds me that role models come in many shapes, sizes, and haircolors. Even, and perhaps especially, red.